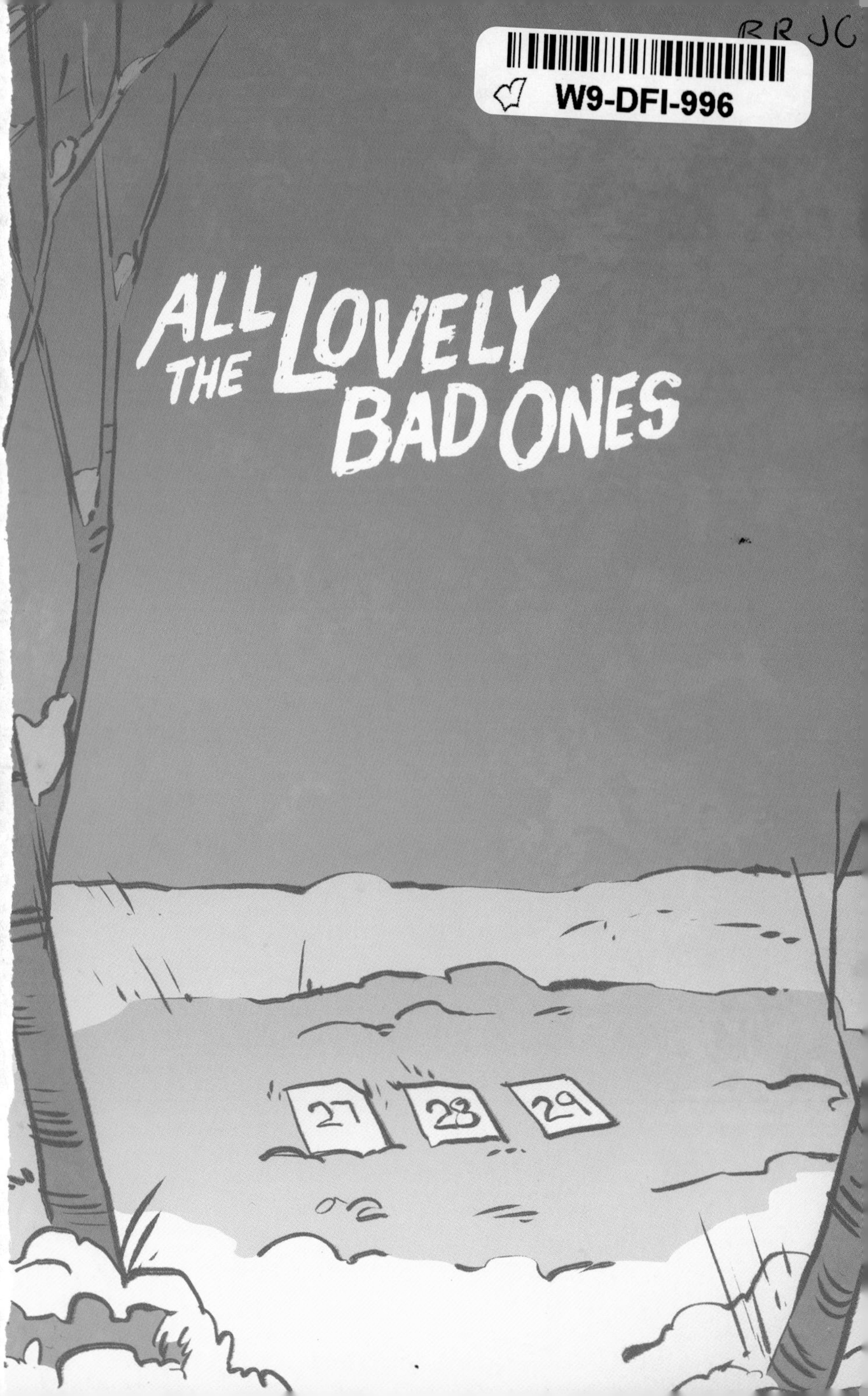
ALL THE LOVELY BAD ONES
27
28
29

Clarion Books is an imprint of HarperCollins Publishers.
HarperAlley is an imprint of HarperCollins Publishers.

ISBN 978-0-35-865014-0 — ISBN 978-0-35-865013-3 (pbk.)

Art Assistant: Irene Yeom
Colors by Brittany Peer
Lettering: Joamette Gil

The artist used Clip Studio Paint EX, a Wacom Cintiq 13HD,
and a Huion Kamvas 22 to create the digital illustrations.
Design by Pete Friedrich

23 24 25 26 27 GPS 10 9 8 7 6 5 4 3 2 1

First Edition

# MARY DOWNING HAHN

# ALL THE LOVELY BAD ONES

## a ghost story graphic novel

*Adapted by* Scott Peterson,
Naomi Franquiz, *and* Brittany Peer

Clarion Books
*Imprints of* HarperCollins*Publishers*

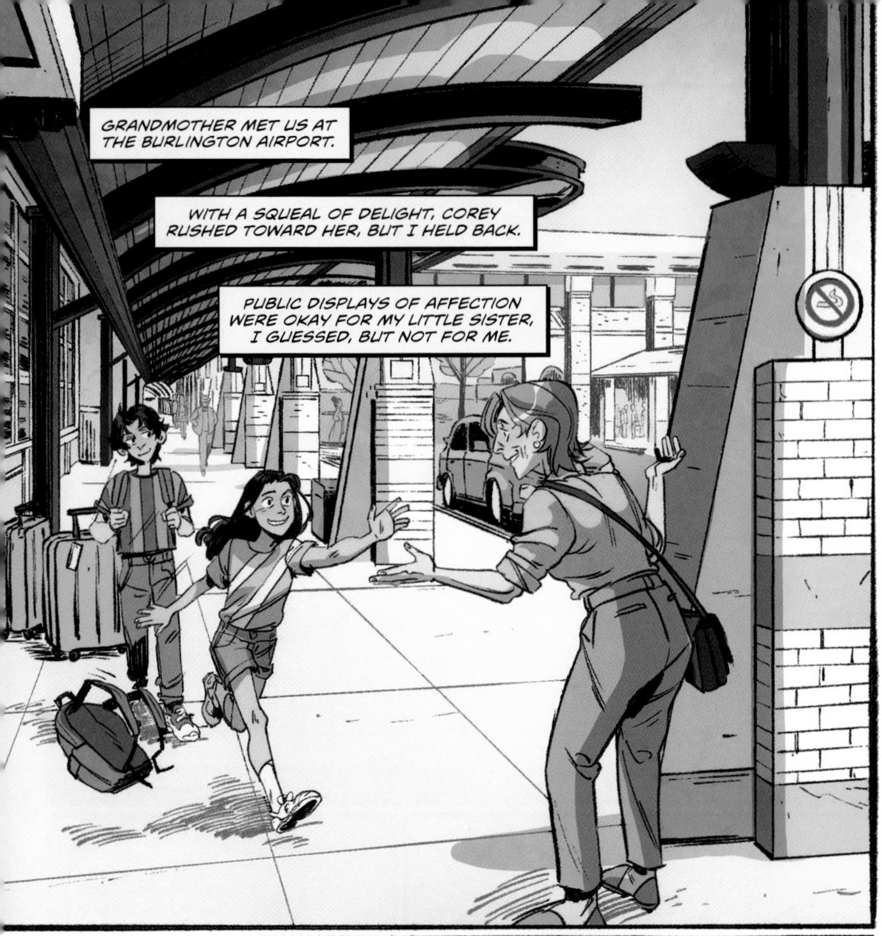
GRANDMOTHER MET US AT THE BURLINGTON AIRPORT.
WITH A SQUEAL OF DELIGHT, COREY RUSHED TOWARD HER, BUT I HELD BACK.
PUBLIC DISPLAYS OF AFFECTION WERE OKAY FOR MY LITTLE SISTER, I GUESSED, BUT NOT FOR ME.
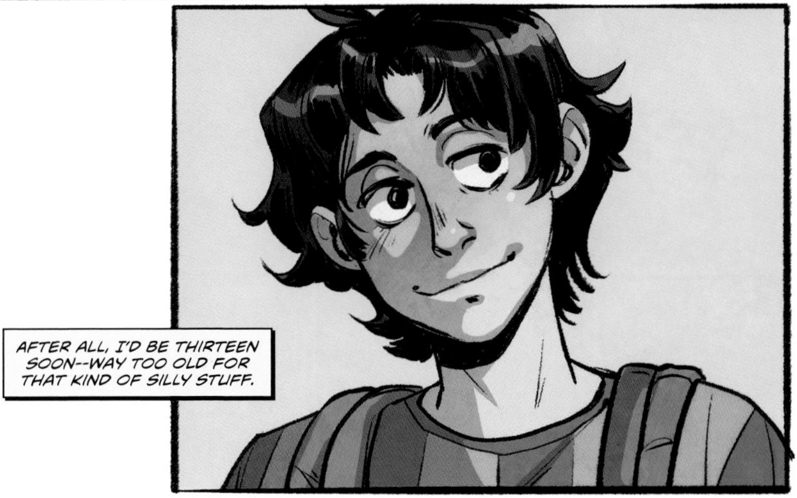
AFTER ALL, I'D BE THIRTEEN SOON--WAY TOO OLD FOR THAT KIND OF SILLY STUFF.

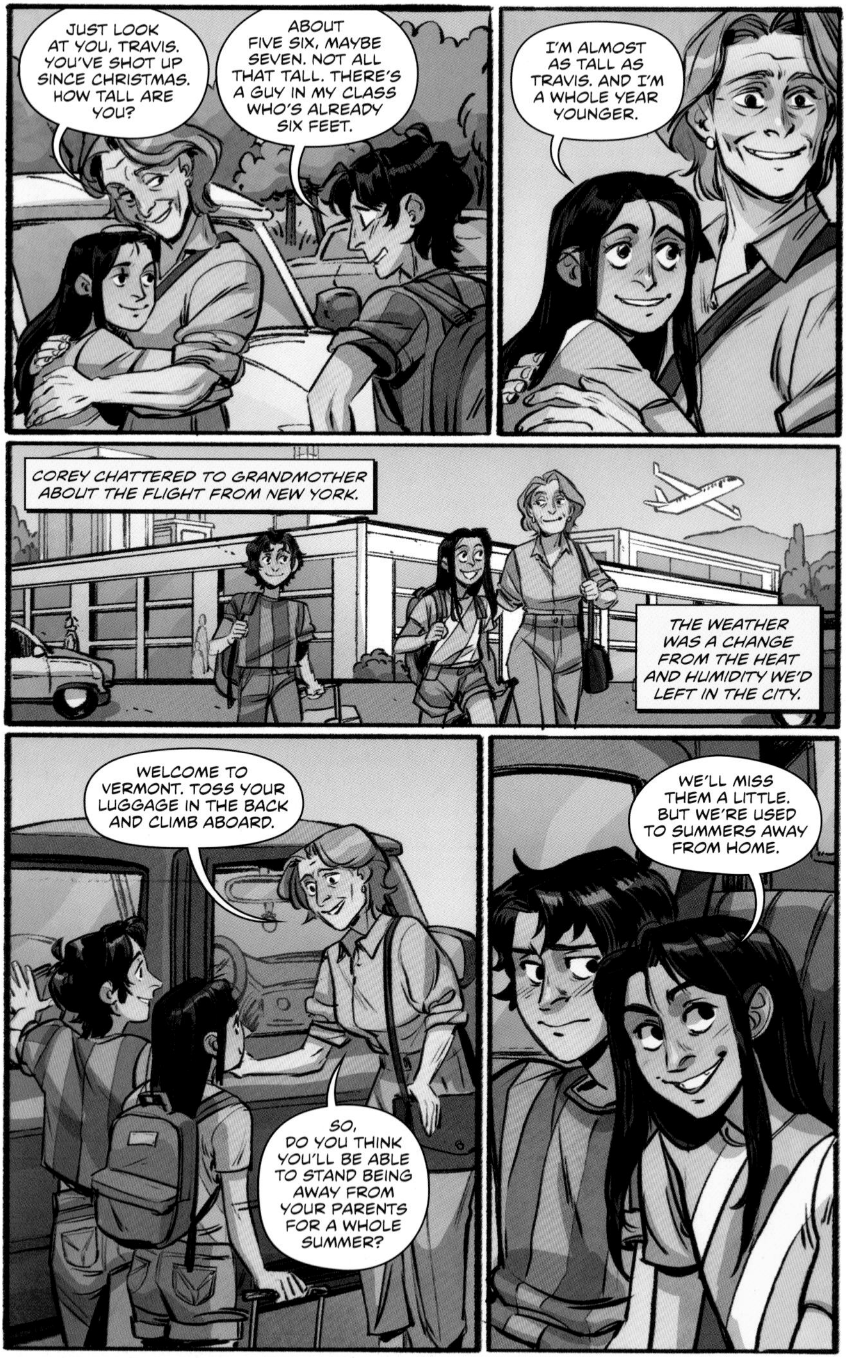
JUST LOOK AT YOU, TRAVIS. YOU'VE SHOT UP SINCE CHRISTMAS. HOW TALL ARE YOU?
ABOUT FIVE SIX, MAYBE SEVEN. NOT ALL THAT TALL. THERE'S A GUY IN MY CLASS WHO'S ALREADY SIX FEET.
I'M ALMOST AS TALL AS TRAVIS. AND I'M A WHOLE YEAR YOUNGER.
COREY CHATTERED TO GRANDMOTHER ABOUT THE FLIGHT FROM NEW YORK.
THE WEATHER WAS A CHANGE FROM THE HEAT AND HUMIDITY WE'D LEFT IN THE CITY.
WELCOME TO VERMONT. TOSS YOUR LUGGAGE IN THE BACK AND CLIMB ABOARD.
SO, DO YOU THINK YOU'LL BE ABLE TO STAND BEING AWAY FROM YOUR PARENTS FOR A WHOLE SUMMER?
WE'LL MISS THEM A LITTLE. BUT WE'RE USED TO SUMMERS AWAY FROM HOME.

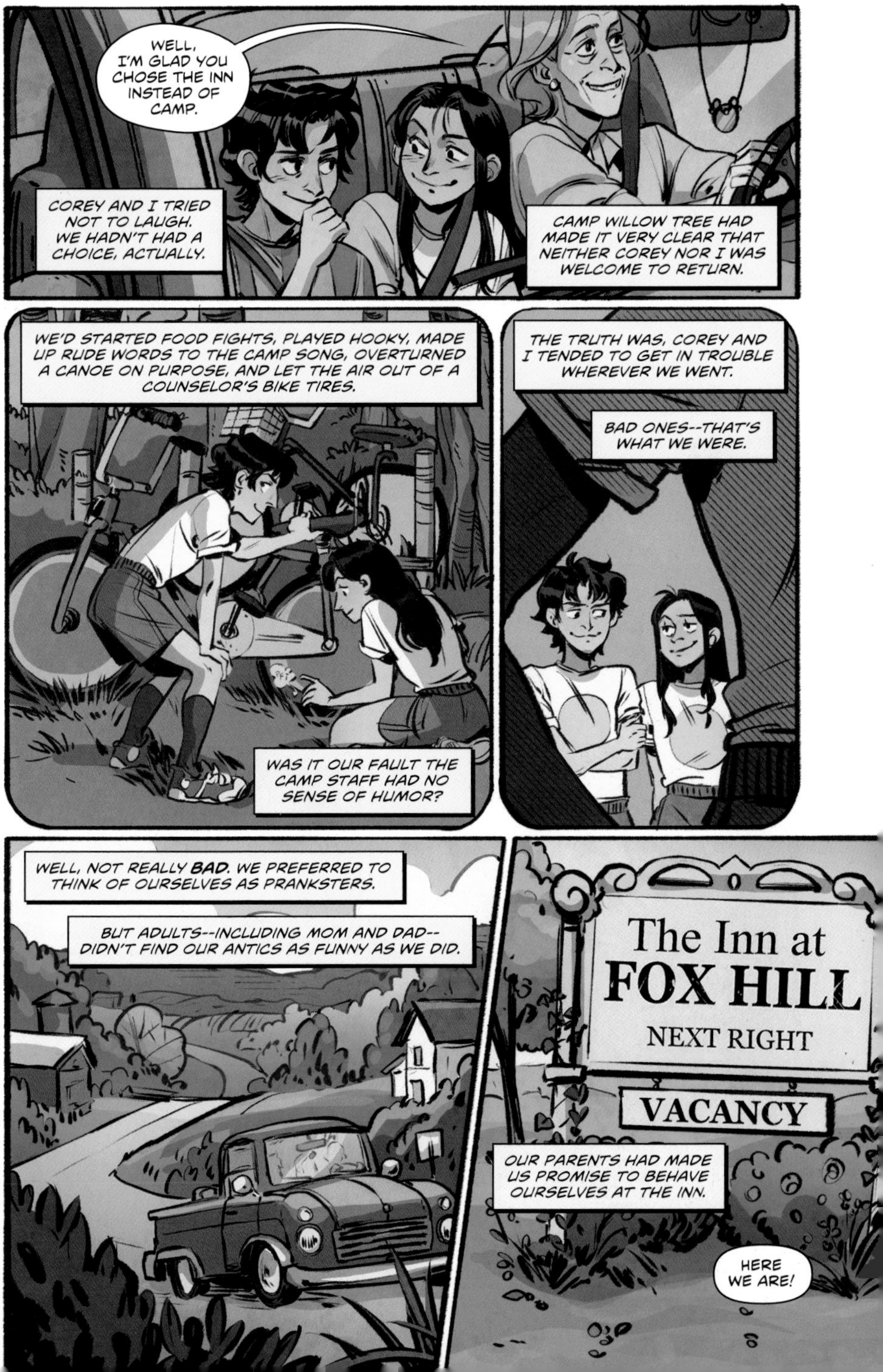
WELL, I'M GLAD YOU CHOSE THE INN INSTEAD OF CAMP.
COREY AND I TRIED NOT TO LAUGH. WE HADN'T HAD A CHOICE, ACTUALLY.
CAMP WILLOW TREE HAD MADE IT VERY CLEAR THAT NEITHER COREY NOR I WAS WELCOME TO RETURN.
WE'D STARTED FOOD FIGHTS, PLAYED HOOKY, MADE UP RUDE WORDS TO THE CAMP SONG, OVERTURNED A CANOE ON PURPOSE, AND LET THE AIR OUT OF A COUNSELOR'S BIKE TIRES.
WAS IT OUR FAULT THE CAMP STAFF HAD NO SENSE OF HUMOR?
THE TRUTH WAS, COREY AND I TENDED TO GET IN TROUBLE WHEREVER WE WENT.
BAD ONES--THAT'S WHAT WE WERE.
WELL, NOT REALLY BAD. WE PREFERRED TO THINK OF OURSELVES AS PRANKSTERS.
BUT ADULTS--INCLUDING MOM AND DAD--DIDN'T FIND OUR ANTICS AS FUNNY AS WE DID.
The Inn at FOX HILL NEXT RIGHT
VACANCY
OUR PARENTS HAD MADE US PROMISE TO BEHAVE OURSELVES AT THE INN.
HERE WE ARE!

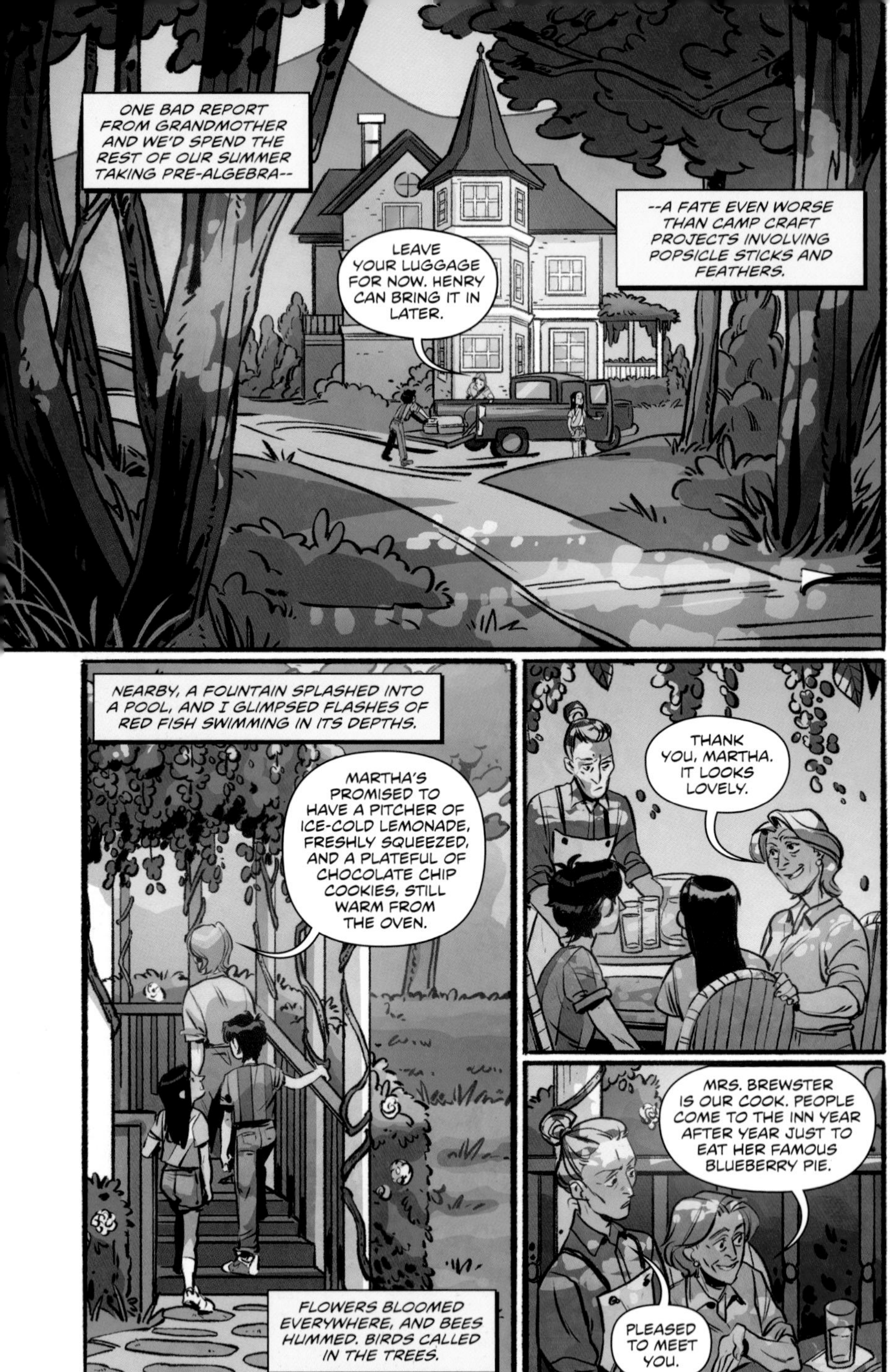
ONE BAD REPORT FROM GRANDMOTHER AND WE'D SPEND THE REST OF OUR SUMMER TAKING PRE-ALGEBRA--
LEAVE YOUR LUGGAGE FOR NOW. HENRY CAN BRING IT IN LATER.
--A FATE EVEN WORSE THAN CAMP CRAFT PROJECTS INVOLVING POPSICLE STICKS AND FEATHERS.
NEARBY, A FOUNTAIN SPLASHED INTO A POOL, AND I GLIMPSED FLASHES OF RED FISH SWIMMING IN ITS DEPTHS.
MARTHA'S PROMISED TO HAVE A PITCHER OF ICE-COLD LEMONADE, FRESHLY SQUEEZED, AND A PLATEFUL OF CHOCOLATE CHIP COOKIES, STILL WARM FROM THE OVEN.
FLOWERS BLOOMED EVERYWHERE, AND BEES HUMMED. BIRDS CALLED IN THE TREES.
THANK YOU, MARTHA. IT LOOKS LOVELY.
MRS. BREWSTER IS OUR COOK. PEOPLE COME TO THE INN YEAR AFTER YEAR JUST TO EAT HER FAMOUS BLUEBERRY PIE.
PLEASED TO MEET YOU.

MARTHA'S A LITTLE STANDOFFISH, BUT SHE AND HER HUSBAND MORE OR LESS CAME WITH THE INN.

AND SHE'S TRULY MAGNIFICENT IN THE KITCHEN.

SHE LOOKS LIKE AN OLD GRUMP.

YOU'LL CHANGE YOUR MIND ABOUT HER WHEN YOU EAT YOUR FIRST MEAL HERE.

IS THAT A SWIMMING POOL?

IT IS. AND IF YOU LIKE TENNIS, THE COURT'S OVER THERE.

IF IT RAINS, THERE'S A LIBRARY, COMPUTER, TV, AND AT LEAST A DOZEN OLD-FASHIONED BOARD GAMES. HOPEFULLY, YOU'LL FIND PLENTY TO DO.

I HAVE BICYCLES FOR THE GUESTS--THE STATE PARK JUST DOWN THE ROAD HAS A GREAT NETWORK OF BIKING AND HIKING TRAILS.

*OUR LEMONADE WAS JUST AS GOOD AS GRANDMOTHER HAD PROMISED.*

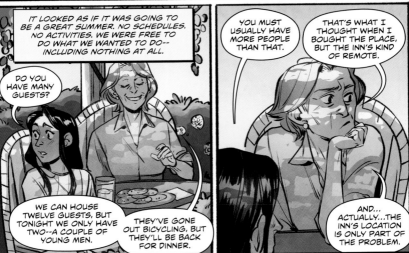

*IT LOOKED AS IF IT WAS GOING TO BE A GREAT SUMMER. NO SCHEDULES. NO ACTIVITIES. WE WERE FREE TO DO WHAT WE WANTED TO DO-- INCLUDING NOTHING AT ALL.*

DO YOU HAVE MANY GUESTS?

WE CAN HOUSE TWELVE GUESTS, BUT TONIGHT WE ONLY HAVE TWO--A COUPLE OF YOUNG MEN.

THEY'VE GONE OUT BICYCLING, BUT THEY'LL BE BACK FOR DINNER.

YOU MUST USUALLY HAVE MORE PEOPLE THAN THAT.

THAT'S WHAT I THOUGHT WHEN I BOUGHT THE PLACE, BUT THE INN'S KIND OF REMOTE.

AND... ACTUALLY...THE INN'S LOCATION IS ONLY PART OF THE PROBLEM.

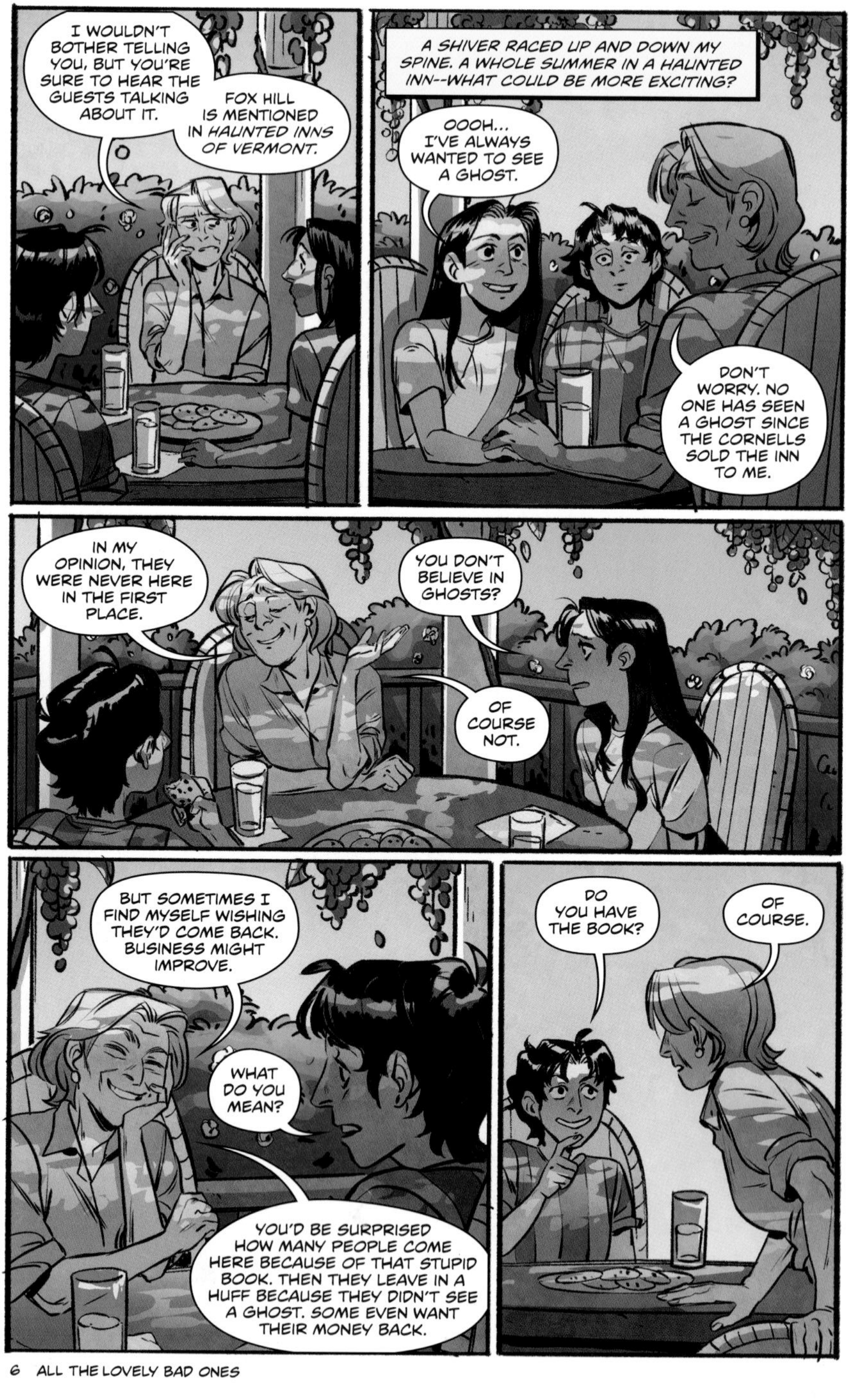
I WOULDN'T BOTHER TELLING YOU, BUT YOU'RE SURE TO HEAR THE GUESTS TALKING ABOUT IT.
FOX HILL IS MENTIONED IN *HAUNTED INNS OF VERMONT.*
*A SHIVER RACED UP AND DOWN MY SPINE. A WHOLE SUMMER IN A HAUNTED INN--WHAT COULD BE MORE EXCITING?*
OOOH... I'VE ALWAYS WANTED TO SEE A GHOST.
DON'T WORRY. NO ONE HAS SEEN A GHOST SINCE THE CORNELLS SOLD THE INN TO ME.
IN MY OPINION, THEY WERE NEVER HERE IN THE FIRST PLACE.
YOU DON'T BELIEVE IN GHOSTS?
OF COURSE NOT.
BUT SOMETIMES I FIND MYSELF WISHING THEY'D COME BACK. BUSINESS MIGHT IMPROVE.
WHAT DO YOU MEAN?
YOU'D BE SURPRISED HOW MANY PEOPLE COME HERE BECAUSE OF THAT STUPID BOOK. THEN THEY LEAVE IN A HUFF BECAUSE THEY DIDN'T SEE A GHOST. SOME EVEN WANT THEIR MONEY BACK.
DO YOU HAVE THE BOOK?
OF COURSE.

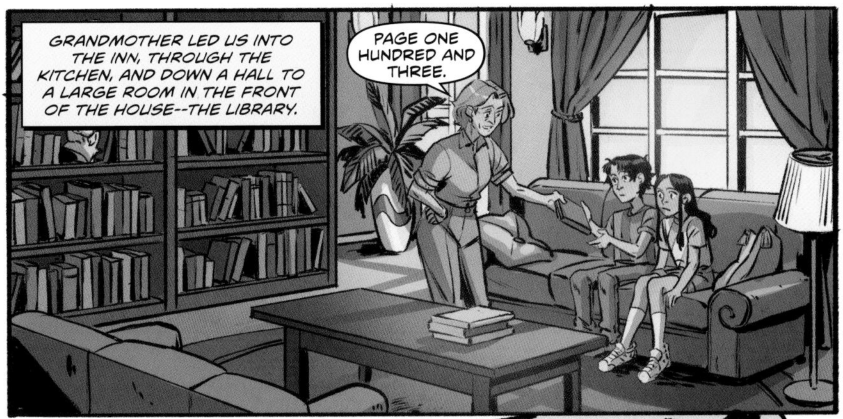
GRANDMOTHER LED US INTO THE INN, THROUGH THE KITCHEN, AND DOWN A HALL TO A LARGE ROOM IN THE FRONT OF THE HOUSE--THE LIBRARY.
PAGE ONE HUNDRED AND THREE.

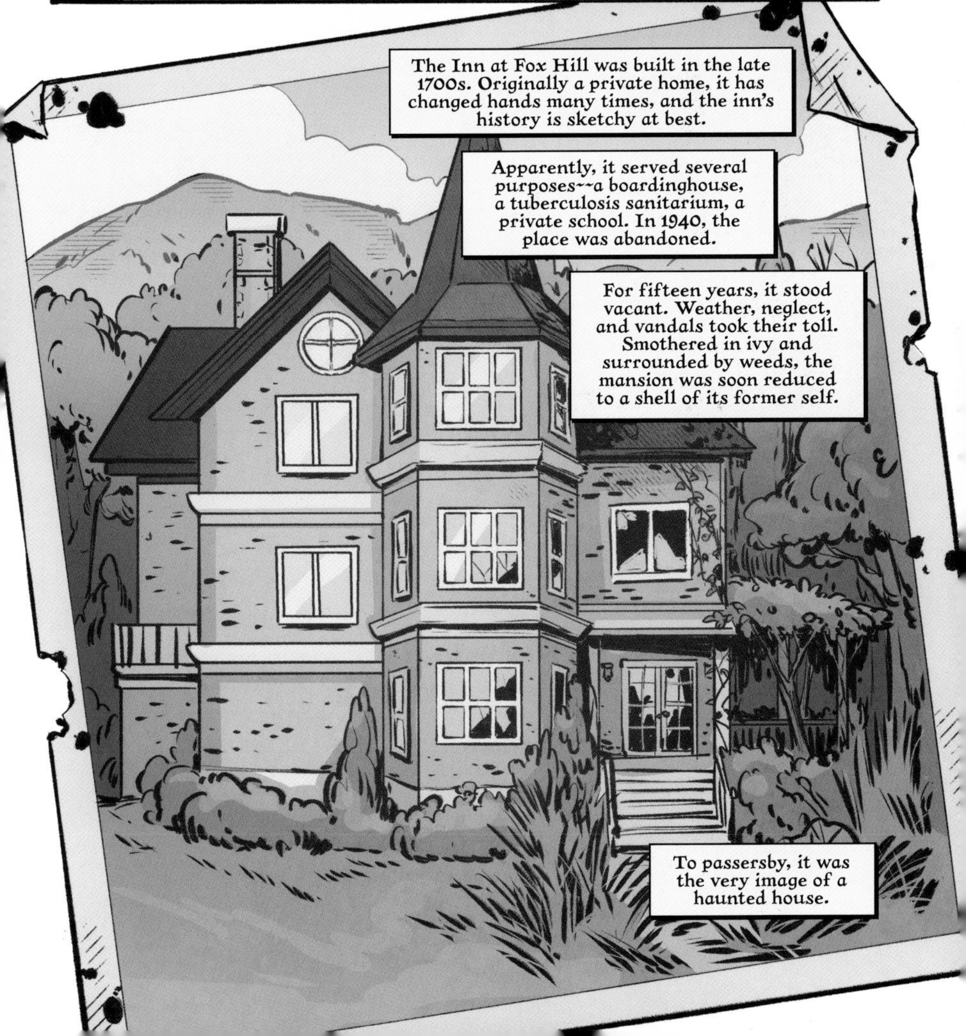
The Inn at Fox Hill was built in the late 1700s. Originally a private home, it has changed hands many times, and the inn's history is sketchy at best.
Apparently, it served several purposes--a boardinghouse, a tuberculosis sanitarium, a private school. In 1940, the place was abandoned.
For fifteen years, it stood vacant. Weather, neglect, and vandals took their toll. Smothered in ivy and surrounded by weeds, the mansion was soon reduced to a shell of its former self.
To passersby, it was the very image of a haunted house.

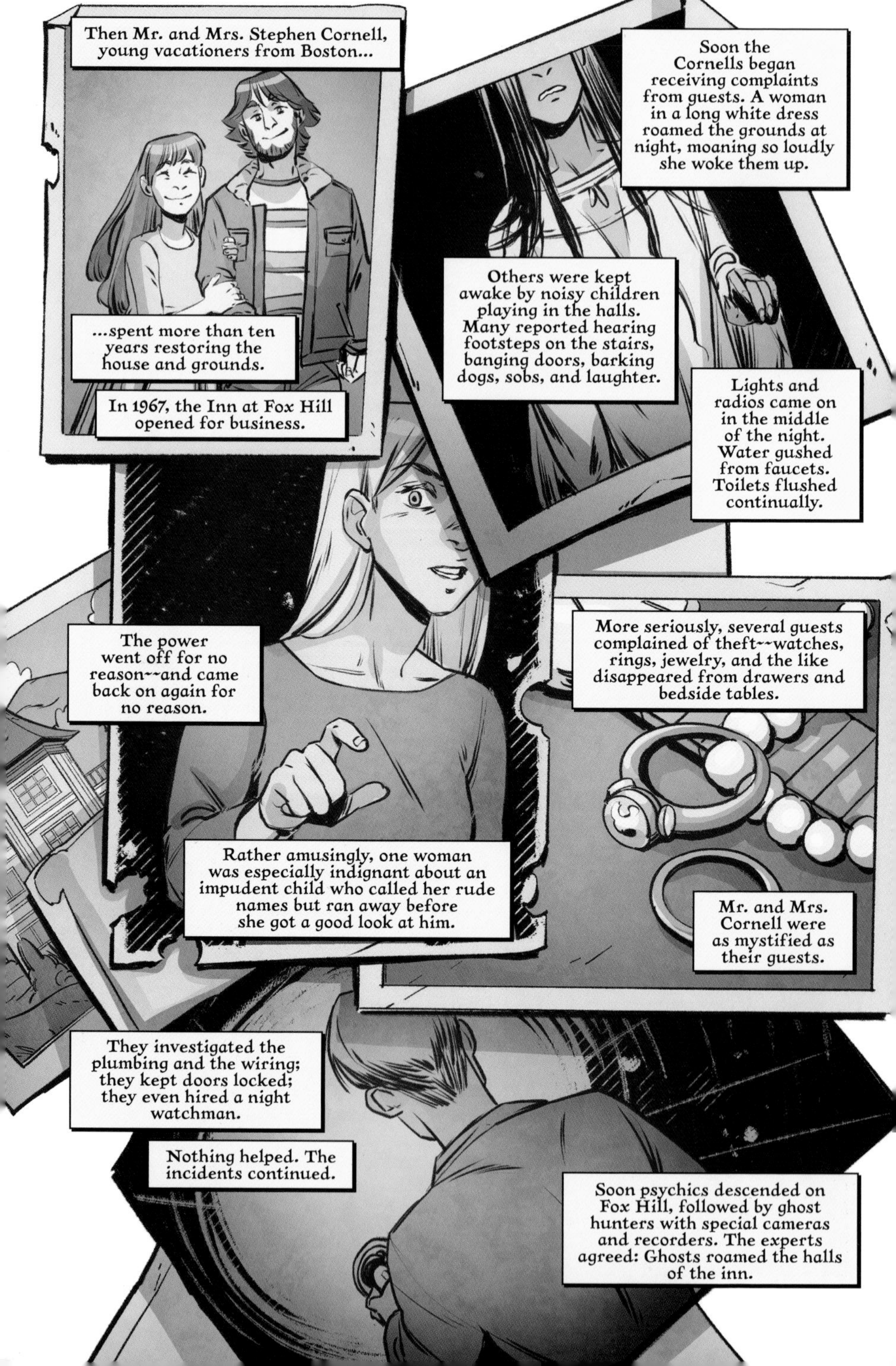
Then Mr. and Mrs. Stephen Cornell, young vacationers from Boston...
...spent more than ten years restoring the house and grounds.
In 1967, the Inn at Fox Hill opened for business.
Soon the Cornells began receiving complaints from guests. A woman in a long white dress roamed the grounds at night, moaning so loudly she woke them up.
Others were kept awake by noisy children playing in the halls. Many reported hearing footsteps on the stairs, banging doors, barking dogs, sobs, and laughter.
Lights and radios came on in the middle of the night. Water gushed from faucets. Toilets flushed continually.
The power went off for no reason--and came back on again for no reason.
More seriously, several guests complained of theft--watches, rings, jewelry, and the like disappeared from drawers and bedside tables.
Rather amusingly, one woman was especially indignant about an impudent child who called her rude names but ran away before she got a good look at him.
Mr. and Mrs. Cornell were as mystified as their guests.
They investigated the plumbing and the wiring; they kept doors locked; they even hired a night watchman.
Nothing helped. The incidents continued.
Soon psychics descended on Fox Hill, followed by ghost hunters with special cameras and recorders. The experts agreed: Ghosts roamed the halls of the inn.

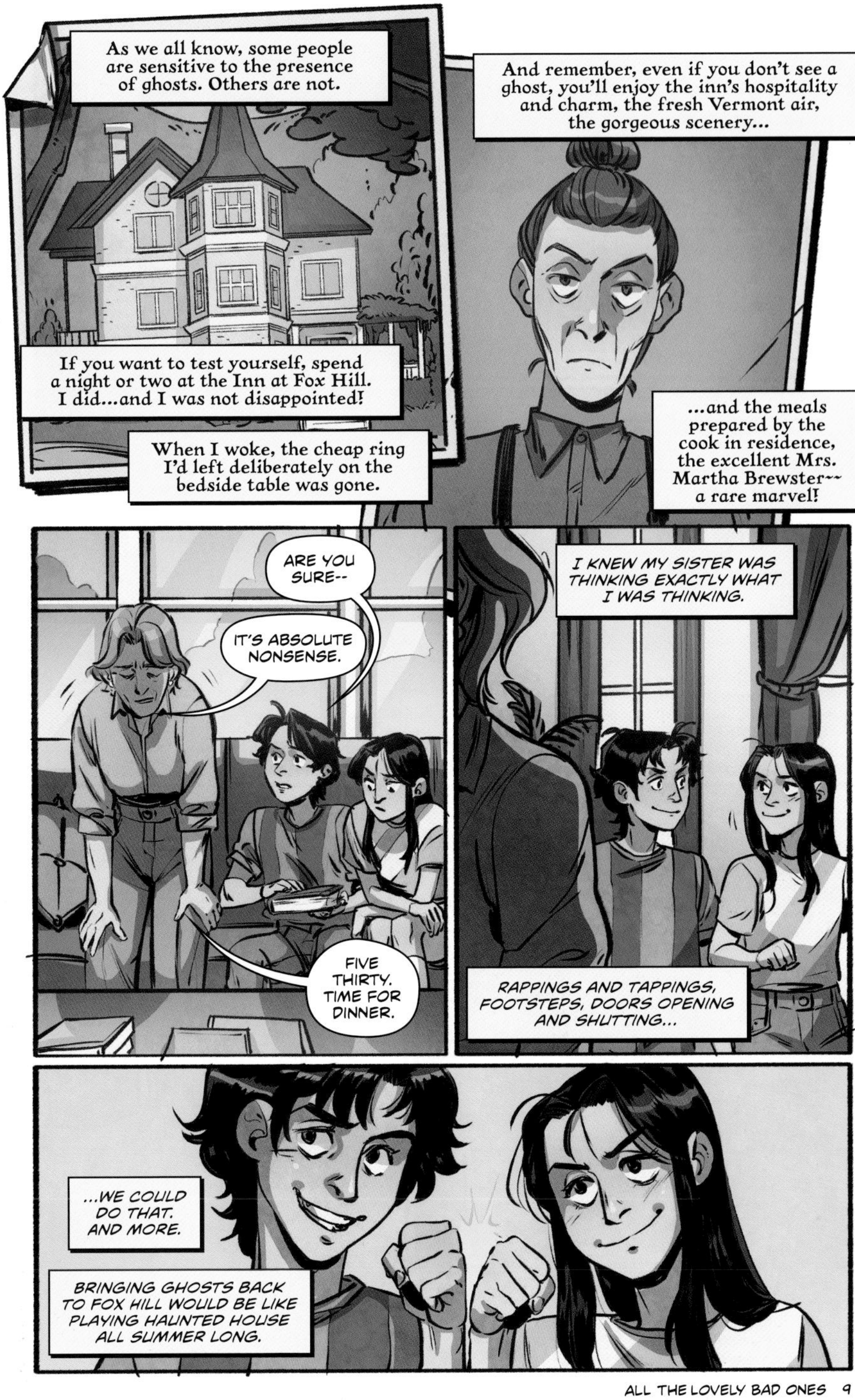

As we all know, some people are sensitive to the presence of ghosts. Others are not.
If you want to test yourself, spend a night or two at the Inn at Fox Hill. I did...and I was not disappointed!
When I woke, the cheap ring I'd left deliberately on the bedside table was gone.
And remember, even if you don't see a ghost, you'll enjoy the inn's hospitality and charm, the fresh Vermont air, the gorgeous scenery...
...and the meals prepared by the cook in residence, the excellent Mrs. Martha Brewster-- a rare marvel!
ARE YOU SURE--
IT'S ABSOLUTE NONSENSE.
FIVE THIRTY. TIME FOR DINNER.
I KNEW MY SISTER WAS THINKING EXACTLY WHAT I WAS THINKING.
RAPPINGS AND TAPPINGS, FOOTSTEPS, DOORS OPENING AND SHUTTING...
...WE COULD DO THAT. AND MORE.
BRINGING GHOSTS BACK TO FOX HILL WOULD BE LIKE PLAYING HAUNTED HOUSE ALL SUMMER LONG.

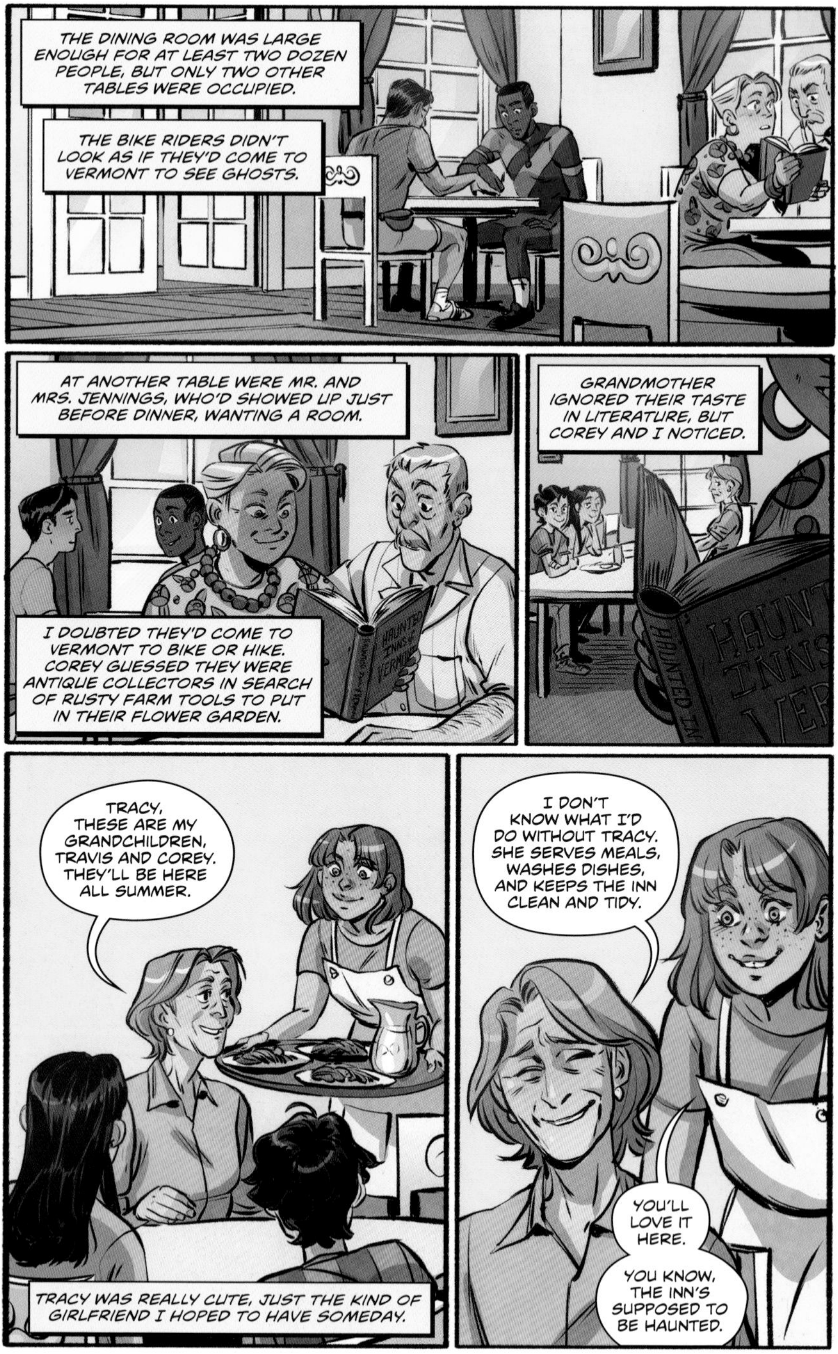
THE DINING ROOM WAS LARGE ENOUGH FOR AT LEAST TWO DOZEN PEOPLE, BUT ONLY TWO OTHER TABLES WERE OCCUPIED.
THE BIKE RIDERS DIDN'T LOOK AS IF THEY'D COME TO VERMONT TO SEE GHOSTS.
AT ANOTHER TABLE WERE MR. AND MRS. JENNINGS, WHO'D SHOWED UP JUST BEFORE DINNER, WANTING A ROOM.
I DOUBTED THEY'D COME TO VERMONT TO BIKE OR HIKE. COREY GUESSED THEY WERE ANTIQUE COLLECTORS IN SEARCH OF RUSTY FARM TOOLS TO PUT IN THEIR FLOWER GARDEN.
GRANDMOTHER IGNORED THEIR TASTE IN LITERATURE, BUT COREY AND I NOTICED.
TRACY, THESE ARE MY GRANDCHILDREN, TRAVIS AND COREY. THEY'LL BE HERE ALL SUMMER.
TRACY WAS REALLY CUTE, JUST THE KIND OF GIRLFRIEND I HOPED TO HAVE SOMEDAY.
I DON'T KNOW WHAT I'D DO WITHOUT TRACY. SHE SERVES MEALS, WASHES DISHES, AND KEEPS THE INN CLEAN AND TIDY.
YOU'LL LOVE IT HERE.
YOU KNOW, THE INN'S SUPPOSED TO BE HAUNTED.

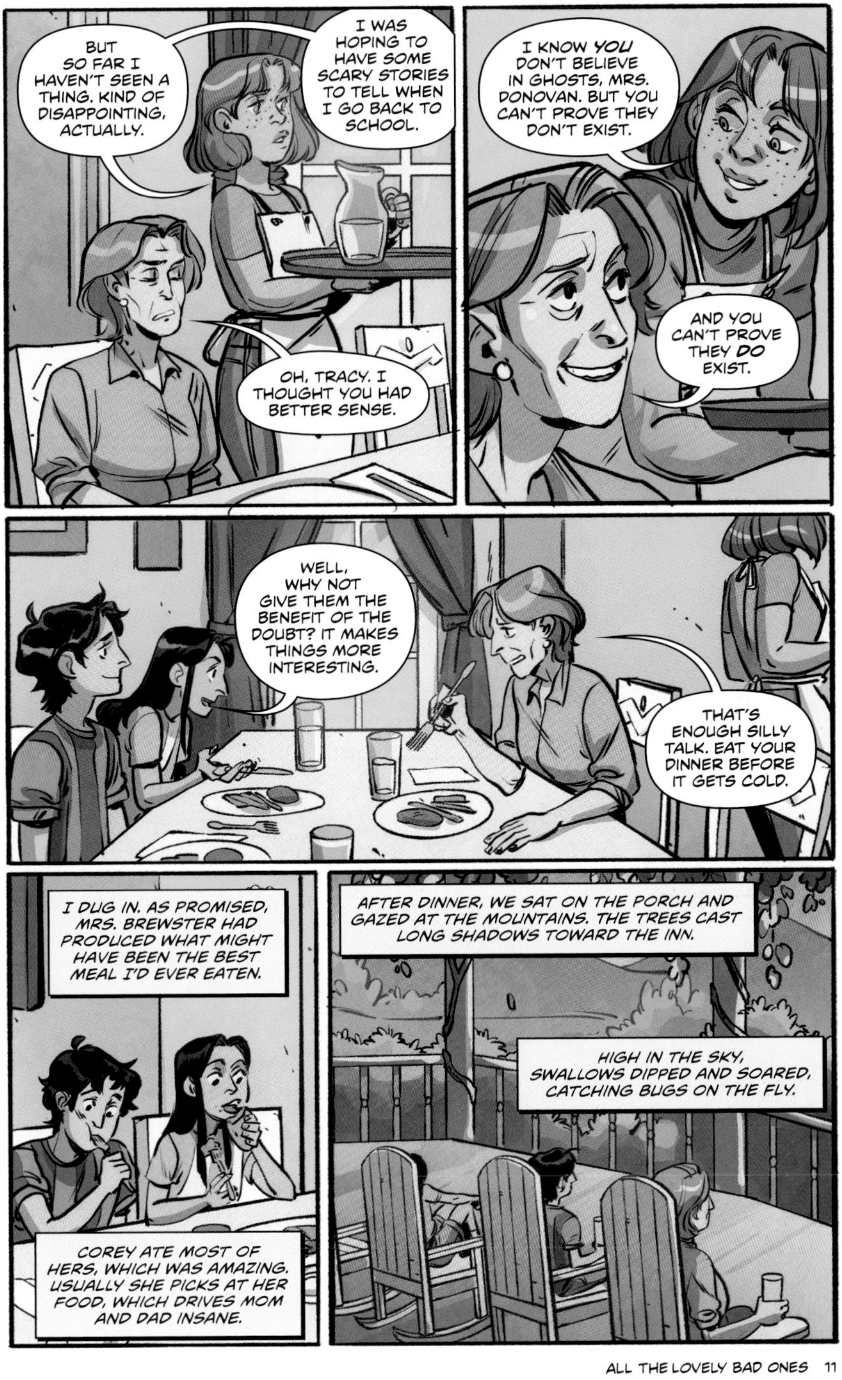

BUT SO FAR I HAVEN'T SEEN A THING. KIND OF DISAPPOINTING, ACTUALLY.
I WAS HOPING TO HAVE SOME SCARY STORIES TO TELL WHEN I GO BACK TO SCHOOL.
OH, TRACY. I THOUGHT YOU HAD BETTER SENSE.
I KNOW *YOU* DON'T BELIEVE IN GHOSTS, MRS. DONOVAN. BUT YOU CAN'T PROVE THEY DON'T EXIST.
AND YOU CAN'T PROVE THEY *DO* EXIST.
WELL, WHY NOT GIVE THEM THE BENEFIT OF THE DOUBT? IT MAKES THINGS MORE INTERESTING.
THAT'S ENOUGH SILLY TALK. EAT YOUR DINNER BEFORE IT GETS COLD.
I DUG IN. AS PROMISED, MRS. BREWSTER HAD PRODUCED WHAT MIGHT HAVE BEEN THE BEST MEAL I'D EVER EATEN.
COREY ATE MOST OF HERS, WHICH WAS AMAZING. USUALLY SHE PICKS AT HER FOOD, WHICH DRIVES MOM AND DAD INSANE.
AFTER DINNER, WE SAT ON THE PORCH AND GAZED AT THE MOUNTAINS. THE TREES CAST LONG SHADOWS TOWARD THE INN.
HIGH IN THE SKY, SWALLOWS DIPPED AND SOARED, CATCHING BUGS ON THE FLY.

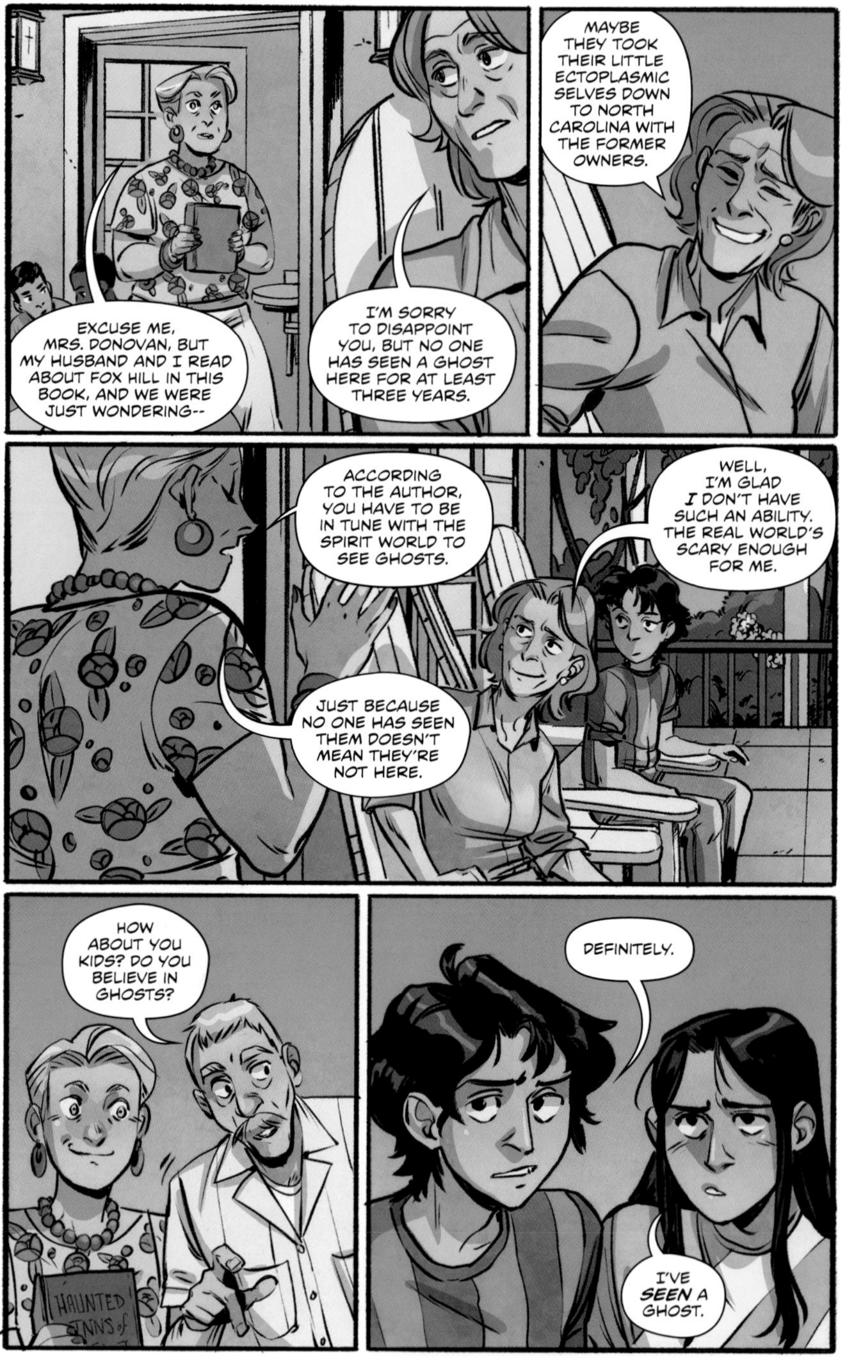
EXCUSE ME, MRS. DONOVAN, BUT MY HUSBAND AND I READ ABOUT FOX HILL IN THIS BOOK, AND WE WERE JUST WONDERING--
I'M SORRY TO DISAPPOINT YOU, BUT NO ONE HAS SEEN A GHOST HERE FOR AT LEAST THREE YEARS.
MAYBE THEY TOOK THEIR LITTLE ECTOPLASMIC SELVES DOWN TO NORTH CAROLINA WITH THE FORMER OWNERS.
ACCORDING TO THE AUTHOR, YOU HAVE TO BE IN TUNE WITH THE SPIRIT WORLD TO SEE GHOSTS.
JUST BECAUSE NO ONE HAS SEEN THEM DOESN'T MEAN THEY'RE NOT HERE.
WELL, I'M GLAD *I* DON'T HAVE SUCH AN ABILITY. THE REAL WORLD'S SCARY ENOUGH FOR ME.
HOW ABOUT YOU KIDS? DO YOU BELIEVE IN GHOSTS?
HAUNTED INNS of
DEFINITELY.
I'VE **SEEN** A GHOST.

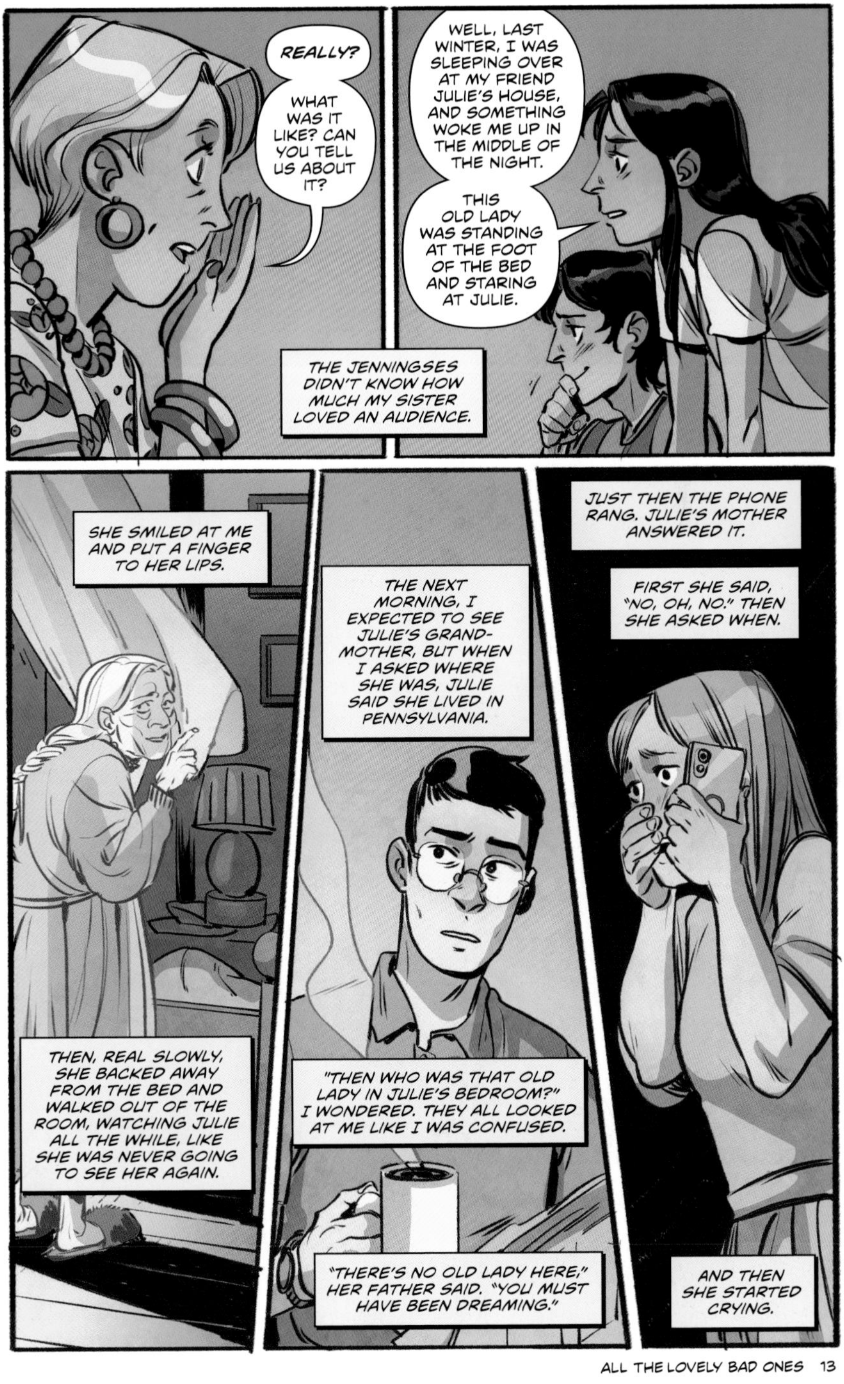

REALLY?
WHAT WAS IT LIKE? CAN YOU TELL US ABOUT IT?
WELL, LAST WINTER, I WAS SLEEPING OVER AT MY FRIEND JULIE'S HOUSE, AND SOMETHING WOKE ME UP IN THE MIDDLE OF THE NIGHT.
THIS OLD LADY WAS STANDING AT THE FOOT OF THE BED AND STARING AT JULIE.
THE JENNINGSES DIDN'T KNOW HOW MUCH MY SISTER LOVED AN AUDIENCE.
SHE SMILED AT ME AND PUT A FINGER TO HER LIPS.
THEN, REAL SLOWLY, SHE BACKED AWAY FROM THE BED AND WALKED OUT OF THE ROOM, WATCHING JULIE ALL THE WHILE, LIKE SHE WAS NEVER GOING TO SEE HER AGAIN.
THE NEXT MORNING, I EXPECTED TO SEE JULIE'S GRAND-MOTHER, BUT WHEN I ASKED WHERE SHE WAS, JULIE SAID SHE LIVED IN PENNSYLVANIA.
"THEN WHO WAS THAT OLD LADY IN JULIE'S BEDROOM?" I WONDERED. THEY ALL LOOKED AT ME LIKE I WAS CONFUSED.
"THERE'S NO OLD LADY HERE," HER FATHER SAID. "YOU MUST HAVE BEEN DREAMING."
JUST THEN THE PHONE RANG. JULIE'S MOTHER ANSWERED IT.
FIRST SHE SAID, "NO, OH, NO." THEN SHE ASKED WHEN.
AND THEN SHE STARTED CRYING.

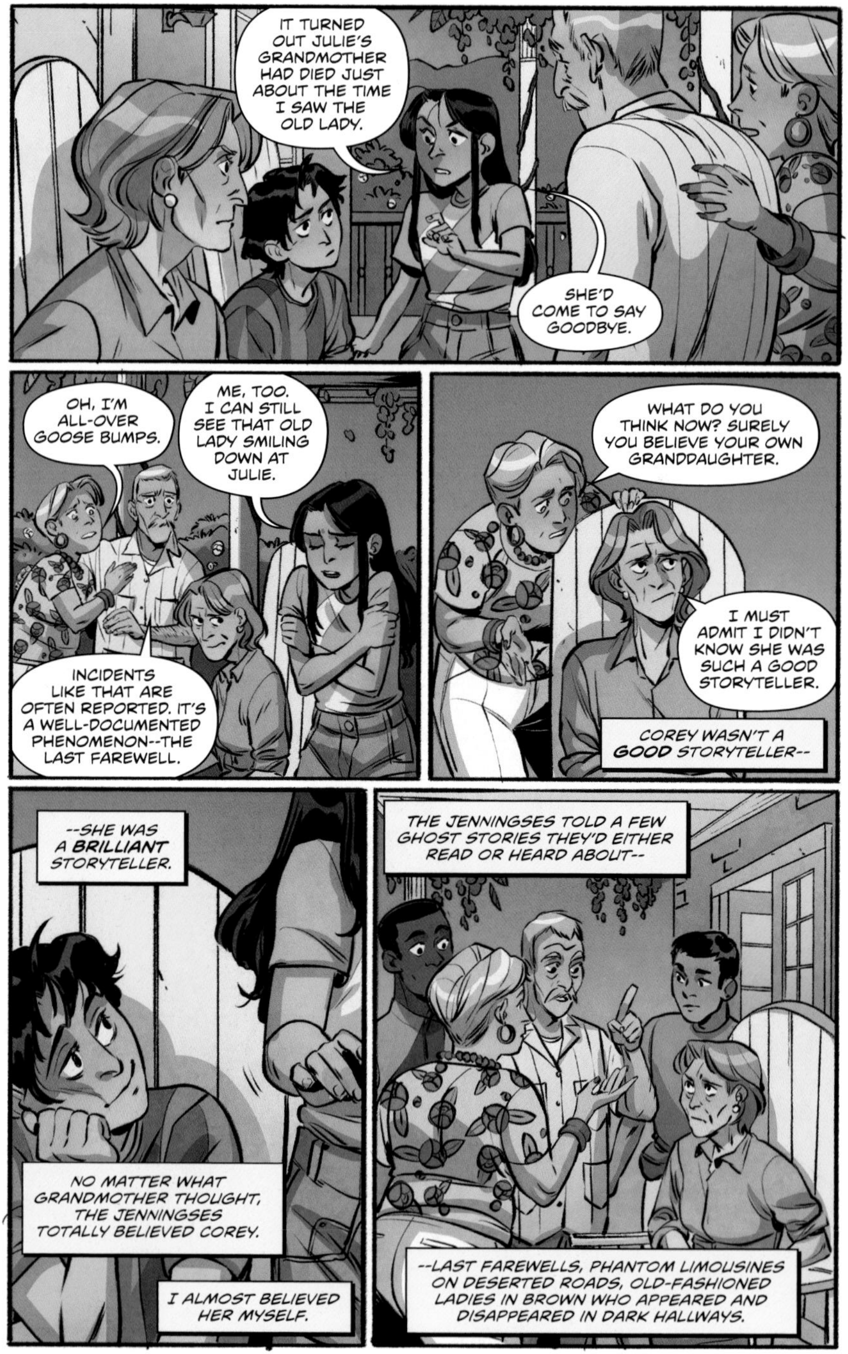
IT TURNED OUT JULIE'S GRANDMOTHER HAD DIED JUST ABOUT THE TIME I SAW THE OLD LADY.
SHE'D COME TO SAY GOODBYE.
OH, I'M ALL-OVER GOOSE BUMPS.
ME, TOO. I CAN STILL SEE THAT OLD LADY SMILING DOWN AT JULIE.
INCIDENTS LIKE THAT ARE OFTEN REPORTED. IT'S A WELL-DOCUMENTED PHENOMENON--THE LAST FAREWELL.
WHAT DO YOU THINK NOW? SURELY YOU BELIEVE YOUR OWN GRANDDAUGHTER.
I MUST ADMIT I DIDN'T KNOW SHE WAS SUCH A GOOD STORYTELLER.
COREY WASN'T A GOOD STORYTELLER--
--SHE WAS A BRILLIANT STORYTELLER.
NO MATTER WHAT GRANDMOTHER THOUGHT, THE JENNINGSES TOTALLY BELIEVED COREY.
I ALMOST BELIEVED HER MYSELF.
THE JENNINGSES TOLD A FEW GHOST STORIES THEY'D EITHER READ OR HEARD ABOUT--
--LAST FAREWELLS, PHANTOM LIMOUSINES ON DESERTED ROADS, OLD-FASHIONED LADIES IN BROWN WHO APPEARED AND DISAPPEARED IN DARK HALLWAYS.

TIM THE BIKER THREW IN A STORY OF MYSTERIOUS BLUE LIGHTS THAT HOVERED OVER A MOUNTAIN DOWN SOUTH SOMEWHERE. HIS BUDDY, ROBERT, SAID HE DIDN'T BELIEVE IN THAT STUFF--

--WHICH EARNED HIM A NOD OF APPROVAL FROM GRANDMOTHER.

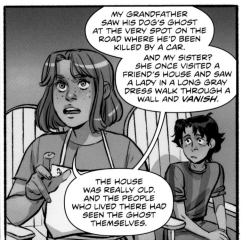

MY GRANDFATHER SAW HIS DOG'S GHOST AT THE VERY SPOT ON THE ROAD WHERE HE'D BEEN KILLED BY A CAR.

AND MY SISTER? SHE ONCE VISITED A FRIEND'S HOUSE AND SAW A LADY IN A LONG GRAY DRESS WALK THROUGH A WALL AND *VANISH*.

THE HOUSE WAS REALLY OLD. AND THE PEOPLE WHO LIVED THERE HAD SEEN THE GHOST THEMSELVES.

GRADUALLY, THE STORIES FADED AWAY AND WE SAT TOGETHER SILENTLY, EACH OF US THINKING OUR OWN THOUGHTS--ABOUT GHOSTS, I GUESSED.

SOME BELIEVING, SOME NOT, AND SOME NOT SURE. STARS STUDDED THE SKY--THOUSANDS, MAYBE MILLIONS, MORE THAN I'D EVER SEEN IN NEW YORK.

IT'S GETTING CHILLY.

BIG DAY AHEAD. AT LEAST SEVENTY-FIVE MILES. AT *LEAST*.

LET'S TAKE A WALK TO LOOK AT THE STARS AWAY FROM THE LIGHTS OF THE INN.

AH, HENRY. THESE ARE MY GRANDCHILDREN, COREY AND TRAVIS.

THEY'LL BE SLEEPING IN THE TWO ROOMS ON THE FIRST FLOOR IN THE BACK. CAN YOU HELP WITH THEIR LUGGAGE?

MR. BREWSTER DIDN'T SAY A WORD, JUST GRUNTED AN ACKNOWLEDGMENT.

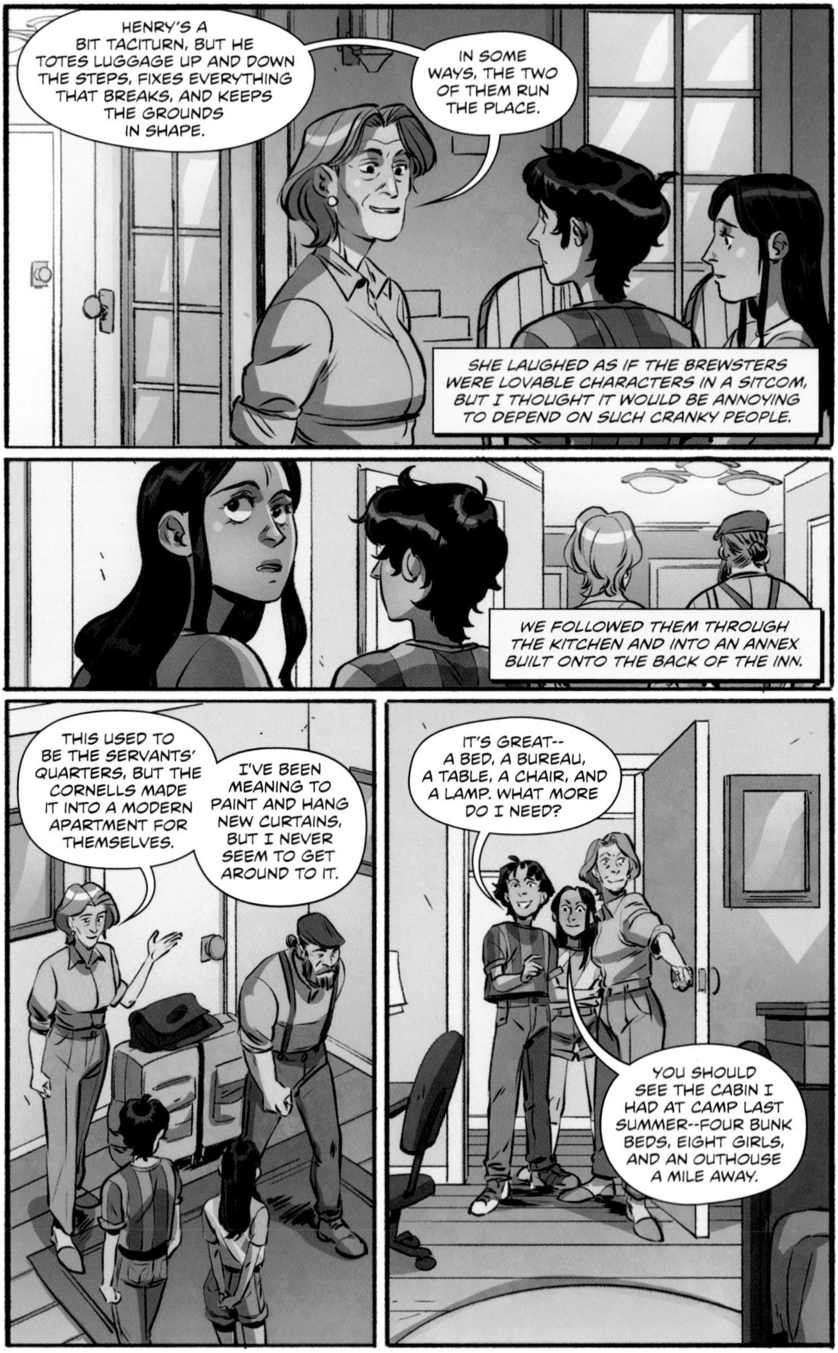
HENRY'S A BIT TACITURN, BUT HE TOTES LUGGAGE UP AND DOWN THE STEPS, FIXES EVERYTHING THAT BREAKS, AND KEEPS THE GROUNDS IN SHAPE.
IN SOME WAYS, THE TWO OF THEM RUN THE PLACE.
SHE LAUGHED AS IF THE BREWSTERS WERE LOVABLE CHARACTERS IN A SITCOM, BUT I THOUGHT IT WOULD BE ANNOYING TO DEPEND ON SUCH CRANKY PEOPLE.
WE FOLLOWED THEM THROUGH THE KITCHEN AND INTO AN ANNEX BUILT ONTO THE BACK OF THE INN.
THIS USED TO BE THE SERVANTS' QUARTERS, BUT THE CORNELLS MADE IT INTO A MODERN APARTMENT FOR THEMSELVES.
I'VE BEEN MEANING TO PAINT AND HANG NEW CURTAINS, BUT I NEVER SEEM TO GET AROUND TO IT.
IT'S GREAT-- A BED, A BUREAU, A TABLE, A CHAIR, AND A LAMP. WHAT MORE DO I NEED?
YOU SHOULD SEE THE CABIN I HAD AT CAMP LAST SUMMER--FOUR BUNK BEDS, EIGHT GIRLS, AND AN OUTHOUSE A MILE AWAY.

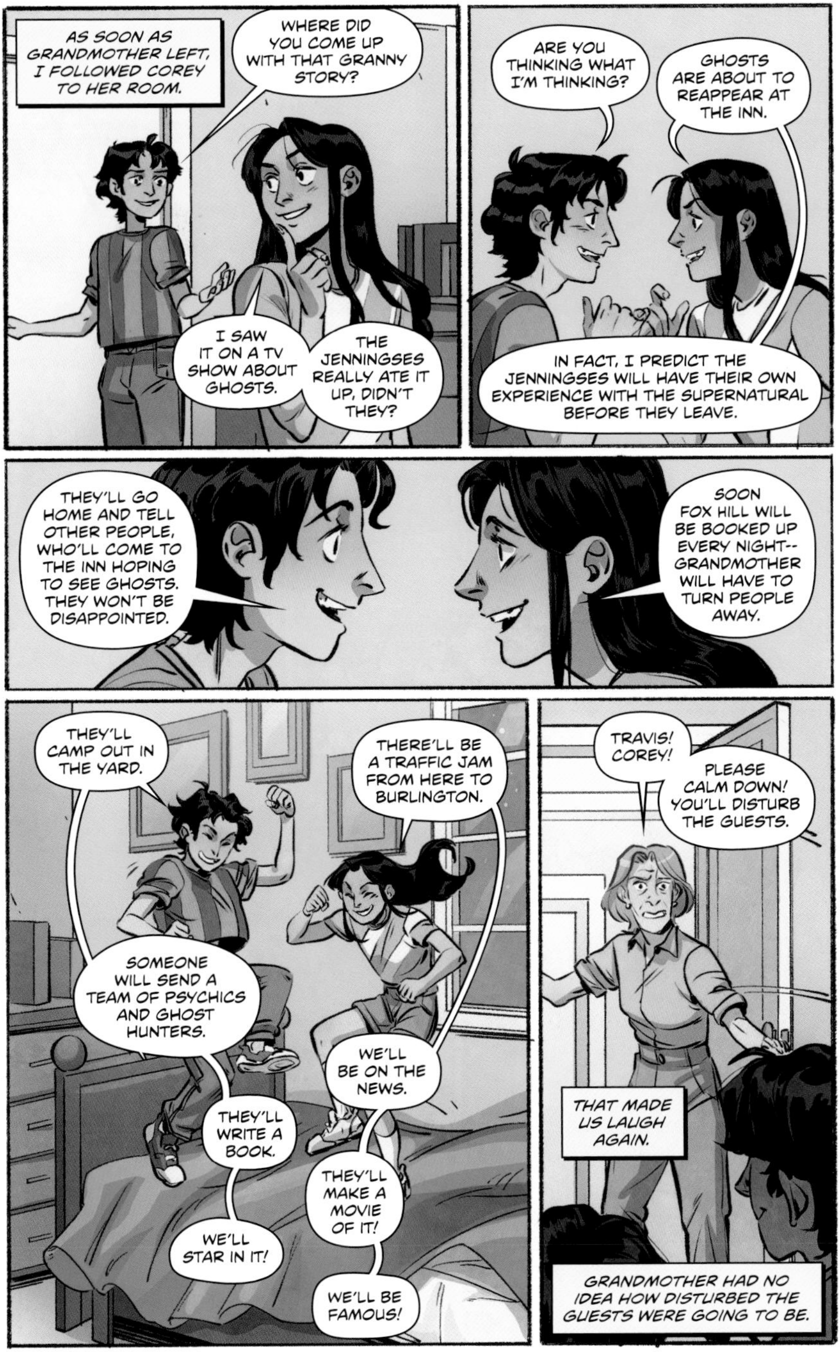
AS SOON AS GRANDMOTHER LEFT, I FOLLOWED COREY TO HER ROOM.
WHERE DID YOU COME UP WITH THAT GRANNY STORY?
I SAW IT ON A TV SHOW ABOUT GHOSTS.
THE JENNINGSES REALLY ATE IT UP, DIDN'T THEY?
ARE YOU THINKING WHAT I'M THINKING?
GHOSTS ARE ABOUT TO REAPPEAR AT THE INN.
IN FACT, I PREDICT THE JENNINGSES WILL HAVE THEIR OWN EXPERIENCE WITH THE SUPERNATURAL BEFORE THEY LEAVE.
THEY'LL GO HOME AND TELL OTHER PEOPLE, WHO'LL COME TO THE INN HOPING TO SEE GHOSTS. THEY WON'T BE DISAPPOINTED.
SOON FOX HILL WILL BE BOOKED UP EVERY NIGHT-- GRANDMOTHER WILL HAVE TO TURN PEOPLE AWAY.
THEY'LL CAMP OUT IN THE YARD.
THERE'LL BE A TRAFFIC JAM FROM HERE TO BURLINGTON.
SOMEONE WILL SEND A TEAM OF PSYCHICS AND GHOST HUNTERS.
WE'LL BE ON THE NEWS.
THEY'LL WRITE A BOOK.
THEY'LL MAKE A MOVIE OF IT!
WE'LL STAR IN IT!
WE'LL BE FAMOUS!
TRAVIS! COREY!
PLEASE CALM DOWN! YOU'LL DISTURB THE GUESTS.
THAT MADE US LAUGH AGAIN.
GRANDMOTHER HAD NO IDEA HOW DISTURBED THE GUESTS WERE GOING TO BE.

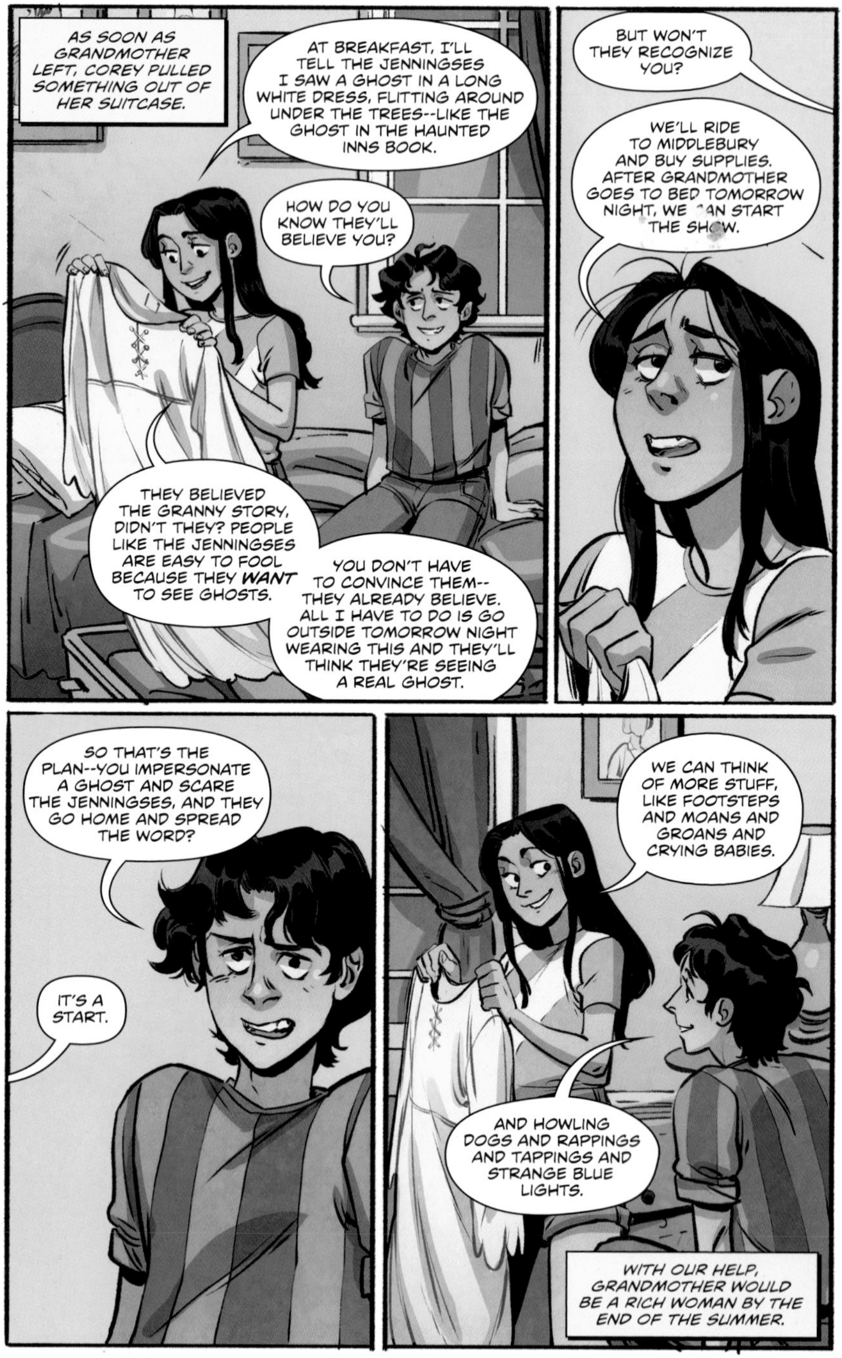
AS SOON AS GRANDMOTHER LEFT, COREY PULLED SOMETHING OUT OF HER SUITCASE.
AT BREAKFAST, I'LL TELL THE JENNINGSES I SAW A GHOST IN A LONG WHITE DRESS, FLITTING AROUND UNDER THE TREES--LIKE THE GHOST IN THE HAUNTED INNS BOOK.
HOW DO YOU KNOW THEY'LL BELIEVE YOU?
THEY BELIEVED THE GRANNY STORY, DIDN'T THEY? PEOPLE LIKE THE JENNINGSES ARE EASY TO FOOL BECAUSE THEY ***WANT*** TO SEE GHOSTS.
YOU DON'T HAVE TO CONVINCE THEM--THEY ALREADY BELIEVE. ALL I HAVE TO DO IS GO OUTSIDE TOMORROW NIGHT WEARING THIS AND THEY'LL THINK THEY'RE SEEING A REAL GHOST.
BUT WON'T THEY RECOGNIZE YOU?
WE'LL RIDE TO MIDDLEBURY AND BUY SUPPLIES. AFTER GRANDMOTHER GOES TO BED TOMORROW NIGHT, WE CAN START THE SHOW.
SO THAT'S THE PLAN--YOU IMPERSONATE A GHOST AND SCARE THE JENNINGSES, AND THEY GO HOME AND SPREAD THE WORD?
IT'S A START.
WE CAN THINK OF MORE STUFF, LIKE FOOTSTEPS AND MOANS AND GROANS AND CRYING BABIES.
AND HOWLING DOGS AND RAPPINGS AND TAPPINGS AND STRANGE BLUE LIGHTS.
WITH OUR HELP, GRANDMOTHER WOULD BE A RICH WOMAN BY THE END OF THE SUMMER.

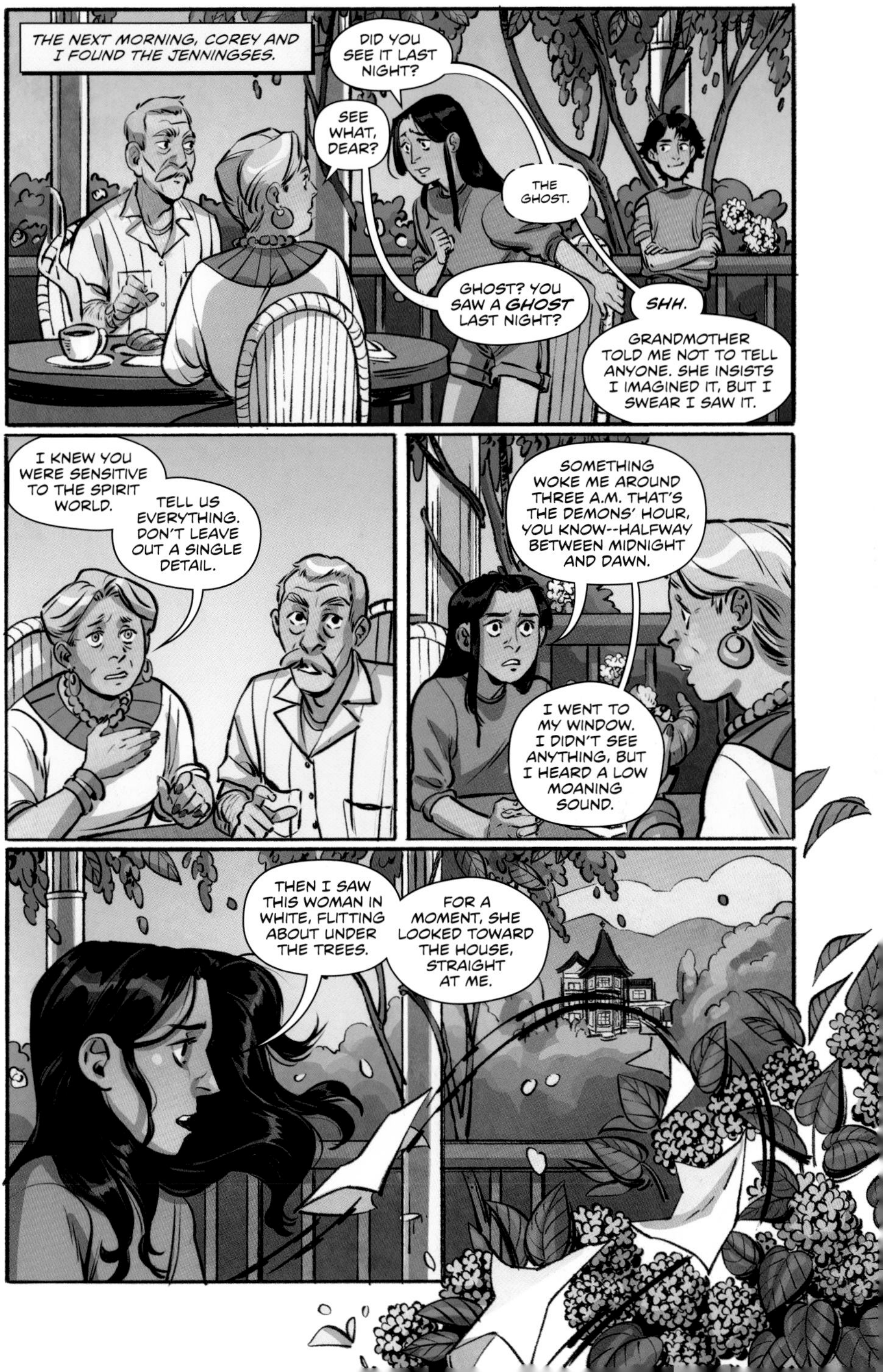
THE NEXT MORNING, COREY AND I FOUND THE JENNINGSES.
DID YOU SEE IT LAST NIGHT?
SEE WHAT, DEAR?
THE GHOST.
GHOST? YOU SAW A *GHOST* LAST NIGHT?
*SHH.*
GRANDMOTHER TOLD ME NOT TO TELL ANYONE. SHE INSISTS I IMAGINED IT, BUT I SWEAR I SAW IT.
I KNEW YOU WERE SENSITIVE TO THE SPIRIT WORLD.
TELL US EVERYTHING. DON'T LEAVE OUT A SINGLE DETAIL.
SOMETHING WOKE ME AROUND THREE A.M. THAT'S THE DEMONS' HOUR, YOU KNOW--HALFWAY BETWEEN MIDNIGHT AND DAWN.
I WENT TO MY WINDOW. I DIDN'T SEE ANYTHING, BUT I HEARD A LOW MOANING SOUND.
THEN I SAW THIS WOMAN IN WHITE, FLITTING ABOUT UNDER THE TREES.
FOR A MOMENT, SHE LOOKED TOWARD THE HOUSE, STRAIGHT AT ME.

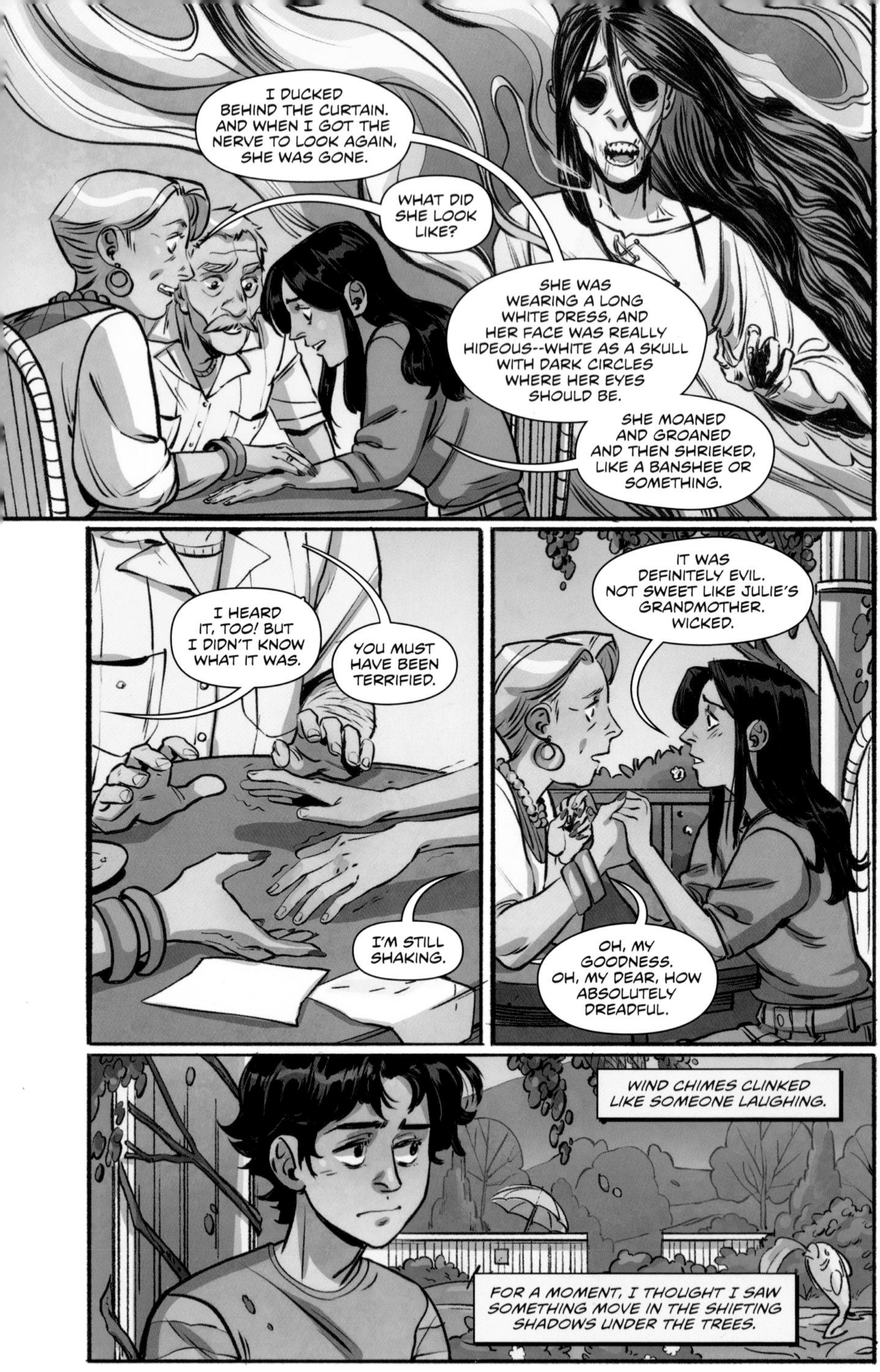
I DUCKED BEHIND THE CURTAIN. AND WHEN I GOT THE NERVE TO LOOK AGAIN, SHE WAS GONE.
WHAT DID SHE LOOK LIKE?
SHE WAS WEARING A LONG WHITE DRESS, AND HER FACE WAS REALLY HIDEOUS--WHITE AS A SKULL WITH DARK CIRCLES WHERE HER EYES SHOULD BE.
SHE MOANED AND GROANED AND THEN SHRIEKED, LIKE A BANSHEE OR SOMETHING.
I HEARD IT, TOO! BUT I DIDN'T KNOW WHAT IT WAS.
YOU MUST HAVE BEEN TERRIFIED.
I'M STILL SHAKING.
IT WAS DEFINITELY EVIL. NOT SWEET LIKE JULIE'S GRANDMOTHER. WICKED.
OH, MY GOODNESS. OH, MY DEAR, HOW ABSOLUTELY DREADFUL.
WIND CHIMES CLINKED LIKE SOMEONE LAUGHING.
FOR A MOMENT, I THOUGHT I SAW SOMETHING MOVE IN THE SHIFTING SHADOWS UNDER THE TREES.

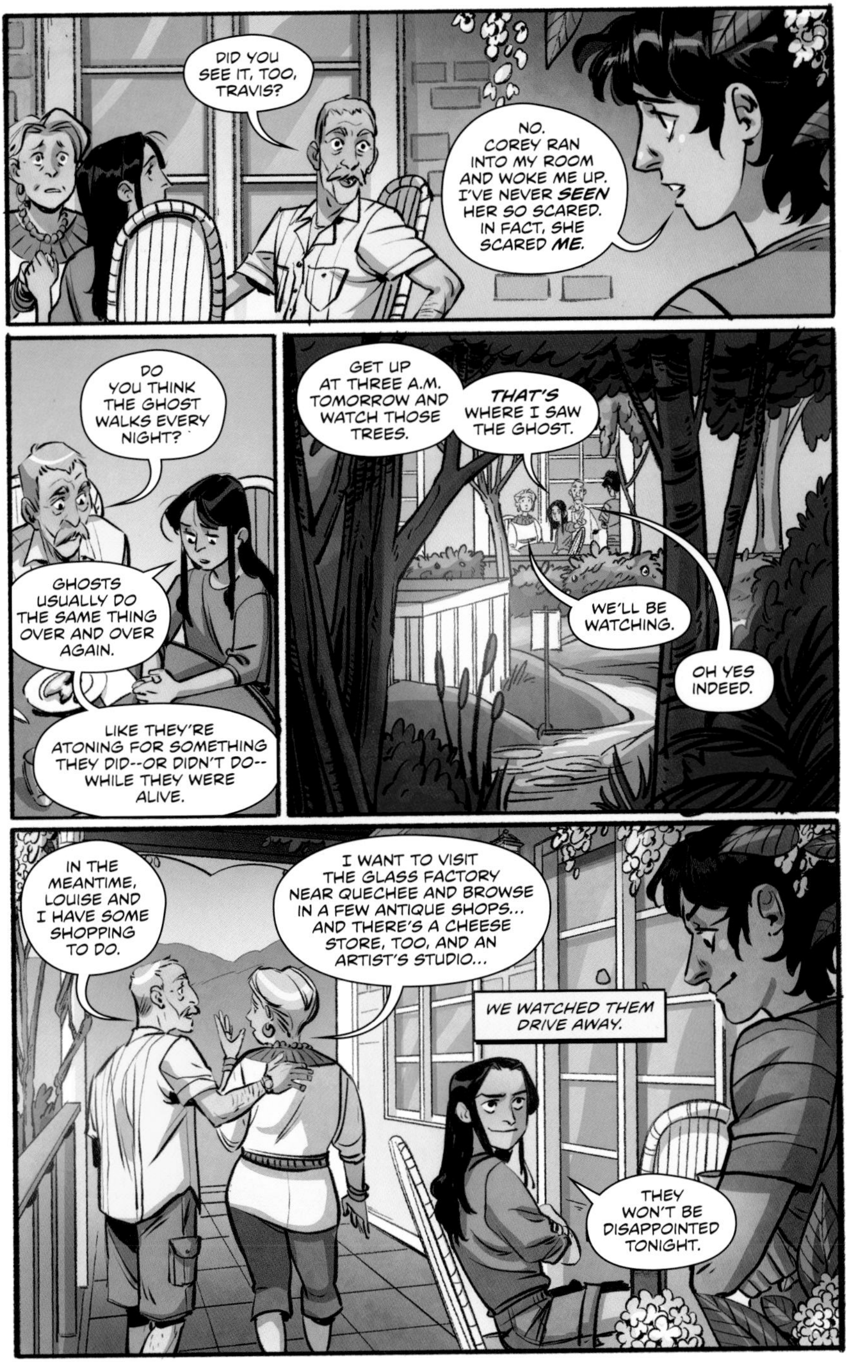
DID YOU SEE IT, TOO, TRAVIS?
NO. COREY RAN INTO MY ROOM AND WOKE ME UP. I'VE NEVER *SEEN* HER SO SCARED. IN FACT, SHE SCARED *ME*.
DO YOU THINK THE GHOST WALKS EVERY NIGHT?
GHOSTS USUALLY DO THE SAME THING OVER AND OVER AGAIN.
LIKE THEY'RE ATONING FOR SOMETHING THEY DID--OR DIDN'T DO--WHILE THEY WERE ALIVE.
GET UP AT THREE A.M. TOMORROW AND WATCH THOSE TREES.
*THAT'S* WHERE I SAW THE GHOST.
WE'LL BE WATCHING.
OH YES INDEED.
IN THE MEANTIME, LOUISE AND I HAVE SOME SHOPPING TO DO.
I WANT TO VISIT THE GLASS FACTORY NEAR QUECHEE AND BROWSE IN A FEW ANTIQUE SHOPS... AND THERE'S A CHEESE STORE, TOO, AND AN ARTIST'S STUDIO...
*WE WATCHED THEM DRIVE AWAY.*
THEY WON'T BE DISAPPOINTED TONIGHT.

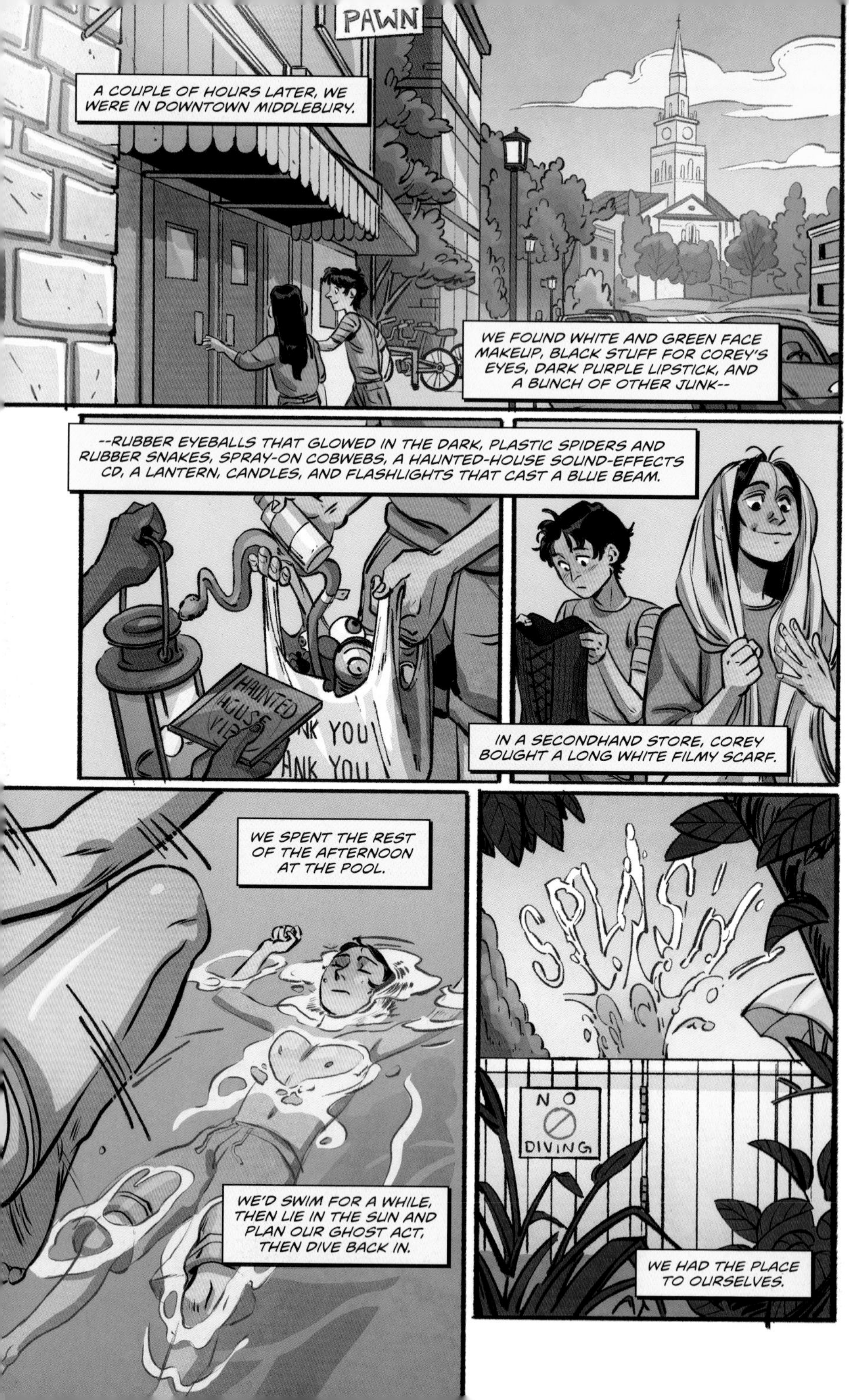
PAWN
A COUPLE OF HOURS LATER, WE WERE IN DOWNTOWN MIDDLEBURY.
WE FOUND WHITE AND GREEN FACE MAKEUP, BLACK STUFF FOR COREY'S EYES, DARK PURPLE LIPSTICK, AND A BUNCH OF OTHER JUNK--
--RUBBER EYEBALLS THAT GLOWED IN THE DARK, PLASTIC SPIDERS AND RUBBER SNAKES, SPRAY-ON COBWEBS, A HAUNTED-HOUSE SOUND-EFFECTS CD, A LANTERN, CANDLES, AND FLASHLIGHTS THAT CAST A BLUE BEAM.
HAUNTED HOUSE
IN A SECONDHAND STORE, COREY BOUGHT A LONG WHITE FILMY SCARF.
WE SPENT THE REST OF THE AFTERNOON AT THE POOL.
WE'D SWIM FOR A WHILE, THEN LIE IN THE SUN AND PLAN OUR GHOST ACT, THEN DIVE BACK IN.
SPLASH!
NO DIVING
WE HAD THE PLACE TO OURSELVES.

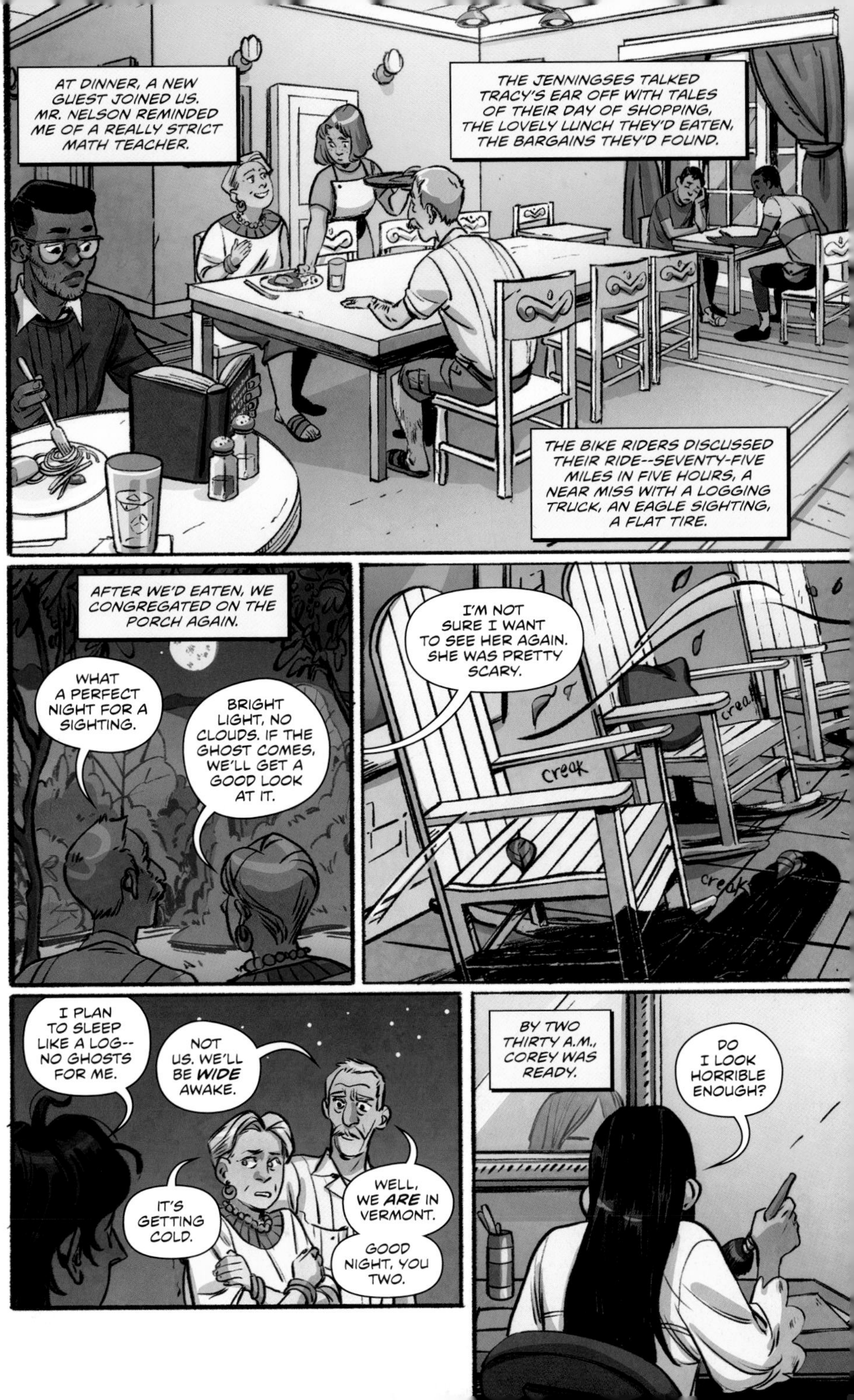
AT DINNER, A NEW GUEST JOINED US. MR. NELSON REMINDED ME OF A REALLY STRICT MATH TEACHER.
THE JENNINGSES TALKED TRACY'S EAR OFF WITH TALES OF THEIR DAY OF SHOPPING, THE LOVELY LUNCH THEY'D EATEN, THE BARGAINS THEY'D FOUND.
THE BIKE RIDERS DISCUSSED THEIR RIDE--SEVENTY-FIVE MILES IN FIVE HOURS, A NEAR MISS WITH A LOGGING TRUCK, AN EAGLE SIGHTING, A FLAT TIRE.
AFTER WE'D EATEN, WE CONGREGATED ON THE PORCH AGAIN.
WHAT A PERFECT NIGHT FOR A SIGHTING.
BRIGHT LIGHT, NO CLOUDS. IF THE GHOST COMES, WE'LL GET A GOOD LOOK AT IT.
I'M NOT SURE I WANT TO SEE HER AGAIN. SHE WAS PRETTY SCARY.
creak
creak
creak
I PLAN TO SLEEP LIKE A LOG-- NO GHOSTS FOR ME.
NOT US. WE'LL BE WIDE AWAKE.
IT'S GETTING COLD.
WELL, WE ARE IN VERMONT.
GOOD NIGHT, YOU TWO.
BY TWO THIRTY A.M., COREY WAS READY.
DO I LOOK HORRIBLE ENOUGH?

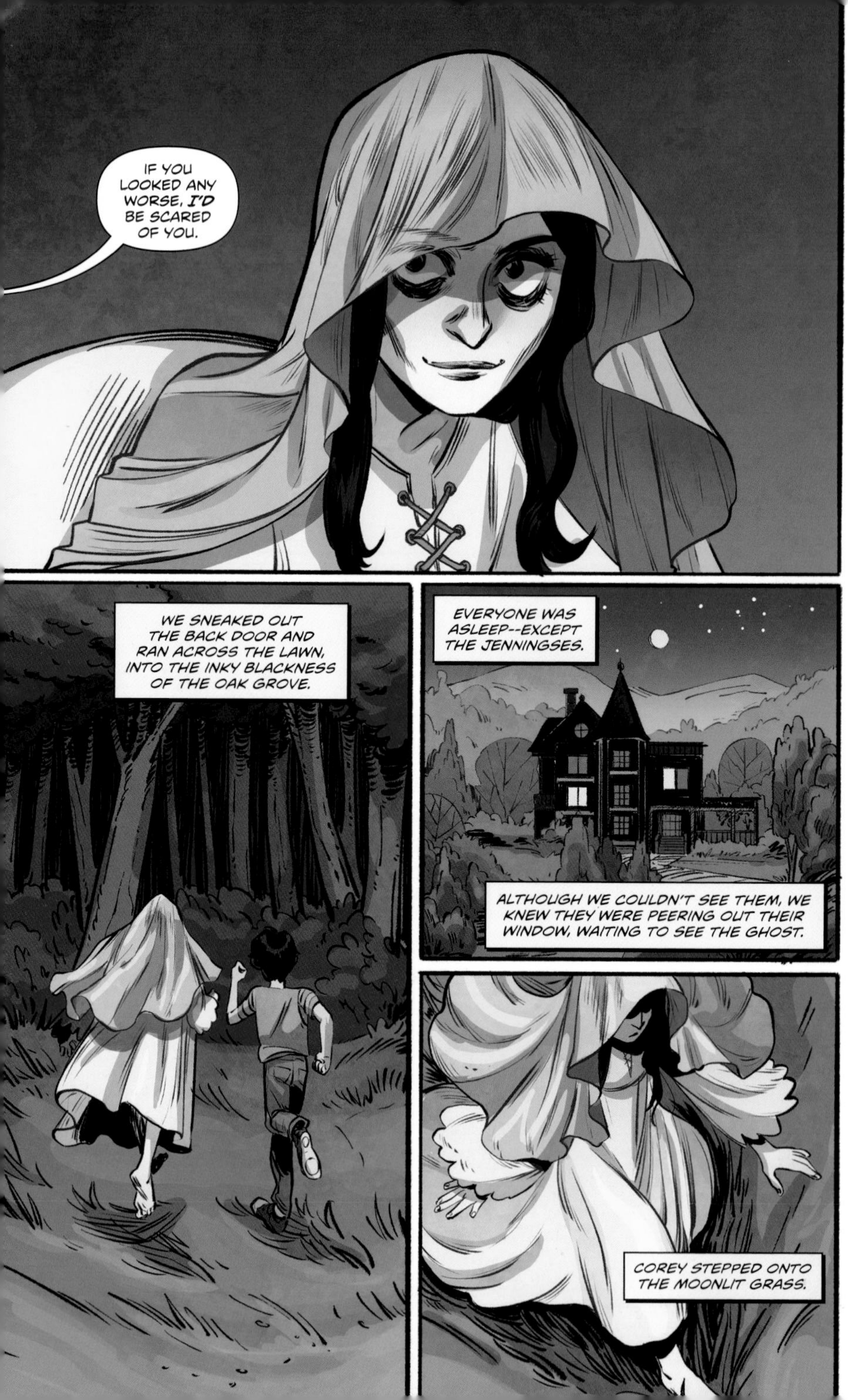
IF YOU LOOKED ANY WORSE, *I'D* BE SCARED OF YOU.
WE SNEAKED OUT THE BACK DOOR AND RAN ACROSS THE LAWN, INTO THE INKY BLACKNESS OF THE OAK GROVE.
EVERYONE WAS ASLEEP--EXCEPT THE JENNINGSES.
ALTHOUGH WE COULDN'T SEE THEM, WE KNEW THEY WERE PEERING OUT THEIR WINDOW, WAITING TO SEE THE GHOST.
COREY STEPPED ONTO THE MOONLIT GRASS.

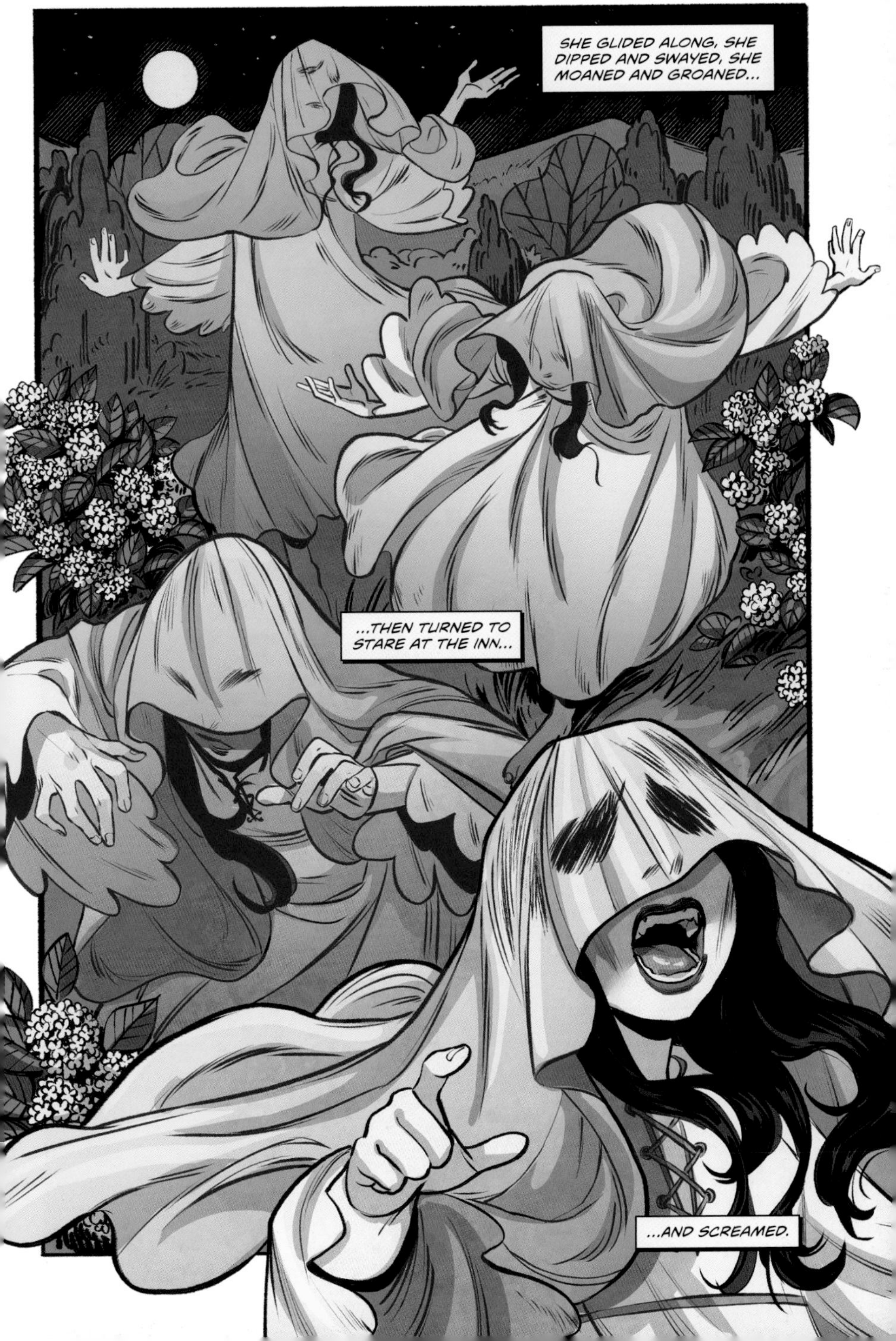
SHE GLIDED ALONG, SHE DIPPED AND SWAYED, SHE MOANED AND GROANED...
...THEN TURNED TO STARE AT THE INN...
...AND SCREAMED.

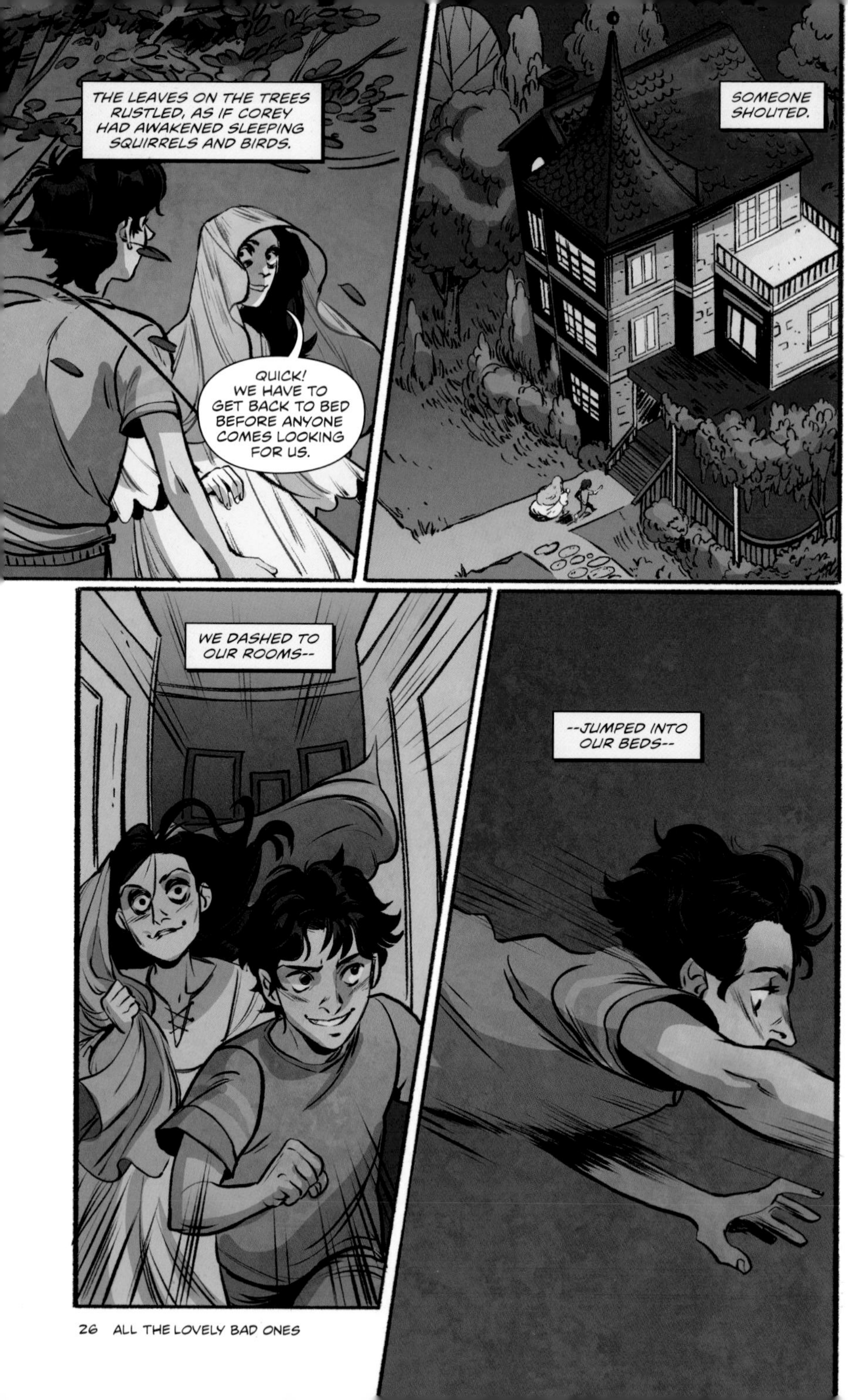
THE LEAVES ON THE TREES RUSTLED, AS IF COREY HAD AWAKENED SLEEPING SQUIRRELS AND BIRDS.
QUICK! WE HAVE TO GET BACK TO BED BEFORE ANYONE COMES LOOKING FOR US.
SOMEONE SHOUTED.
WE DASHED TO OUR ROOMS--
--JUMPED INTO OUR BEDS--

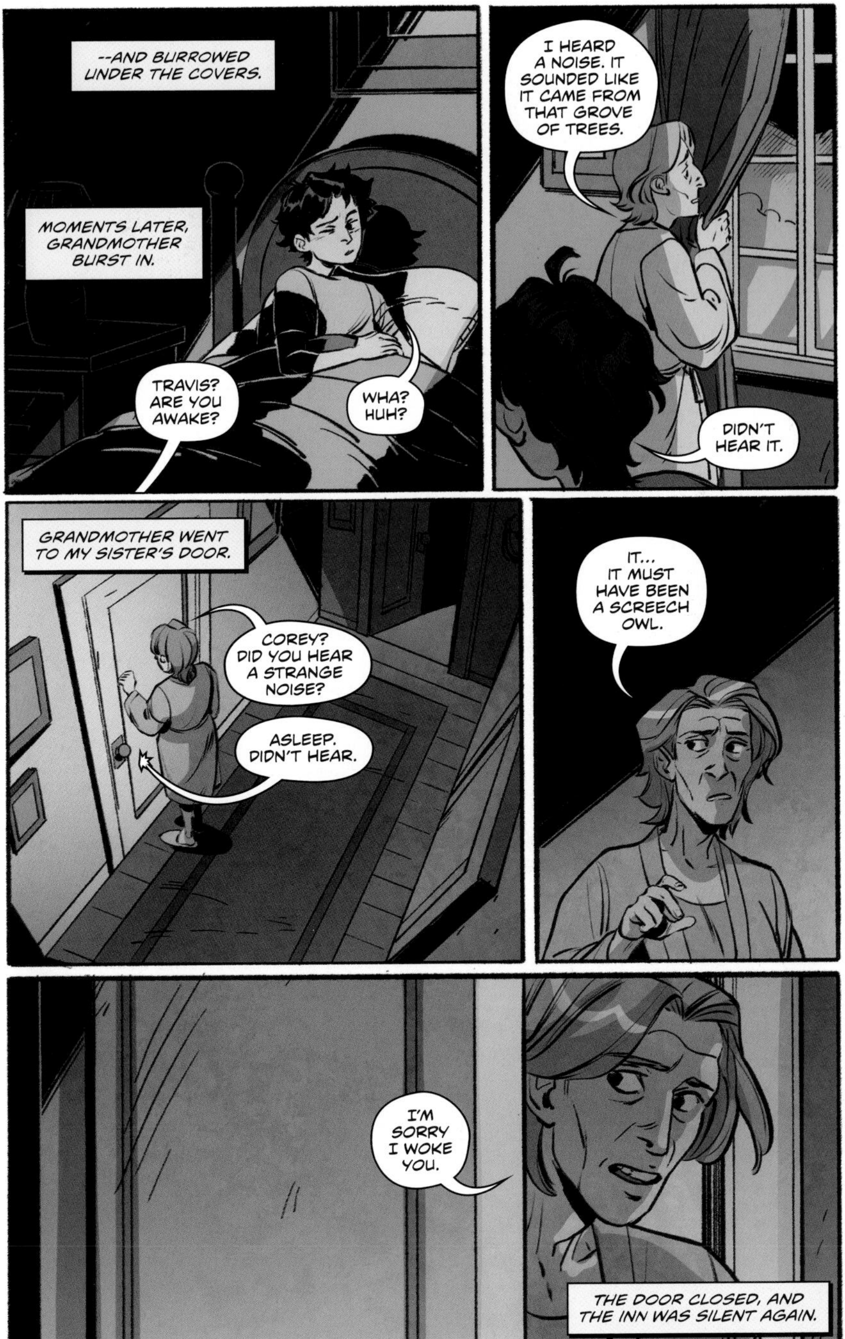
--AND BURROWED UNDER THE COVERS.
MOMENTS LATER, GRANDMOTHER BURST IN.
TRAVIS? ARE YOU AWAKE?
WHA? HUH?
I HEARD A NOISE. IT SOUNDED LIKE IT CAME FROM THAT GROVE OF TREES.
DIDN'T HEAR IT.
GRANDMOTHER WENT TO MY SISTER'S DOOR.
COREY? DID YOU HEAR A STRANGE NOISE?
ASLEEP. DIDN'T HEAR.
IT... IT MUST HAVE BEEN A SCREECH OWL.
I'M SORRY I WOKE YOU.
THE DOOR CLOSED, AND THE INN WAS SILENT AGAIN.

WE'D DONE IT--

--GHOSTS HAD RETURNED TO FOX HILL.

AFTER A WHILE, I HEARD COREY TIPTOEING DOWN THE HALL TO THE BATHROOM.

SHE WAS IN THERE A LONG TIME BEFORE SHE CAME TO SEE ME.

BOY, WAS THAT STUFF HARD TO GET OFF. MY WHOLE FACE STINGS.

YOU WERE GREAT.

I THINK I WOKE UP *EVERYBODY* WITH THAT SCREAM.

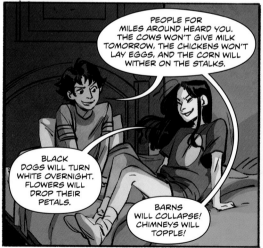

PEOPLE FOR MILES AROUND HEARD YOU. THE COWS WON'T GIVE MILK TOMORROW, THE CHICKENS WON'T LAY EGGS, AND THE CORN WILL WITHER ON THE STALKS.

BLACK DOGS WILL TURN WHITE OVERNIGHT. FLOWERS WILL DROP THEIR PETALS.

BARNS WILL COLLAPSE! CHIMNEYS WILL TOPPLE!

I CAN'T WAIT TO HEAR WHAT EVERYBODY SAYS TOMORROW!

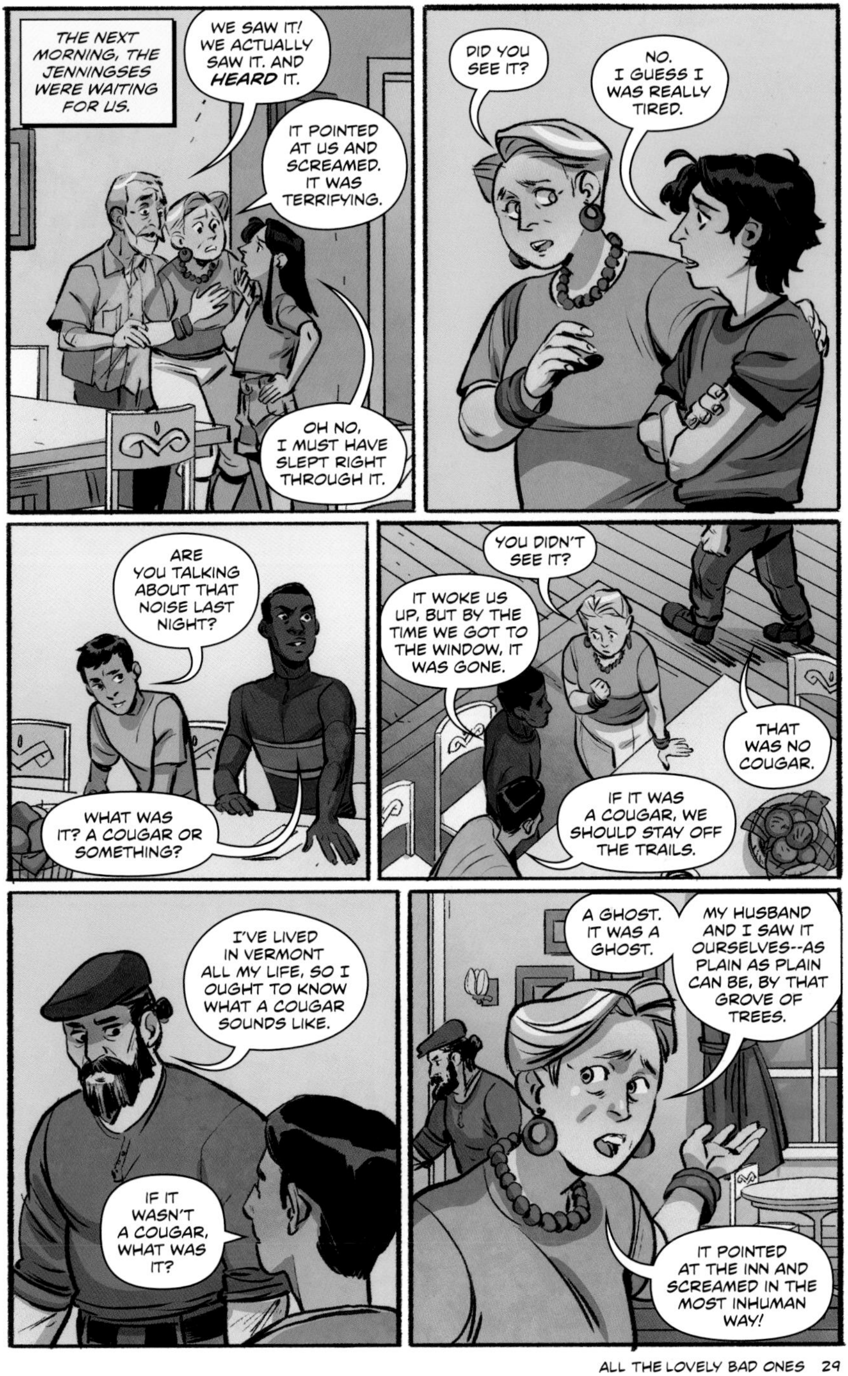
THE NEXT MORNING, THE JENNINGSES WERE WAITING FOR US.
WE SAW IT! WE ACTUALLY SAW IT. AND HEARD IT.
IT POINTED AT US AND SCREAMED. IT WAS TERRIFYING.
OH NO, I MUST HAVE SLEPT RIGHT THROUGH IT.
DID YOU SEE IT?
NO. I GUESS I WAS REALLY TIRED.
ARE YOU TALKING ABOUT THAT NOISE LAST NIGHT?
WHAT WAS IT? A COUGAR OR SOMETHING?
YOU DIDN'T SEE IT?
IT WOKE US UP, BUT BY THE TIME WE GOT TO THE WINDOW, IT WAS GONE.
THAT WAS NO COUGAR.
IF IT WAS A COUGAR, WE SHOULD STAY OFF THE TRAILS.
I'VE LIVED IN VERMONT ALL MY LIFE, SO I OUGHT TO KNOW WHAT A COUGAR SOUNDS LIKE.
IF IT WASN'T A COUGAR, WHAT WAS IT?
A GHOST. IT WAS A GHOST.
MY HUSBAND AND I SAW IT OURSELVES--AS PLAIN AS PLAIN CAN BE, BY THAT GROVE OF TREES.
IT POINTED AT THE INN AND SCREAMED IN THE MOST INHUMAN WAY!

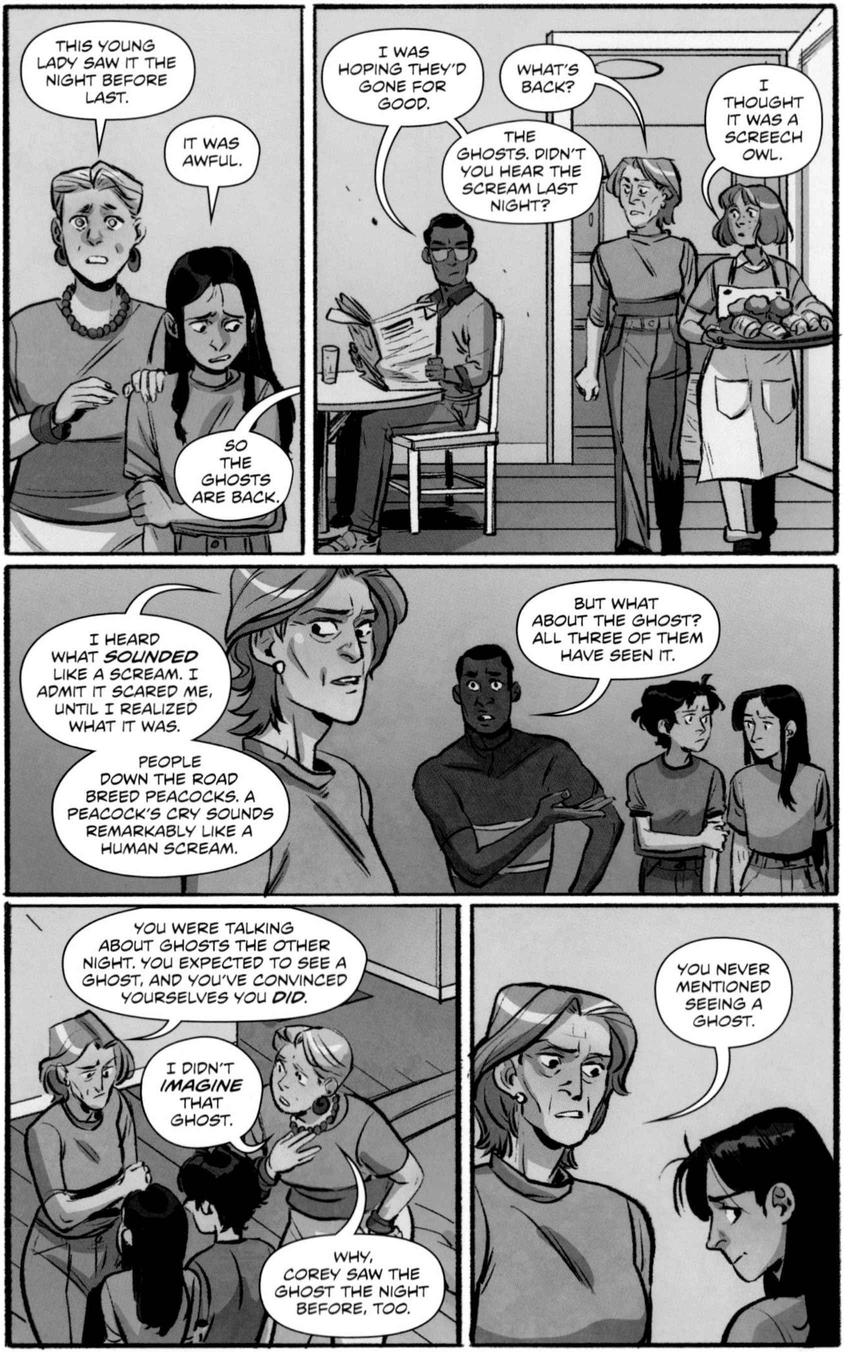
THIS YOUNG LADY SAW IT THE NIGHT BEFORE LAST.
IT WAS AWFUL.
SO THE GHOSTS ARE BACK.
I WAS HOPING THEY'D GONE FOR GOOD.
WHAT'S BACK?
THE GHOSTS. DIDN'T YOU HEAR THE SCREAM LAST NIGHT?
I THOUGHT IT WAS A SCREECH OWL.
I HEARD WHAT *SOUNDED* LIKE A SCREAM. I ADMIT IT SCARED ME, UNTIL I REALIZED WHAT IT WAS.
PEOPLE DOWN THE ROAD BREED PEACOCKS. A PEACOCK'S CRY SOUNDS REMARKABLY LIKE A HUMAN SCREAM.
BUT WHAT ABOUT THE GHOST? ALL THREE OF THEM HAVE SEEN IT.
YOU WERE TALKING ABOUT GHOSTS THE OTHER NIGHT. YOU EXPECTED TO SEE A GHOST, AND YOU'VE CONVINCED YOURSELVES YOU *DID*.
I DIDN'T *IMAGINE* THAT GHOST.
WHY, COREY SAW THE GHOST THE NIGHT BEFORE, TOO.
YOU NEVER MENTIONED SEEING A GHOST.

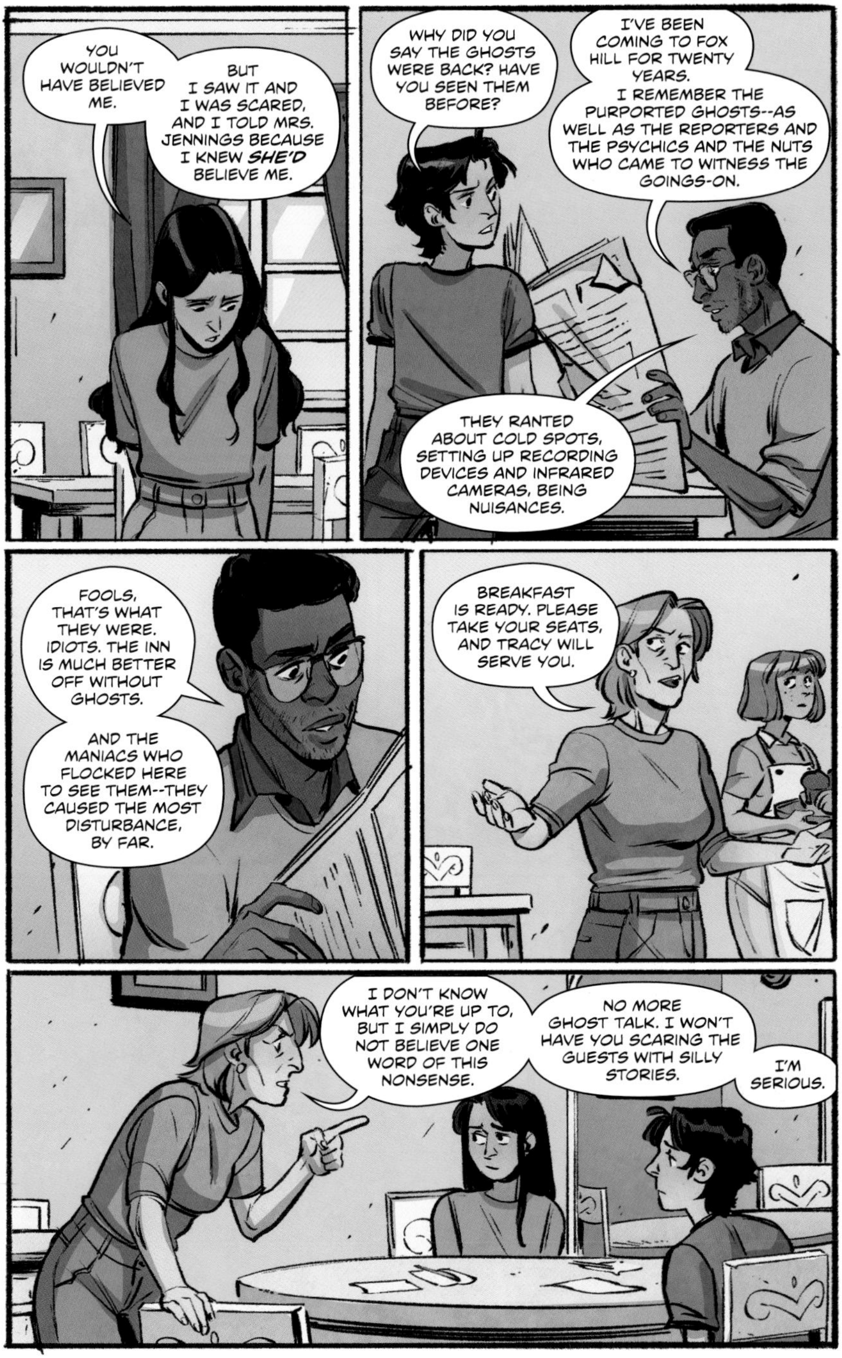
YOU WOULDN'T HAVE BELIEVED ME.
BUT I SAW IT AND I WAS SCARED, AND I TOLD MRS. JENNINGS BECAUSE I KNEW *SHE'D* BELIEVE ME.
WHY DID YOU SAY THE GHOSTS WERE BACK? HAVE YOU SEEN THEM BEFORE?
I'VE BEEN COMING TO FOX HILL FOR TWENTY YEARS.
I REMEMBER THE PURPORTED GHOSTS--AS WELL AS THE REPORTERS AND THE PSYCHICS AND THE NUTS WHO CAME TO WITNESS THE GOINGS-ON.
THEY RANTED ABOUT COLD SPOTS, SETTING UP RECORDING DEVICES AND INFRARED CAMERAS, BEING NUISANCES.
FOOLS, THAT'S WHAT THEY WERE. IDIOTS. THE INN IS MUCH BETTER OFF WITHOUT GHOSTS.
AND THE MANIACS WHO FLOCKED HERE TO SEE THEM--THEY CAUSED THE MOST DISTURBANCE, BY FAR.
BREAKFAST IS READY. PLEASE TAKE YOUR SEATS, AND TRACY WILL SERVE YOU.
I DON'T KNOW WHAT YOU'RE UP TO, BUT I SIMPLY DO NOT BELIEVE ONE WORD OF THIS NONSENSE.
NO MORE GHOST TALK. I WON'T HAVE YOU SCARING THE GUESTS WITH SILLY STORIES.
I'M SERIOUS.

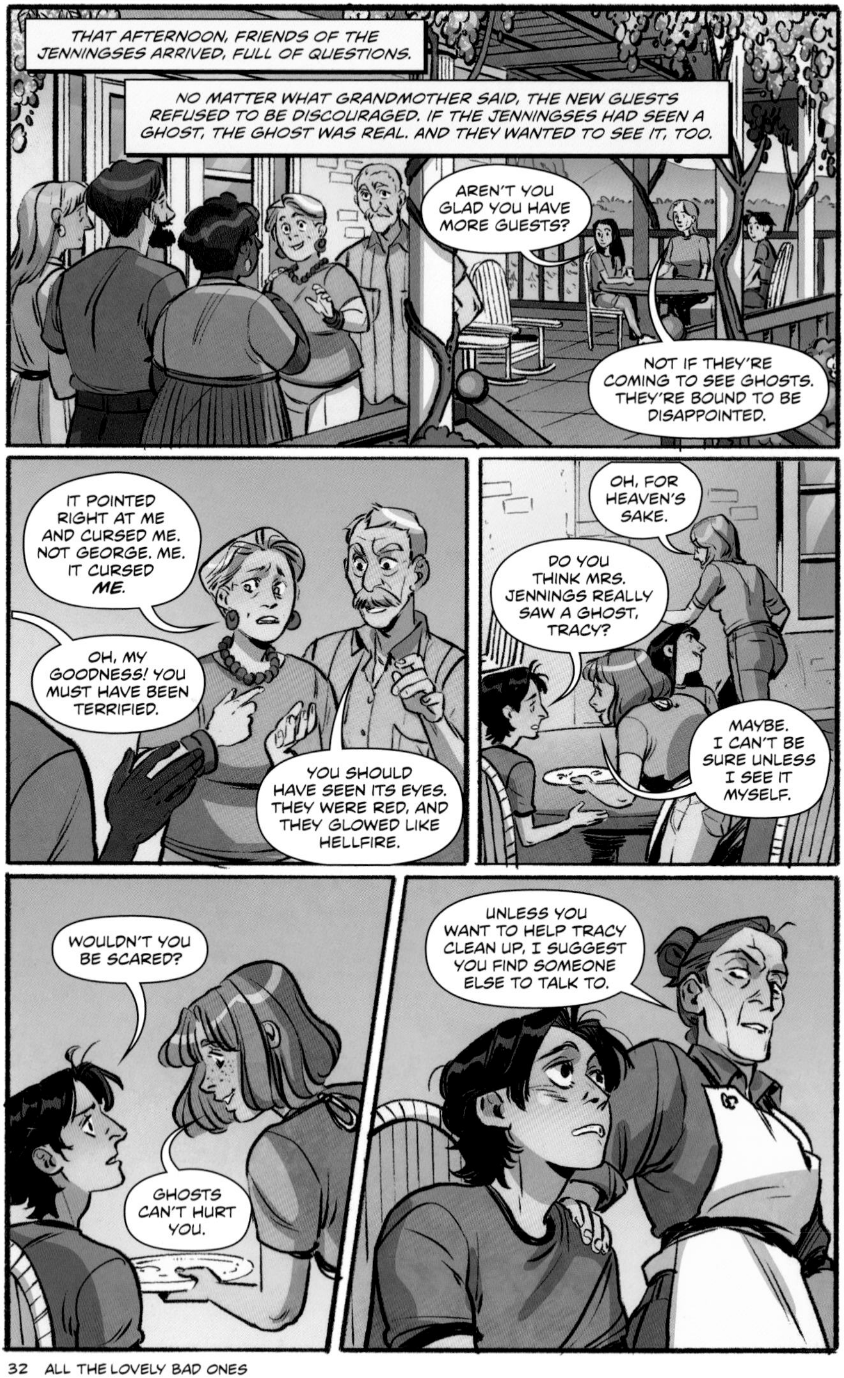
THAT AFTERNOON, FRIENDS OF THE JENNINGSES ARRIVED, FULL OF QUESTIONS.
NO MATTER WHAT GRANDMOTHER SAID, THE NEW GUESTS REFUSED TO BE DISCOURAGED. IF THE JENNINGSES HAD SEEN A GHOST, THE GHOST WAS REAL. AND THEY WANTED TO SEE IT, TOO.
AREN'T YOU GLAD YOU HAVE MORE GUESTS?
NOT IF THEY'RE COMING TO SEE GHOSTS. THEY'RE BOUND TO BE DISAPPOINTED.
IT POINTED RIGHT AT ME AND CURSED ME. NOT GEORGE. ME. IT CURSED ***ME.***
OH, MY GOODNESS! YOU MUST HAVE BEEN TERRIFIED.
YOU SHOULD HAVE SEEN ITS EYES. THEY WERE RED, AND THEY GLOWED LIKE HELLFIRE.
OH, FOR HEAVEN'S SAKE.
DO YOU THINK MRS. JENNINGS REALLY SAW A GHOST, TRACY?
MAYBE. I CAN'T BE SURE UNLESS I SEE IT MYSELF.
WOULDN'T YOU BE SCARED?
GHOSTS CAN'T HURT YOU.
UNLESS YOU WANT TO HELP TRACY CLEAN UP, I SUGGEST YOU FIND SOMEONE ELSE TO TALK TO.

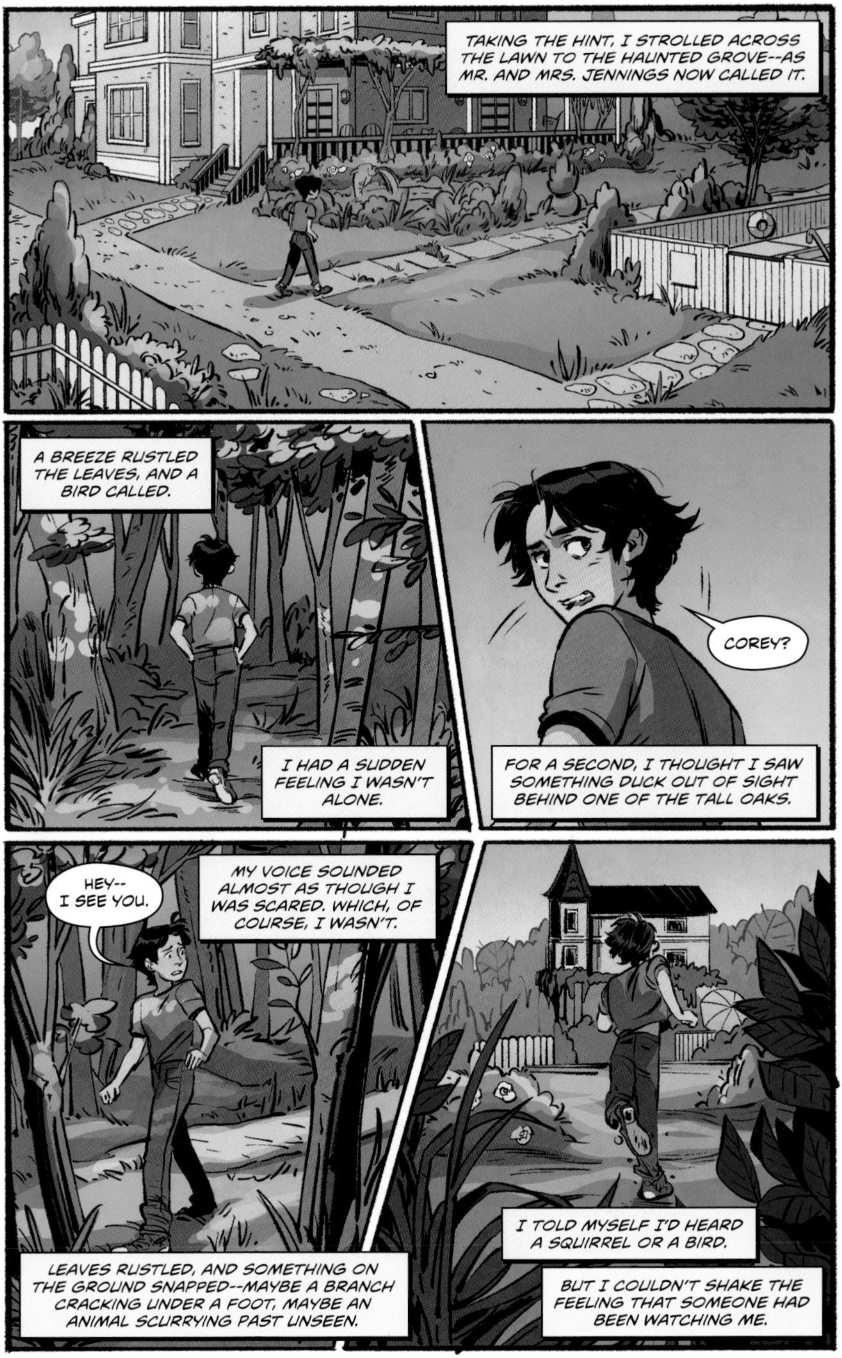
TAKING THE HINT, I STROLLED ACROSS THE LAWN TO THE HAUNTED GROVE--AS MR. AND MRS. JENNINGS NOW CALLED IT.
A BREEZE RUSTLED THE LEAVES, AND A BIRD CALLED.
I HAD A SUDDEN FEELING I WASN'T ALONE.
COREY?
FOR A SECOND, I THOUGHT I SAW SOMETHING DUCK OUT OF SIGHT BEHIND ONE OF THE TALL OAKS.
HEY-- I SEE YOU.
MY VOICE SOUNDED ALMOST AS THOUGH I WAS SCARED. WHICH, OF COURSE, I WASN'T.
LEAVES RUSTLED, AND SOMETHING ON THE GROUND SNAPPED--MAYBE A BRANCH CRACKING UNDER A FOOT, MAYBE AN ANIMAL SCURRYING PAST UNSEEN.
I TOLD MYSELF I'D HEARD A SQUIRREL OR A BIRD.
BUT I COULDN'T SHAKE THE FEELING THAT SOMEONE HAD BEEN WATCHING ME.

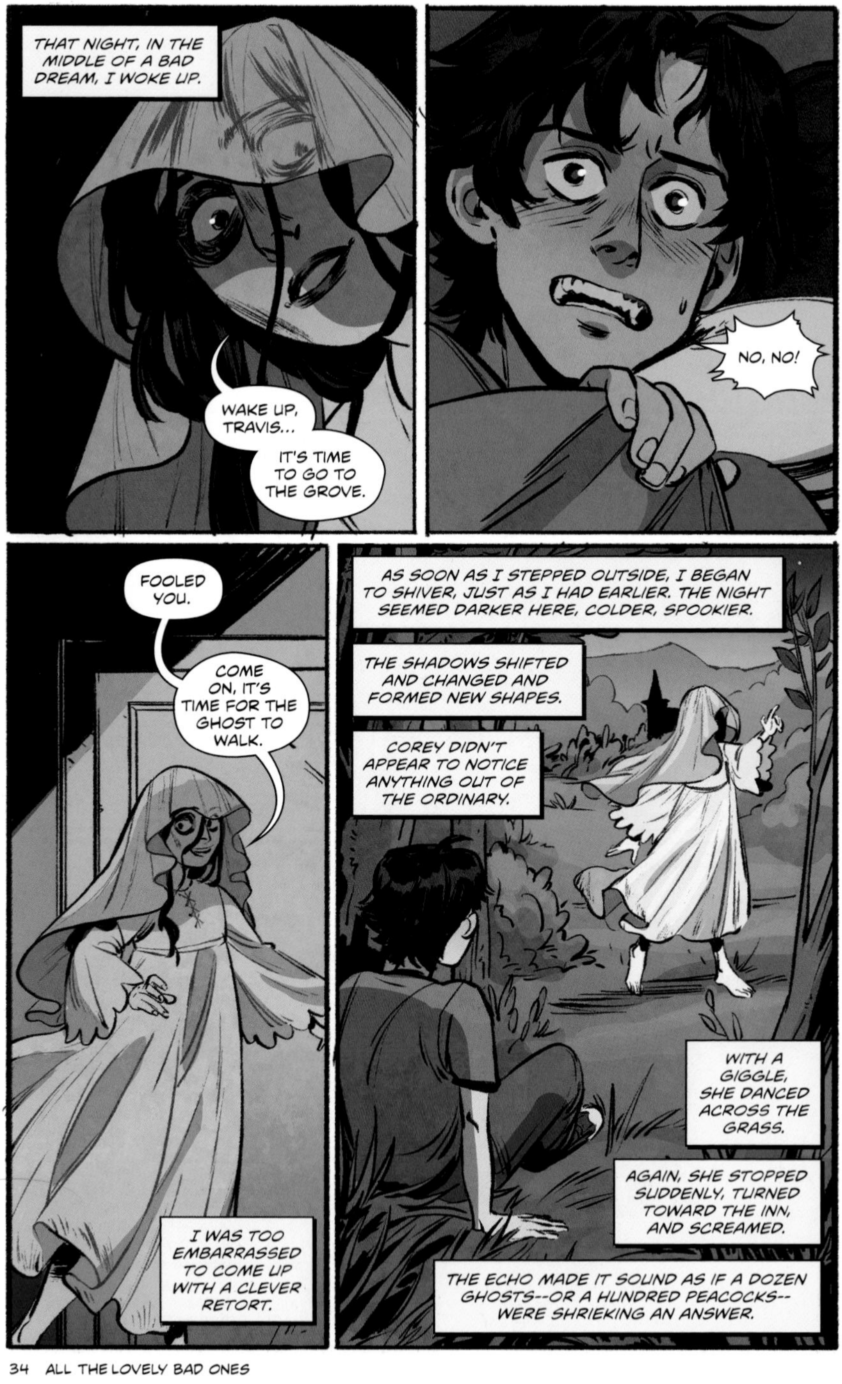
THAT NIGHT, IN THE MIDDLE OF A BAD DREAM, I WOKE UP.
WAKE UP, TRAVIS...
IT'S TIME TO GO TO THE GROVE.
NO, NO!
FOOLED YOU.
COME ON, IT'S TIME FOR THE GHOST TO WALK.
I WAS TOO EMBARRASSED TO COME UP WITH A CLEVER RETORT.
AS SOON AS I STEPPED OUTSIDE, I BEGAN TO SHIVER, JUST AS I HAD EARLIER. THE NIGHT SEEMED DARKER HERE, COLDER, SPOOKIER.
THE SHADOWS SHIFTED AND CHANGED AND FORMED NEW SHAPES.
COREY DIDN'T APPEAR TO NOTICE ANYTHING OUT OF THE ORDINARY.
WITH A GIGGLE, SHE DANCED ACROSS THE GRASS.
AGAIN, SHE STOPPED SUDDENLY, TURNED TOWARD THE INN, AND SCREAMED.
THE ECHO MADE IT SOUND AS IF A DOZEN GHOSTS--OR A HUNDRED PEACOCKS--WERE SHRIEKING AN ANSWER.

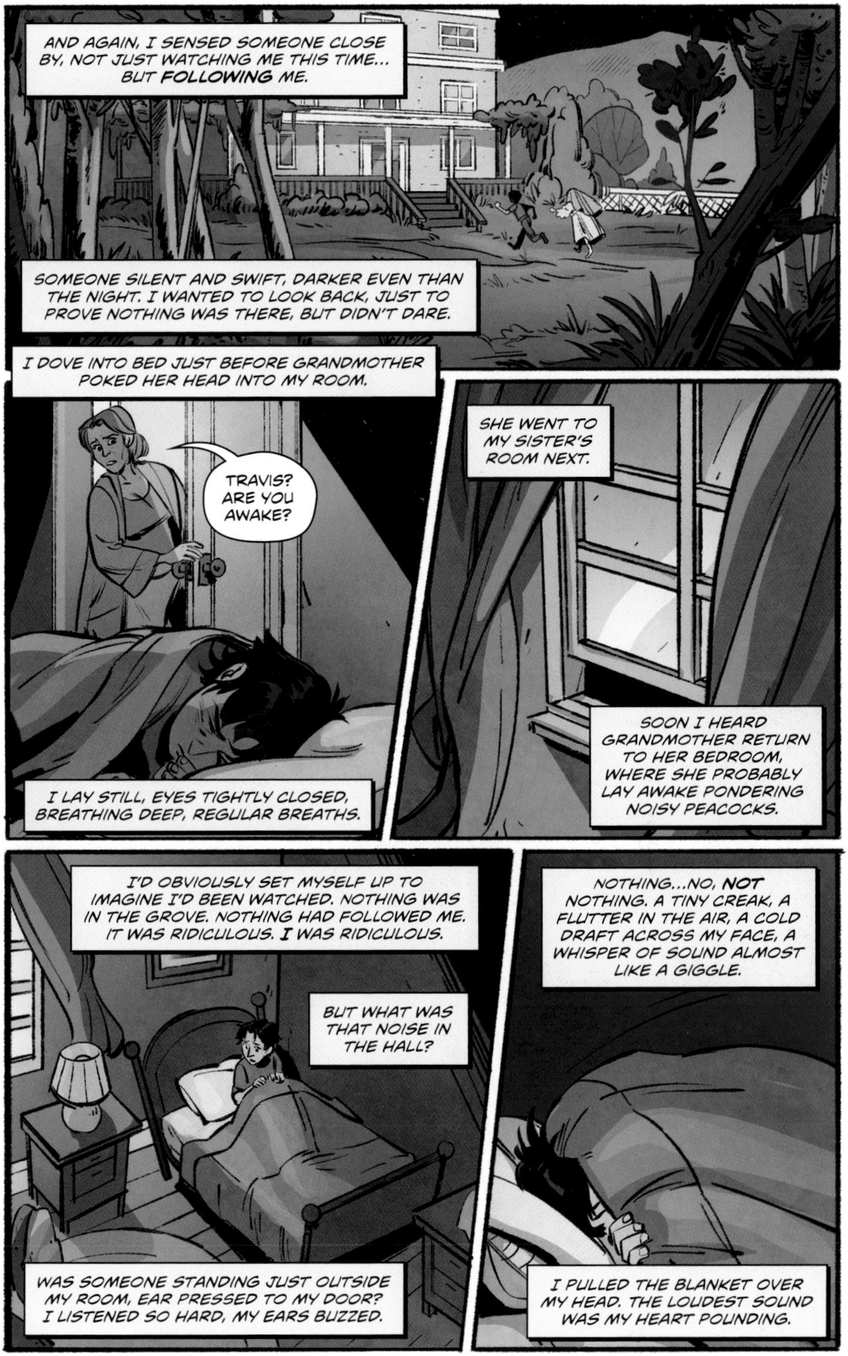
AND AGAIN, I SENSED SOMEONE CLOSE BY, NOT JUST WATCHING ME THIS TIME... BUT **FOLLOWING** ME.
SOMEONE SILENT AND SWIFT, DARKER EVEN THAN THE NIGHT. I WANTED TO LOOK BACK, JUST TO PROVE NOTHING WAS THERE, BUT DIDN'T DARE.
I DOVE INTO BED JUST BEFORE GRANDMOTHER POKED HER HEAD INTO MY ROOM.
TRAVIS? ARE YOU AWAKE?
I LAY STILL, EYES TIGHTLY CLOSED, BREATHING DEEP, REGULAR BREATHS.
SHE WENT TO MY SISTER'S ROOM NEXT.
SOON I HEARD GRANDMOTHER RETURN TO HER BEDROOM, WHERE SHE PROBABLY LAY AWAKE PONDERING NOISY PEACOCKS.
I'D OBVIOUSLY SET MYSELF UP TO IMAGINE I'D BEEN WATCHED. NOTHING WAS IN THE GROVE. NOTHING HAD FOLLOWED ME. IT WAS RIDICULOUS. **I** WAS RIDICULOUS.
BUT WHAT WAS THAT NOISE IN THE HALL?
WAS SOMEONE STANDING JUST OUTSIDE MY ROOM, EAR PRESSED TO MY DOOR? I LISTENED SO HARD, MY EARS BUZZED.
NOTHING...NO, **NOT** NOTHING. A TINY CREAK, A FLUTTER IN THE AIR, A COLD DRAFT ACROSS MY FACE, A WHISPER OF SOUND ALMOST LIKE A GIGGLE.
I PULLED THE BLANKET OVER MY HEAD. THE LOUDEST SOUND WAS MY HEART POUNDING.

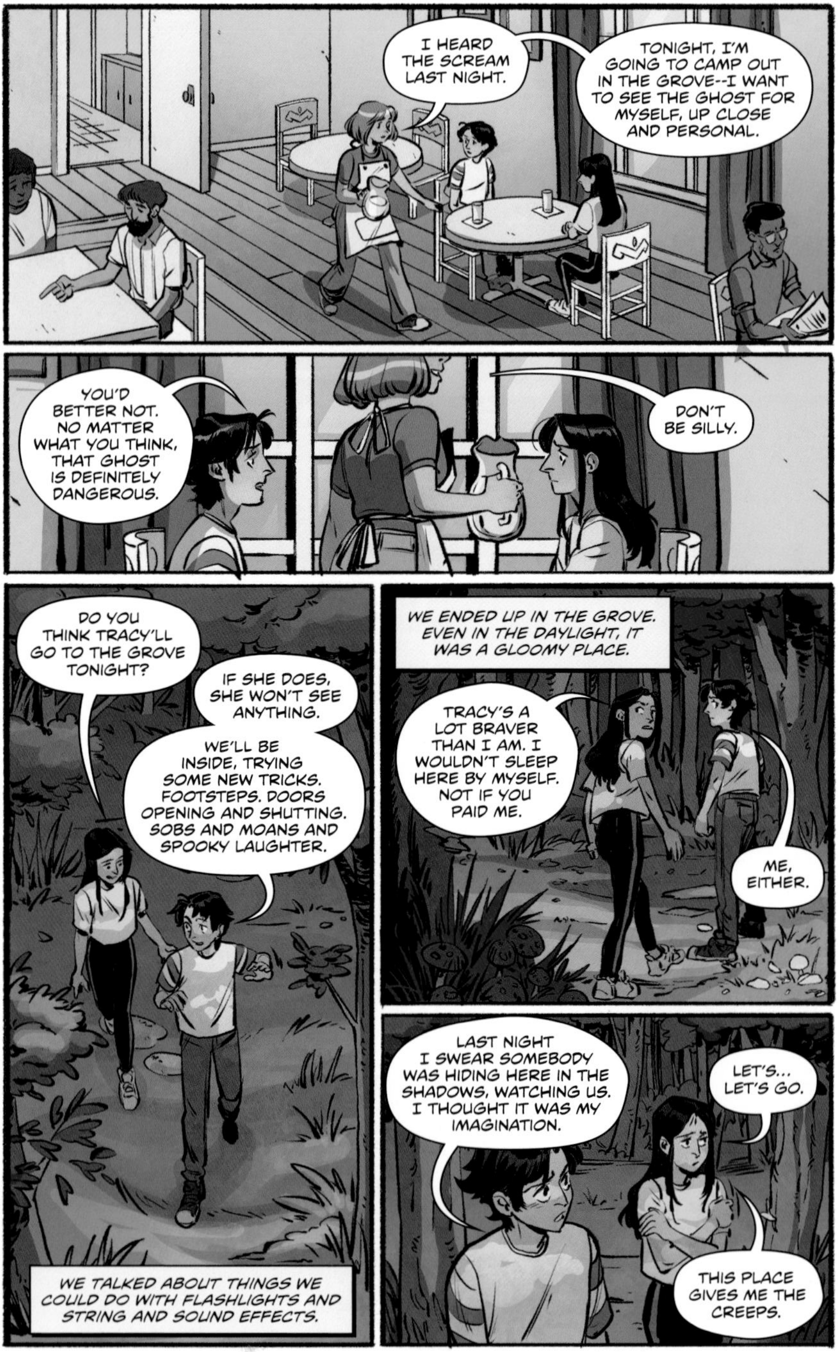
I HEARD THE SCREAM LAST NIGHT.
TONIGHT, I'M GOING TO CAMP OUT IN THE GROVE--I WANT TO SEE THE GHOST FOR MYSELF, UP CLOSE AND PERSONAL.
YOU'D BETTER NOT. NO MATTER WHAT YOU THINK, THAT GHOST IS DEFINITELY DANGEROUS.
DON'T BE SILLY.
DO YOU THINK TRACY'LL GO TO THE GROVE TONIGHT?
IF SHE DOES, SHE WON'T SEE ANYTHING.
WE'LL BE INSIDE, TRYING SOME NEW TRICKS. FOOTSTEPS. DOORS OPENING AND SHUTTING. SOBS AND MOANS AND SPOOKY LAUGHTER.
WE TALKED ABOUT THINGS WE COULD DO WITH FLASHLIGHTS AND STRING AND SOUND EFFECTS.
WE ENDED UP IN THE GROVE. EVEN IN THE DAYLIGHT, IT WAS A GLOOMY PLACE.
TRACY'S A LOT BRAVER THAN I AM. I WOULDN'T SLEEP HERE BY MYSELF. NOT IF YOU PAID ME.
ME, EITHER.
LAST NIGHT I SWEAR SOMEBODY WAS HIDING HERE IN THE SHADOWS, WATCHING US. I THOUGHT IT WAS MY IMAGINATION.
LET'S... LET'S GO.
THIS PLACE GIVES ME THE CREEPS.

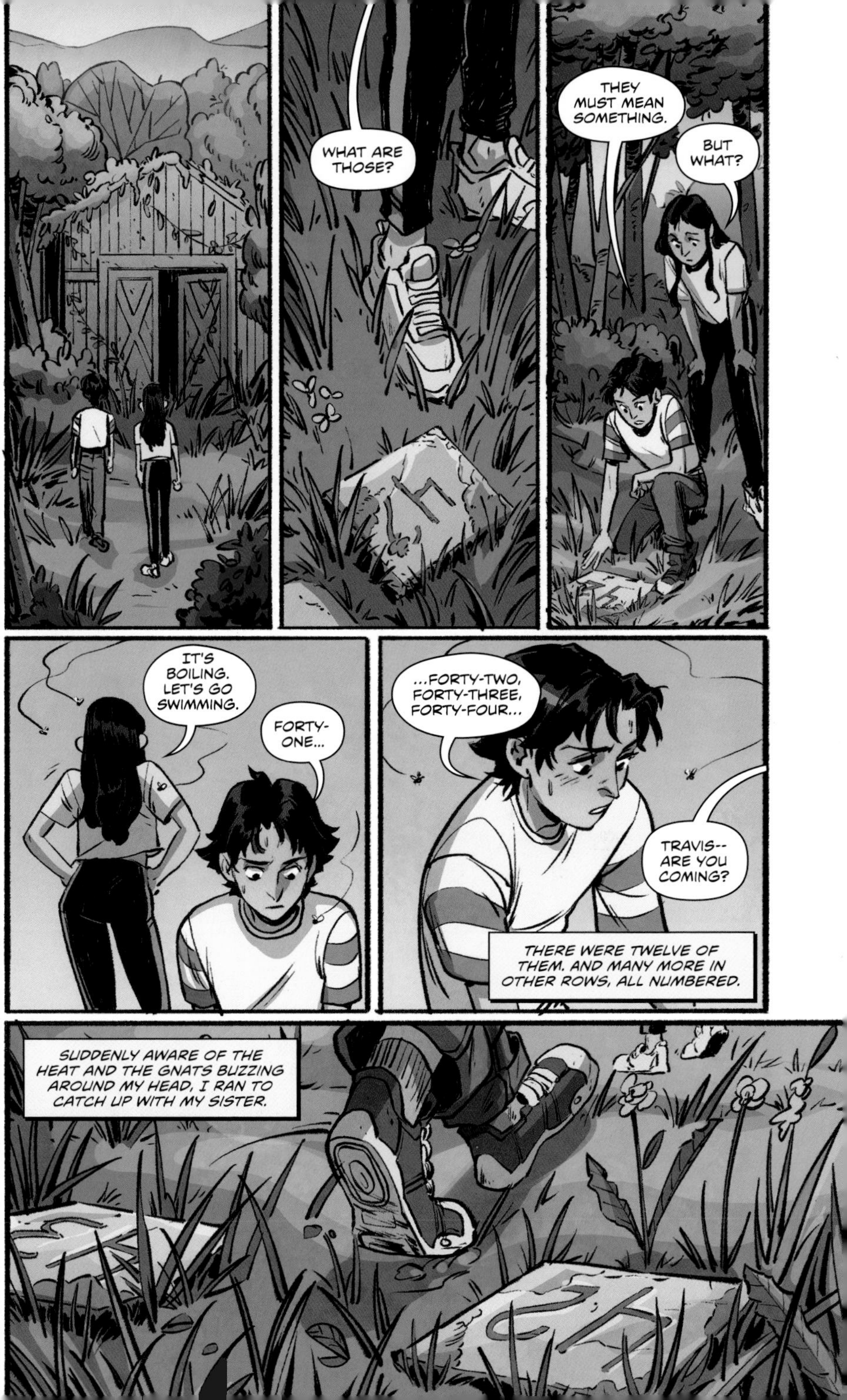
WHAT ARE THOSE?
THEY MUST MEAN SOMETHING.
BUT WHAT?
IT'S BOILING. LET'S GO SWIMMING.
FORTY-ONE...
...FORTY-TWO, FORTY-THREE, FORTY-FOUR...
TRAVIS-- ARE YOU COMING?
THERE WERE TWELVE OF THEM. AND MANY MORE IN OTHER ROWS, ALL NUMBERED.
SUDDENLY AWARE OF THE HEAT AND THE GNATS BUZZING AROUND MY HEAD, I RAN TO CATCH UP WITH MY SISTER.

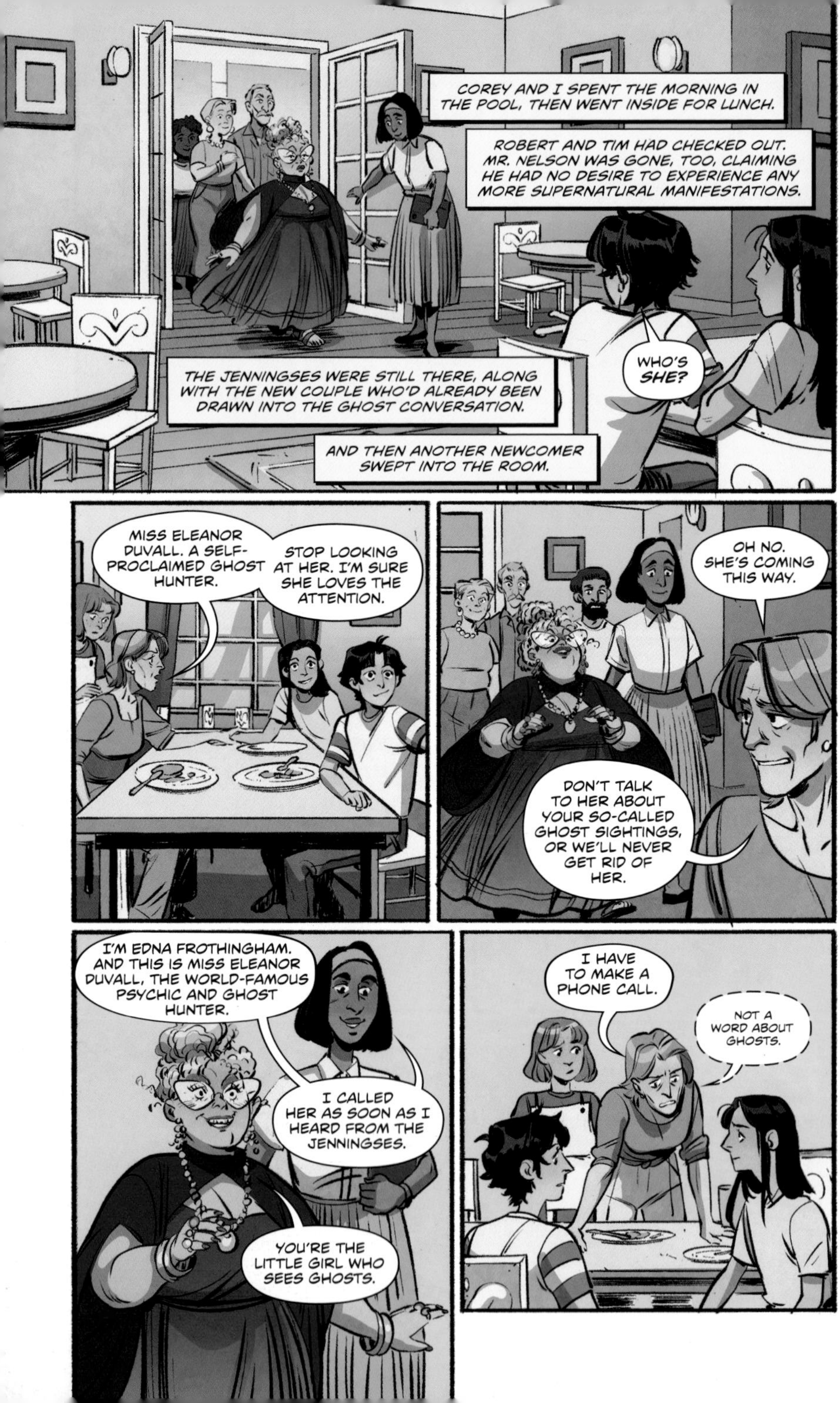
COREY AND I SPENT THE MORNING IN THE POOL, THEN WENT INSIDE FOR LUNCH.
ROBERT AND TIM HAD CHECKED OUT. MR. NELSON WAS GONE, TOO, CLAIMING HE HAD NO DESIRE TO EXPERIENCE ANY MORE SUPERNATURAL MANIFESTATIONS.
THE JENNINGSES WERE STILL THERE, ALONG WITH THE NEW COUPLE WHO'D ALREADY BEEN DRAWN INTO THE GHOST CONVERSATION.
AND THEN ANOTHER NEWCOMER SWEPT INTO THE ROOM.
WHO'S SHE?
MISS ELEANOR DUVALL. A SELF-PROCLAIMED GHOST HUNTER.
STOP LOOKING AT HER. I'M SURE SHE LOVES THE ATTENTION.
OH NO. SHE'S COMING THIS WAY.
DON'T TALK TO HER ABOUT YOUR SO-CALLED GHOST SIGHTINGS, OR WE'LL NEVER GET RID OF HER.
I'M EDNA FROTHINGHAM. AND THIS IS MISS ELEANOR DUVALL, THE WORLD-FAMOUS PSYCHIC AND GHOST HUNTER.
I CALLED HER AS SOON AS I HEARD FROM THE JENNINGSES.
YOU'RE THE LITTLE GIRL WHO SEES GHOSTS.
I HAVE TO MAKE A PHONE CALL.
NOT A WORD ABOUT GHOSTS.

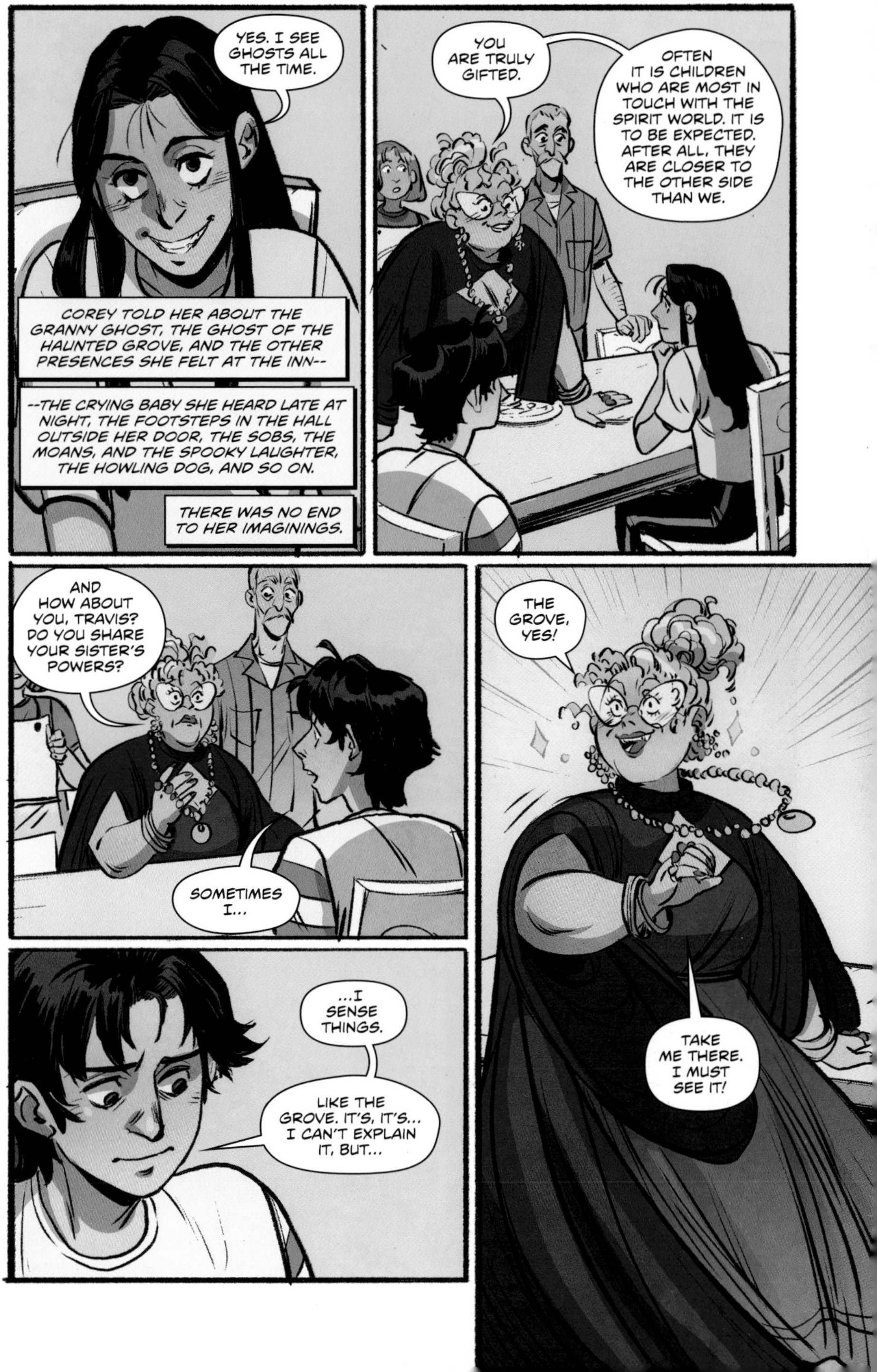
YES. I SEE GHOSTS ALL THE TIME.
COREY TOLD HER ABOUT THE GRANNY GHOST, THE GHOST OF THE HAUNTED GROVE, AND THE OTHER PRESENCES SHE FELT AT THE INN--
--THE CRYING BABY SHE HEARD LATE AT NIGHT, THE FOOTSTEPS IN THE HALL OUTSIDE HER DOOR, THE SOBS, THE MOANS, AND THE SPOOKY LAUGHTER, THE HOWLING DOG, AND SO ON.
THERE WAS NO END TO HER IMAGININGS.
YOU ARE TRULY GIFTED.
OFTEN IT IS CHILDREN WHO ARE MOST IN TOUCH WITH THE SPIRIT WORLD. IT IS TO BE EXPECTED. AFTER ALL, THEY ARE CLOSER TO THE OTHER SIDE THAN WE.
AND HOW ABOUT YOU, TRAVIS? DO YOU SHARE YOUR SISTER'S POWERS?
SOMETIMES I...
...I SENSE THINGS.
LIKE THE GROVE. IT'S, IT'S... I CAN'T EXPLAIN IT, BUT...
THE GROVE, YES!
TAKE ME THERE. I MUST SEE IT!

WITH RELUCTANCE, COREY AND I LED THE WHOLE GROUP INTO THE GROVE.

IMMEDIATELY, THEY ALL BEGAN TO SHIVER. MRS. JENNINGS SAID SHE FELT FAINT.

ARE YOU ALL RIGHT, ELEANOR?

COME FORTH. SHOW YOURSELF, SPIRIT OF DARKNESS. I FEAR YOU NOT.

NOTHING HAPPENED.

BUT SOMETHING WAS THERE. SOMETHING THAT SENT SHIVERS RACING UP AND DOWN MY SPINE.

IT IS HERE, JUST AS THE CHILD SAID. BUT IT DOES NOT WISH TO REVEAL ITSELF. PERHAPS THERE ARE TOO MANY OF US.

COME. WE'LL RETURN TOMORROW WHEN CHESTER ARRIVES.

CHESTER?

CHESTER COAKLEY, MY ASSOCIATE. HE WAS DELAYED BY A NASTY PIECE OF BUSINESS IN SALEM BUT SHOULD ARRIVE TOMORROW WITH OUR EQUIPMENT.

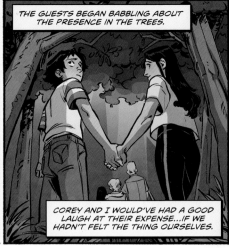

THE GUESTS BEGAN BABBLING ABOUT THE PRESENCE IN THE TREES.

COREY AND I WOULD'VE HAD A GOOD LAUGH AT THEIR EXPENSE...IF WE HADN'T FELT THE THING OURSELVES.

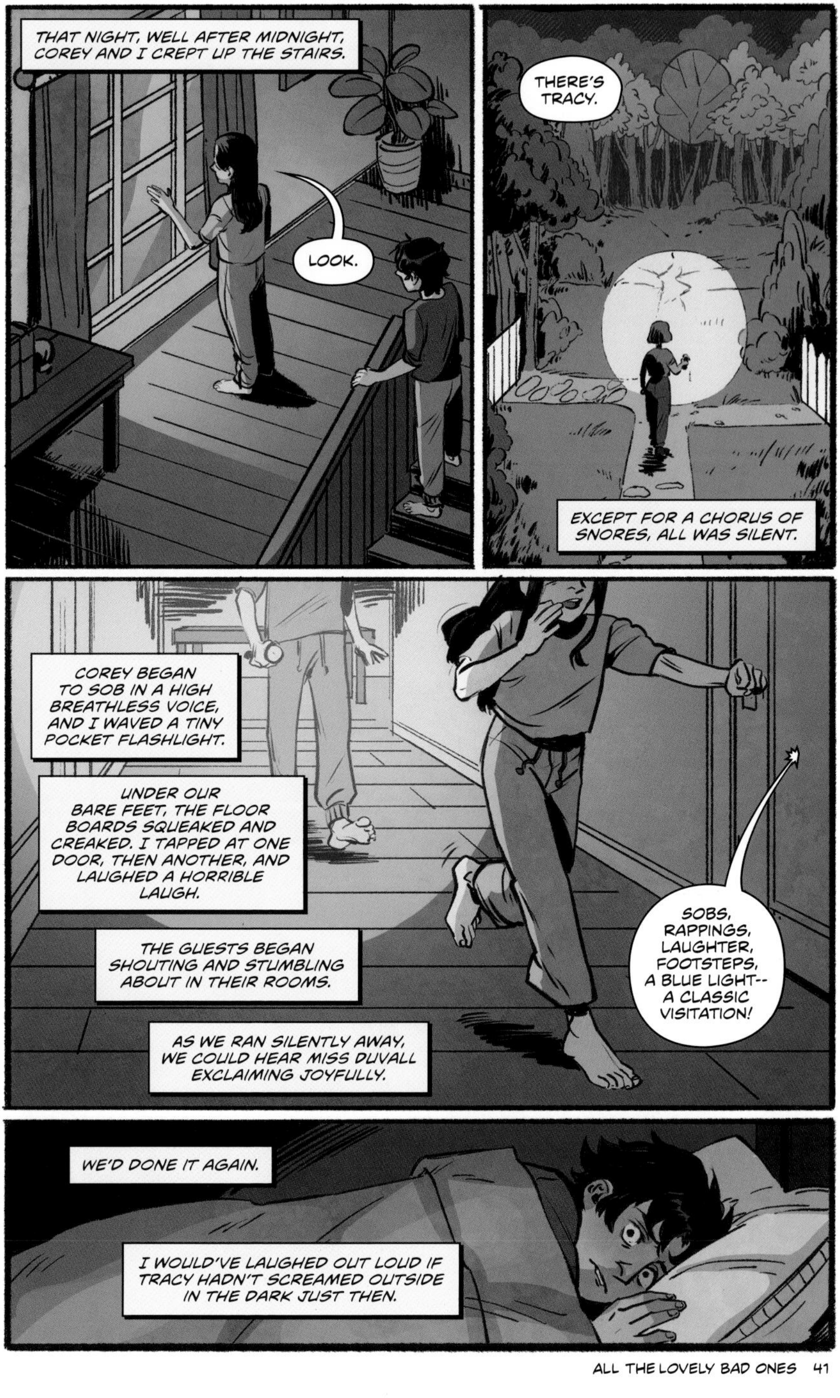
THAT NIGHT, WELL AFTER MIDNIGHT, COREY AND I CREPT UP THE STAIRS.
LOOK.
THERE'S TRACY.
EXCEPT FOR A CHORUS OF SNORES, ALL WAS SILENT.
COREY BEGAN TO SOB IN A HIGH BREATHLESS VOICE, AND I WAVED A TINY POCKET FLASHLIGHT.
UNDER OUR BARE FEET, THE FLOOR BOARDS SQUEAKED AND CREAKED. I TAPPED AT ONE DOOR, THEN ANOTHER, AND LAUGHED A HORRIBLE LAUGH.
THE GUESTS BEGAN SHOUTING AND STUMBLING ABOUT IN THEIR ROOMS.
AS WE RAN SILENTLY AWAY, WE COULD HEAR MISS DUVALL EXCLAIMING JOYFULLY.
SOBS, RAPPINGS, LAUGHTER, FOOTSTEPS, A BLUE LIGHT-- A CLASSIC VISITATION!
WE'D DONE IT AGAIN.
I WOULD'VE LAUGHED OUT LOUD IF TRACY HADN'T SCREAMED OUTSIDE IN THE DARK JUST THEN.

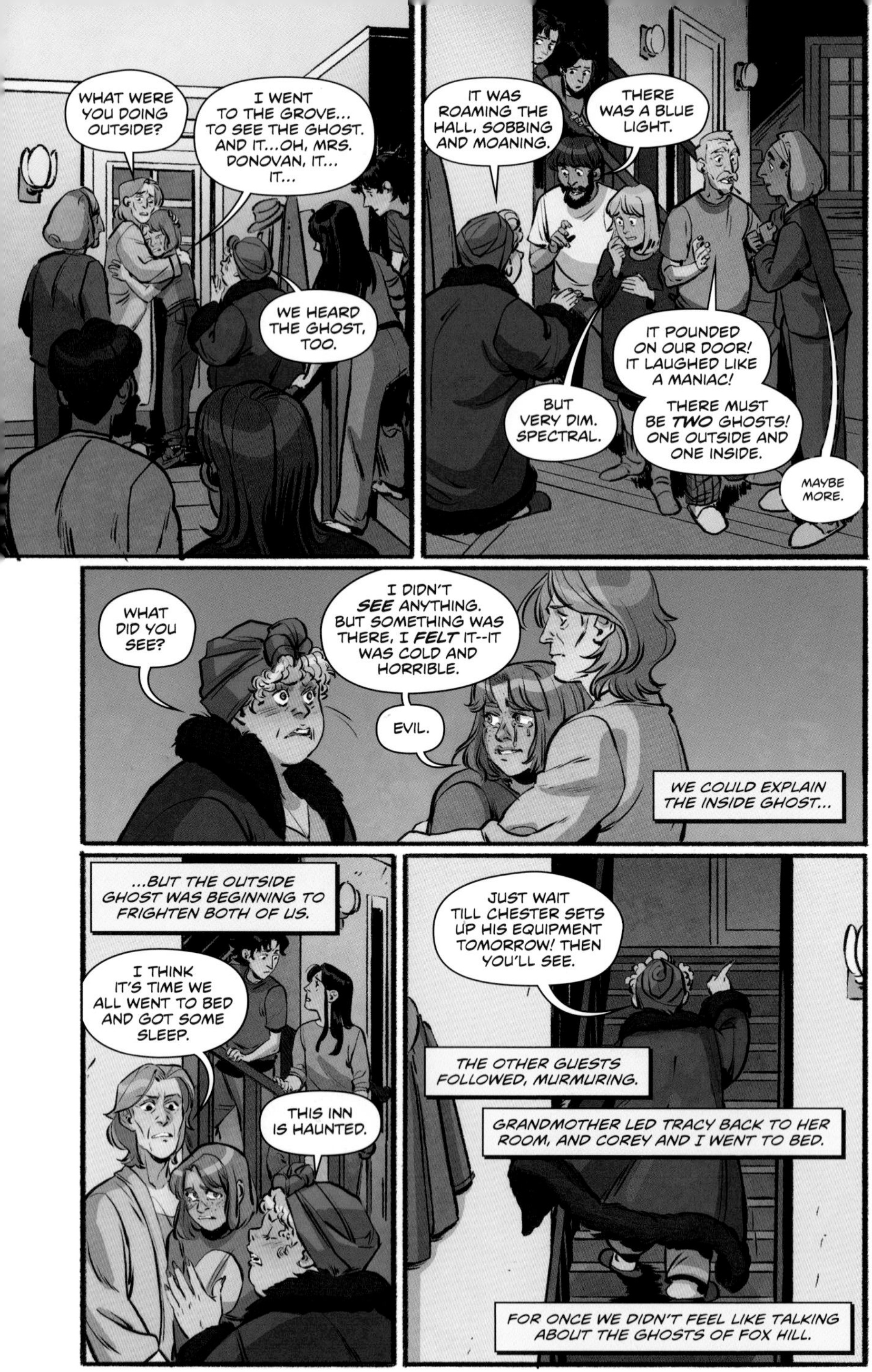
WHAT WERE YOU DOING OUTSIDE?
I WENT TO THE GROVE... TO SEE THE GHOST. AND IT...OH, MRS. DONOVAN, IT... IT...
WE HEARD THE GHOST, TOO.
IT WAS ROAMING THE HALL, SOBBING AND MOANING.
THERE WAS A BLUE LIGHT.
BUT VERY DIM. SPECTRAL.
IT POUNDED ON OUR DOOR! IT LAUGHED LIKE A MANIAC!
THERE MUST BE TWO GHOSTS! ONE OUTSIDE AND ONE INSIDE.
MAYBE MORE.
WHAT DID YOU SEE?
I DIDN'T SEE ANYTHING. BUT SOMETHING WAS THERE, I FELT IT--IT WAS COLD AND HORRIBLE.
EVIL.
WE COULD EXPLAIN THE INSIDE GHOST...
...BUT THE OUTSIDE GHOST WAS BEGINNING TO FRIGHTEN BOTH OF US.
I THINK IT'S TIME WE ALL WENT TO BED AND GOT SOME SLEEP.
THIS INN IS HAUNTED.
JUST WAIT TILL CHESTER SETS UP HIS EQUIPMENT TOMORROW! THEN YOU'LL SEE.
THE OTHER GUESTS FOLLOWED, MURMURING.
GRANDMOTHER LED TRACY BACK TO HER ROOM, AND COREY AND I WENT TO BED.
FOR ONCE WE DIDN'T FEEL LIKE TALKING ABOUT THE GHOSTS OF FOX HILL.

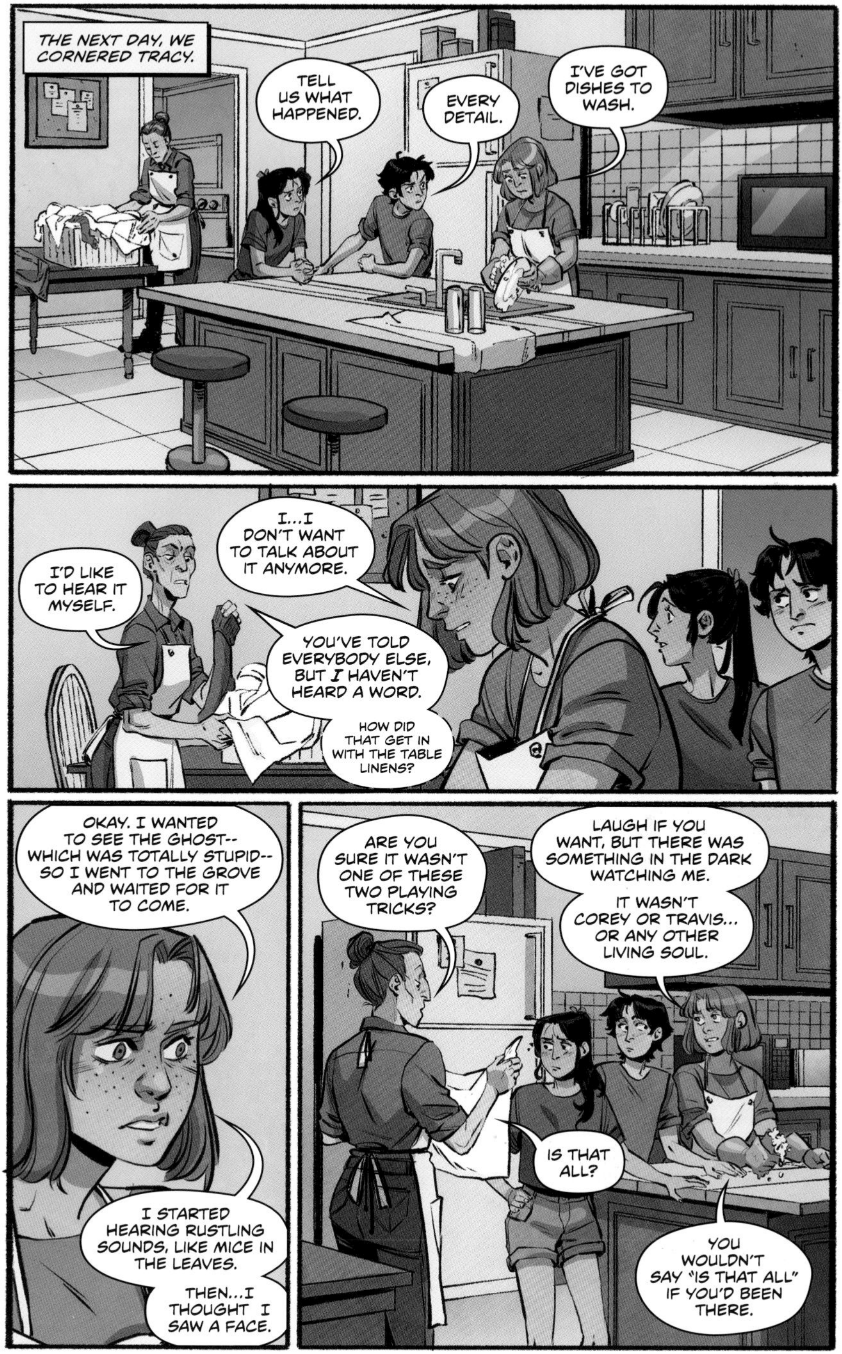
THE NEXT DAY, WE CORNERED TRACY.
TELL US WHAT HAPPENED.
EVERY DETAIL.
I'VE GOT DISHES TO WASH.
I'D LIKE TO HEAR IT MYSELF.
I...I DON'T WANT TO TALK ABOUT IT ANYMORE.
YOU'VE TOLD EVERYBODY ELSE, BUT *I* HAVEN'T HEARD A WORD.
HOW DID THAT GET IN WITH THE TABLE LINENS?
OKAY. I WANTED TO SEE THE GHOST-- WHICH WAS TOTALLY STUPID-- SO I WENT TO THE GROVE AND WAITED FOR IT TO COME.
I STARTED HEARING RUSTLING SOUNDS, LIKE MICE IN THE LEAVES.
THEN...I THOUGHT I SAW A FACE.
ARE YOU SURE IT WASN'T ONE OF THESE TWO PLAYING TRICKS?
LAUGH IF YOU WANT, BUT THERE WAS SOMETHING IN THE DARK WATCHING ME.
IT WASN'T COREY OR TRAVIS... OR ANY OTHER LIVING SOUL.
IS THAT ALL?
YOU WOULDN'T SAY "IS THAT ALL" IF YOU'D BEEN THERE.

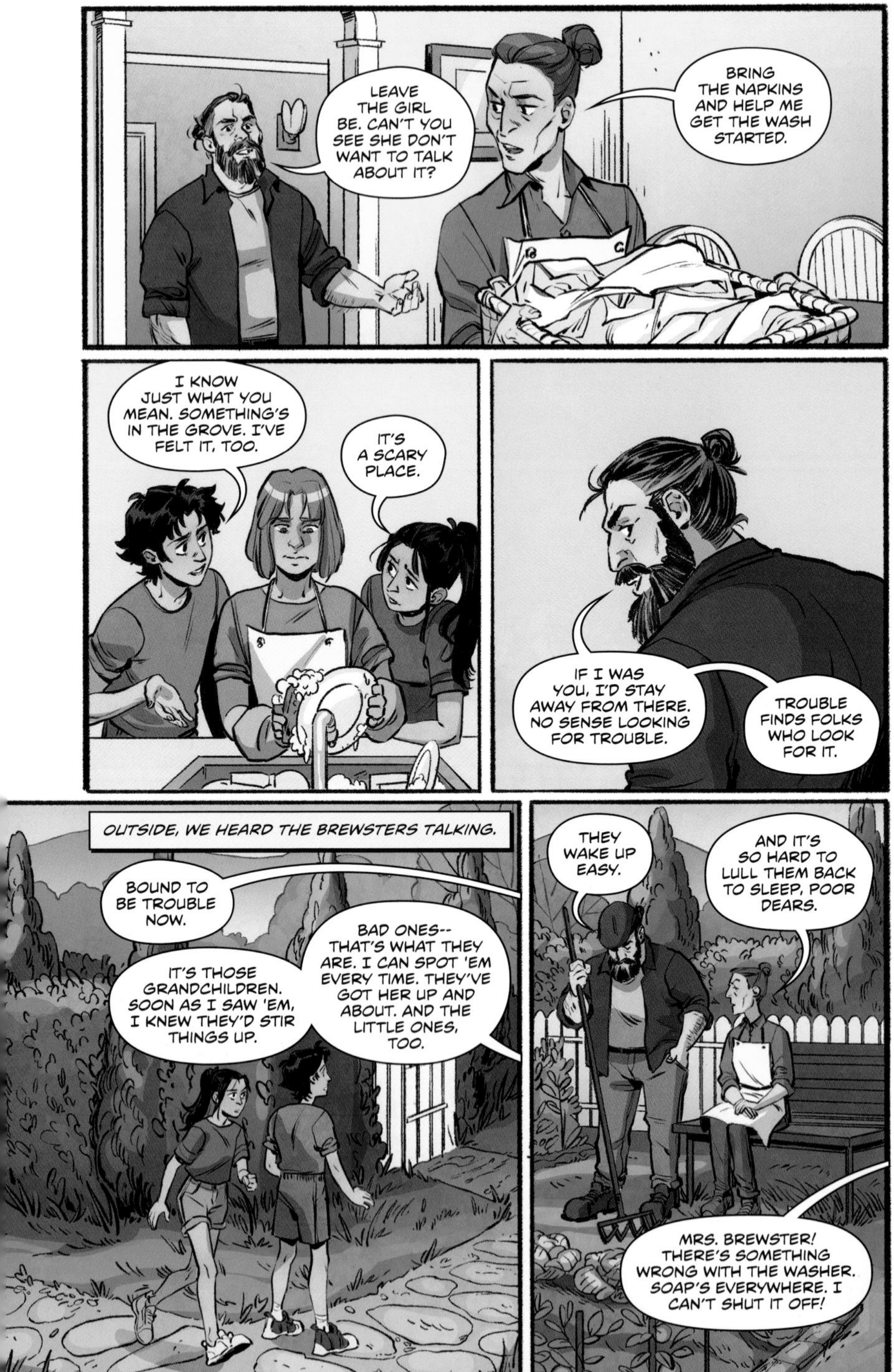
LEAVE THE GIRL BE. CAN'T YOU SEE SHE DON'T WANT TO TALK ABOUT IT?
BRING THE NAPKINS AND HELP ME GET THE WASH STARTED.
I KNOW JUST WHAT YOU MEAN. SOMETHING'S IN THE GROVE. I'VE FELT IT, TOO.
IT'S A SCARY PLACE.
IF I WAS YOU, I'D STAY AWAY FROM THERE. NO SENSE LOOKING FOR TROUBLE.
TROUBLE FINDS FOLKS WHO LOOK FOR IT.
OUTSIDE, WE HEARD THE BREWSTERS TALKING.
BOUND TO BE TROUBLE NOW.
IT'S THOSE GRANDCHILDREN. SOON AS I SAW 'EM, I KNEW THEY'D STIR THINGS UP.
BAD ONES--THAT'S WHAT THEY ARE. I CAN SPOT 'EM EVERY TIME. THEY'VE GOT HER UP AND ABOUT. AND THE LITTLE ONES, TOO.
THEY WAKE UP EASY.
AND IT'S SO HARD TO LULL THEM BACK TO SLEEP, POOR DEARS.
MRS. BREWSTER! THERE'S SOMETHING WRONG WITH THE WASHER. SOAP'S EVERYWHERE. I CAN'T SHUT IT OFF!

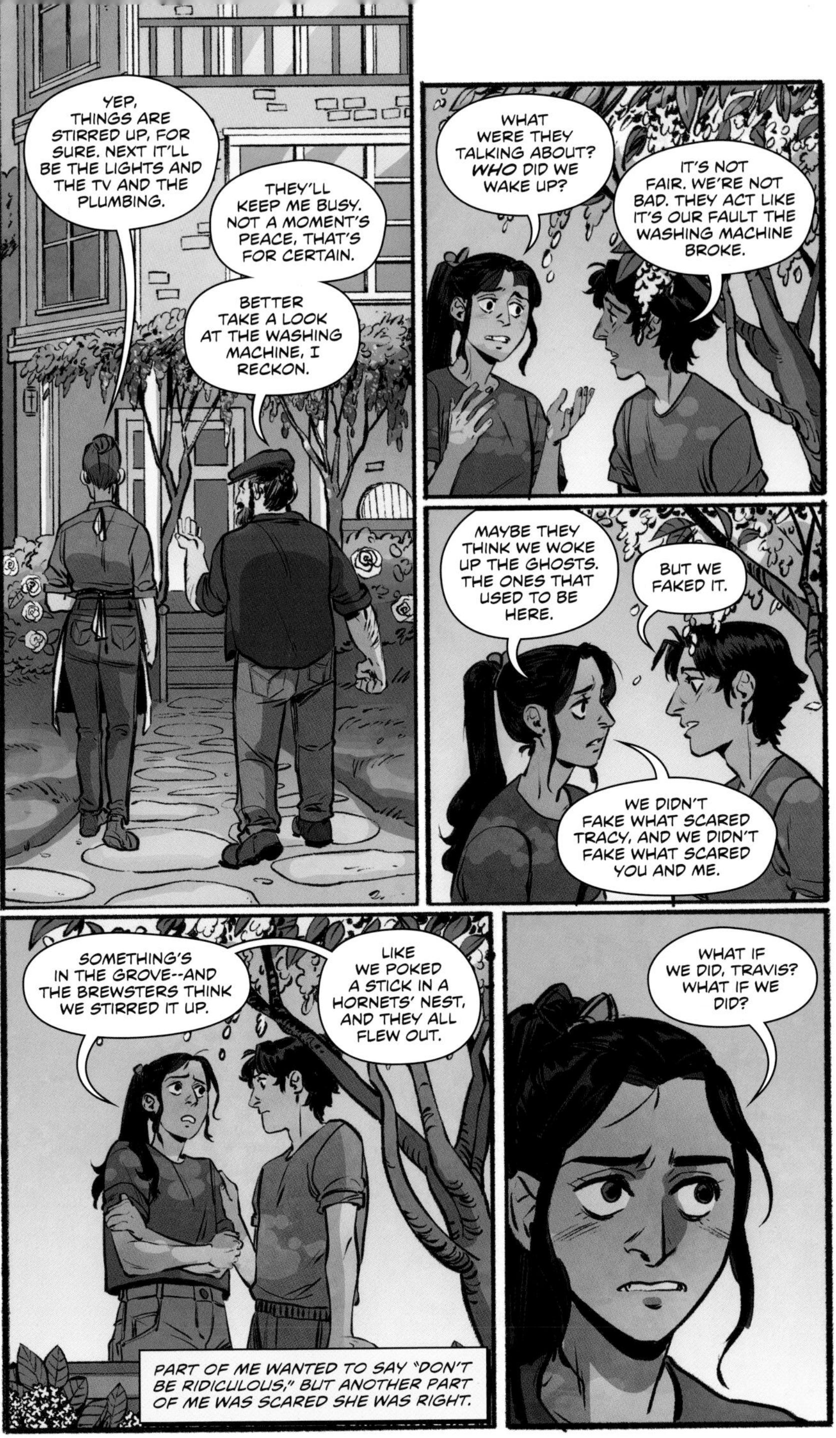

YEP, THINGS ARE STIRRED UP, FOR SURE. NEXT IT'LL BE THE LIGHTS AND THE TV AND THE PLUMBING.
THEY'LL KEEP ME BUSY. NOT A MOMENT'S PEACE, THAT'S FOR CERTAIN.
BETTER TAKE A LOOK AT THE WASHING MACHINE, I RECKON.
WHAT WERE THEY TALKING ABOUT? *WHO* DID WE WAKE UP?
IT'S NOT FAIR. WE'RE NOT BAD. THEY ACT LIKE IT'S OUR FAULT THE WASHING MACHINE BROKE.
MAYBE THEY THINK WE WOKE UP THE GHOSTS. THE ONES THAT USED TO BE HERE.
BUT WE FAKED IT.
WE DIDN'T FAKE WHAT SCARED TRACY, AND WE DIDN'T FAKE WHAT SCARED YOU AND ME.
SOMETHING'S IN THE GROVE--AND THE BREWSTERS THINK WE STIRRED IT UP.
LIKE WE POKED A STICK IN A HORNETS' NEST, AND THEY ALL FLEW OUT.
PART OF ME WANTED TO SAY "DON'T BE RIDICULOUS," BUT ANOTHER PART OF ME WAS SCARED SHE WAS RIGHT.
WHAT IF WE DID, TRAVIS? WHAT IF WE DID?

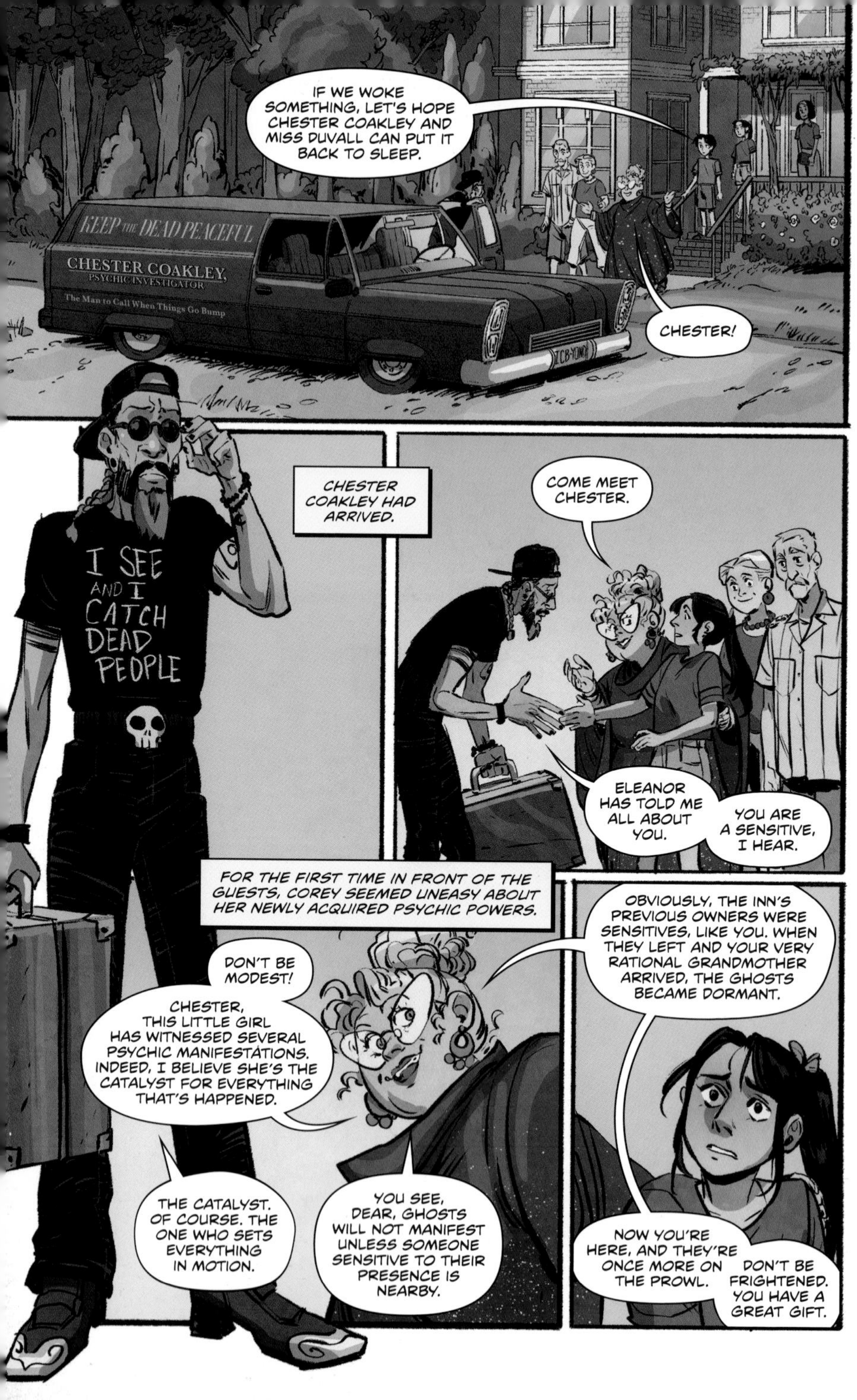
IF WE WOKE SOMETHING, LET'S HOPE CHESTER COAKLEY AND MISS DUVALL CAN PUT IT BACK TO SLEEP.
KEEP THE DEAD PEACEFUL
CHESTER COAKLEY, PSYCHIC INVESTIGATOR
The Man to Call When Things Go Bump
CHESTER!
I SEE AND I CATCH DEAD PEOPLE
CHESTER COAKLEY HAD ARRIVED.
COME MEET CHESTER.
ELEANOR HAS TOLD ME ALL ABOUT YOU.
YOU ARE A SENSITIVE, I HEAR.
FOR THE FIRST TIME IN FRONT OF THE GUESTS, COREY SEEMED UNEASY ABOUT HER NEWLY ACQUIRED PSYCHIC POWERS.
DON'T BE MODEST!
CHESTER, THIS LITTLE GIRL HAS WITNESSED SEVERAL PSYCHIC MANIFESTATIONS. INDEED, I BELIEVE SHE'S THE CATALYST FOR EVERYTHING THAT'S HAPPENED.
THE CATALYST. OF COURSE. THE ONE WHO SETS EVERYTHING IN MOTION.
YOU SEE, DEAR, GHOSTS WILL NOT MANIFEST UNLESS SOMEONE SENSITIVE TO THEIR PRESENCE IS NEARBY.
OBVIOUSLY, THE INN'S PREVIOUS OWNERS WERE SENSITIVES, LIKE YOU. WHEN THEY LEFT AND YOUR VERY RATIONAL GRANDMOTHER ARRIVED, THE GHOSTS BECAME DORMANT.
NOW YOU'RE HERE, AND THEY'RE ONCE MORE ON THE PROWL.
DON'T BE FRIGHTENED. YOU HAVE A GREAT GIFT.

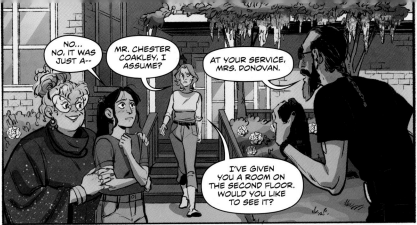

NO... NO, IT WAS JUST A--

MR. CHESTER COAKLEY, I ASSUME?

AT YOUR SERVICE, MRS. DONOVAN.

I'VE GIVEN YOU A ROOM ON THE SECOND FLOOR. WOULD YOU LIKE TO SEE IT?

"OH, SHE'S A CATALYST--THERE HAS TO BE A CATALYST."

HEY... WHERE ARE YOU GOING?

TO MY ROOM. I WANT TO BE ALONE FOR A WHILE.

SHE DIDN'T LOOK BACK.

SO I WALKED TO THE PLACE WHERE I'D FOUND THE ROW OF STONES.

I STARED AT THEM, STILL PUZZLED.

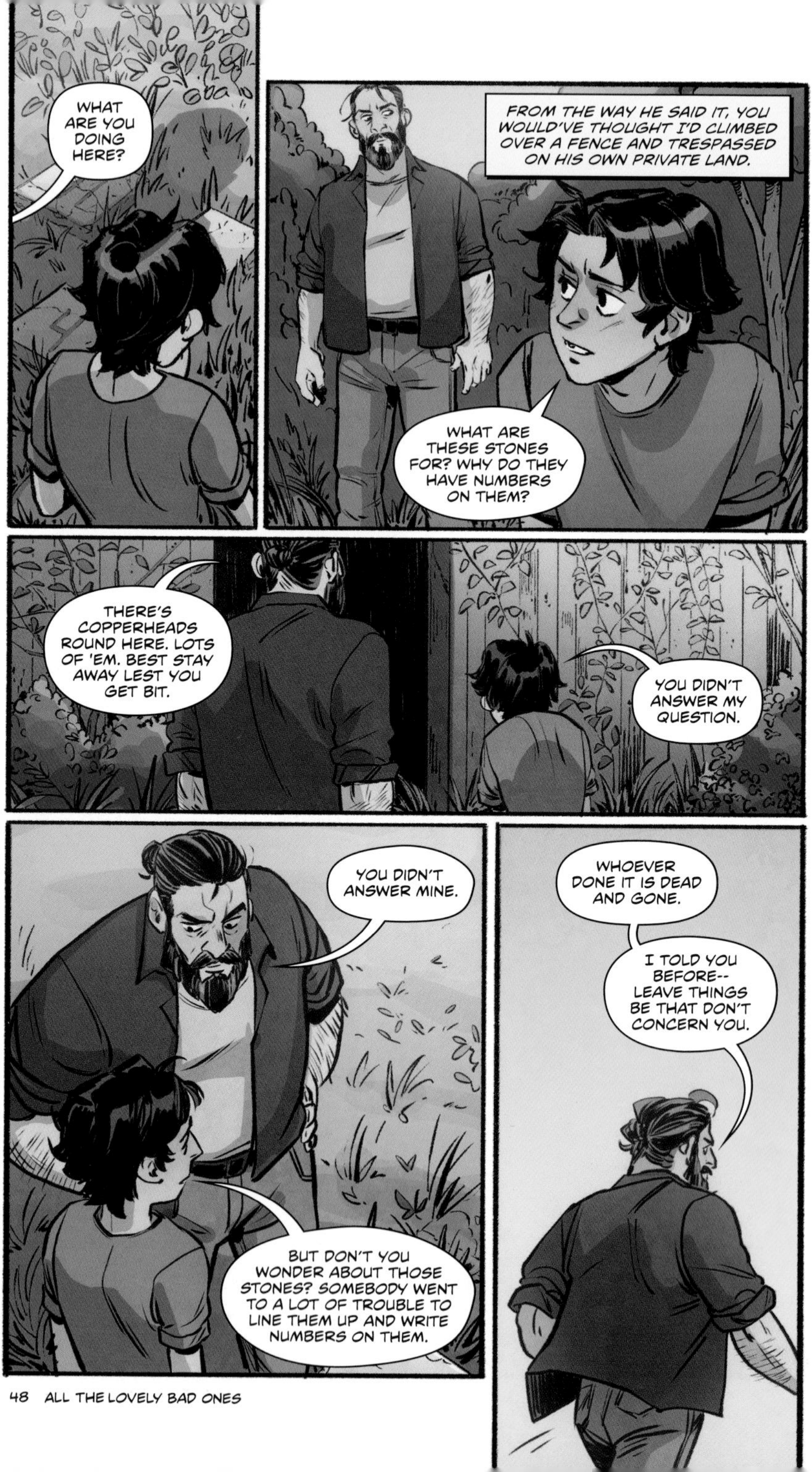
WHAT ARE YOU DOING HERE?
FROM THE WAY HE SAID IT, YOU WOULD'VE THOUGHT I'D CLIMBED OVER A FENCE AND TRESPASSED ON HIS OWN PRIVATE LAND.
WHAT ARE THESE STONES FOR? WHY DO THEY HAVE NUMBERS ON THEM?
THERE'S COPPERHEADS ROUND HERE. LOTS OF 'EM. BEST STAY AWAY LEST YOU GET BIT.
YOU DIDN'T ANSWER MY QUESTION.
YOU DIDN'T ANSWER MINE.
BUT DON'T YOU WONDER ABOUT THOSE STONES? SOMEBODY WENT TO A LOT OF TROUBLE TO LINE THEM UP AND WRITE NUMBERS ON THEM.
WHOEVER DONE IT IS DEAD AND GONE.
I TOLD YOU BEFORE-- LEAVE THINGS BE THAT DON'T CONCERN YOU.

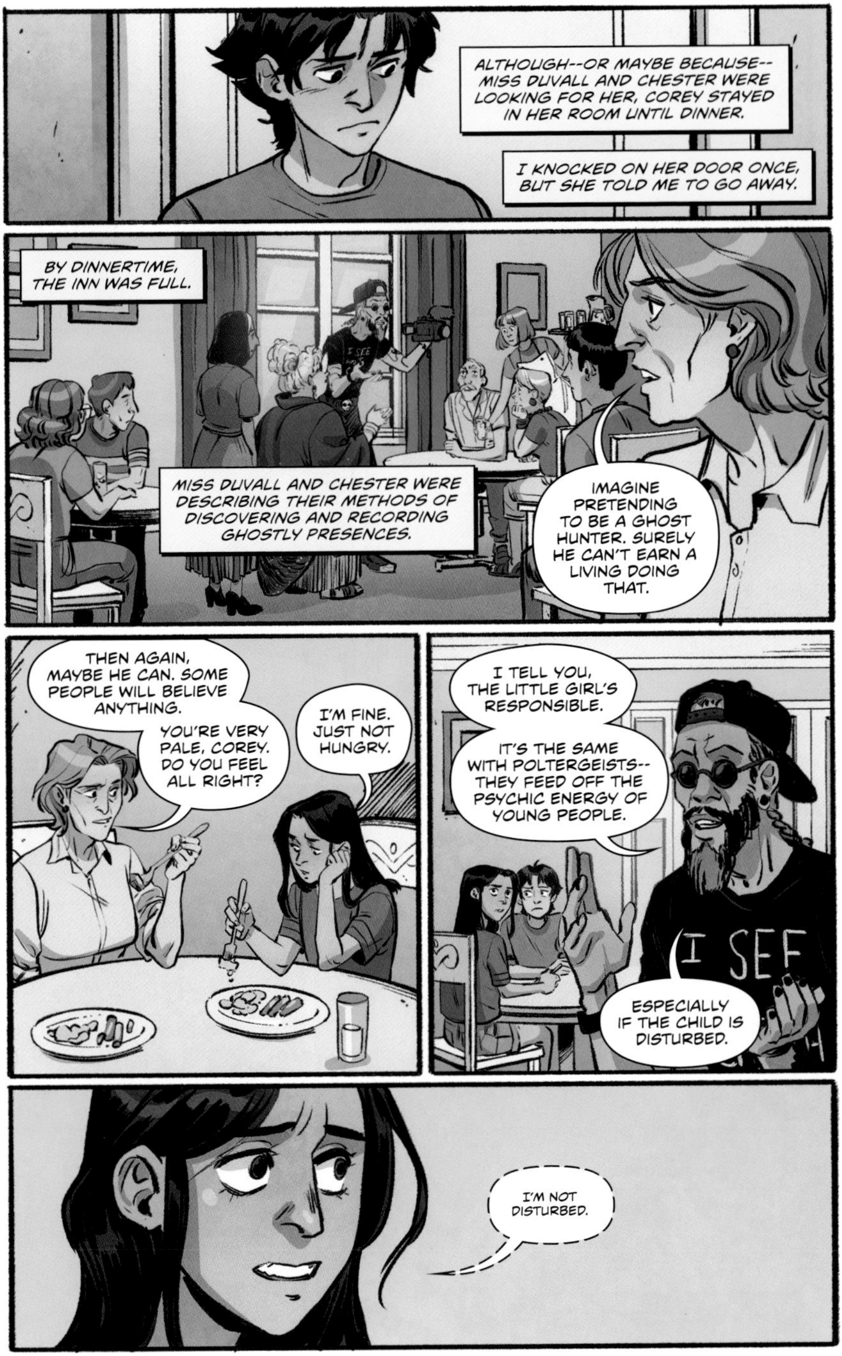
ALTHOUGH--OR MAYBE BECAUSE--MISS DUVALL AND CHESTER WERE LOOKING FOR HER, COREY STAYED IN HER ROOM UNTIL DINNER.
I KNOCKED ON HER DOOR ONCE, BUT SHE TOLD ME TO GO AWAY.
BY DINNERTIME, THE INN WAS FULL.
MISS DUVALL AND CHESTER WERE DESCRIBING THEIR METHODS OF DISCOVERING AND RECORDING GHOSTLY PRESENCES.
IMAGINE PRETENDING TO BE A GHOST HUNTER. SURELY HE CAN'T EARN A LIVING DOING THAT.
THEN AGAIN, MAYBE HE CAN. SOME PEOPLE WILL BELIEVE ANYTHING.
YOU'RE VERY PALE, COREY. DO YOU FEEL ALL RIGHT?
I'M FINE. JUST NOT HUNGRY.
I TELL YOU, THE LITTLE GIRL'S RESPONSIBLE.
IT'S THE SAME WITH POLTERGEISTS--THEY FEED OFF THE PSYCHIC ENERGY OF YOUNG PEOPLE.
I SEE
ESPECIALLY IF THE CHILD IS DISTURBED.
I'M NOT DISTURBED.

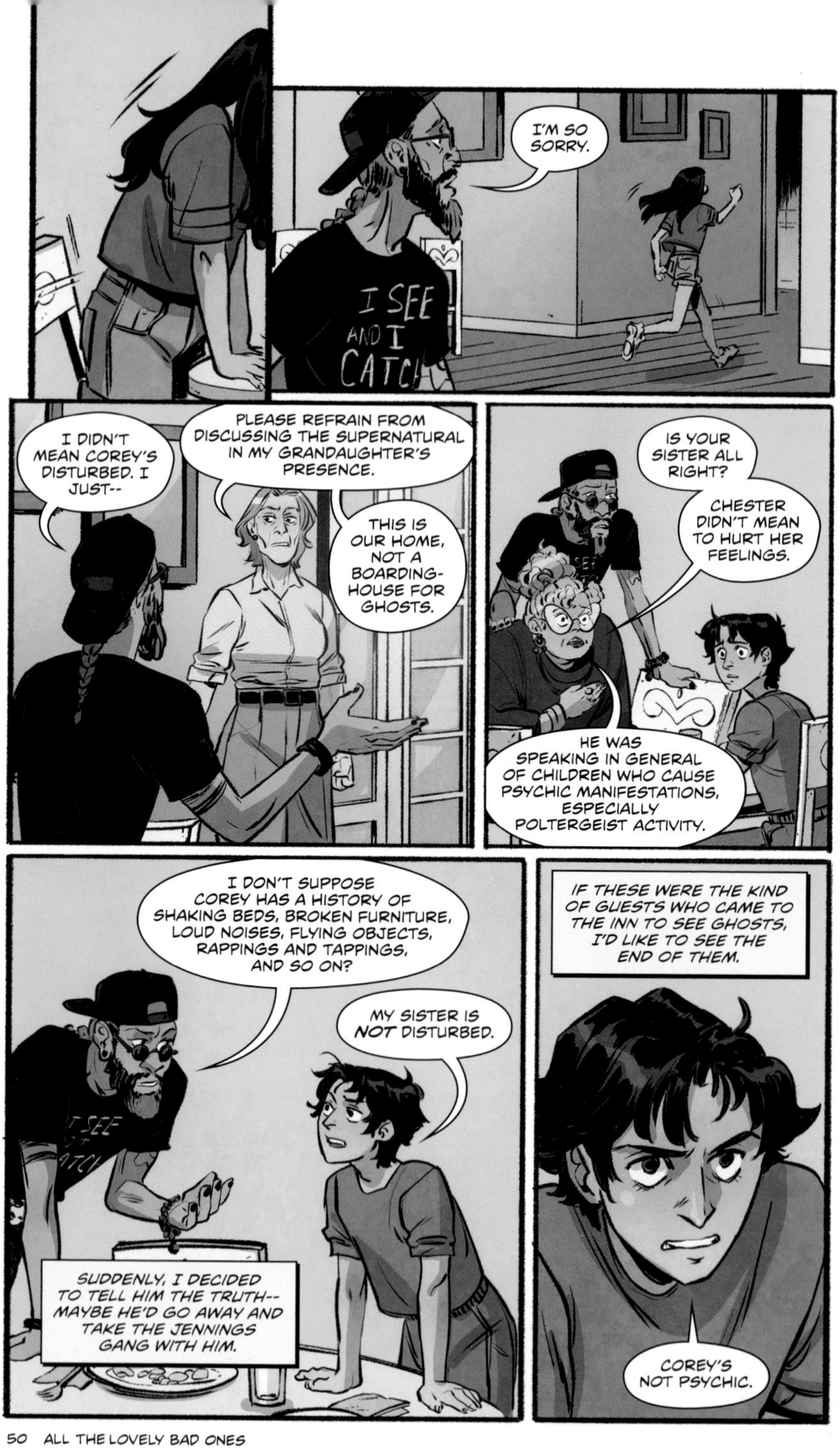
I'M SO SORRY.
I SEE AND I CATCH
I DIDN'T MEAN COREY'S DISTURBED. I JUST--
PLEASE REFRAIN FROM DISCUSSING THE SUPERNATURAL IN MY GRANDAUGHTER'S PRESENCE.
THIS IS OUR HOME, NOT A BOARDING-HOUSE FOR GHOSTS.
IS YOUR SISTER ALL RIGHT?
CHESTER DIDN'T MEAN TO HURT HER FEELINGS.
HE WAS SPEAKING IN GENERAL OF CHILDREN WHO CAUSE PSYCHIC MANIFESTATIONS, ESPECIALLY POLTERGEIST ACTIVITY.
I DON'T SUPPOSE COREY HAS A HISTORY OF SHAKING BEDS, BROKEN FURNITURE, LOUD NOISES, FLYING OBJECTS, RAPPINGS AND TAPPINGS, AND SO ON?
MY SISTER IS *NOT* DISTURBED.
SUDDENLY, I DECIDED TO TELL HIM THE TRUTH--MAYBE HE'D GO AWAY AND TAKE THE JENNINGS GANG WITH HIM.
IF THESE WERE THE KIND OF GUESTS WHO CAME TO THE INN TO SEE GHOSTS, I'D LIKE TO SEE THE END OF THEM.
COREY'S NOT PSYCHIC.

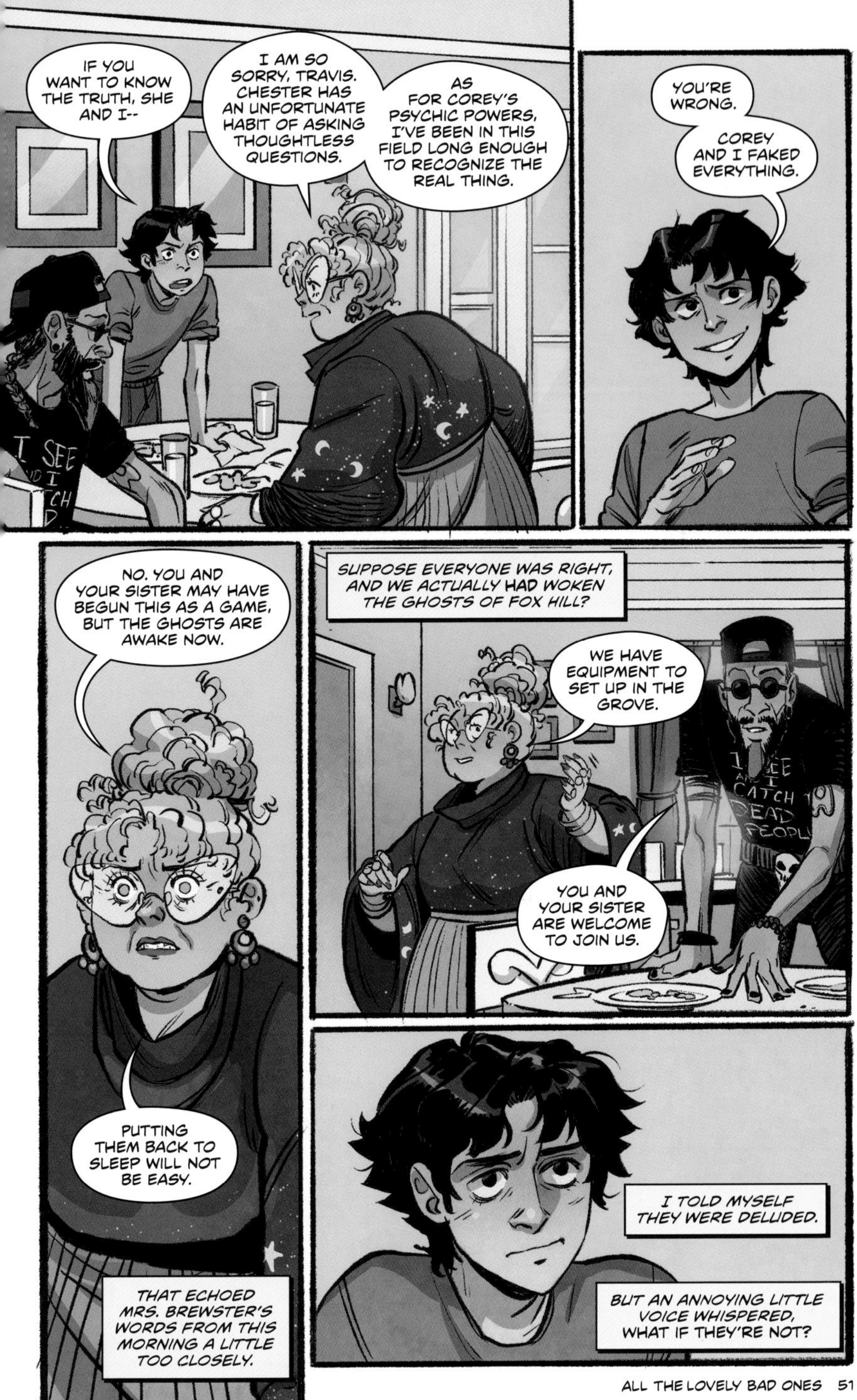
IF YOU WANT TO KNOW THE TRUTH, SHE AND I--
I AM SO SORRY, TRAVIS. CHESTER HAS AN UNFORTUNATE HABIT OF ASKING THOUGHTLESS QUESTIONS.
AS FOR COREY'S PSYCHIC POWERS, I'VE BEEN IN THIS FIELD LONG ENOUGH TO RECOGNIZE THE REAL THING.
I SEE AND I CATCH D
YOU'RE WRONG.
COREY AND I FAKED EVERYTHING.
NO. YOU AND YOUR SISTER MAY HAVE BEGUN THIS AS A GAME, BUT THE GHOSTS ARE AWAKE NOW.
PUTTING THEM BACK TO SLEEP WILL NOT BE EASY.
THAT ECHOED MRS. BREWSTER'S WORDS FROM THIS MORNING A LITTLE TOO CLOSELY.
SUPPOSE EVERYONE WAS RIGHT, AND WE ACTUALLY HAD WOKEN THE GHOSTS OF FOX HILL?
WE HAVE EQUIPMENT TO SET UP IN THE GROVE.
I SEE AND I CATCH DEAD PEOPLE
YOU AND YOUR SISTER ARE WELCOME TO JOIN US.
I TOLD MYSELF THEY WERE DELUDED.
BUT AN ANNOYING LITTLE VOICE WHISPERED, WHAT IF THEY'RE NOT?

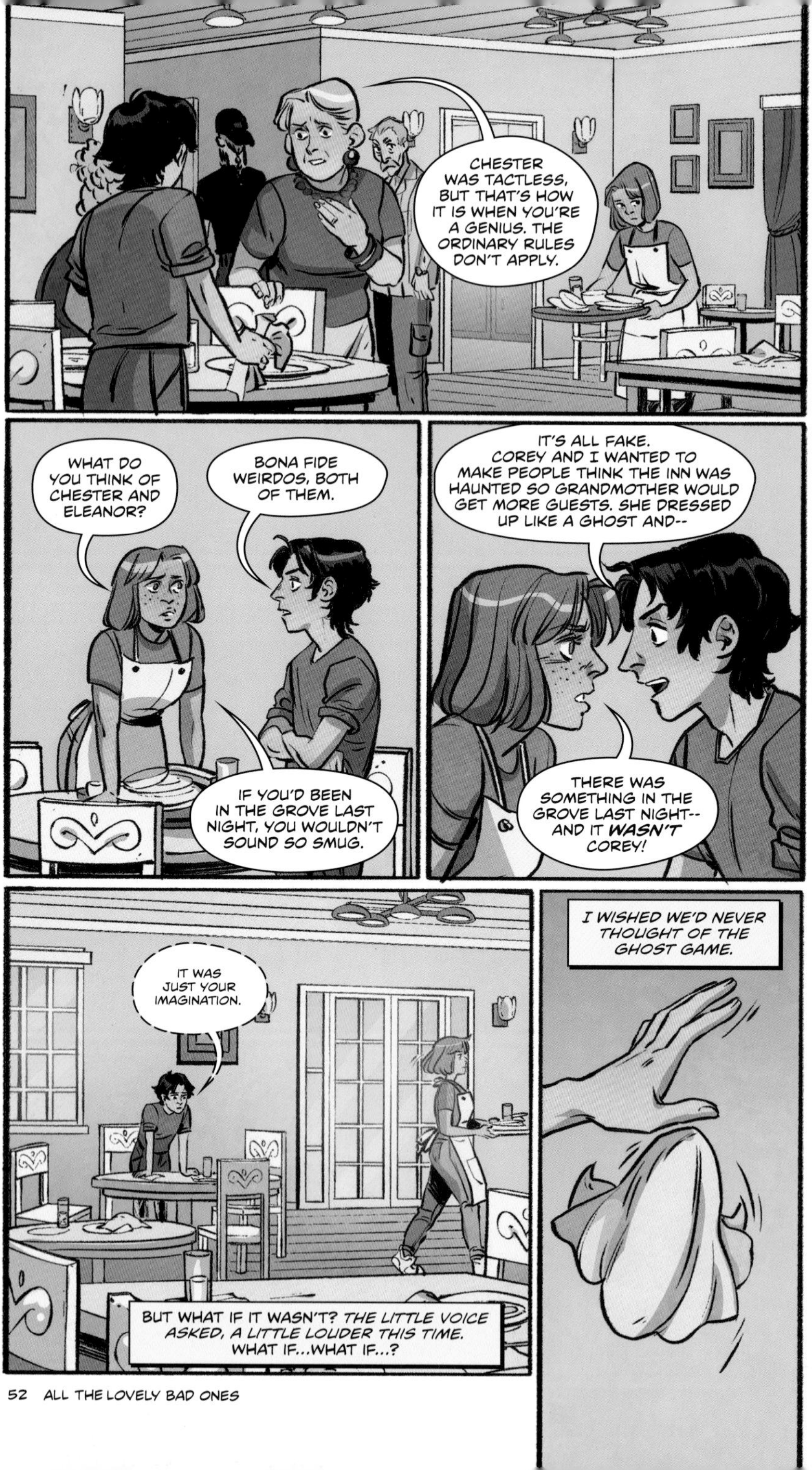
CHESTER WAS TACTLESS, BUT THAT'S HOW IT IS WHEN YOU'RE A GENIUS. THE ORDINARY RULES DON'T APPLY.
WHAT DO YOU THINK OF CHESTER AND ELEANOR?
BONA FIDE WEIRDOS, BOTH OF THEM.
IF YOU'D BEEN IN THE GROVE LAST NIGHT, YOU WOULDN'T SOUND SO SMUG.
IT'S ALL FAKE. COREY AND I WANTED TO MAKE PEOPLE THINK THE INN WAS HAUNTED SO GRANDMOTHER WOULD GET MORE GUESTS. SHE DRESSED UP LIKE A GHOST AND--
THERE WAS SOMETHING IN THE GROVE LAST NIGHT-- AND IT ***WASN'T*** COREY!
IT WAS JUST YOUR IMAGINATION.
BUT WHAT IF IT WASN'T? *THE LITTLE VOICE ASKED, A LITTLE LOUDER THIS TIME.* WHAT IF...WHAT IF...?
*I WISHED WE'D NEVER THOUGHT OF THE GHOST GAME.*

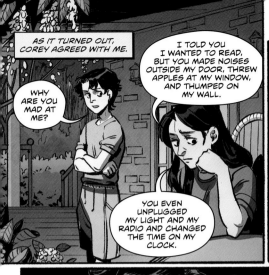

AS IT TURNED OUT, COREY AGREED WITH ME.

WHY ARE YOU MAD AT ME?

I TOLD YOU I WANTED TO READ, BUT YOU MADE NOISES OUTSIDE MY DOOR, THREW APPLES AT MY WINDOW, AND THUMPED ON MY WALL.

YOU EVEN UNPLUGGED MY LIGHT AND MY RADIO AND CHANGED THE TIME ON MY CLOCK.

I KNOCKED ON YOUR DOOR *ONCE*, YOU TOLD ME TO GO AWAY--AND I *DID*. I NEVER MADE NOISES OR THREW APPLES OR ANYTHING. I SWEAR.

OH, THEN IT MUST HAVE BEEN THE GHOST.

NO JOKE.

NO. NO JOKE.

I HEARD SOMETHING THAT SOUNDED LIKE A MUFFLED GIGGLE.

DID YOU HEAR THAT?

A MOUSE. A CAT, A BIRD. NOTHING TO BE SCARED OF.

ADMIT IT--YOU *ARE* SCARED...AND SO AM I.

WE HEARD A WHISPERING IN THE BUSHES AND THEN THE GIGGLE--LOUDER THIS TIME, FOLLOWED BY COLD AIR THAT TOUSLED OUR HAIR.

LET'S GO INSIDE.

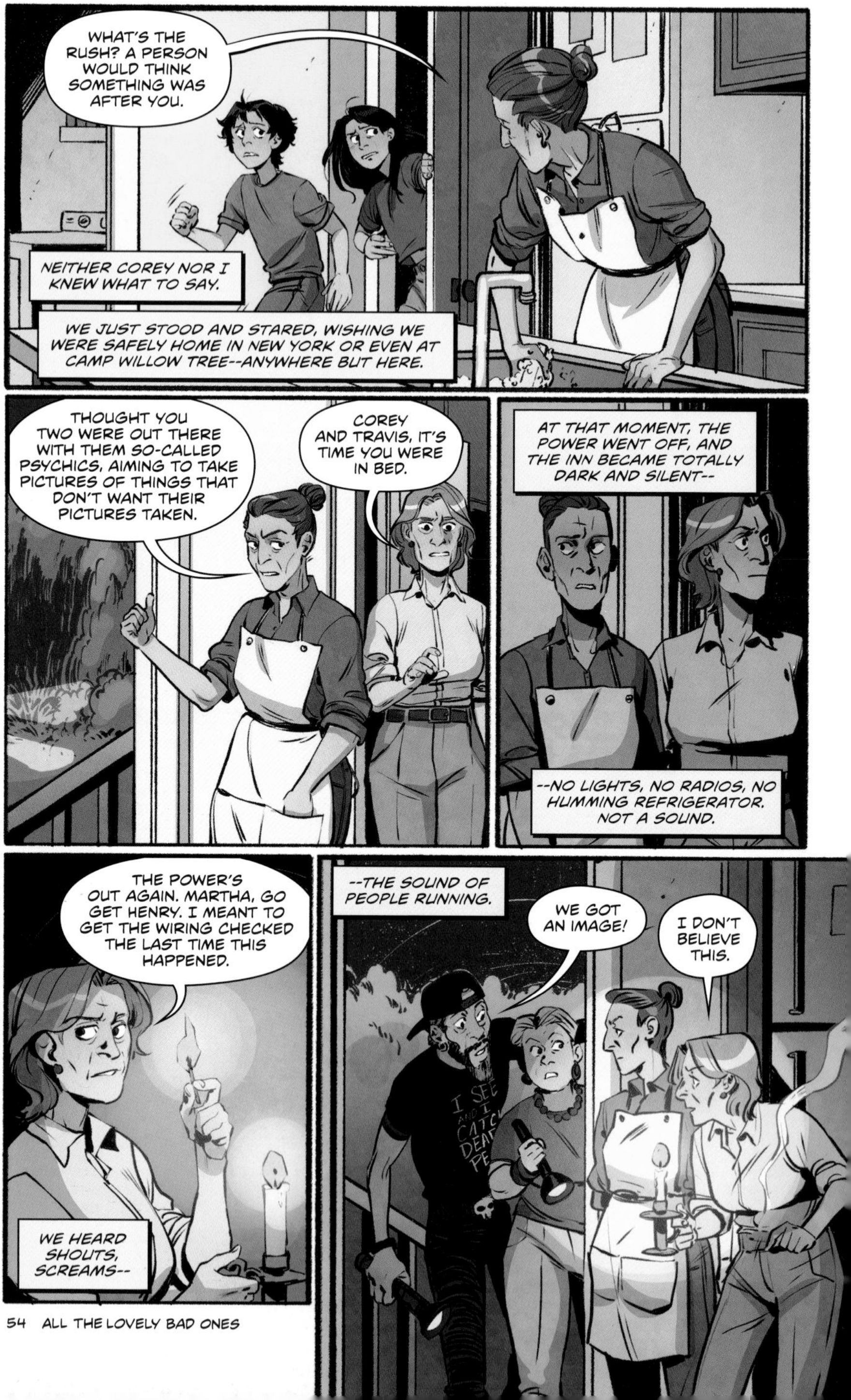
WHAT'S THE RUSH? A PERSON WOULD THINK SOMETHING WAS AFTER YOU.
NEITHER COREY NOR I KNEW WHAT TO SAY.
WE JUST STOOD AND STARED, WISHING WE WERE SAFELY HOME IN NEW YORK OR EVEN AT CAMP WILLOW TREE--ANYWHERE BUT HERE.
THOUGHT YOU TWO WERE OUT THERE WITH THEM SO-CALLED PSYCHICS, AIMING TO TAKE PICTURES OF THINGS THAT DON'T WANT THEIR PICTURES TAKEN.
COREY AND TRAVIS, IT'S TIME YOU WERE IN BED.
AT THAT MOMENT, THE POWER WENT OFF, AND THE INN BECAME TOTALLY DARK AND SILENT--
--NO LIGHTS, NO RADIOS, NO HUMMING REFRIGERATOR. NOT A SOUND.
THE POWER'S OUT AGAIN. MARTHA, GO GET HENRY. I MEANT TO GET THE WIRING CHECKED THE LAST TIME THIS HAPPENED.
WE HEARD SHOUTS, SCREAMS--
--THE SOUND OF PEOPLE RUNNING.
WE GOT AN IMAGE!
I DON'T BELIEVE THIS.

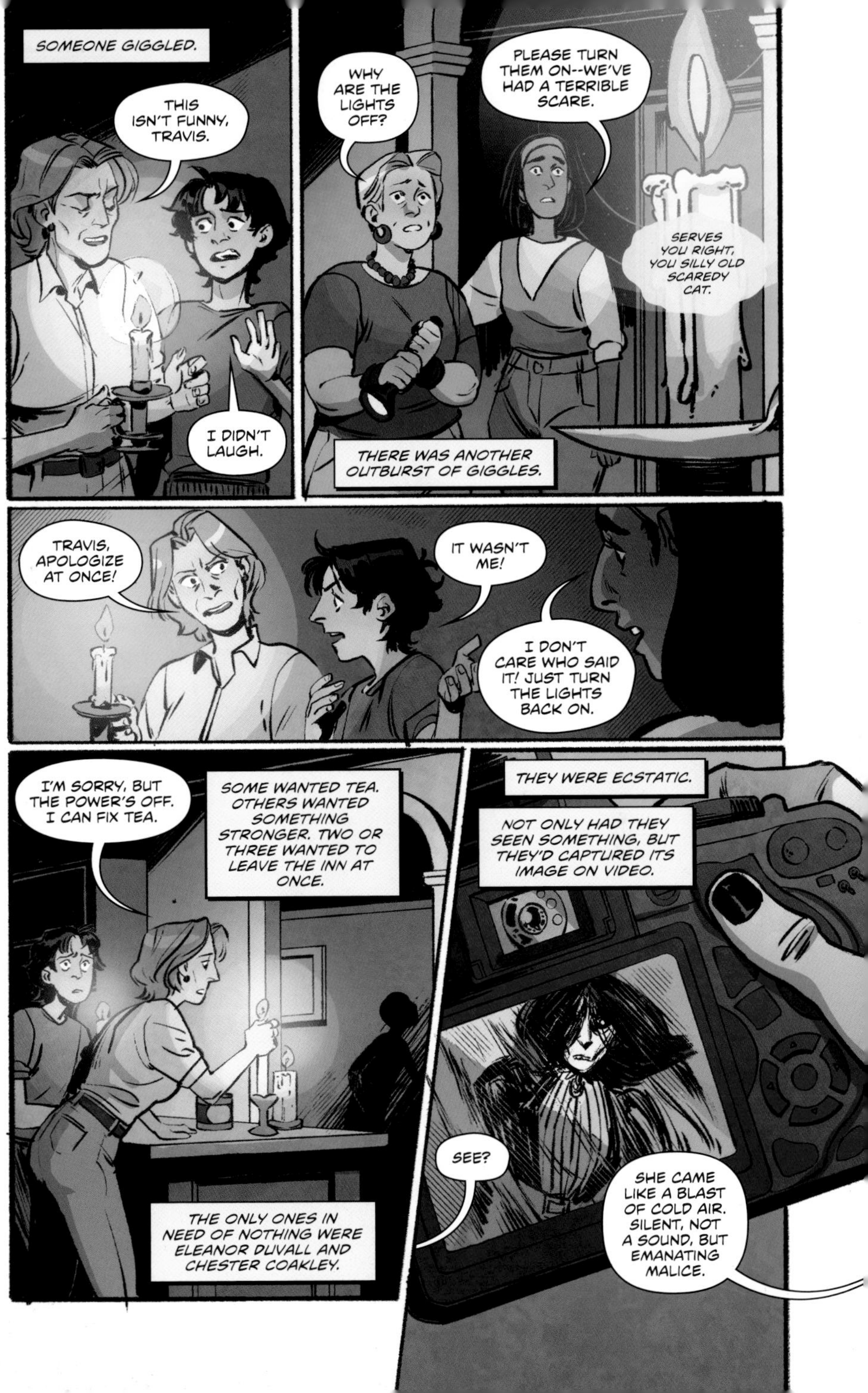

SOMEONE GIGGLED.
THIS ISN'T FUNNY, TRAVIS.
I DIDN'T LAUGH.
WHY ARE THE LIGHTS OFF?
PLEASE TURN THEM ON--WE'VE HAD A TERRIBLE SCARE.
SERVES YOU RIGHT, YOU SILLY OLD SCAREDY CAT.
THERE WAS ANOTHER OUTBURST OF GIGGLES.
TRAVIS, APOLOGIZE AT ONCE!
IT WASN'T ME!
I DON'T CARE WHO SAID IT! JUST TURN THE LIGHTS BACK ON.
I'M SORRY, BUT THE POWER'S OFF. I CAN FIX TEA.
SOME WANTED TEA. OTHERS WANTED SOMETHING STRONGER. TWO OR THREE WANTED TO LEAVE THE INN AT ONCE.
THE ONLY ONES IN NEED OF NOTHING WERE ELEANOR DUVALL AND CHESTER COAKLEY.
THEY WERE ECSTATIC.
NOT ONLY HAD THEY SEEN SOMETHING, BUT THEY'D CAPTURED ITS IMAGE ON VIDEO.
SEE?
SHE CAME LIKE A BLAST OF COLD AIR. SILENT, NOT A SOUND, BUT EMANATING MALICE.

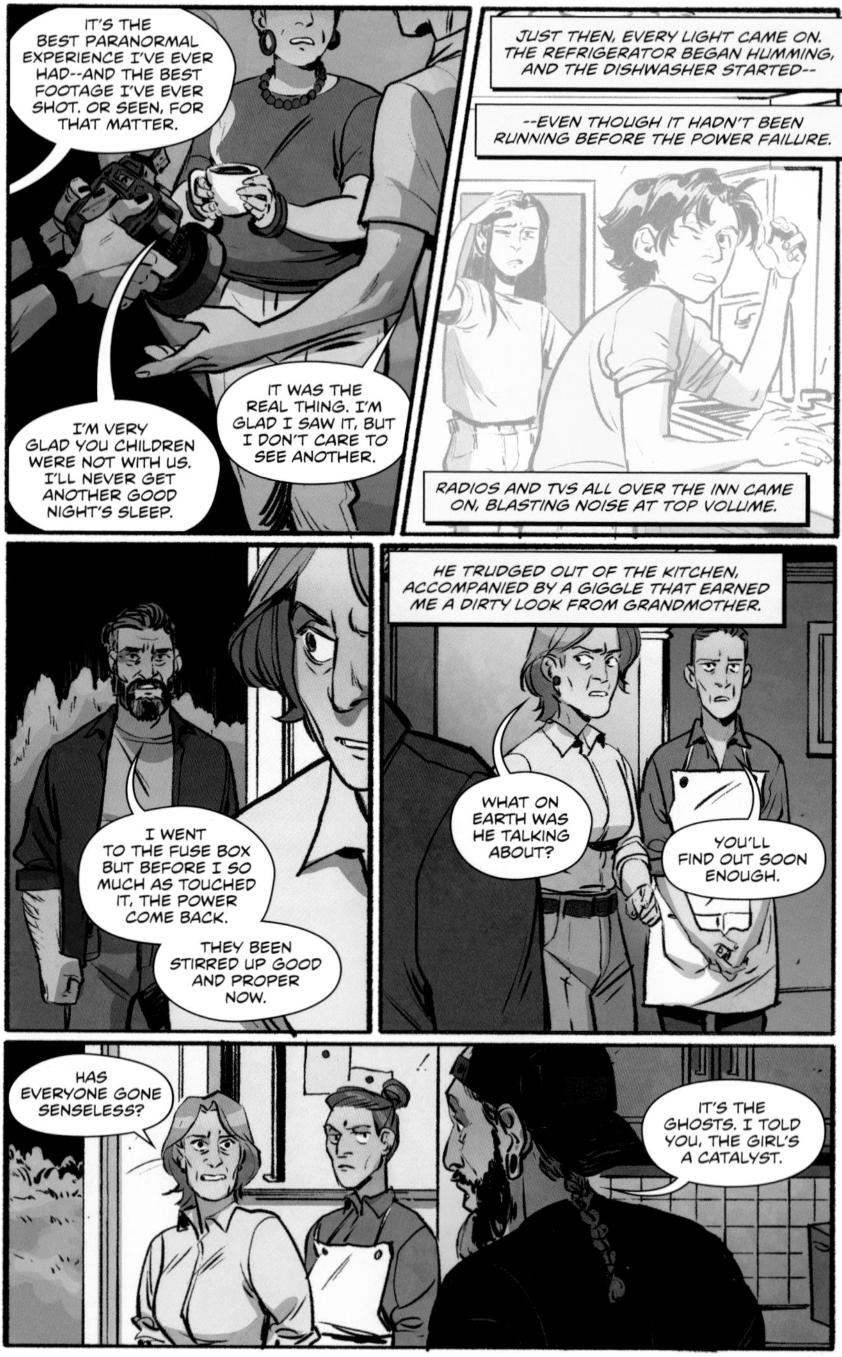
IT'S THE BEST PARANORMAL EXPERIENCE I'VE EVER HAD--AND THE BEST FOOTAGE I'VE EVER SHOT. OR SEEN, FOR THAT MATTER.
I'M VERY GLAD YOU CHILDREN WERE NOT WITH US. I'LL NEVER GET ANOTHER GOOD NIGHT'S SLEEP.
IT WAS THE REAL THING. I'M GLAD I SAW IT, BUT I DON'T CARE TO SEE ANOTHER.
JUST THEN, EVERY LIGHT CAME ON. THE REFRIGERATOR BEGAN HUMMING, AND THE DISHWASHER STARTED--
--EVEN THOUGH IT HADN'T BEEN RUNNING BEFORE THE POWER FAILURE.
RADIOS AND TVS ALL OVER THE INN CAME ON, BLASTING NOISE AT TOP VOLUME.
I WENT TO THE FUSE BOX BUT BEFORE I SO MUCH AS TOUCHED IT, THE POWER COME BACK.
THEY BEEN STIRRED UP GOOD AND PROPER NOW.
HE TRUDGED OUT OF THE KITCHEN, ACCOMPANIED BY A GIGGLE THAT EARNED ME A DIRTY LOOK FROM GRANDMOTHER.
WHAT ON EARTH WAS HE TALKING ABOUT?
YOU'LL FIND OUT SOON ENOUGH.
HAS EVERYONE GONE SENSELESS?
IT'S THE GHOSTS. I TOLD YOU, THE GIRL'S A CATALYST.

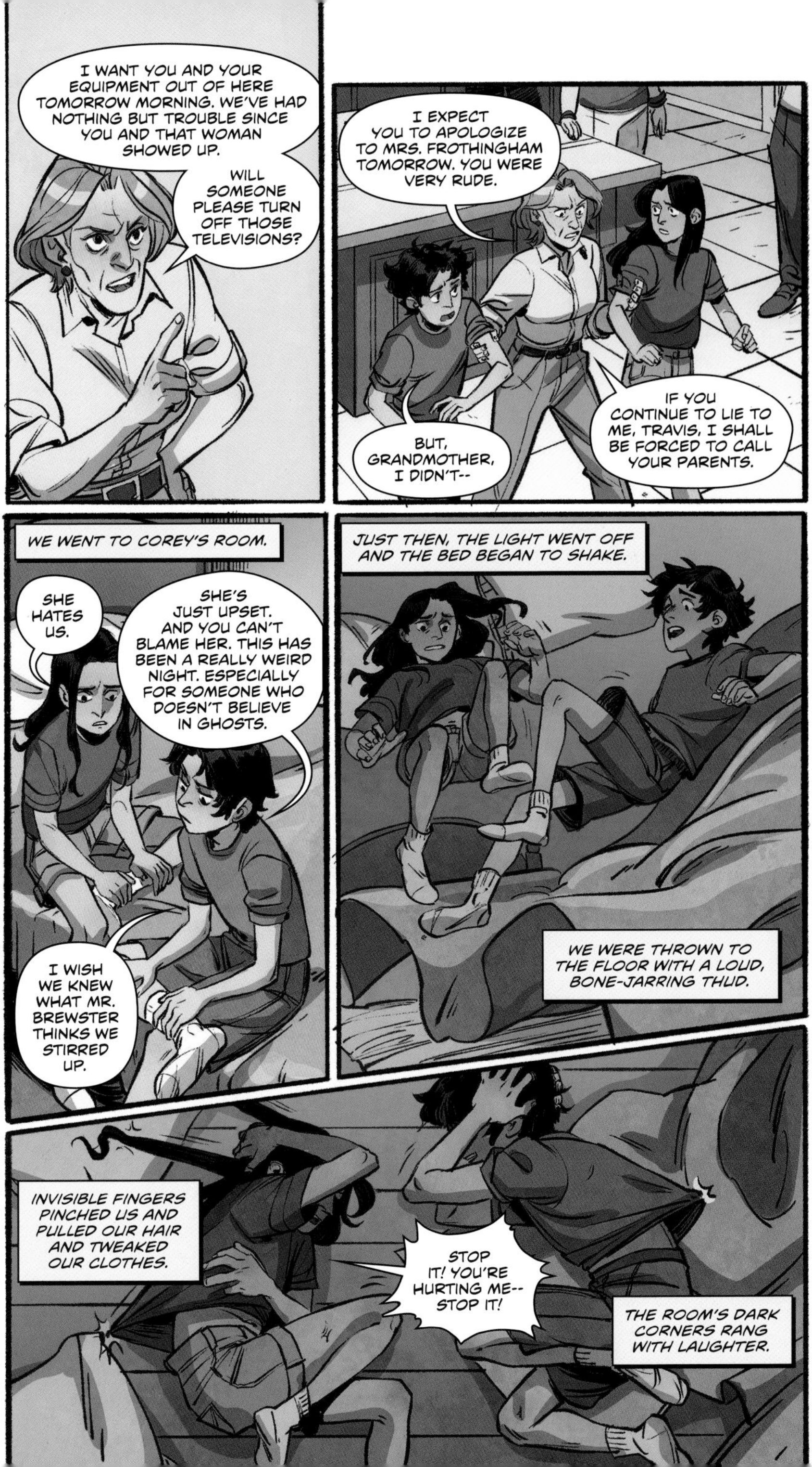
I WANT YOU AND YOUR EQUIPMENT OUT OF HERE TOMORROW MORNING. WE'VE HAD NOTHING BUT TROUBLE SINCE YOU AND THAT WOMAN SHOWED UP.
WILL SOMEONE PLEASE TURN OFF THOSE TELEVISIONS?
I EXPECT YOU TO APOLOGIZE TO MRS. FROTHINGHAM TOMORROW. YOU WERE VERY RUDE.
BUT, GRANDMOTHER, I DIDN'T--
IF YOU CONTINUE TO LIE TO ME, TRAVIS, I SHALL BE FORCED TO CALL YOUR PARENTS.
WE WENT TO COREY'S ROOM.
SHE HATES US.
SHE'S JUST UPSET. AND YOU CAN'T BLAME HER. THIS HAS BEEN A REALLY WEIRD NIGHT. ESPECIALLY FOR SOMEONE WHO DOESN'T BELIEVE IN GHOSTS.
I WISH WE KNEW WHAT MR. BREWSTER THINKS WE STIRRED UP.
JUST THEN, THE LIGHT WENT OFF AND THE BED BEGAN TO SHAKE.
WE WERE THROWN TO THE FLOOR WITH A LOUD, BONE-JARRING THUD.
INVISIBLE FINGERS PINCHED US AND PULLED OUR HAIR AND TWEAKED OUR CLOTHES.
STOP IT! YOU'RE HURTING ME-- STOP IT!
THE ROOM'S DARK CORNERS RANG WITH LAUGHTER.

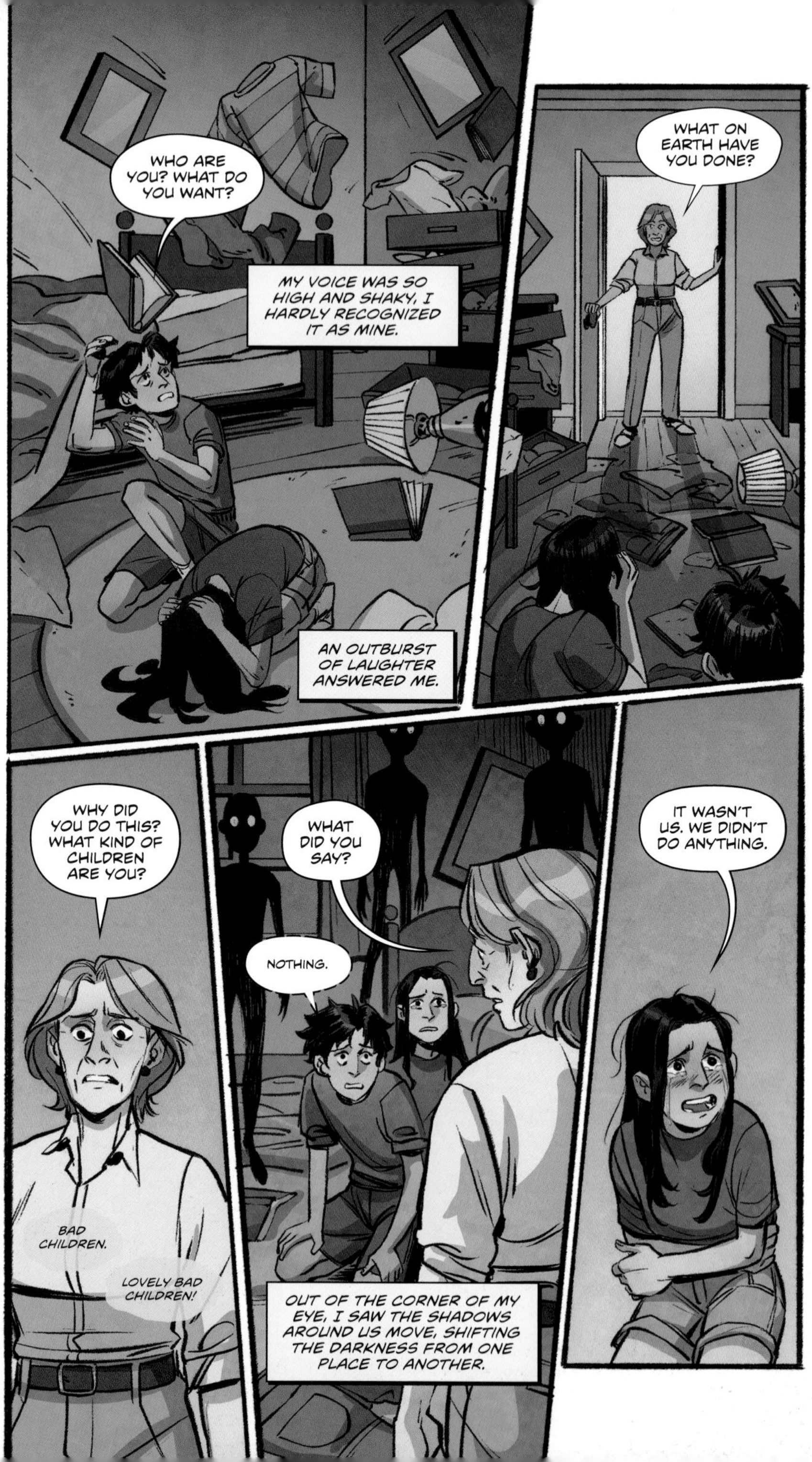
WHO ARE YOU? WHAT DO YOU WANT?
MY VOICE WAS SO HIGH AND SHAKY, I HARDLY RECOGNIZED IT AS MINE.
AN OUTBURST OF LAUGHTER ANSWERED ME.
WHAT ON EARTH HAVE YOU DONE?
WHY DID YOU DO THIS? WHAT KIND OF CHILDREN ARE YOU?
BAD CHILDREN.
LOVELY BAD CHILDREN!
WHAT DID YOU SAY?
NOTHING.
OUT OF THE CORNER OF MY EYE, I SAW THE SHADOWS AROUND US MOVE, SHIFTING THE DARKNESS FROM ONE PLACE TO ANOTHER.
IT WASN'T US. WE DIDN'T DO ANYTHING.

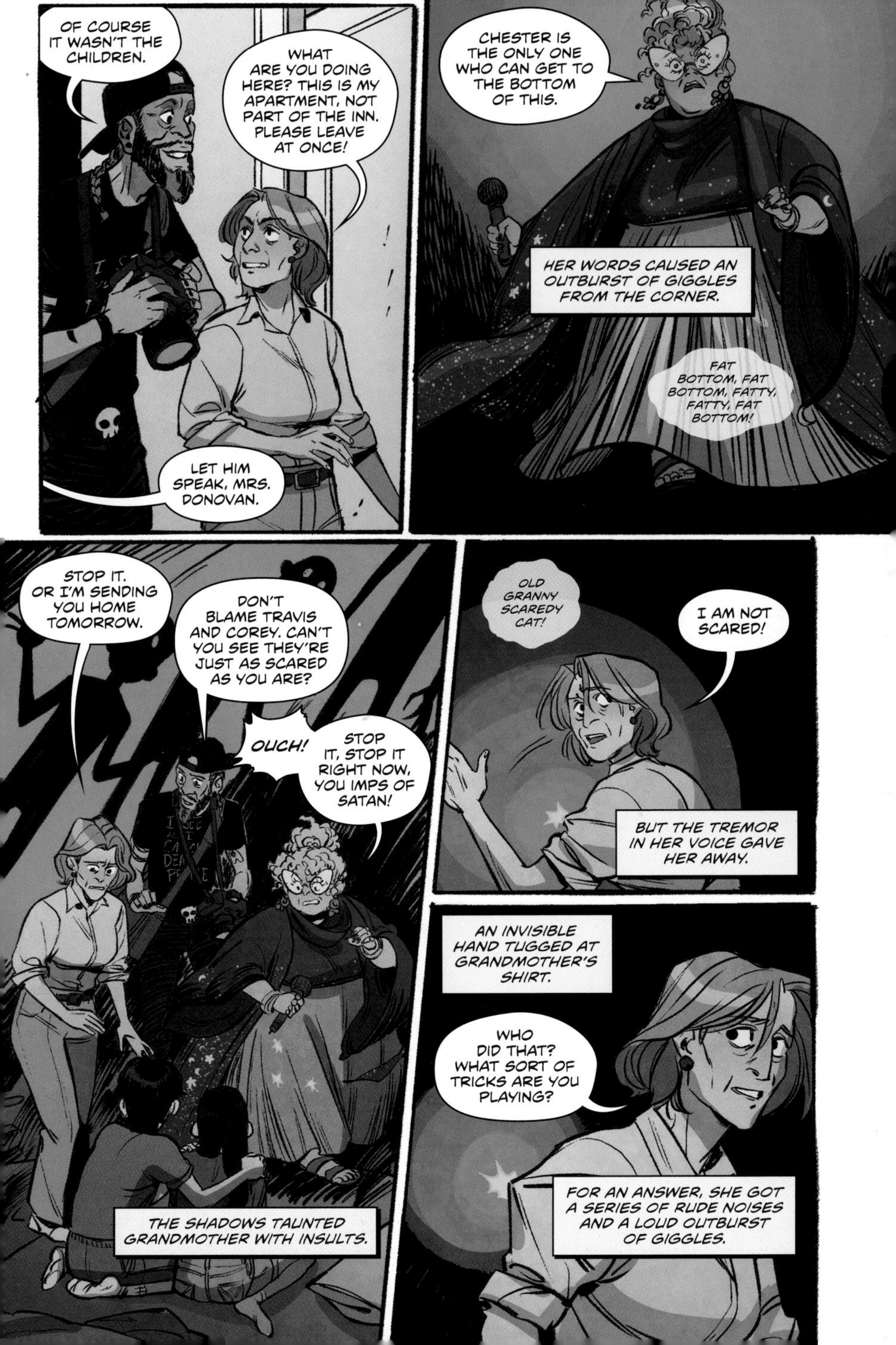
OF COURSE IT WASN'T THE CHILDREN.
WHAT ARE YOU DOING HERE? THIS IS MY APARTMENT, NOT PART OF THE INN. PLEASE LEAVE AT ONCE!
LET HIM SPEAK, MRS. DONOVAN.
CHESTER IS THE ONLY ONE WHO CAN GET TO THE BOTTOM OF THIS.
HER WORDS CAUSED AN OUTBURST OF GIGGLES FROM THE CORNER.
FAT BOTTOM, FAT BOTTOM, FATTY, FATTY, FAT BOTTOM!
STOP IT. OR I'M SENDING YOU HOME TOMORROW.
DON'T BLAME TRAVIS AND COREY. CAN'T YOU SEE THEY'RE JUST AS SCARED AS YOU ARE?
OUCH!
STOP IT, STOP IT RIGHT NOW, YOU IMPS OF SATAN!
THE SHADOWS TAUNTED GRANDMOTHER WITH INSULTS.
OLD GRANNY SCAREDY CAT!
I AM NOT SCARED!
BUT THE TREMOR IN HER VOICE GAVE HER AWAY.
AN INVISIBLE HAND TUGGED AT GRANDMOTHER'S SHIRT.
WHO DID THAT? WHAT SORT OF TRICKS ARE YOU PLAYING?
FOR AN ANSWER, SHE GOT A SERIES OF RUDE NOISES AND A LOUD OUTBURST OF GIGGLES.

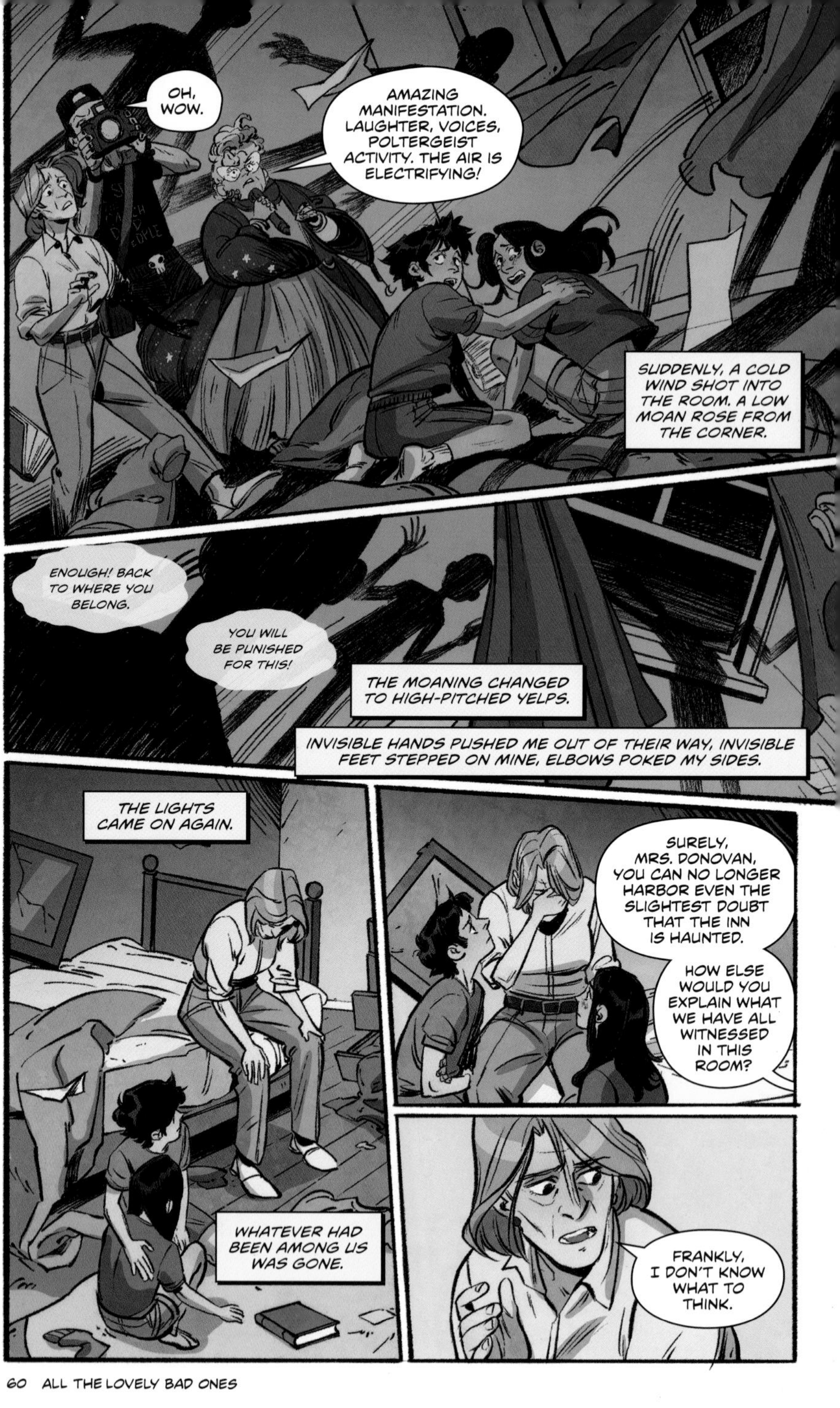
OH, WOW.
AMAZING MANIFESTATION. LAUGHTER, VOICES, POLTERGEIST ACTIVITY. THE AIR IS ELECTRIFYING!
SUDDENLY, A COLD WIND SHOT INTO THE ROOM. A LOW MOAN ROSE FROM THE CORNER.
ENOUGH! BACK TO WHERE YOU BELONG.
YOU WILL BE PUNISHED FOR THIS!
THE MOANING CHANGED TO HIGH-PITCHED YELPS.
INVISIBLE HANDS PUSHED ME OUT OF THEIR WAY, INVISIBLE FEET STEPPED ON MINE, ELBOWS POKED MY SIDES.
THE LIGHTS CAME ON AGAIN.
WHATEVER HAD BEEN AMONG US WAS GONE.
SURELY, MRS. DONOVAN, YOU CAN NO LONGER HARBOR EVEN THE SLIGHTEST DOUBT THAT THE INN IS HAUNTED.
HOW ELSE WOULD YOU EXPLAIN WHAT WE HAVE ALL WITNESSED IN THIS ROOM?
FRANKLY, I DON'T KNOW WHAT TO THINK.

BUT IF YOU AND MR. COAKLEY ARE RESPONSIBLE FOR THIS, I WILL BRING A LAWSUIT.

I ASSURE YOU NEITHER CHESTER NOR I--

BUT--

PLEASE GO BACK TO YOUR ROOMS. BY CHECKOUT TIME TOMORROW, I EXPECT YOU BOTH GONE.

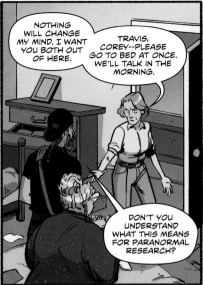

NOTHING WILL CHANGE MY MIND. I WANT YOU BOTH OUT OF HERE.

TRAVIS, COREY--PLEASE GO TO BED AT ONCE. WE'LL TALK IN THE MORNING.

DON'T YOU UNDERSTAND WHAT THIS MEANS FOR PARANORMAL RESEARCH?

PLEASE DON'T LEAVE ME BY MYSELF, TRAVIS.

I'M SCARED TO DEATH THEY'LL COME BACK.

SHE TOSSED ME A BLANKET AND AN EXTRA PILLOW, AND I TRIED TO MAKE MYSELF COMFORTABLE ON THE FLOOR. I DIDN'T WANT TO BE ALONE ANY MORE THAN MY SISTER DID.

I KIND OF WISH GRANDMOTHER **WOULD** SEND US HOME. I DON'T LIKE IT HERE ANYMORE.

EVEN CAMP DOESN'T SEEM SO BAD NOW.

SWIMMING IN A FREEZING LAKE AT SEVEN A.M., EATING MYSTERY MEAT AND MUSHY LIMA BEANS, HIKING TEN MILES UPHILL.

SINGING THOSE DUMB CAMP SONGS, STRIKING OUT IN SOFTBALL...

I COULDN'T RELAX. EVERY SOUND FRIGHTENED ME-- A SIGH OF WIND, THE TAP OF A BRANCH AGAINST THE WINDOW, A CREAK IN THE HALL OUTSIDE THE DOOR.

I EXPECTED TO HEAR GIGGLES AND FEEL THE PINCH OF INVISIBLE FINGERS.

WORSE YET, WHAT IF THE THING FROM THE GROVE CAME HOWLING THROUGH THE WINDOW?

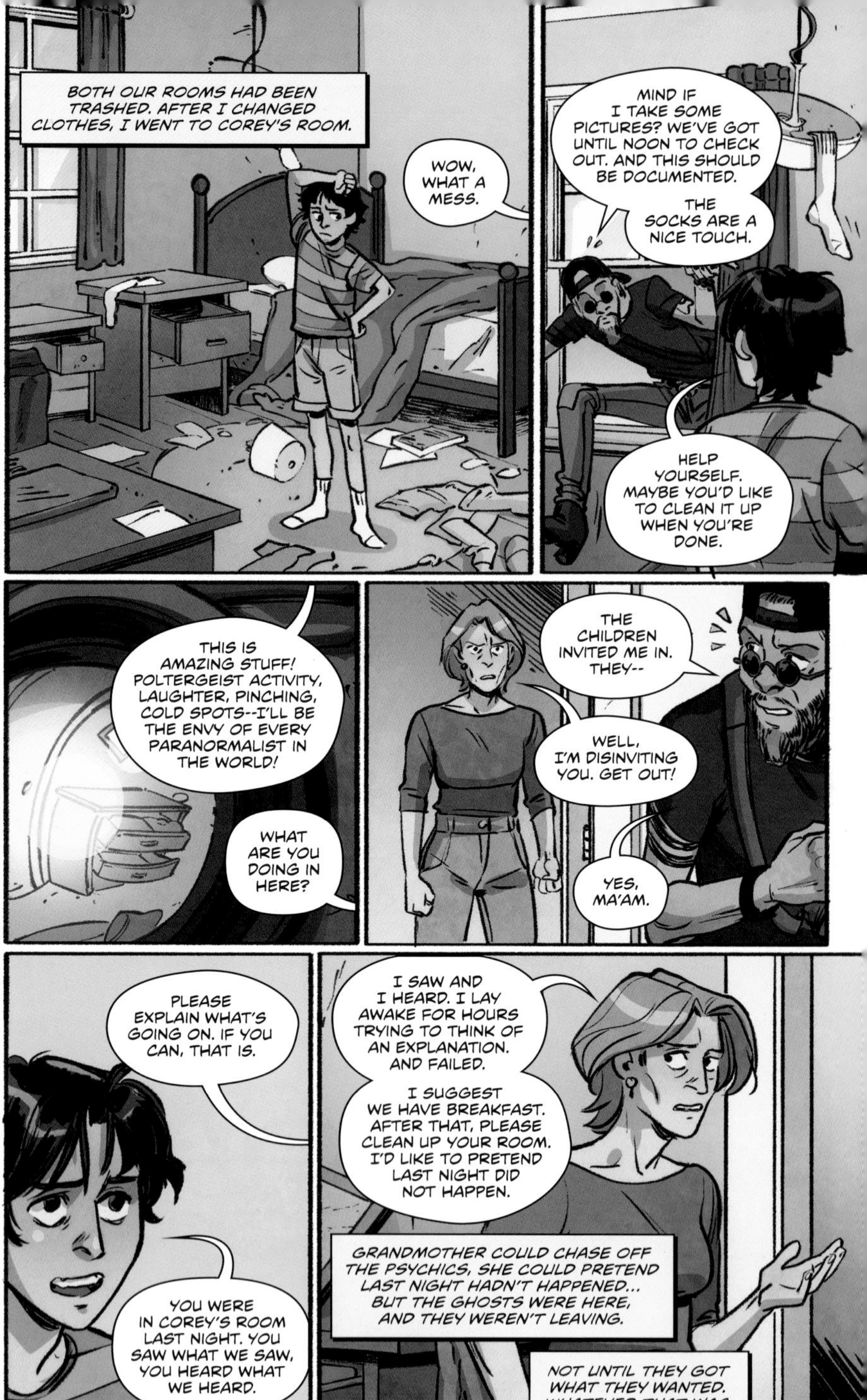
BOTH OUR ROOMS HAD BEEN TRASHED. AFTER I CHANGED CLOTHES, I WENT TO COREY'S ROOM.
WOW, WHAT A MESS.
MIND IF I TAKE SOME PICTURES? WE'VE GOT UNTIL NOON TO CHECK OUT. AND THIS SHOULD BE DOCUMENTED.
THE SOCKS ARE A NICE TOUCH.
HELP YOURSELF. MAYBE YOU'D LIKE TO CLEAN IT UP WHEN YOU'RE DONE.
THIS IS AMAZING STUFF! POLTERGEIST ACTIVITY, LAUGHTER, PINCHING, COLD SPOTS--I'LL BE THE ENVY OF EVERY PARANORMALIST IN THE WORLD!
WHAT ARE YOU DOING IN HERE?
THE CHILDREN INVITED ME IN. THEY--
WELL, I'M DISINVITING YOU. GET OUT!
YES, MA'AM.
PLEASE EXPLAIN WHAT'S GOING ON. IF YOU CAN, THAT IS.
YOU WERE IN COREY'S ROOM LAST NIGHT. YOU SAW WHAT WE SAW, YOU HEARD WHAT WE HEARD.
I SAW AND I HEARD. I LAY AWAKE FOR HOURS TRYING TO THINK OF AN EXPLANATION. AND FAILED.
I SUGGEST WE HAVE BREAKFAST. AFTER THAT, PLEASE CLEAN UP YOUR ROOM. I'D LIKE TO PRETEND LAST NIGHT DID NOT HAPPEN.
GRANDMOTHER COULD CHASE OFF THE PSYCHICS, SHE COULD PRETEND LAST NIGHT HADN'T HAPPENED... BUT THE GHOSTS WERE HERE, AND THEY WEREN'T LEAVING.
NOT UNTIL THEY GOT WHAT THEY WANTED. WHATEVER THAT WAS.

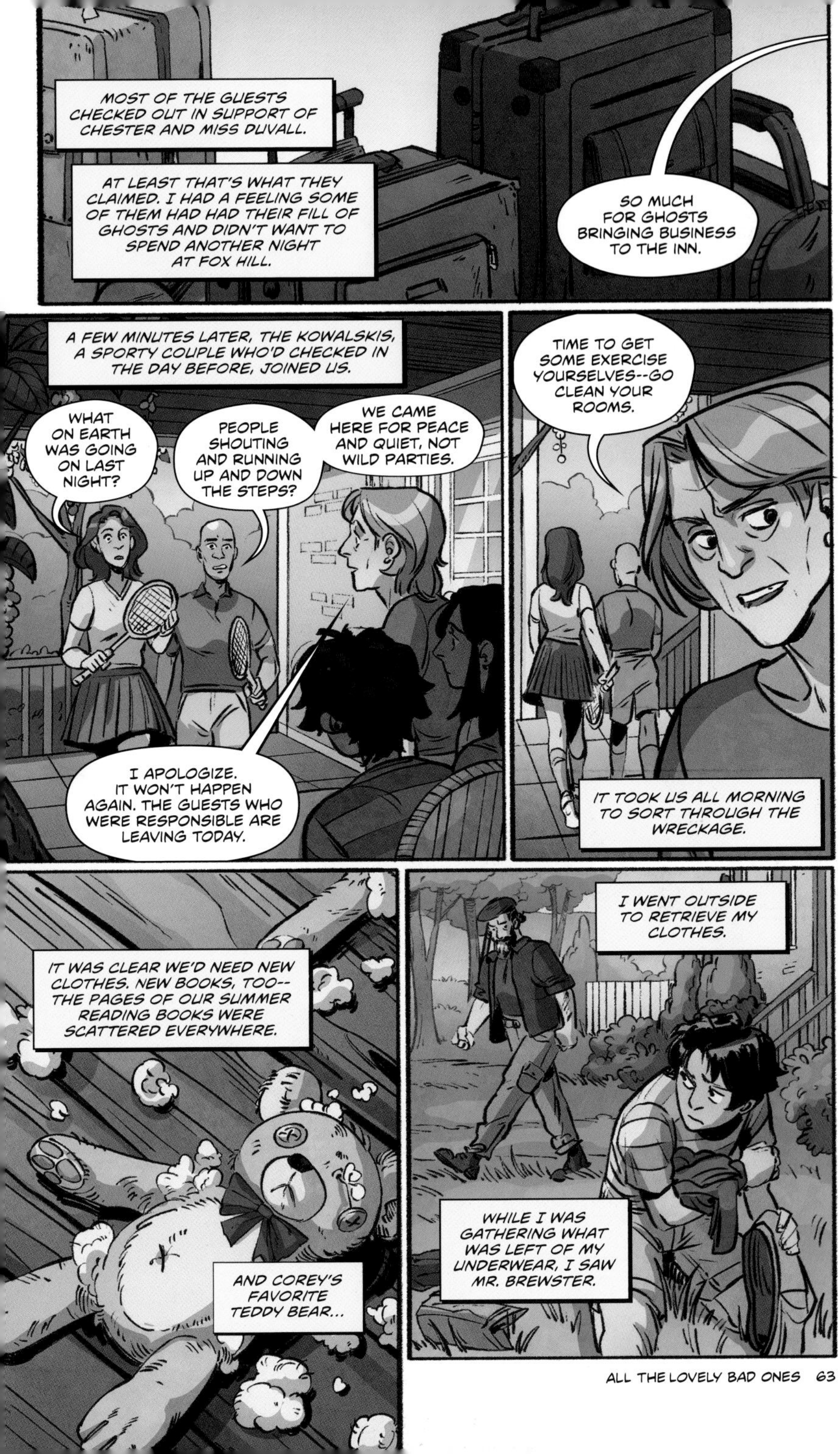
MOST OF THE GUESTS CHECKED OUT IN SUPPORT OF CHESTER AND MISS DUVALL.
AT LEAST THAT'S WHAT THEY CLAIMED. I HAD A FEELING SOME OF THEM HAD HAD THEIR FILL OF GHOSTS AND DIDN'T WANT TO SPEND ANOTHER NIGHT AT FOX HILL.
SO MUCH FOR GHOSTS BRINGING BUSINESS TO THE INN.
A FEW MINUTES LATER, THE KOWALSKIS, A SPORTY COUPLE WHO'D CHECKED IN THE DAY BEFORE, JOINED US.
WHAT ON EARTH WAS GOING ON LAST NIGHT?
PEOPLE SHOUTING AND RUNNING UP AND DOWN THE STEPS?
WE CAME HERE FOR PEACE AND QUIET, NOT WILD PARTIES.
I APOLOGIZE. IT WON'T HAPPEN AGAIN. THE GUESTS WHO WERE RESPONSIBLE ARE LEAVING TODAY.
TIME TO GET SOME EXERCISE YOURSELVES--GO CLEAN YOUR ROOMS.
IT TOOK US ALL MORNING TO SORT THROUGH THE WRECKAGE.
IT WAS CLEAR WE'D NEED NEW CLOTHES. NEW BOOKS, TOO--THE PAGES OF OUR SUMMER READING BOOKS WERE SCATTERED EVERYWHERE.
AND COREY'S FAVORITE TEDDY BEAR...
I WENT OUTSIDE TO RETRIEVE MY CLOTHES.
WHILE I WAS GATHERING WHAT WAS LEFT OF MY UNDERWEAR, I SAW MR. BREWSTER.

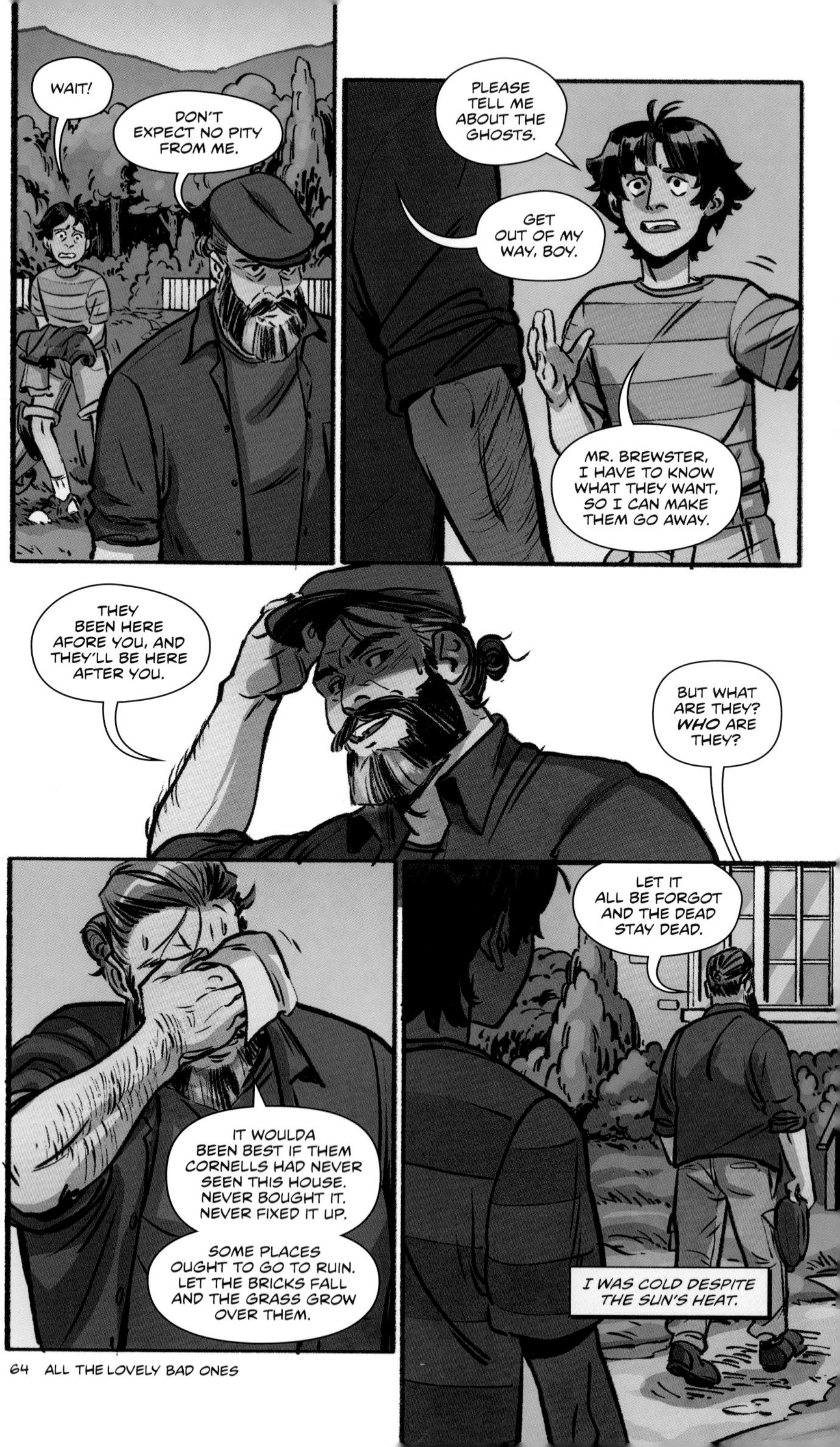
WAIT!
DON'T EXPECT NO PITY FROM ME.
PLEASE TELL ME ABOUT THE GHOSTS.
GET OUT OF MY WAY, BOY.
MR. BREWSTER, I HAVE TO KNOW WHAT THEY WANT, SO I CAN MAKE THEM GO AWAY.
THEY BEEN HERE AFORE YOU, AND THEY'LL BE HERE AFTER YOU.
BUT WHAT ARE THEY? *WHO* ARE THEY?
IT WOULDA BEEN BEST IF THEM CORNELLS HAD NEVER SEEN THIS HOUSE. NEVER BOUGHT IT. NEVER FIXED IT UP.
SOME PLACES OUGHT TO GO TO RUIN. LET THE BRICKS FALL AND THE GRASS GROW OVER THEM.
LET IT ALL BE FORGOT AND THE DEAD STAY DEAD.
*I WAS COLD DESPITE THE SUN'S HEAT.*

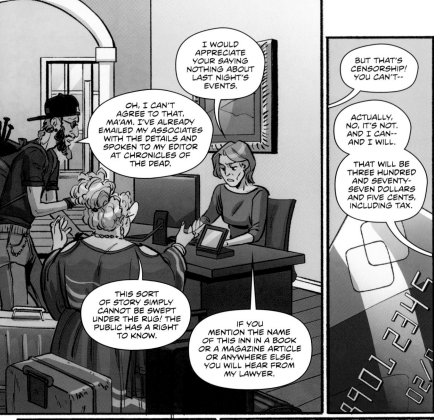

I WOULD APPRECIATE YOUR SAYING NOTHING ABOUT LAST NIGHT'S EVENTS.

OH, I CAN'T AGREE TO THAT, MA'AM. I'VE ALREADY EMAILED MY ASSOCIATES WITH THE DETAILS AND SPOKEN TO MY EDITOR AT CHRONICLES OF THE DEAD.

BUT THAT'S CENSORSHIP! YOU CAN'T--

ACTUALLY, NO, IT'S NOT. AND I CAN-- AND I WILL.

THAT WILL BE THREE HUNDRED AND SEVENTY-SEVEN DOLLARS AND FIVE CENTS, INCLUDING TAX.

THIS SORT OF STORY SIMPLY CANNOT BE SWEPT UNDER THE RUG! THE PUBLIC HAS A RIGHT TO KNOW.

IF YOU MENTION THE NAME OF THIS INN IN A BOOK OR A MAGAZINE ARTICLE OR ANYWHERE ELSE, YOU WILL HEAR FROM MY LAWYER.

BUT THINK OF THE FREE PUBLICITY.

I AM.

I FEEL BETTER ALREADY.

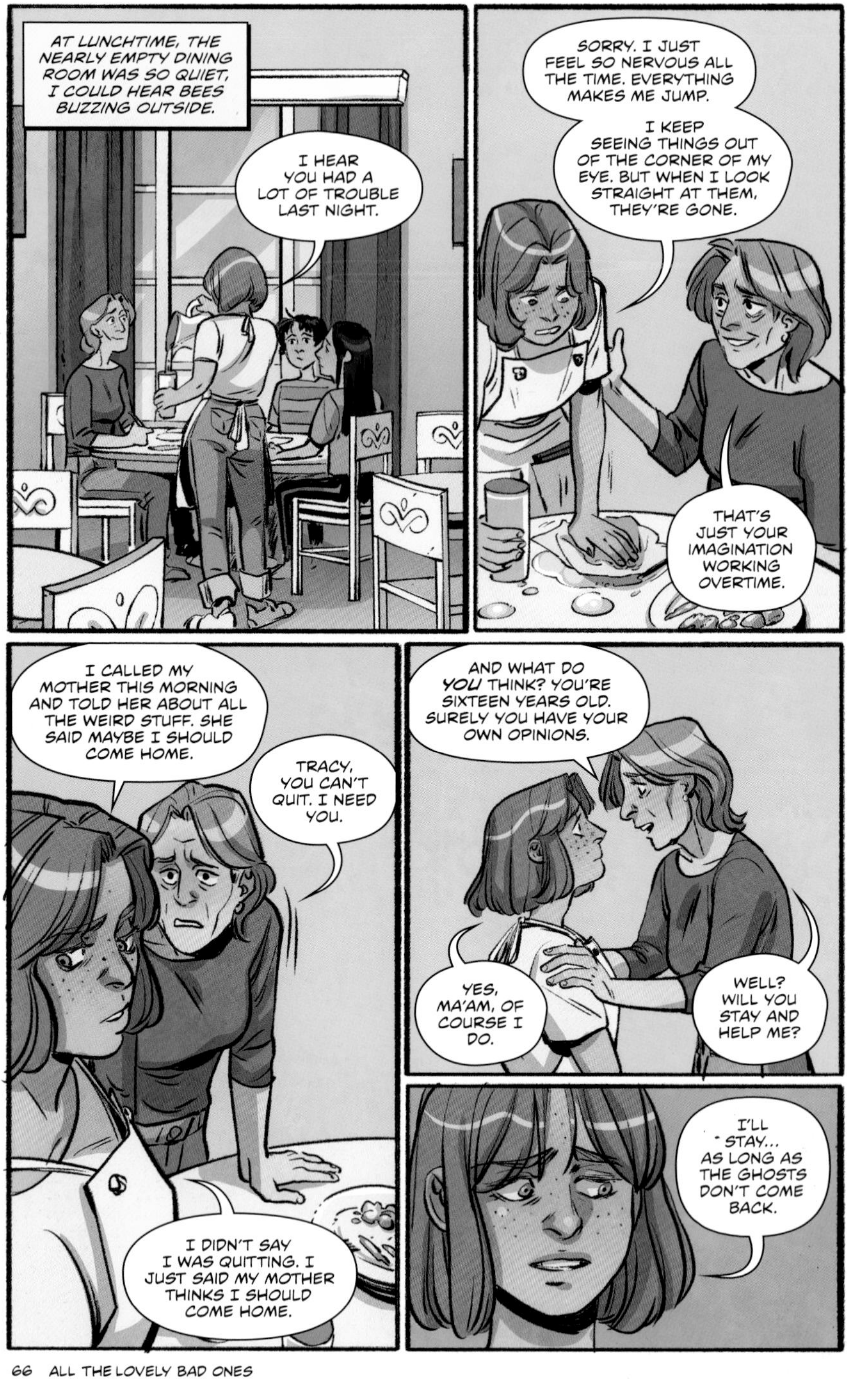
AT LUNCHTIME, THE NEARLY EMPTY DINING ROOM WAS SO QUIET, I COULD HEAR BEES BUZZING OUTSIDE.
I HEAR YOU HAD A LOT OF TROUBLE LAST NIGHT.
SORRY. I JUST FEEL SO NERVOUS ALL THE TIME. EVERYTHING MAKES ME JUMP.
I KEEP SEEING THINGS OUT OF THE CORNER OF MY EYE. BUT WHEN I LOOK STRAIGHT AT THEM, THEY'RE GONE.
THAT'S JUST YOUR IMAGINATION WORKING OVERTIME.
I CALLED MY MOTHER THIS MORNING AND TOLD HER ABOUT ALL THE WEIRD STUFF. SHE SAID MAYBE I SHOULD COME HOME.
TRACY, YOU CAN'T QUIT. I NEED YOU.
I DIDN'T SAY I WAS QUITTING. I JUST SAID MY MOTHER THINKS I SHOULD COME HOME.
AND WHAT DO *YOU* THINK? YOU'RE SIXTEEN YEARS OLD. SURELY YOU HAVE YOUR OWN OPINIONS.
YES, MA'AM, OF COURSE I DO.
WELL? WILL YOU STAY AND HELP ME?
I'LL STAY... AS LONG AS THE GHOSTS DON'T COME BACK.

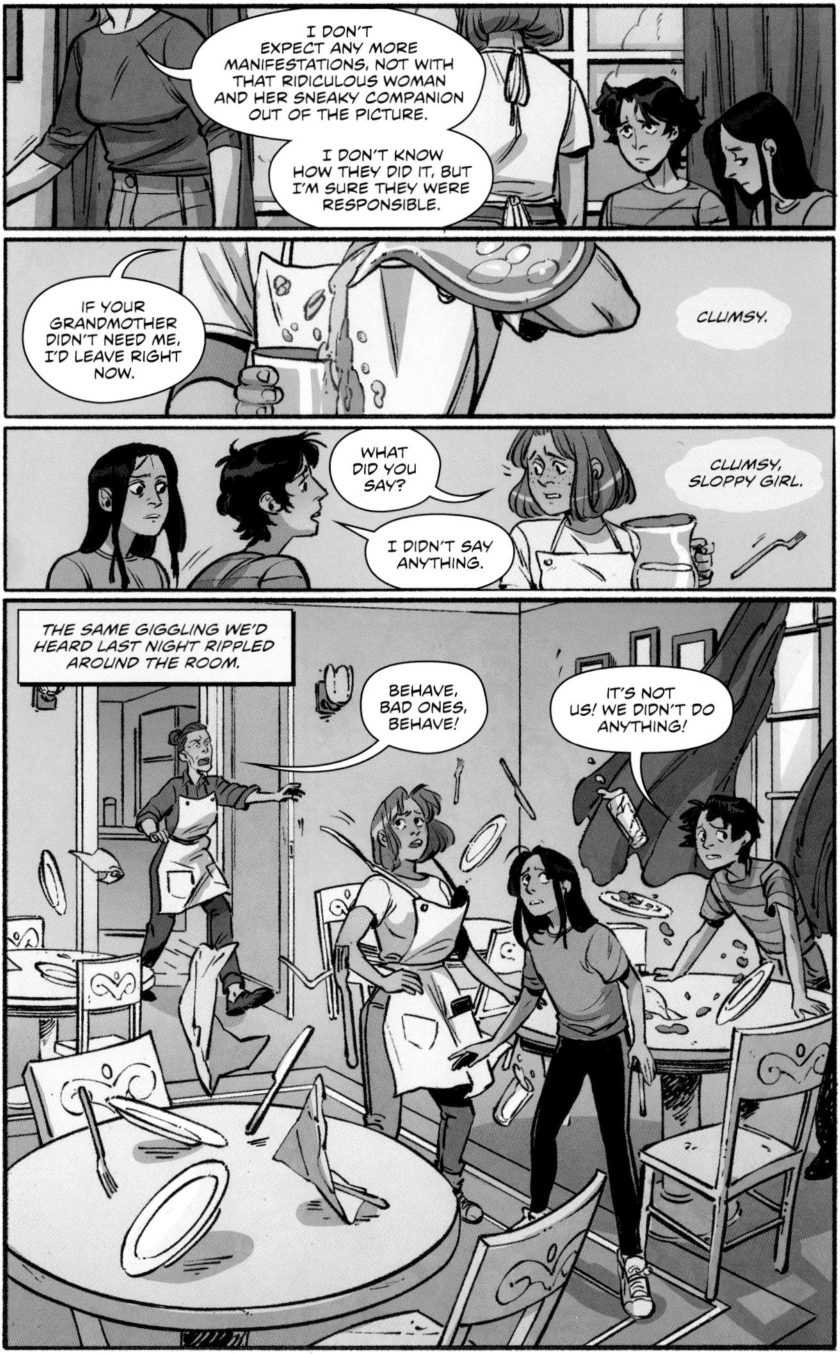
I DON'T EXPECT ANY MORE MANIFESTATIONS, NOT WITH THAT RIDICULOUS WOMAN AND HER SNEAKY COMPANION OUT OF THE PICTURE.
I DON'T KNOW HOW THEY DID IT, BUT I'M SURE THEY WERE RESPONSIBLE.
IF YOUR GRANDMOTHER DIDN'T NEED ME, I'D LEAVE RIGHT NOW.
CLUMSY.
WHAT DID YOU SAY?
I DIDN'T SAY ANYTHING.
CLUMSY, SLOPPY GIRL.
THE SAME GIGGLING WE'D HEARD LAST NIGHT RIPPLED AROUND THE ROOM.
BEHAVE, BAD ONES, BEHAVE!
IT'S NOT US! WE DIDN'T DO ANYTHING!

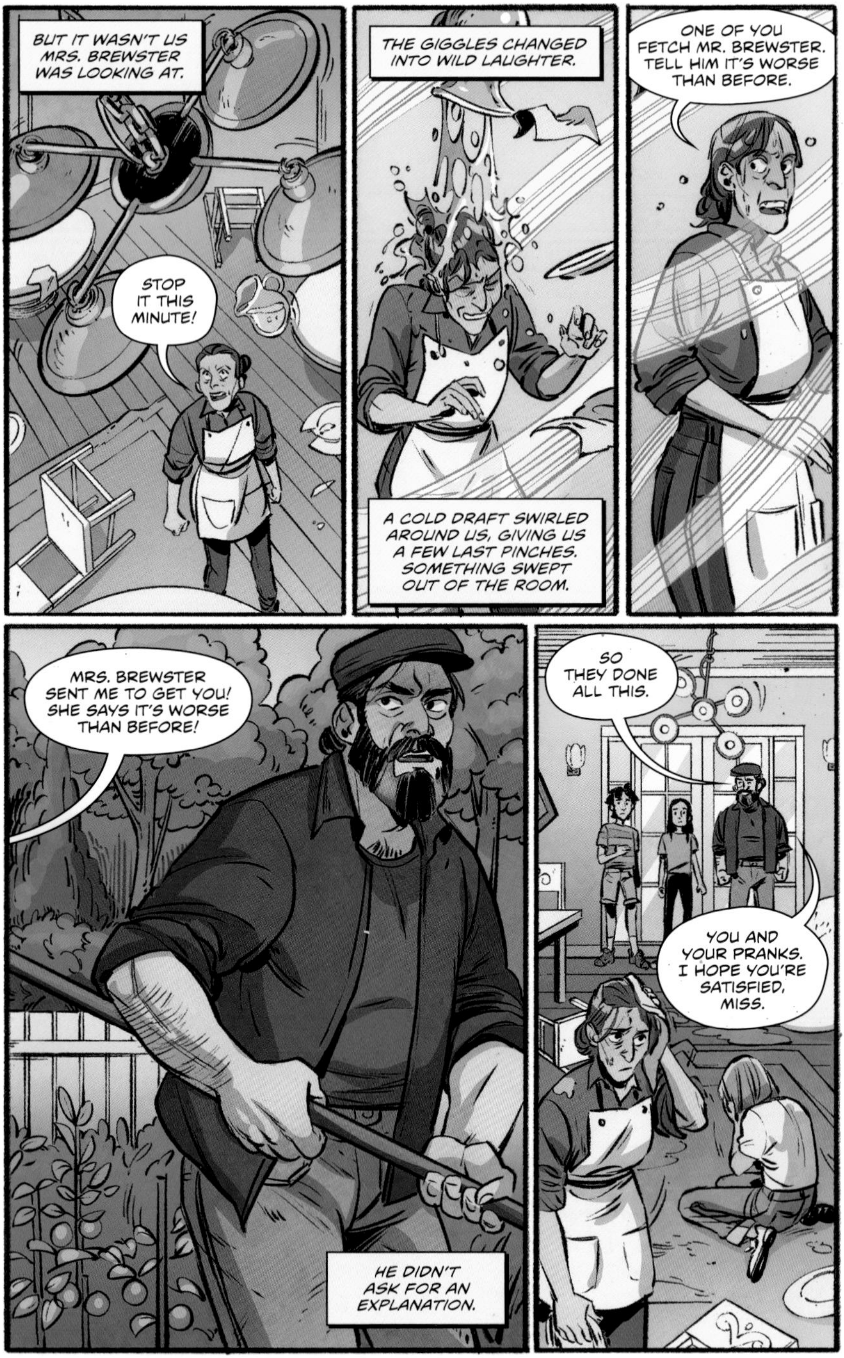
BUT IT WASN'T US MRS. BREWSTER WAS LOOKING AT.
STOP IT THIS MINUTE!
THE GIGGLES CHANGED INTO WILD LAUGHTER.
A COLD DRAFT SWIRLED AROUND US, GIVING US A FEW LAST PINCHES. SOMETHING SWEPT OUT OF THE ROOM.
ONE OF YOU FETCH MR. BREWSTER. TELL HIM IT'S WORSE THAN BEFORE.
MRS. BREWSTER SENT ME TO GET YOU! SHE SAYS IT'S WORSE THAN BEFORE!
HE DIDN'T ASK FOR AN EXPLANATION.
SO THEY DONE ALL THIS.
YOU AND YOUR PRANKS. I HOPE YOU'RE SATISFIED, MISS.

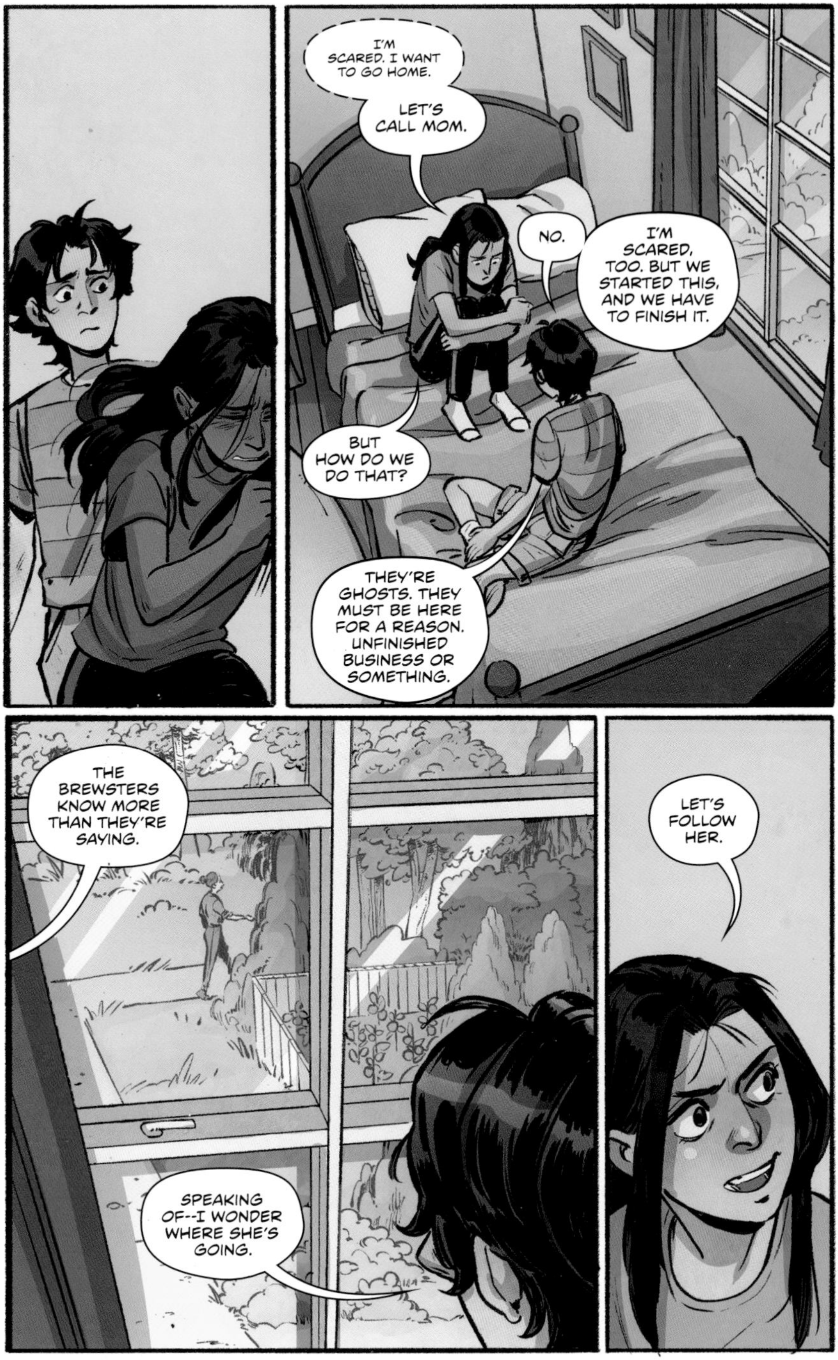
I'M SCARED. I WANT TO GO HOME.
LET'S CALL MOM.
NO.
I'M SCARED, TOO. BUT WE STARTED THIS, AND WE HAVE TO FINISH IT.
BUT HOW DO WE DO THAT?
THEY'RE GHOSTS. THEY MUST BE HERE FOR A REASON. UNFINISHED BUSINESS OR SOMETHING.
THE BREWSTERS KNOW MORE THAN THEY'RE SAYING.
SPEAKING OF--I WONDER WHERE SHE'S GOING.
LET'S FOLLOW HER.

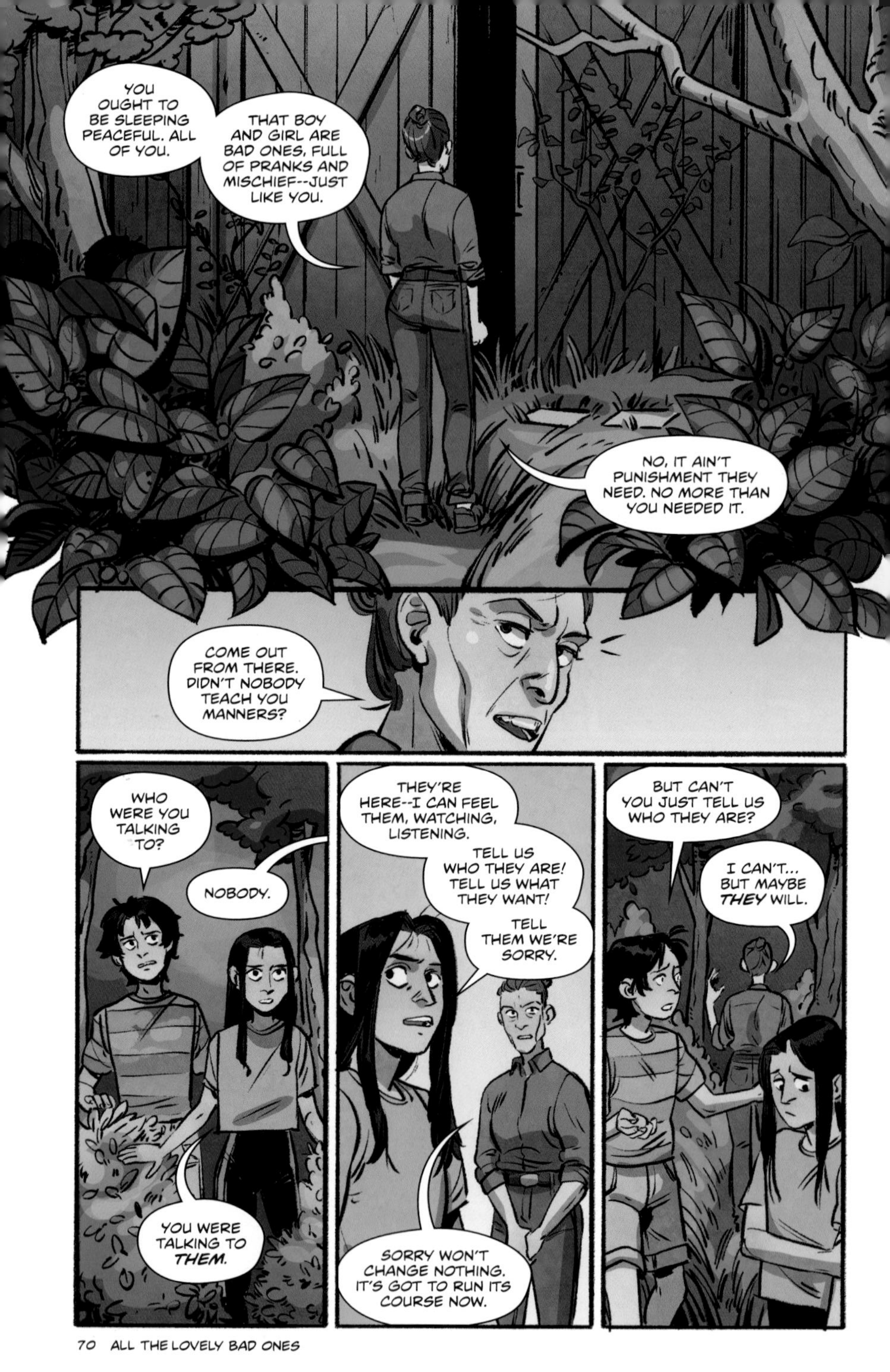
YOU OUGHT TO BE SLEEPING PEACEFUL. ALL OF YOU.
THAT BOY AND GIRL ARE BAD ONES, FULL OF PRANKS AND MISCHIEF--JUST LIKE YOU.
NO, IT AIN'T PUNISHMENT THEY NEED. NO MORE THAN YOU NEEDED IT.
COME OUT FROM THERE. DIDN'T NOBODY TEACH YOU MANNERS?
WHO WERE YOU TALKING TO?
NOBODY.
YOU WERE TALKING TO *THEM*.
THEY'RE HERE--I CAN FEEL THEM, WATCHING, LISTENING.
TELL US WHO THEY ARE! TELL US WHAT THEY WANT!
TELL THEM WE'RE SORRY.
SORRY WON'T CHANGE NOTHING. IT'S GOT TO RUN ITS COURSE NOW.
BUT CAN'T YOU JUST TELL US WHO THEY ARE?
I CAN'T... BUT MAYBE *THEY* WILL.

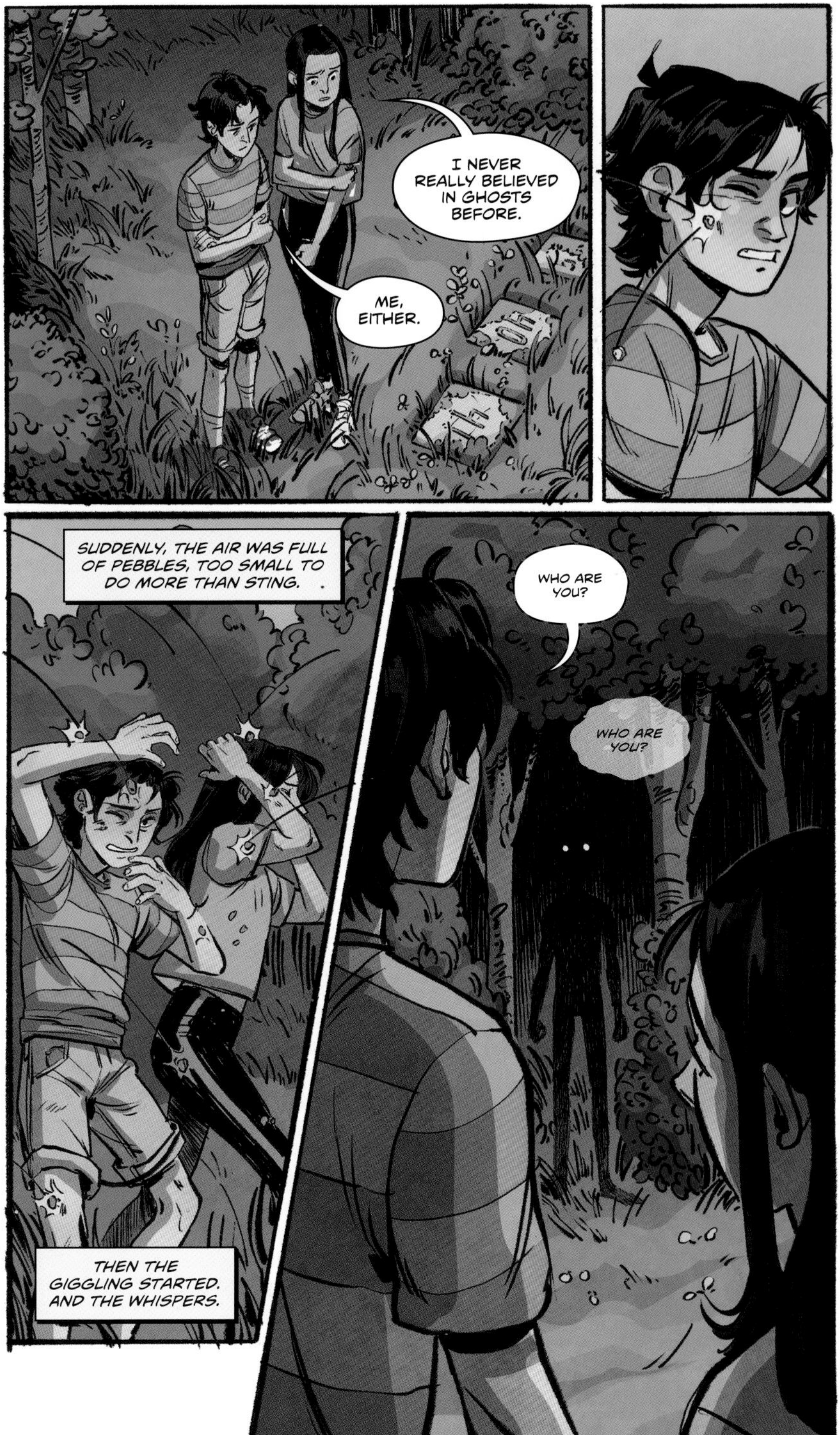
I NEVER REALLY BELIEVED IN GHOSTS BEFORE.
ME, EITHER.
SUDDENLY, THE AIR WAS FULL OF PEBBLES, TOO SMALL TO DO MORE THAN STING.
THEN THE GIGGLING STARTED. AND THE WHISPERS.
WHO ARE YOU?
WHO ARE YOU?

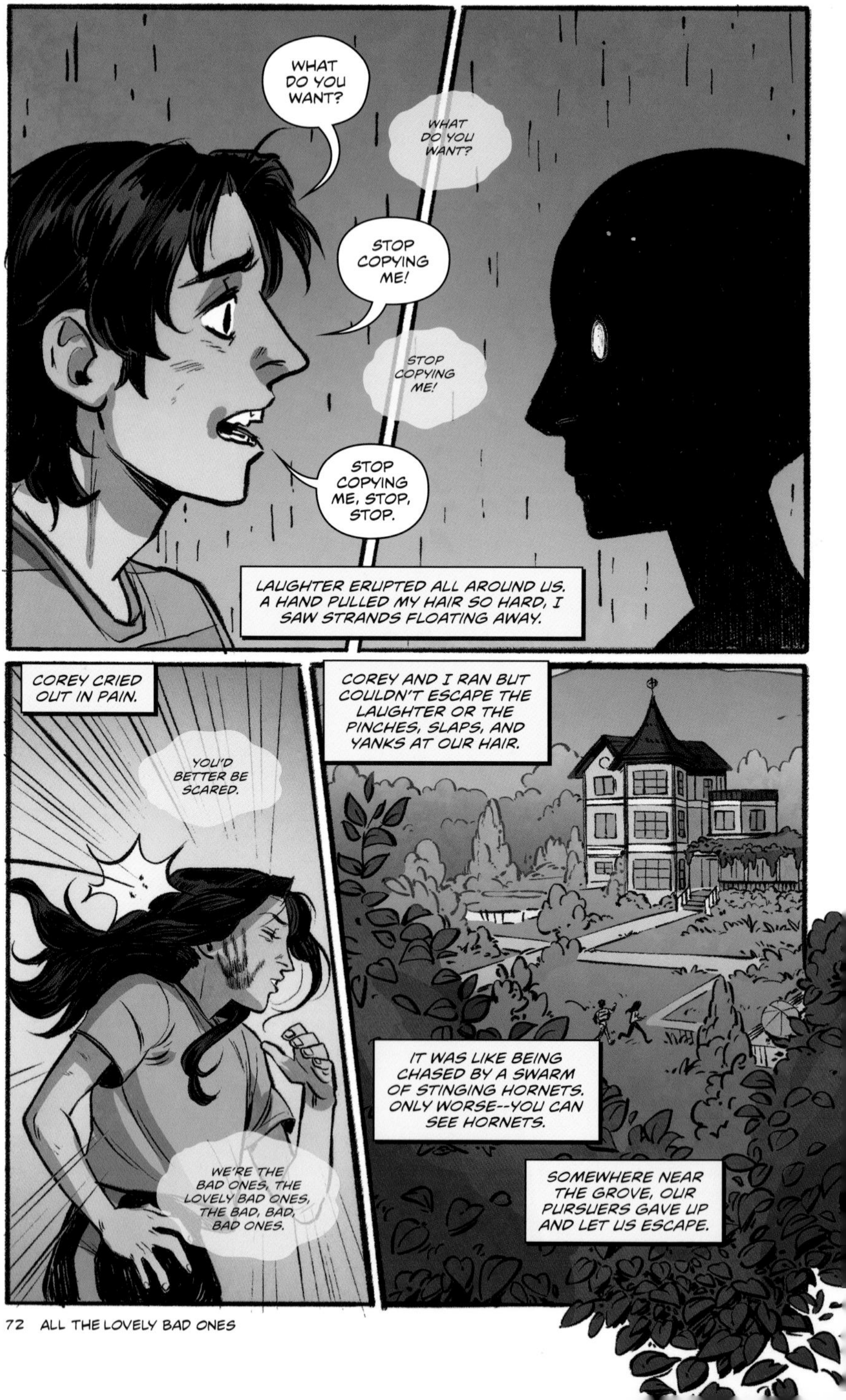
WHAT DO YOU WANT?
WHAT DO YOU WANT?
STOP COPYING ME!
STOP COPYING ME!
STOP COPYING ME, STOP, STOP.
LAUGHTER ERUPTED ALL AROUND US. A HAND PULLED MY HAIR SO HARD, I SAW STRANDS FLOATING AWAY.
COREY CRIED OUT IN PAIN.
YOU'D BETTER BE SCARED.
WE'RE THE BAD ONES, THE LOVELY BAD ONES, THE BAD, BAD, BAD ONES.
COREY AND I RAN BUT COULDN'T ESCAPE THE LAUGHTER OR THE PINCHES, SLAPS, AND YANKS AT OUR HAIR.
IT WAS LIKE BEING CHASED BY A SWARM OF STINGING HORNETS. ONLY WORSE--YOU CAN SEE HORNETS.
SOMEWHERE NEAR THE GROVE, OUR PURSUERS GAVE UP AND LET US ESCAPE.

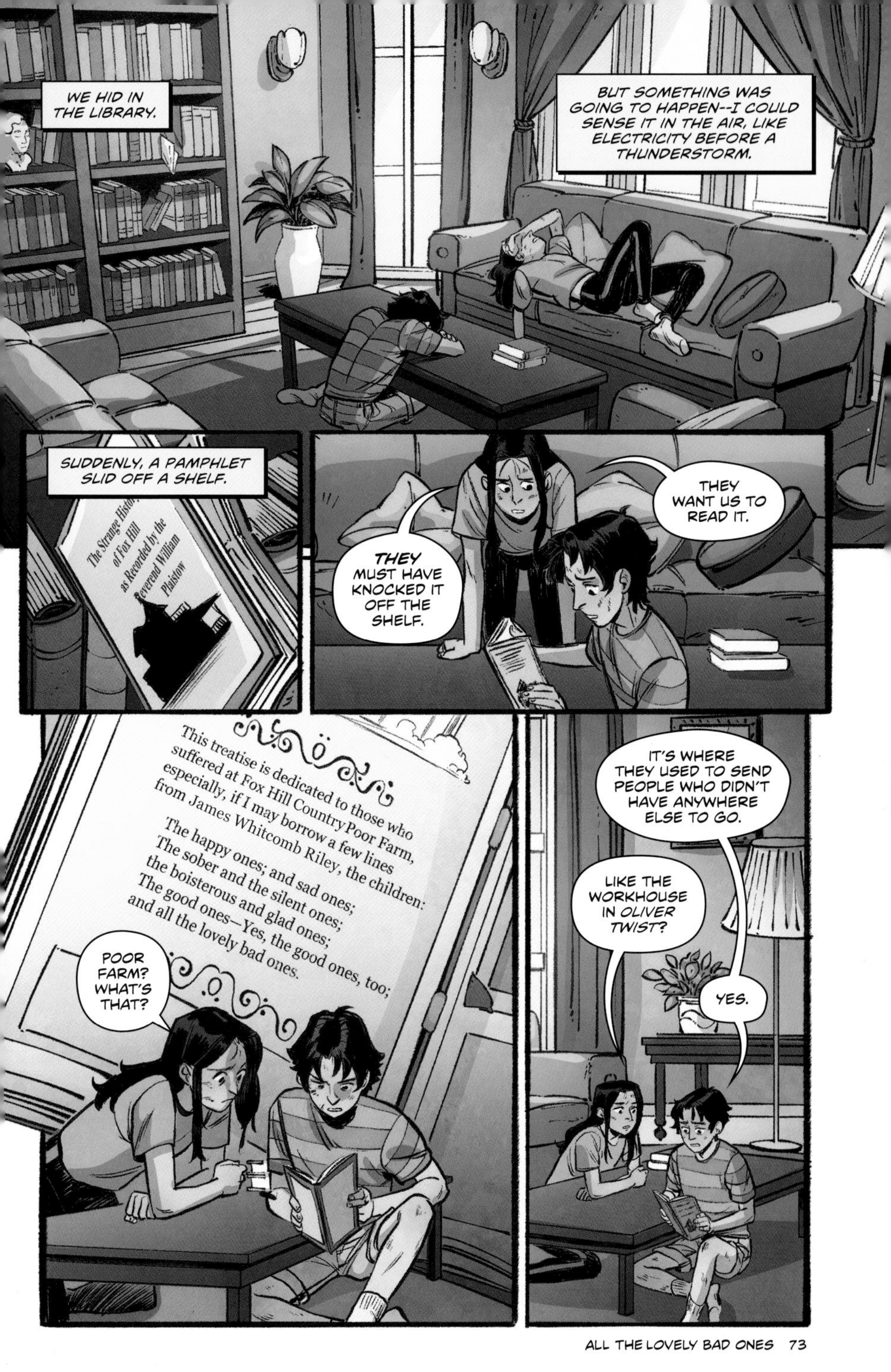
WE HID IN THE LIBRARY.
BUT SOMETHING WAS GOING TO HAPPEN--I COULD SENSE IT IN THE AIR, LIKE ELECTRICITY BEFORE A THUNDERSTORM.
SUDDENLY, A PAMPHLET SLID OFF A SHELF.
The Strange History of Fox Hill as Recorded by the Reverend William Plaistow
*THEY* MUST HAVE KNOCKED IT OFF THE SHELF.
THEY WANT US TO READ IT.
This treatise is dedicated to those who suffered at Fox Hill Country Poor Farm, especially, if I may borrow a few lines from James Whitcomb Riley, the children:
The happy ones; and sad ones;
The sober and the silent ones;
the boisterous and glad ones;
The good ones—Yes, the good ones, too;
and all the lovely bad ones.
POOR FARM? WHAT'S THAT?
IT'S WHERE THEY USED TO SEND PEOPLE WHO DIDN'T HAVE ANYWHERE ELSE TO GO.
LIKE THE WORKHOUSE IN *OLIVER TWIST*?
YES.

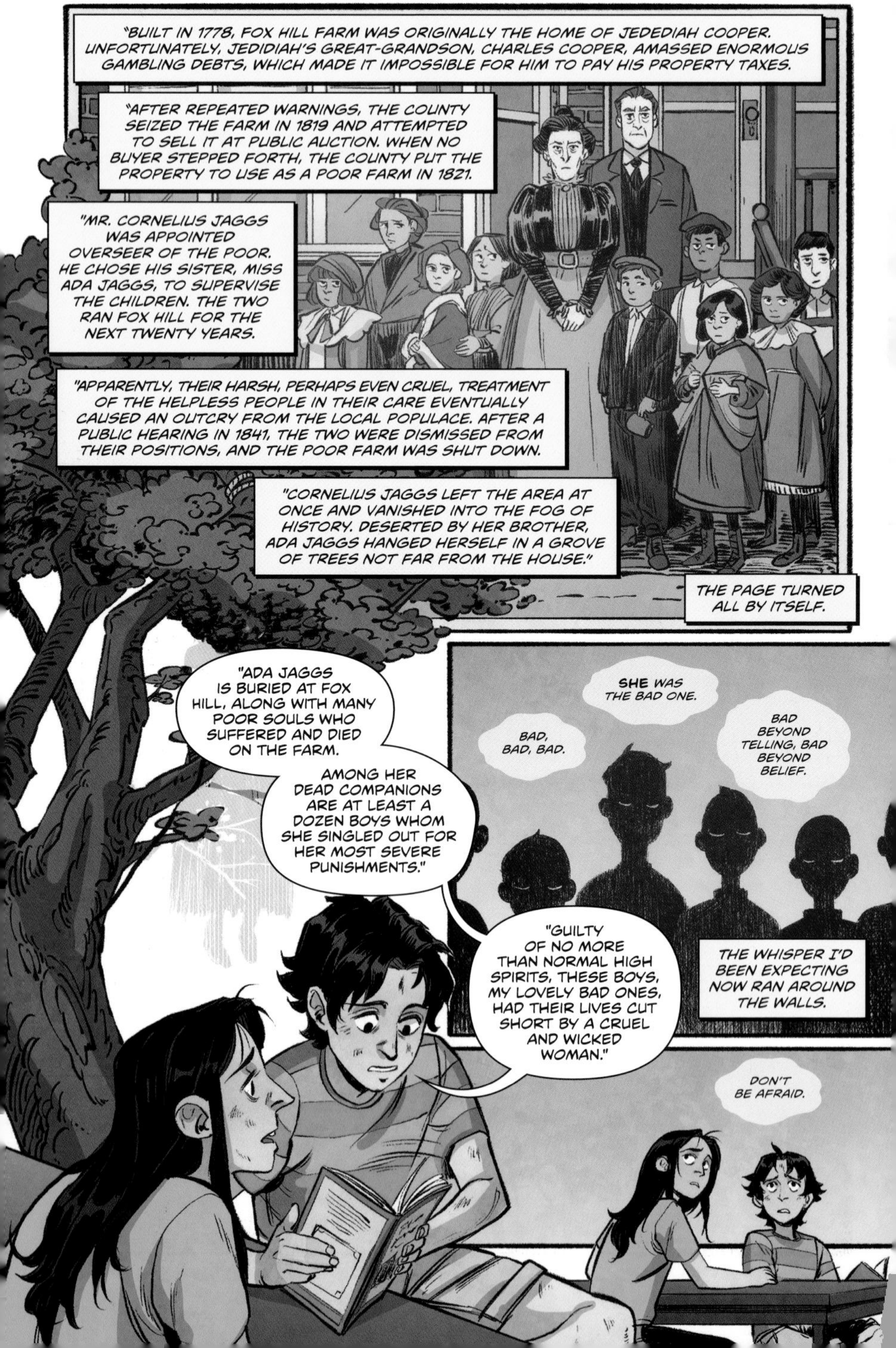
"BUILT IN 1778, FOX HILL FARM WAS ORIGINALLY THE HOME OF JEDEDIAH COOPER. UNFORTUNATELY, JEDIDIAH'S GREAT-GRANDSON, CHARLES COOPER, AMASSED ENORMOUS GAMBLING DEBTS, WHICH MADE IT IMPOSSIBLE FOR HIM TO PAY HIS PROPERTY TAXES.
"AFTER REPEATED WARNINGS, THE COUNTY SEIZED THE FARM IN 1819 AND ATTEMPTED TO SELL IT AT PUBLIC AUCTION. WHEN NO BUYER STEPPED FORTH, THE COUNTY PUT THE PROPERTY TO USE AS A POOR FARM IN 1821.
"MR. CORNELIUS JAGGS WAS APPOINTED OVERSEER OF THE POOR. HE CHOSE HIS SISTER, MISS ADA JAGGS, TO SUPERVISE THE CHILDREN. THE TWO RAN FOX HILL FOR THE NEXT TWENTY YEARS.
"APPARENTLY, THEIR HARSH, PERHAPS EVEN CRUEL, TREATMENT OF THE HELPLESS PEOPLE IN THEIR CARE EVENTUALLY CAUSED AN OUTCRY FROM THE LOCAL POPULACE. AFTER A PUBLIC HEARING IN 1841, THE TWO WERE DISMISSED FROM THEIR POSITIONS, AND THE POOR FARM WAS SHUT DOWN.
"CORNELIUS JAGGS LEFT THE AREA AT ONCE AND VANISHED INTO THE FOG OF HISTORY. DESERTED BY HER BROTHER, ADA JAGGS HANGED HERSELF IN A GROVE OF TREES NOT FAR FROM THE HOUSE."
THE PAGE TURNED ALL BY ITSELF.
"ADA JAGGS IS BURIED AT FOX HILL, ALONG WITH MANY POOR SOULS WHO SUFFERED AND DIED ON THE FARM.
AMONG HER DEAD COMPANIONS ARE AT LEAST A DOZEN BOYS WHOM SHE SINGLED OUT FOR HER MOST SEVERE PUNISHMENTS."
"GUILTY OF NO MORE THAN NORMAL HIGH SPIRITS, THESE BOYS, MY LOVELY BAD ONES, HAD THEIR LIVES CUT SHORT BY A CRUEL AND WICKED WOMAN."
SHE WAS THE BAD ONE.
BAD, BAD, BAD.
BAD BEYOND TELLING, BAD BEYOND BELIEF.
THE WHISPER I'D BEEN EXPECTING NOW RAN AROUND THE WALLS.
DON'T BE AFRAID.

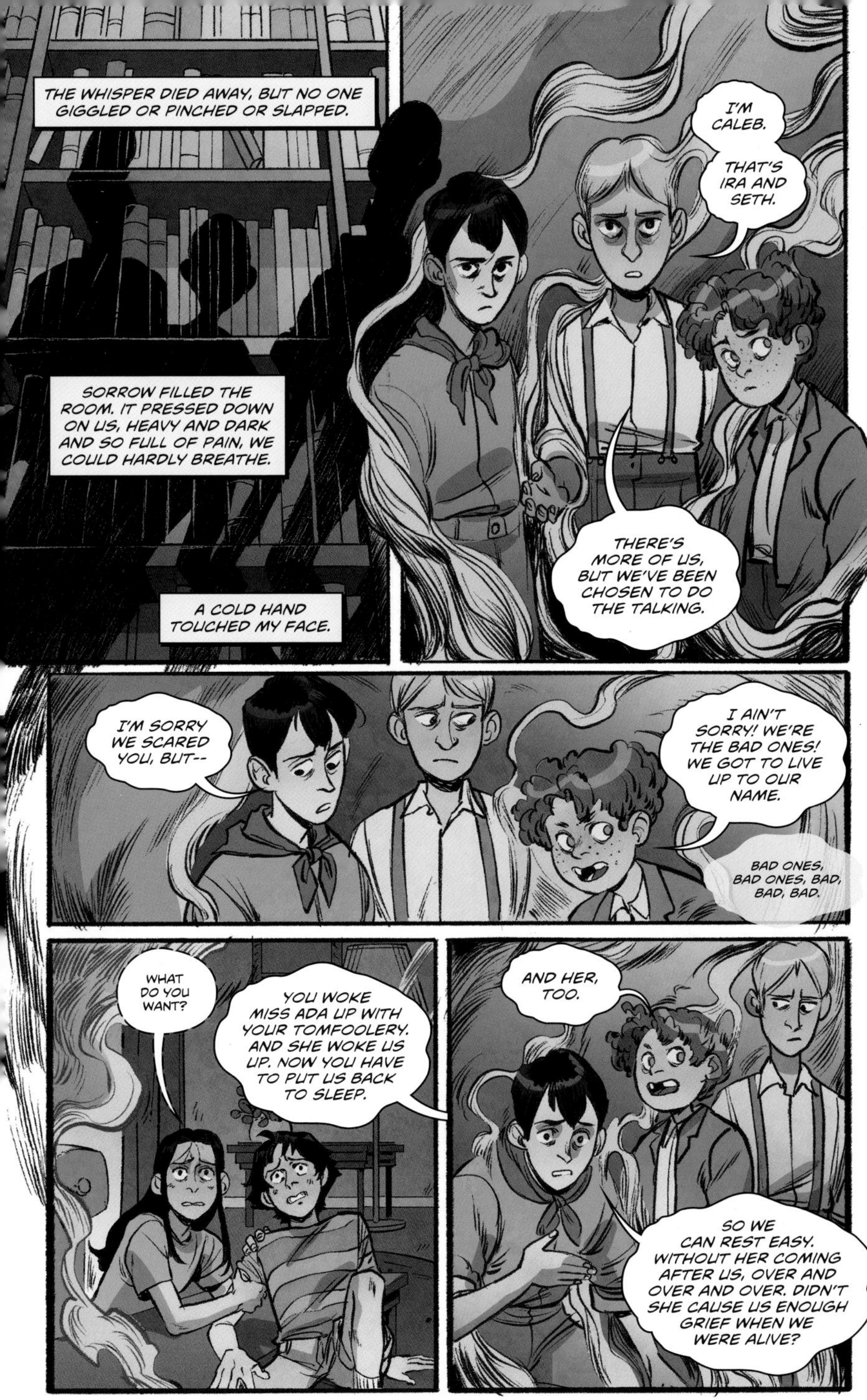
THE WHISPER DIED AWAY, BUT NO ONE GIGGLED OR PINCHED OR SLAPPED.
SORROW FILLED THE ROOM. IT PRESSED DOWN ON US, HEAVY AND DARK AND SO FULL OF PAIN, WE COULD HARDLY BREATHE.
A COLD HAND TOUCHED MY FACE.
I'M CALEB.
THAT'S IRA AND SETH.
THERE'S MORE OF US, BUT WE'VE BEEN CHOSEN TO DO THE TALKING.
I'M SORRY WE SCARED YOU, BUT--
I AIN'T SORRY! WE'RE THE BAD ONES! WE GOT TO LIVE UP TO OUR NAME.
BAD ONES, BAD ONES, BAD, BAD, BAD.
WHAT DO YOU WANT?
YOU WOKE MISS ADA UP WITH YOUR TOMFOOLERY. AND SHE WOKE US UP. NOW YOU HAVE TO PUT US BACK TO SLEEP.
AND HER, TOO.
SO WE CAN REST EASY. WITHOUT HER COMING AFTER US, OVER AND OVER AND OVER. DIDN'T SHE CAUSE US ENOUGH GRIEF WHEN WE WERE ALIVE?

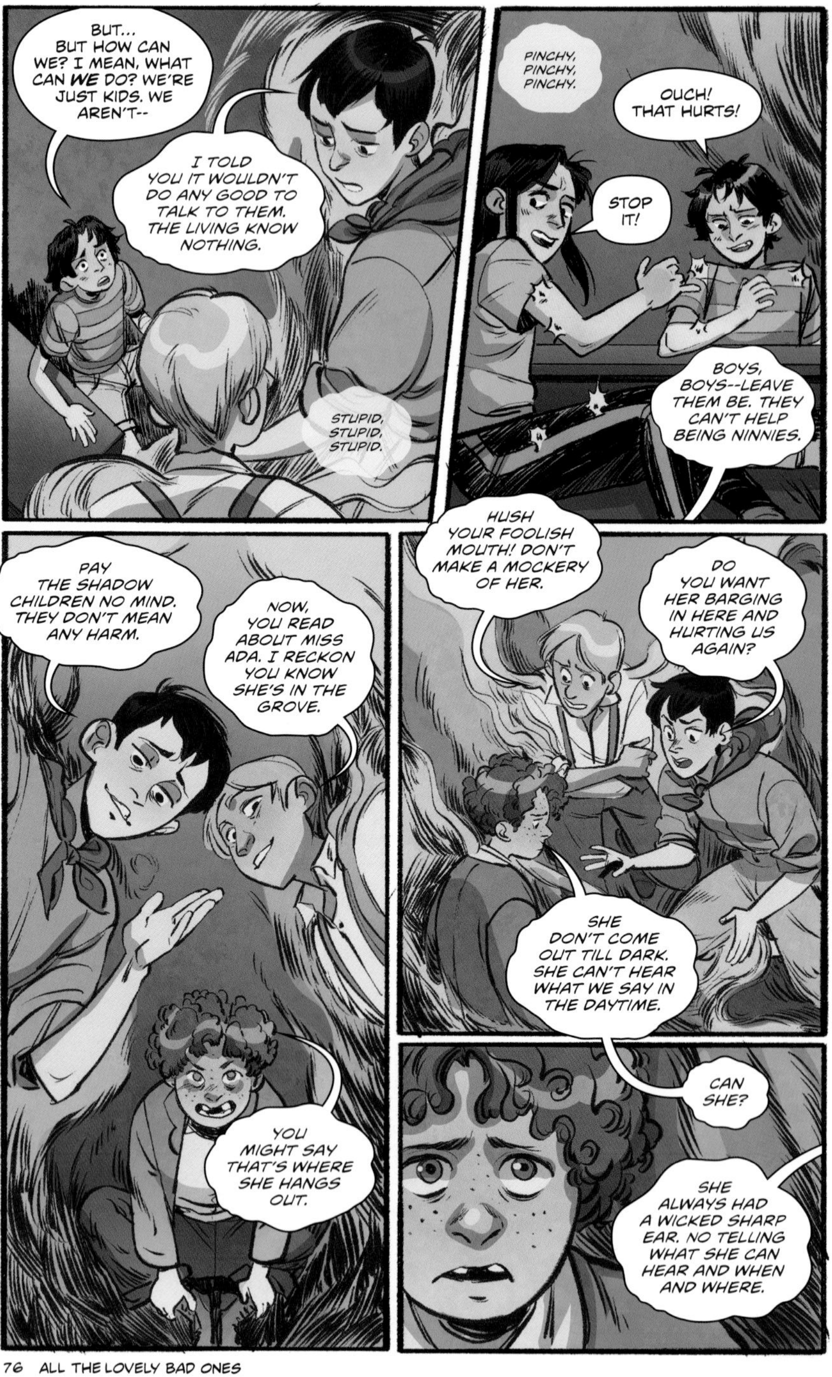
BUT... BUT HOW CAN WE? I MEAN, WHAT CAN WE DO? WE'RE JUST KIDS. WE AREN'T--
I TOLD YOU IT WOULDN'T DO ANY GOOD TO TALK TO THEM. THE LIVING KNOW NOTHING.
STUPID, STUPID, STUPID.
PINCHY, PINCHY, PINCHY.
OUCH! THAT HURTS!
STOP IT!
BOYS, BOYS--LEAVE THEM BE. THEY CAN'T HELP BEING NINNIES.
PAY THE SHADOW CHILDREN NO MIND. THEY DON'T MEAN ANY HARM.
NOW, YOU READ ABOUT MISS ADA. I RECKON YOU KNOW SHE'S IN THE GROVE.
YOU MIGHT SAY THAT'S WHERE SHE HANGS OUT.
HUSH YOUR FOOLISH MOUTH! DON'T MAKE A MOCKERY OF HER.
DO YOU WANT HER BARGING IN HERE AND HURTING US AGAIN?
SHE DON'T COME OUT TILL DARK. SHE CAN'T HEAR WHAT WE SAY IN THE DAYTIME.
CAN SHE?
SHE ALWAYS HAD A WICKED SHARP EAR. NO TELLING WHAT SHE CAN HEAR AND WHEN AND WHERE.

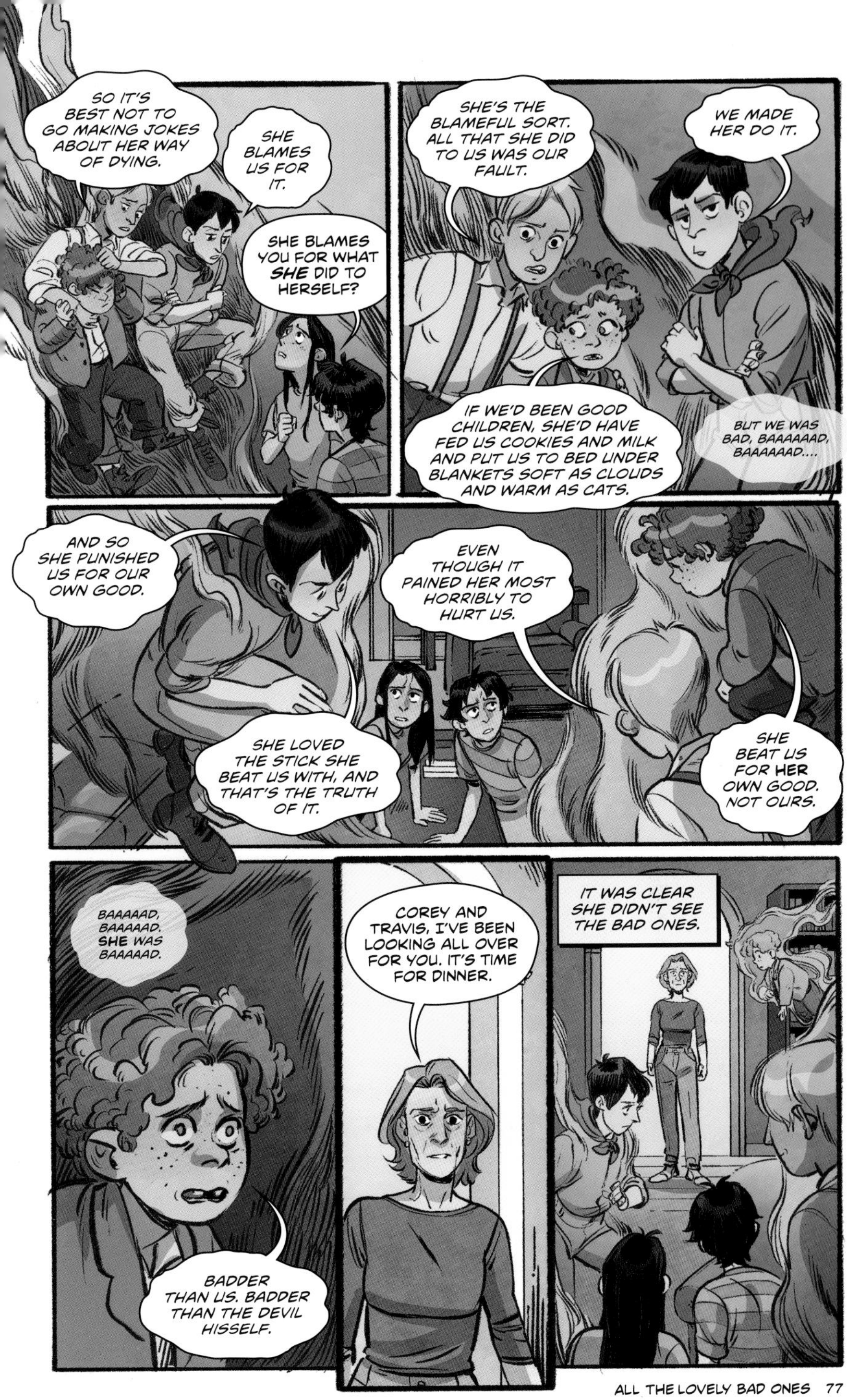
SO IT'S BEST NOT TO GO MAKING JOKES ABOUT HER WAY OF DYING.
SHE BLAMES US FOR IT.
SHE BLAMES YOU FOR WHAT **SHE** DID TO HERSELF?
SHE'S THE BLAMEFUL SORT. ALL THAT SHE DID TO US WAS OUR FAULT.
WE MADE HER DO IT.
IF WE'D BEEN GOOD CHILDREN, SHE'D HAVE FED US COOKIES AND MILK AND PUT US TO BED UNDER BLANKETS SOFT AS CLOUDS AND WARM AS CATS.
BUT WE WAS BAD, BAAAAAAD, BAAAAAAD....
AND SO SHE PUNISHED US FOR OUR OWN GOOD.
EVEN THOUGH IT PAINED HER MOST HORRIBLY TO HURT US.
SHE LOVED THE STICK SHE BEAT US WITH, AND THAT'S THE TRUTH OF IT.
SHE BEAT US FOR **HER** OWN GOOD. NOT OURS.
BAAAAAD, BAAAAAD. **SHE** WAS BAAAAAD.
BADDER THAN US. BADDER THAN THE DEVIL HISSELF.
COREY AND TRAVIS, I'VE BEEN LOOKING ALL OVER FOR YOU. IT'S TIME FOR DINNER.
IT WAS CLEAR SHE DIDN'T SEE THE BAD ONES.

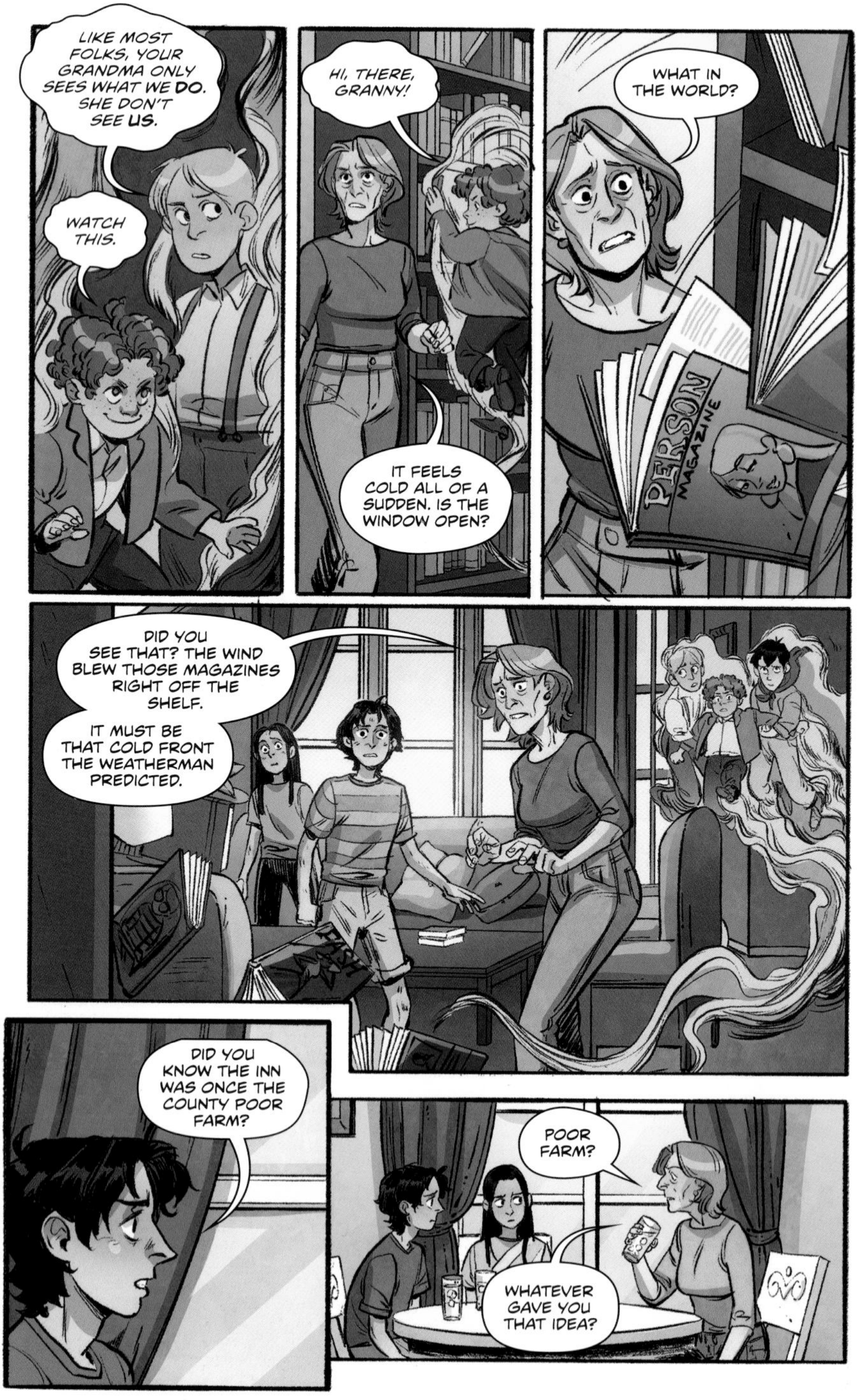
LIKE MOST FOLKS, YOUR GRANDMA ONLY SEES WHAT WE DO. SHE DON'T SEE US.
WATCH THIS.
HI, THERE, GRANNY!
IT FEELS COLD ALL OF A SUDDEN. IS THE WINDOW OPEN?
WHAT IN THE WORLD?
PERSON MAGAZINE
DID YOU SEE THAT? THE WIND BLEW THOSE MAGAZINES RIGHT OFF THE SHELF.
IT MUST BE THAT COLD FRONT THE WEATHERMAN PREDICTED.
DID YOU KNOW THE INN WAS ONCE THE COUNTY POOR FARM?
POOR FARM?
WHATEVER GAVE YOU THAT IDEA?

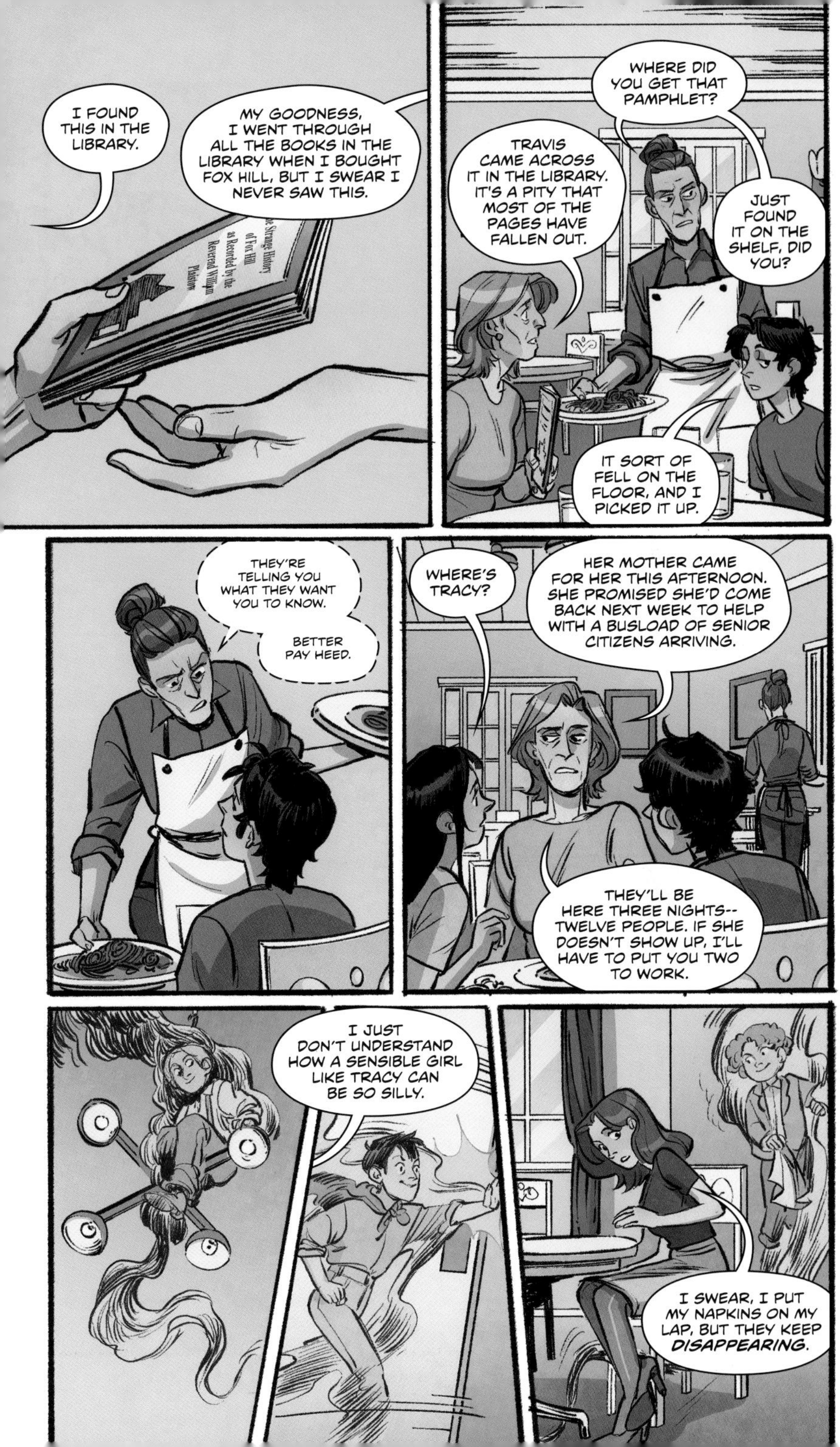
I FOUND THIS IN THE LIBRARY.
MY GOODNESS, I WENT THROUGH ALL THE BOOKS IN THE LIBRARY WHEN I BOUGHT FOX HILL, BUT I SWEAR I NEVER SAW THIS.
WHERE DID YOU GET THAT PAMPHLET?
TRAVIS CAME ACROSS IT IN THE LIBRARY. IT'S A PITY THAT MOST OF THE PAGES HAVE FALLEN OUT.
JUST FOUND IT ON THE SHELF, DID YOU?
IT SORT OF FELL ON THE FLOOR, AND I PICKED IT UP.
THEY'RE TELLING YOU WHAT THEY WANT YOU TO KNOW.
BETTER PAY HEED.
WHERE'S TRACY?
HER MOTHER CAME FOR HER THIS AFTERNOON. SHE PROMISED SHE'D COME BACK NEXT WEEK TO HELP WITH A BUSLOAD OF SENIOR CITIZENS ARRIVING.
THEY'LL BE HERE THREE NIGHTS-- TWELVE PEOPLE. IF SHE DOESN'T SHOW UP, I'LL HAVE TO PUT YOU TWO TO WORK.
I JUST DON'T UNDERSTAND HOW A SENSIBLE GIRL LIKE TRACY CAN BE SO SILLY.
I SWEAR, I PUT MY NAPKINS ON MY LAP, BUT THEY KEEP *DISAPPEARING*.

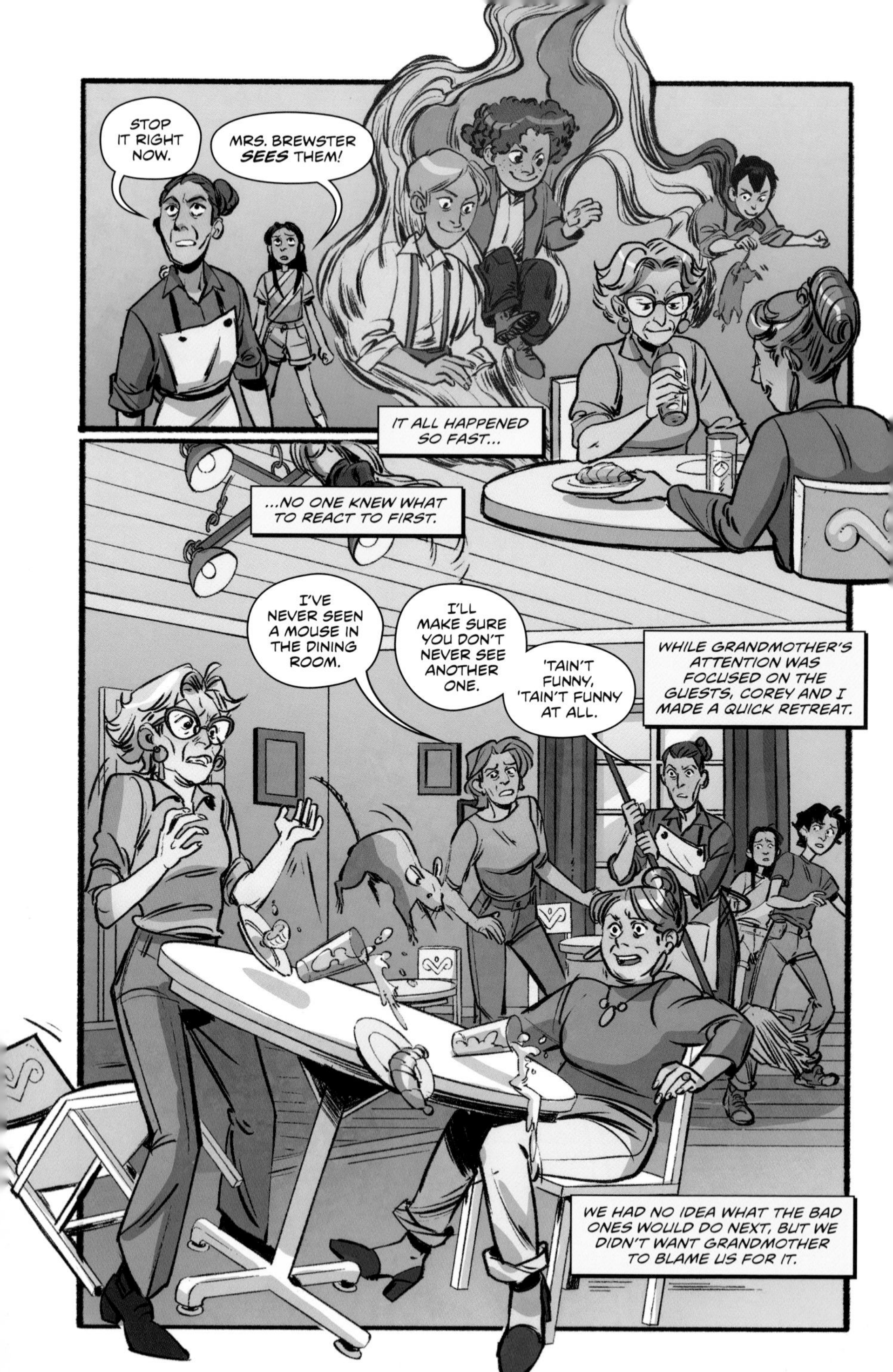
STOP IT RIGHT NOW.
MRS. BREWSTER SEES THEM!
IT ALL HAPPENED SO FAST...
...NO ONE KNEW WHAT TO REACT TO FIRST.
I'VE NEVER SEEN A MOUSE IN THE DINING ROOM.
I'LL MAKE SURE YOU DON'T NEVER SEE ANOTHER ONE.
'TAIN'T FUNNY, 'TAIN'T FUNNY AT ALL.
WHILE GRANDMOTHER'S ATTENTION WAS FOCUSED ON THE GUESTS, COREY AND I MADE A QUICK RETREAT.
WE HAD NO IDEA WHAT THE BAD ONES WOULD DO NEXT, BUT WE DIDN'T WANT GRANDMOTHER TO BLAME US FOR IT.

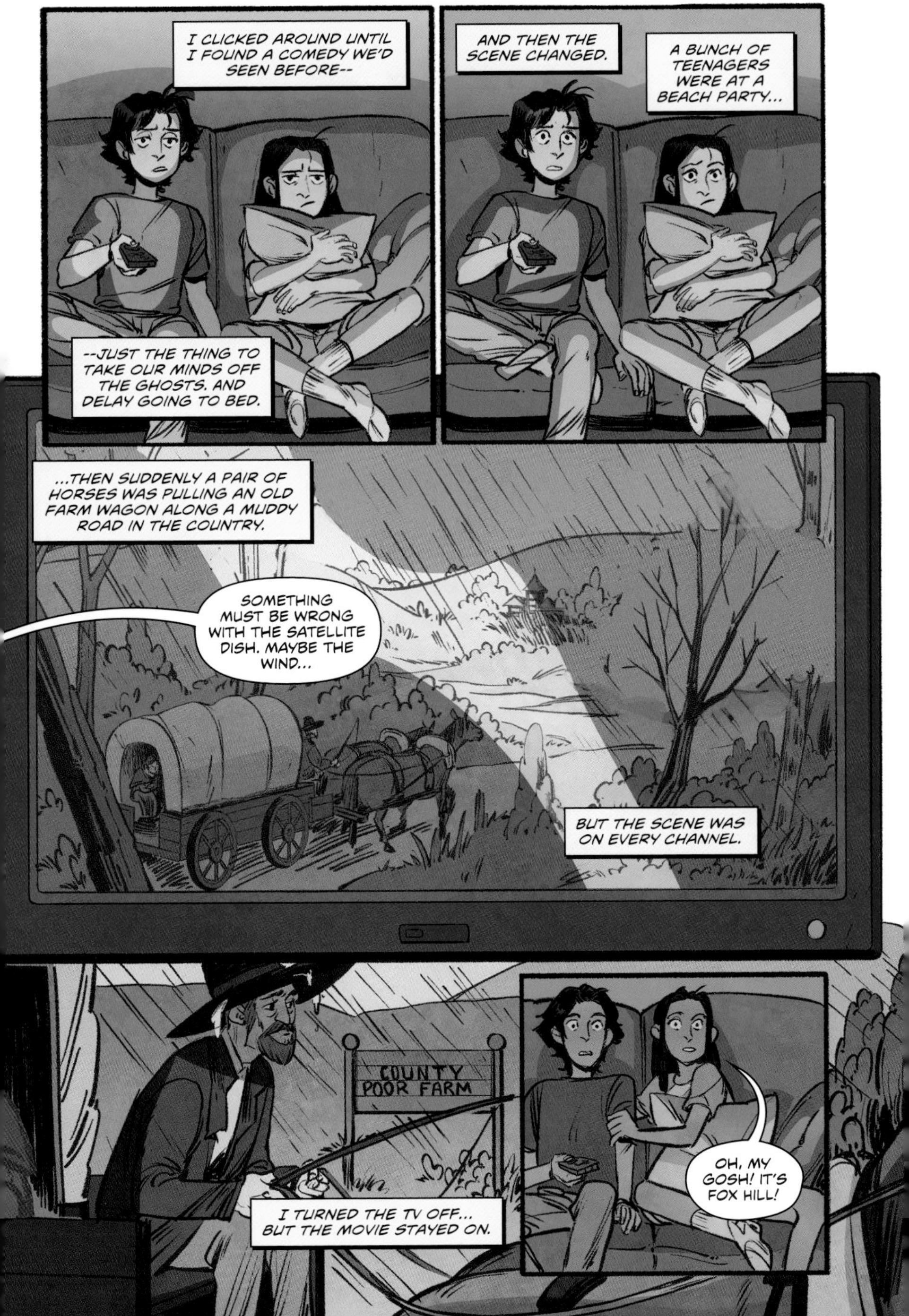
I CLICKED AROUND UNTIL I FOUND A COMEDY WE'D SEEN BEFORE--
--JUST THE THING TO TAKE OUR MINDS OFF THE GHOSTS. AND DELAY GOING TO BED.
AND THEN THE SCENE CHANGED.
A BUNCH OF TEENAGERS WERE AT A BEACH PARTY...
...THEN SUDDENLY A PAIR OF HORSES WAS PULLING AN OLD FARM WAGON ALONG A MUDDY ROAD IN THE COUNTRY.
SOMETHING MUST BE WRONG WITH THE SATELLITE DISH. MAYBE THE WIND...
BUT THE SCENE WAS ON EVERY CHANNEL.
COUNTY POOR FARM
I TURNED THE TV OFF... BUT THE MOVIE STAYED ON.
OH, MY GOSH! IT'S FOX HILL!

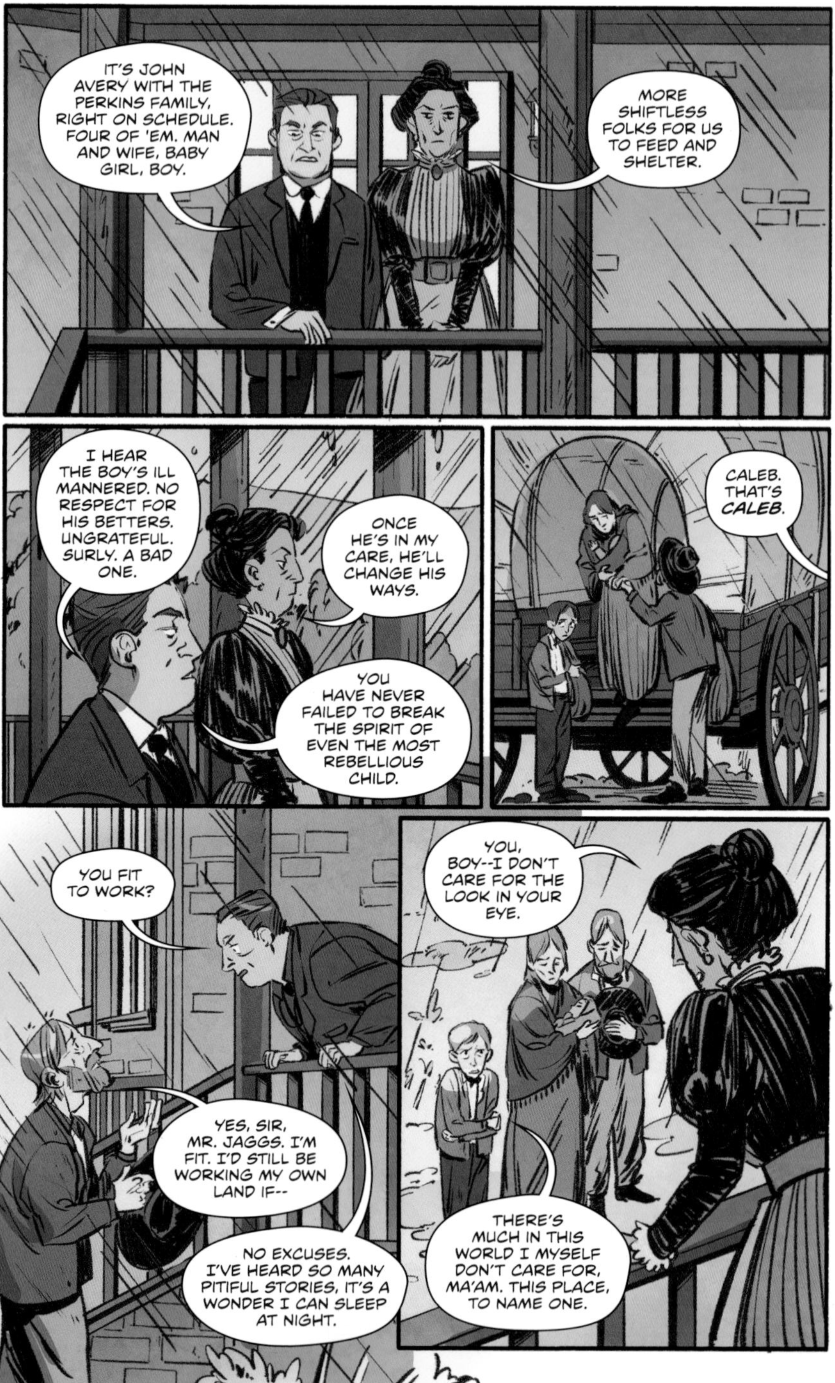
IT'S JOHN AVERY WITH THE PERKINS FAMILY, RIGHT ON SCHEDULE. FOUR OF 'EM. MAN AND WIFE, BABY GIRL, BOY.
MORE SHIFTLESS FOLKS FOR US TO FEED AND SHELTER.
I HEAR THE BOY'S ILL MANNERED. NO RESPECT FOR HIS BETTERS. UNGRATEFUL. SURLY. A BAD ONE.
ONCE HE'S IN MY CARE, HE'LL CHANGE HIS WAYS.
YOU HAVE NEVER FAILED TO BREAK THE SPIRIT OF EVEN THE MOST REBELLIOUS CHILD.
CALEB. THAT'S *CALEB*.
YOU FIT TO WORK?
YES, SIR, MR. JAGGS. I'M FIT. I'D STILL BE WORKING MY OWN LAND IF--
NO EXCUSES. I'VE HEARD SO MANY PITIFUL STORIES, IT'S A WONDER I CAN SLEEP AT NIGHT.
YOU, BOY--I DON'T CARE FOR THE LOOK IN YOUR EYE.
THERE'S MUCH IN THIS WORLD I MYSELF DON'T CARE FOR, MA'AM. THIS PLACE, TO NAME ONE.

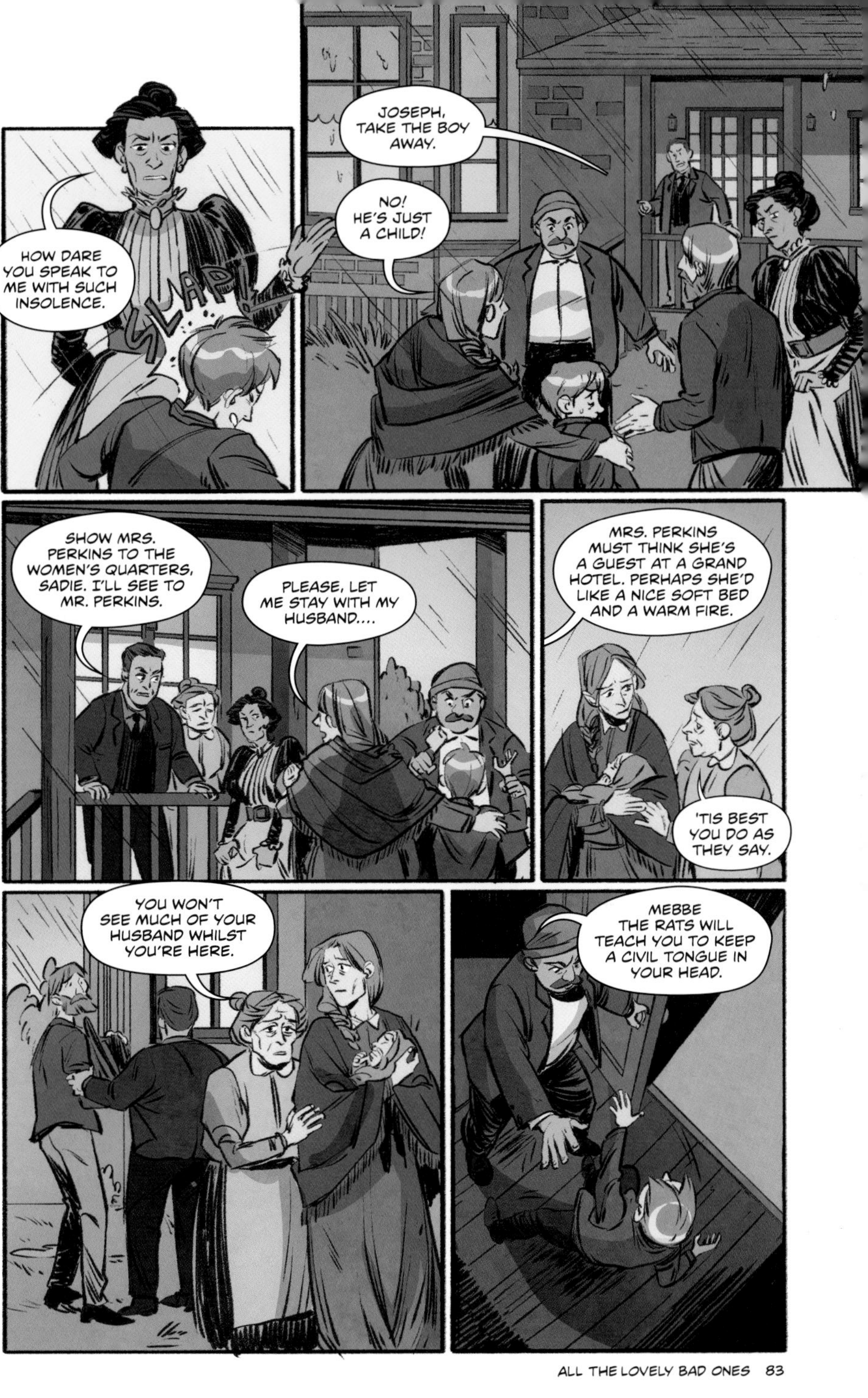
HOW DARE YOU SPEAK TO ME WITH SUCH INSOLENCE.
SLAP!
JOSEPH, TAKE THE BOY AWAY.
NO! HE'S JUST A CHILD!
SHOW MRS. PERKINS TO THE WOMEN'S QUARTERS, SADIE. I'LL SEE TO MR. PERKINS.
PLEASE, LET ME STAY WITH MY HUSBAND....
MRS. PERKINS MUST THINK SHE'S A GUEST AT A GRAND HOTEL. PERHAPS SHE'D LIKE A NICE SOFT BED AND A WARM FIRE.
'TIS BEST YOU DO AS THEY SAY.
YOU WON'T SEE MUCH OF YOUR HUSBAND WHILST YOU'RE HERE.
MEBBE THE RATS WILL TEACH YOU TO KEEP A CIVIL TONGUE IN YOUR HEAD.

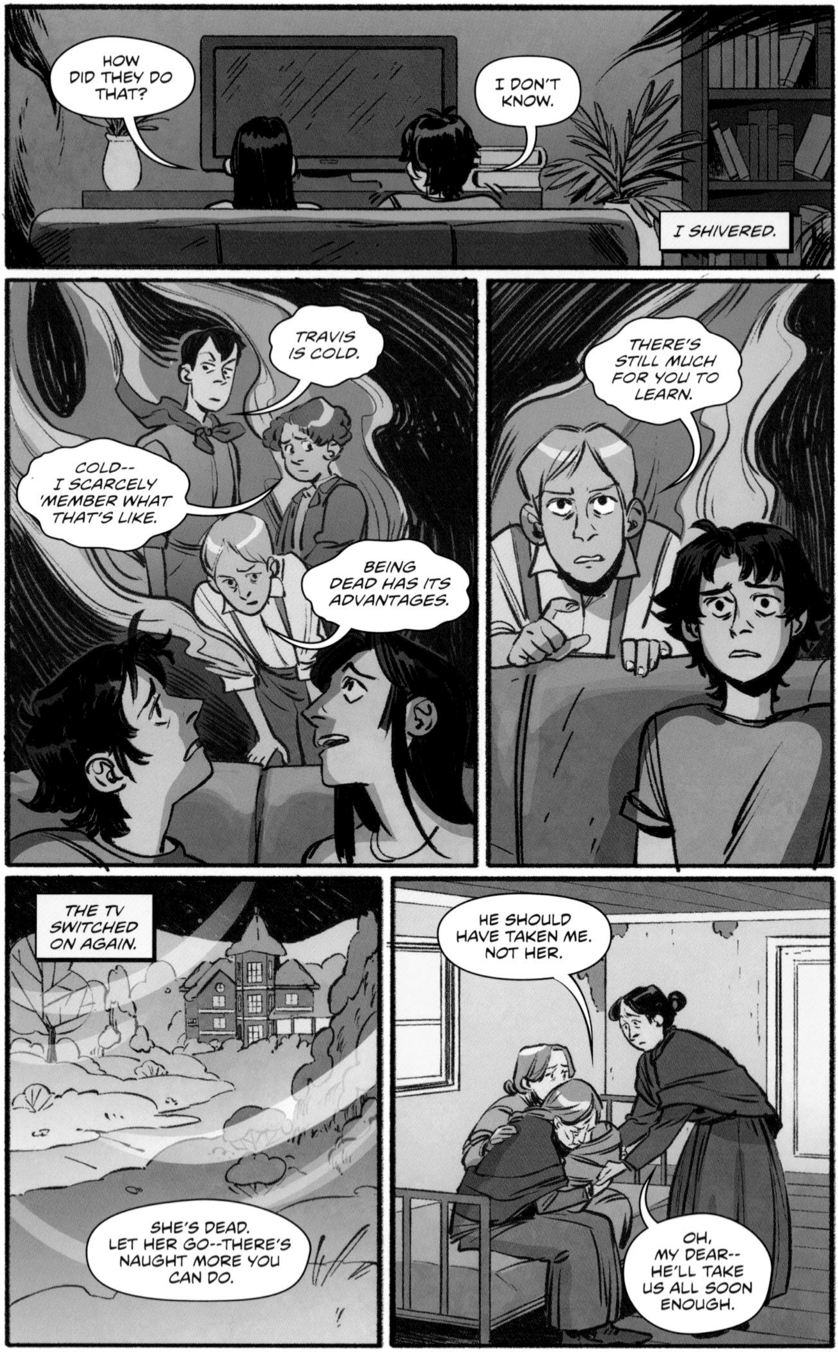
HOW DID THEY DO THAT?
I DON'T KNOW.
I SHIVERED.
TRAVIS IS COLD.
COLD-- I SCARCELY 'MEMBER WHAT THAT'S LIKE.
BEING DEAD HAS ITS ADVANTAGES.
THERE'S STILL MUCH FOR YOU TO LEARN.
THE TV SWITCHED ON AGAIN.
SHE'S DEAD. LET HER GO--THERE'S NAUGHT MORE YOU CAN DO.
HE SHOULD HAVE TAKEN ME. NOT HER.
OH, MY DEAR-- HE'LL TAKE US ALL SOON ENOUGH.

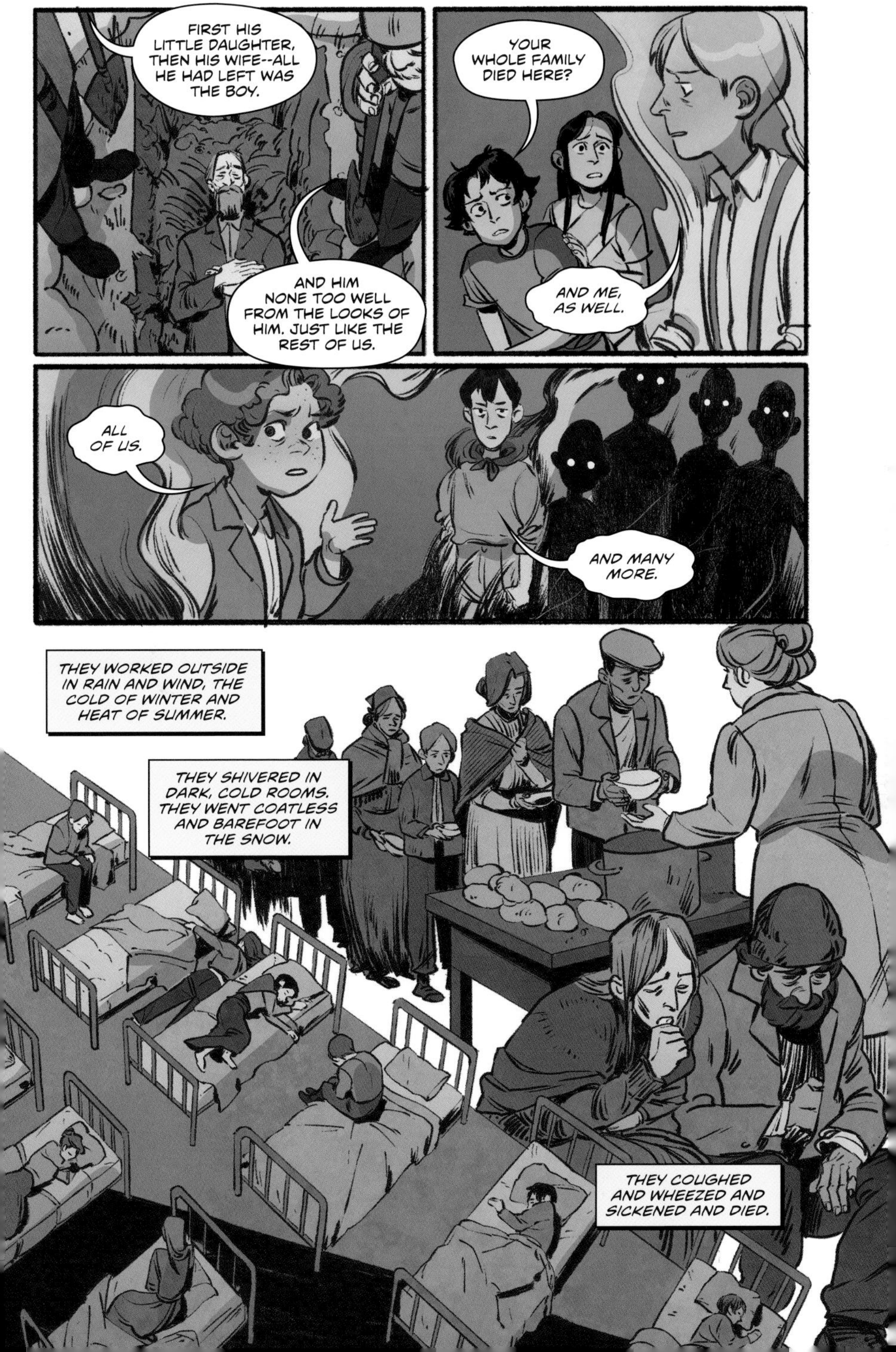

FIRST HIS LITTLE DAUGHTER, THEN HIS WIFE--ALL HE HAD LEFT WAS THE BOY.
AND HIM NONE TOO WELL FROM THE LOOKS OF HIM. JUST LIKE THE REST OF US.
YOUR WHOLE FAMILY DIED HERE?
AND ME, AS WELL.
ALL OF US.
AND MANY MORE.
THEY WORKED OUTSIDE IN RAIN AND WIND, THE COLD OF WINTER AND HEAT OF SUMMER.
THEY SHIVERED IN DARK, COLD ROOMS. THEY WENT COATLESS AND BAREFOOT IN THE SNOW.
THEY COUGHED AND WHEEZED AND SICKENED AND DIED.

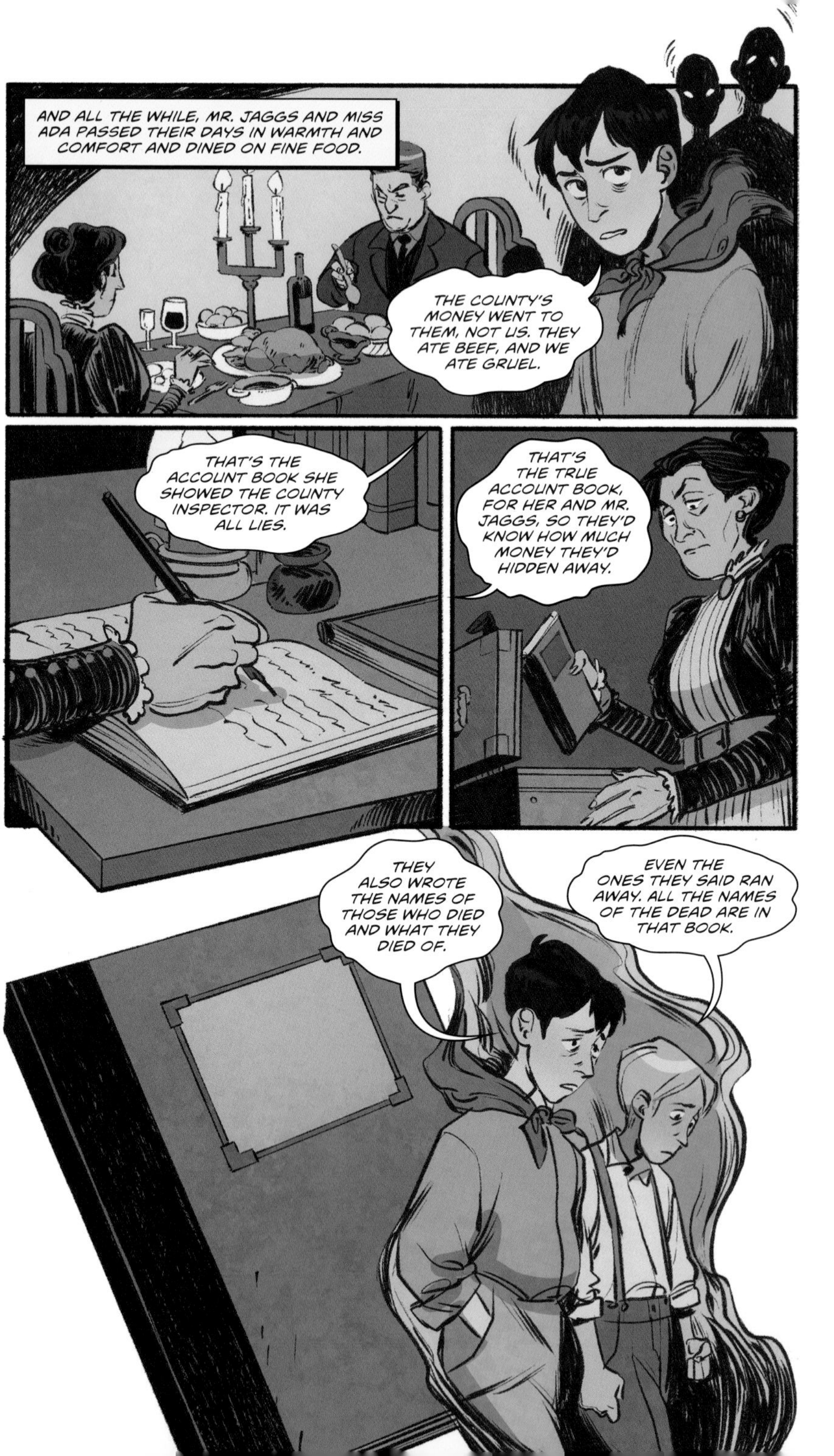
AND ALL THE WHILE, MR. JAGGS AND MISS ADA PASSED THEIR DAYS IN WARMTH AND COMFORT AND DINED ON FINE FOOD.
THE COUNTY'S MONEY WENT TO THEM, NOT US. THEY ATE BEEF, AND WE ATE GRUEL.
THAT'S THE ACCOUNT BOOK SHE SHOWED THE COUNTY INSPECTOR. IT WAS ALL LIES.
THAT'S THE TRUE ACCOUNT BOOK, FOR HER AND MR. JAGGS, SO THEY'D KNOW HOW MUCH MONEY THEY'D HIDDEN AWAY.
THEY ALSO WROTE THE NAMES OF THOSE WHO DIED AND WHAT THEY DIED OF.
EVEN THE ONES THEY SAID RAN AWAY. ALL THE NAMES OF THE DEAD ARE IN THAT BOOK.

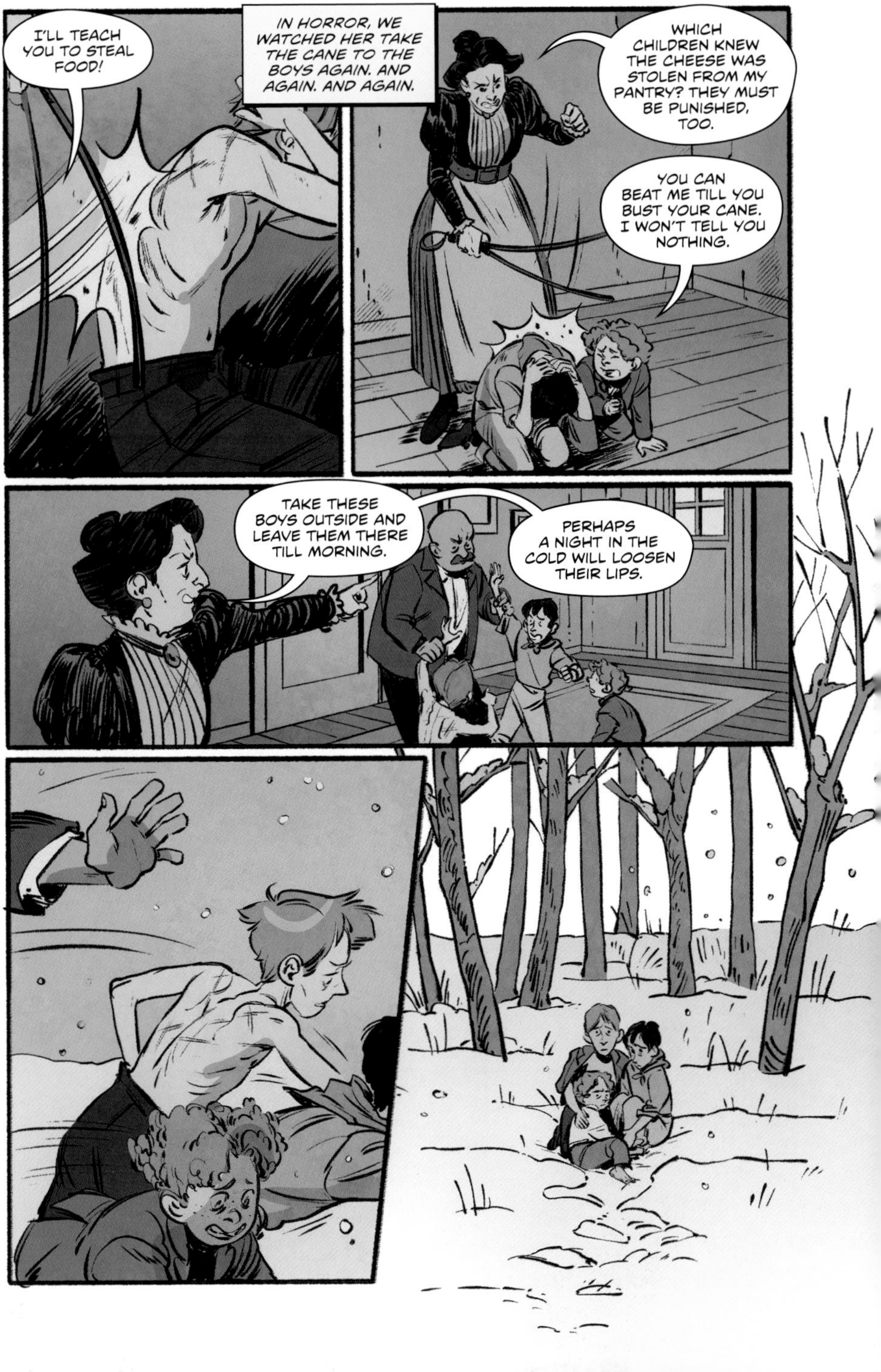
I'LL TEACH YOU TO STEAL FOOD!
IN HORROR, WE WATCHED HER TAKE THE CANE TO THE BOYS AGAIN. AND AGAIN. AND AGAIN.
WHICH CHILDREN KNEW THE CHEESE WAS STOLEN FROM MY PANTRY? THEY MUST BE PUNISHED, TOO.
YOU CAN BEAT ME TILL YOU BUST YOUR CANE. I WON'T TELL YOU NOTHING.
TAKE THESE BOYS OUTSIDE AND LEAVE THEM THERE TILL MORNING.
PERHAPS A NIGHT IN THE COLD WILL LOOSEN THEIR LIPS.

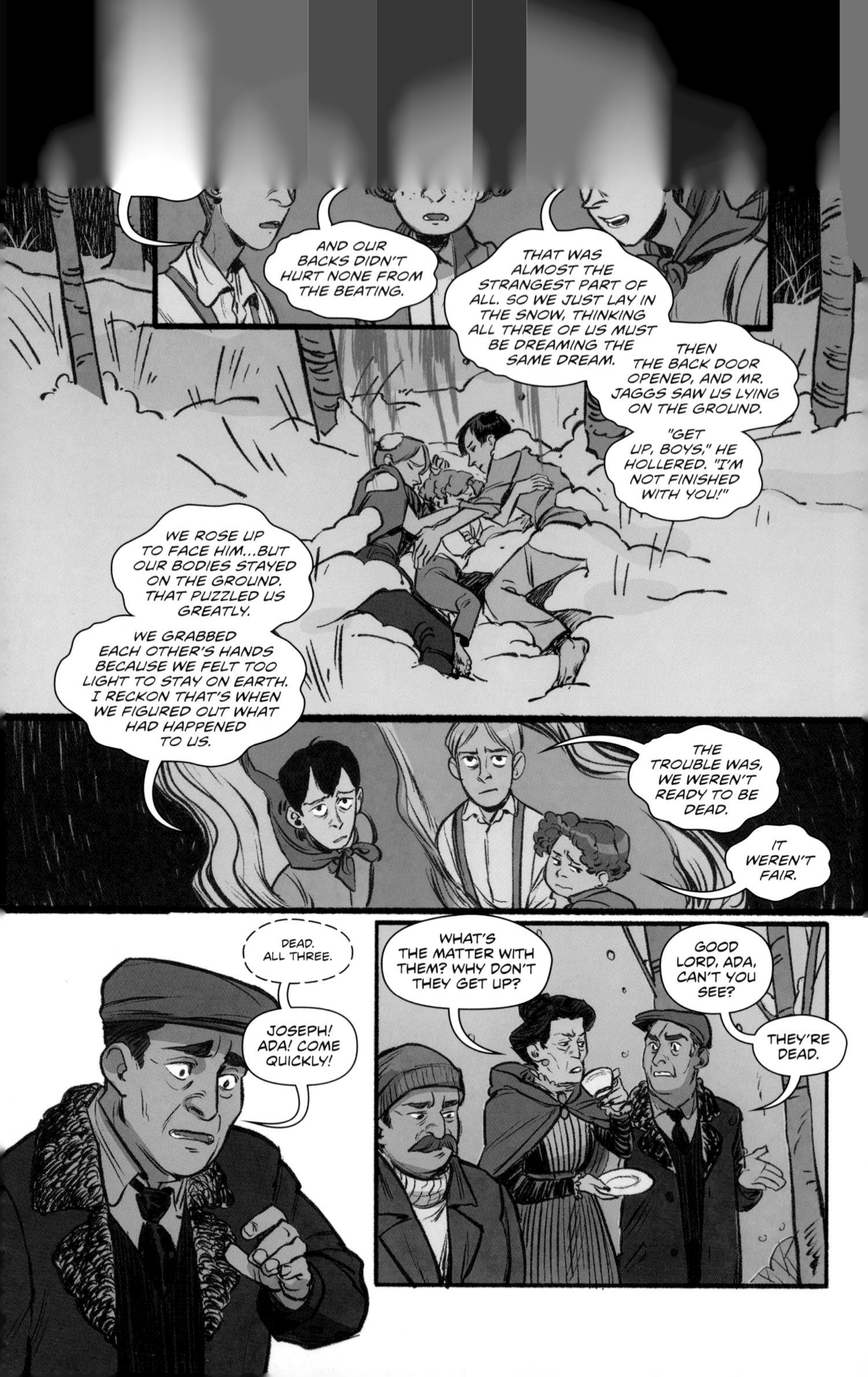
AND OUR BACKS DIDN'T HURT NONE FROM THE BEATING.
THAT WAS ALMOST THE STRANGEST PART OF ALL. SO WE JUST LAY IN THE SNOW, THINKING ALL THREE OF US MUST BE DREAMING THE SAME DREAM.
THEN THE BACK DOOR OPENED, AND MR. JAGGS SAW US LYING ON THE GROUND.
"GET UP, BOYS," HE HOLLERED. "I'M NOT FINISHED WITH YOU!"
WE ROSE UP TO FACE HIM...BUT OUR BODIES STAYED ON THE GROUND. THAT PUZZLED US GREATLY.
WE GRABBED EACH OTHER'S HANDS BECAUSE WE FELT TOO LIGHT TO STAY ON EARTH. I RECKON THAT'S WHEN WE FIGURED OUT WHAT HAD HAPPENED TO US.
THE TROUBLE WAS, WE WEREN'T READY TO BE DEAD.
IT WEREN'T FAIR.
DEAD. ALL THREE.
JOSEPH! ADA! COME QUICKLY!
WHAT'S THE MATTER WITH THEM? WHY DON'T THEY GET UP?
GOOD LORD, ADA, CAN'T YOU SEE?
THEY'RE DEAD.

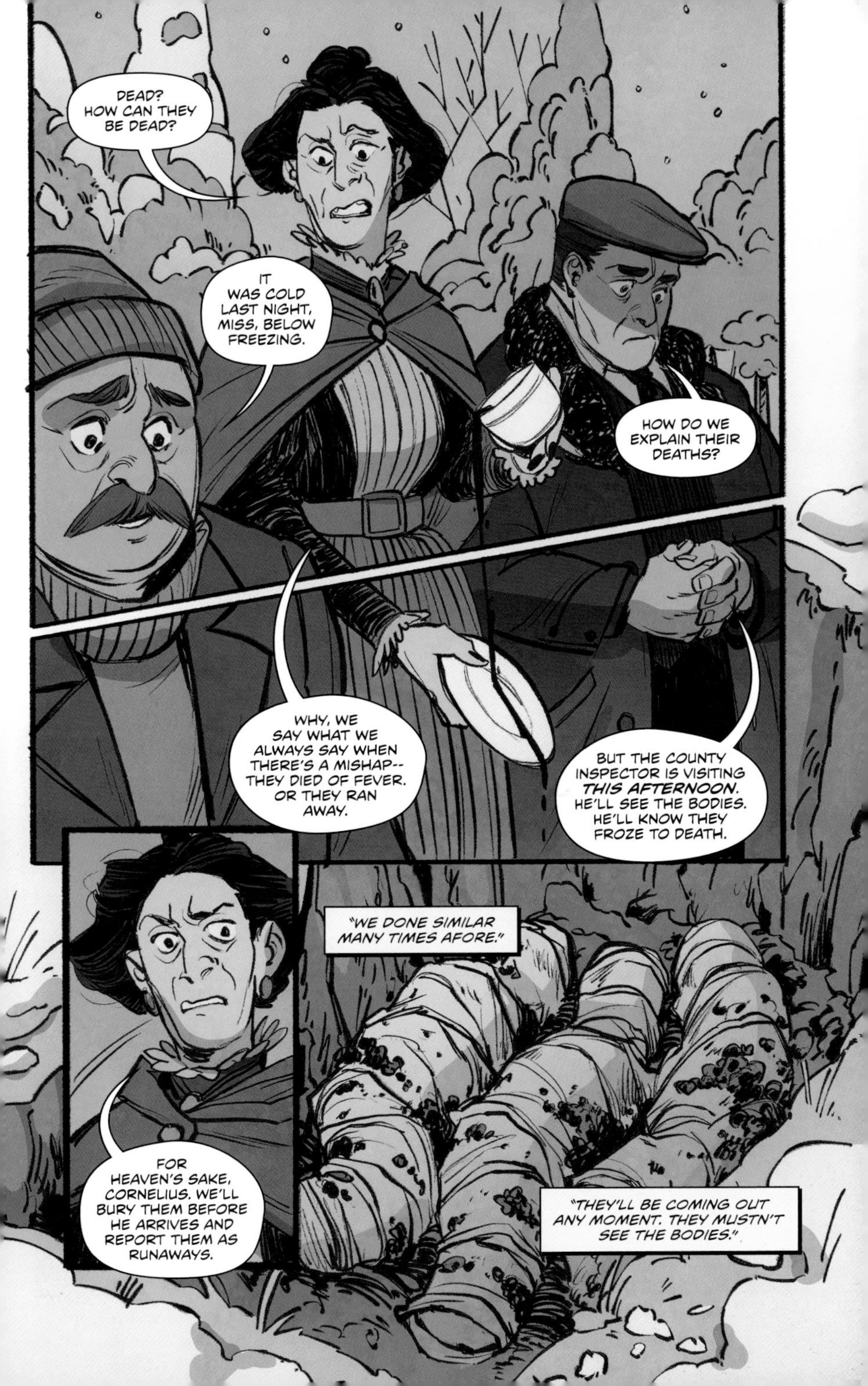
DEAD? HOW CAN THEY BE DEAD?
IT WAS COLD LAST NIGHT, MISS, BELOW FREEZING.
HOW DO WE EXPLAIN THEIR DEATHS?
WHY, WE SAY WHAT WE ALWAYS SAY WHEN THERE'S A MISHAP-- THEY DIED OF FEVER. OR THEY RAN AWAY.
BUT THE COUNTY INSPECTOR IS VISITING *THIS AFTERNOON.* HE'LL SEE THE BODIES. HE'LL KNOW THEY FROZE TO DEATH.
FOR HEAVEN'S SAKE, CORNELIUS. WE'LL BURY THEM BEFORE HE ARRIVES AND REPORT THEM AS RUNAWAYS.
"WE DONE SIMILAR MANY TIMES AFORE."
"THEY'LL BE COMING OUT ANY MOMENT. THEY MUSTN'T SEE THE BODIES."

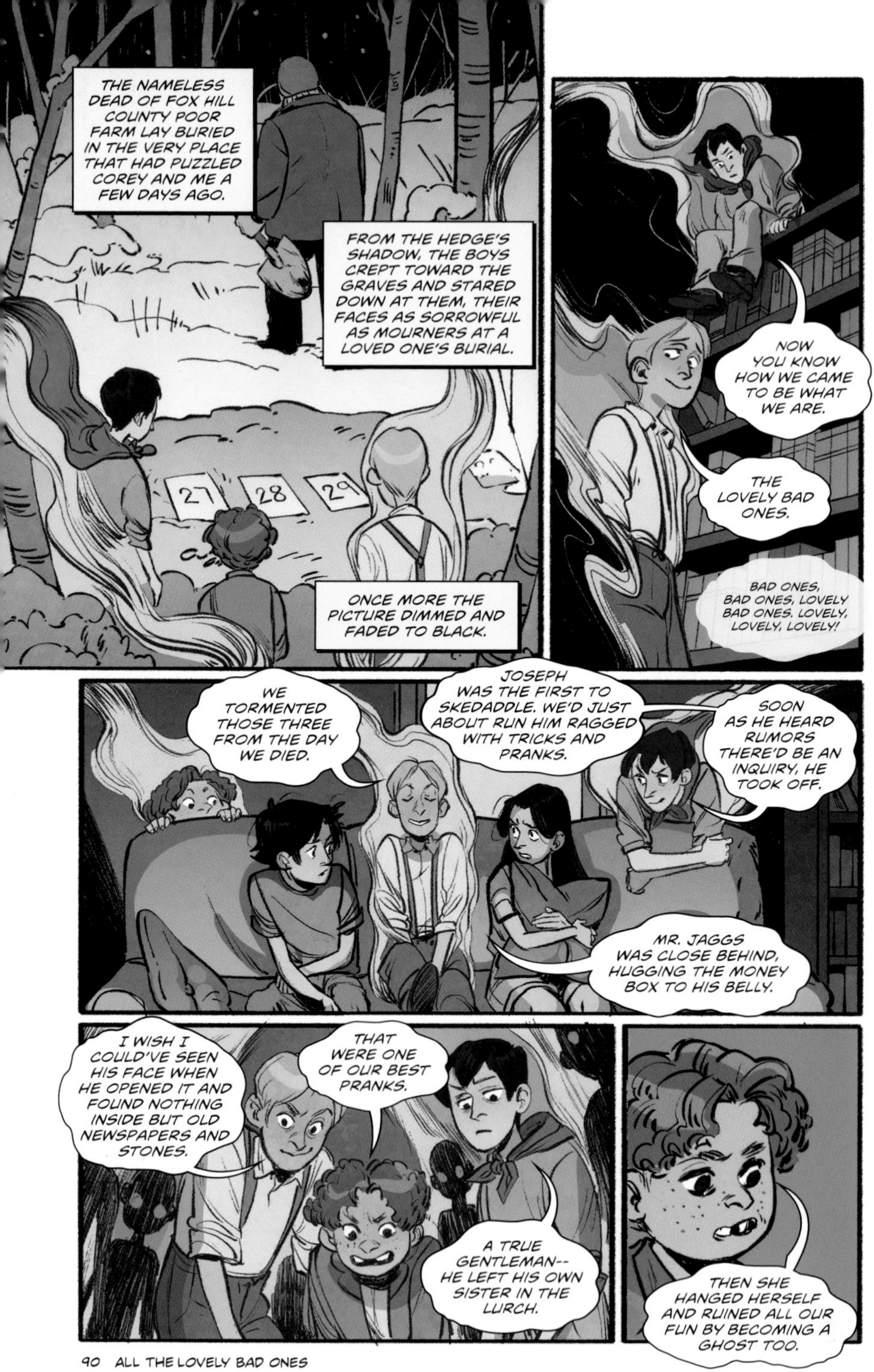
THE NAMELESS DEAD OF FOX HILL COUNTY POOR FARM LAY BURIED IN THE VERY PLACE THAT HAD PUZZLED COREY AND ME A FEW DAYS AGO.
FROM THE HEDGE'S SHADOW, THE BOYS CREPT TOWARD THE GRAVES AND STARED DOWN AT THEM, THEIR FACES AS SORROWFUL AS MOURNERS AT A LOVED ONE'S BURIAL.
27
28
29
ONCE MORE THE PICTURE DIMMED AND FADED TO BLACK.
NOW YOU KNOW HOW WE CAME TO BE WHAT WE ARE.
THE LOVELY BAD ONES.
BAD ONES, BAD ONES, LOVELY BAD ONES. LOVELY, LOVELY, LOVELY!
WE TORMENTED THOSE THREE FROM THE DAY WE DIED.
JOSEPH WAS THE FIRST TO SKEDADDLE. WE'D JUST ABOUT RUN HIM RAGGED WITH TRICKS AND PRANKS.
SOON AS HE HEARD RUMORS THERE'D BE AN INQUIRY, HE TOOK OFF.
MR. JAGGS WAS CLOSE BEHIND, HUGGING THE MONEY BOX TO HIS BELLY.
I WISH I COULD'VE SEEN HIS FACE WHEN HE OPENED IT AND FOUND NOTHING INSIDE BUT OLD NEWSPAPERS AND STONES.
THAT WERE ONE OF OUR BEST PRANKS.
A TRUE GENTLEMAN-- HE LEFT HIS OWN SISTER IN THE LURCH.
THEN SHE HANGED HERSELF AND RUINED ALL OUR FUN BY BECOMING A GHOST TOO.

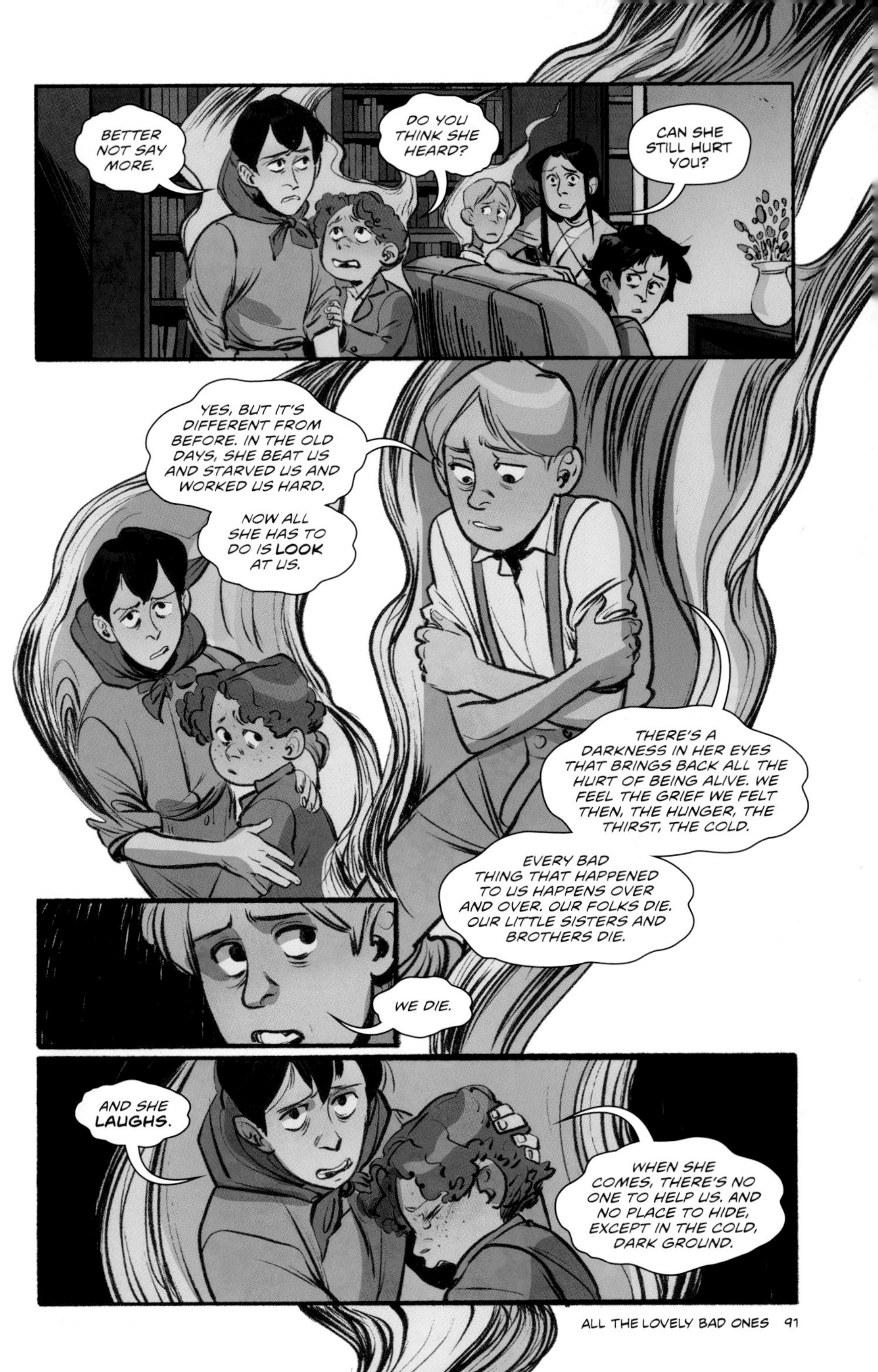
BETTER NOT SAY MORE.
DO YOU THINK SHE HEARD?
CAN SHE STILL HURT YOU?
YES, BUT IT'S DIFFERENT FROM BEFORE. IN THE OLD DAYS, SHE BEAT US AND STARVED US AND WORKED US HARD.
NOW ALL SHE HAS TO DO IS **LOOK** AT US.
THERE'S A DARKNESS IN HER EYES THAT BRINGS BACK ALL THE HURT OF BEING ALIVE. WE FEEL THE GRIEF WE FELT THEN, THE HUNGER, THE THIRST, THE COLD.
EVERY BAD THING THAT HAPPENED TO US HAPPENS OVER AND OVER. OUR FOLKS DIE. OUR LITTLE SISTERS AND BROTHERS DIE.
WE DIE.
AND SHE **LAUGHS**.
WHEN SHE COMES, THERE'S NO ONE TO HELP US. AND NO PLACE TO HIDE, EXCEPT IN THE COLD, DARK GROUND.

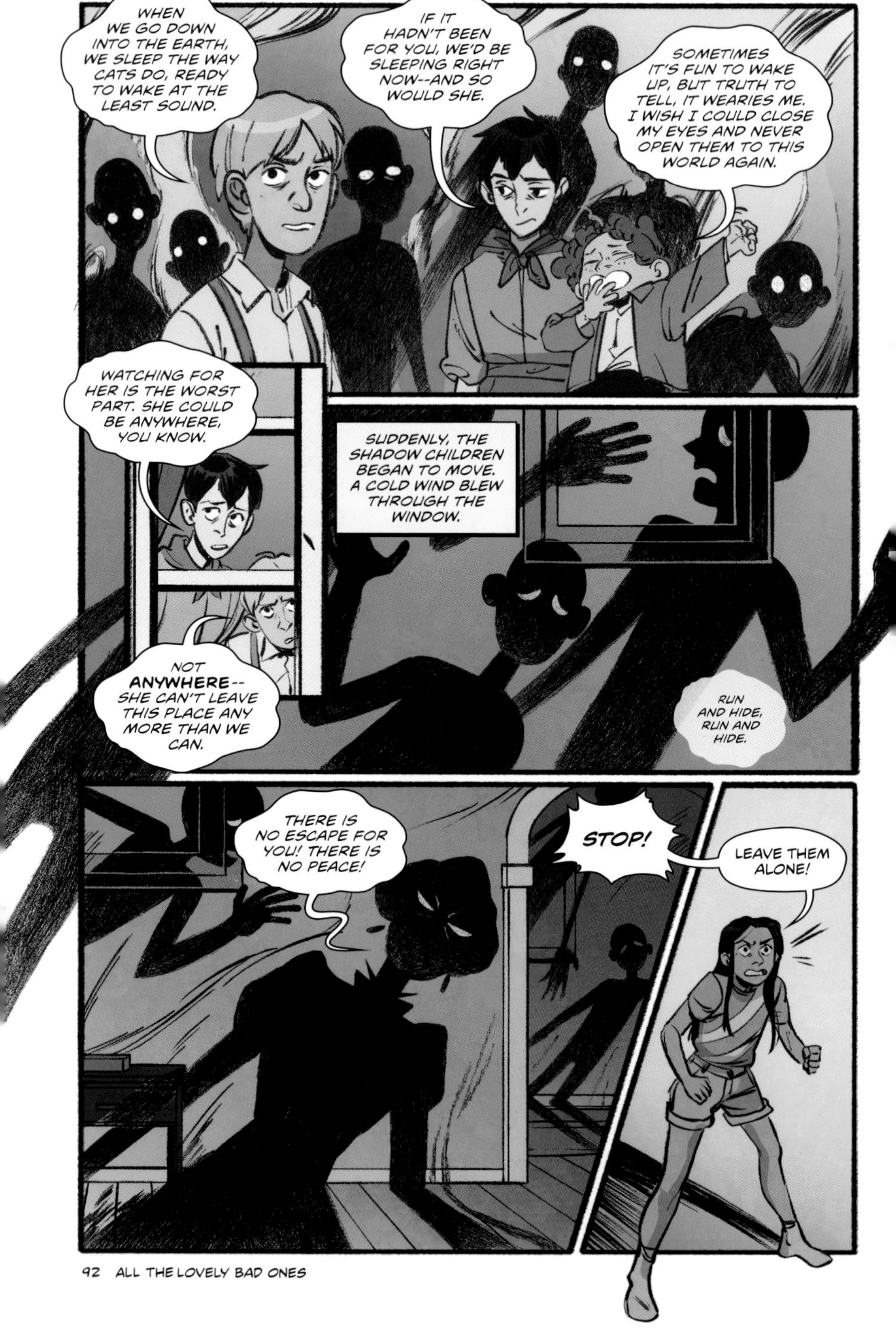
WHEN WE GO DOWN INTO THE EARTH, WE SLEEP THE WAY CATS DO, READY TO WAKE AT THE LEAST SOUND.
IF IT HADN'T BEEN FOR YOU, WE'D BE SLEEPING RIGHT NOW--AND SO WOULD SHE.
SOMETIMES IT'S FUN TO WAKE UP, BUT TRUTH TO TELL, IT WEARIES ME. I WISH I COULD CLOSE MY EYES AND NEVER OPEN THEM TO THIS WORLD AGAIN.
WATCHING FOR HER IS THE WORST PART. SHE COULD BE ANYWHERE, YOU KNOW.
NOT **ANYWHERE**--SHE CAN'T LEAVE THIS PLACE ANY MORE THAN WE CAN.
SUDDENLY, THE SHADOW CHILDREN BEGAN TO MOVE. A COLD WIND BLEW THROUGH THE WINDOW.
RUN AND HIDE, RUN AND HIDE.
THERE IS NO ESCAPE FOR YOU! THERE IS NO PEACE!
STOP!
LEAVE THEM ALONE!

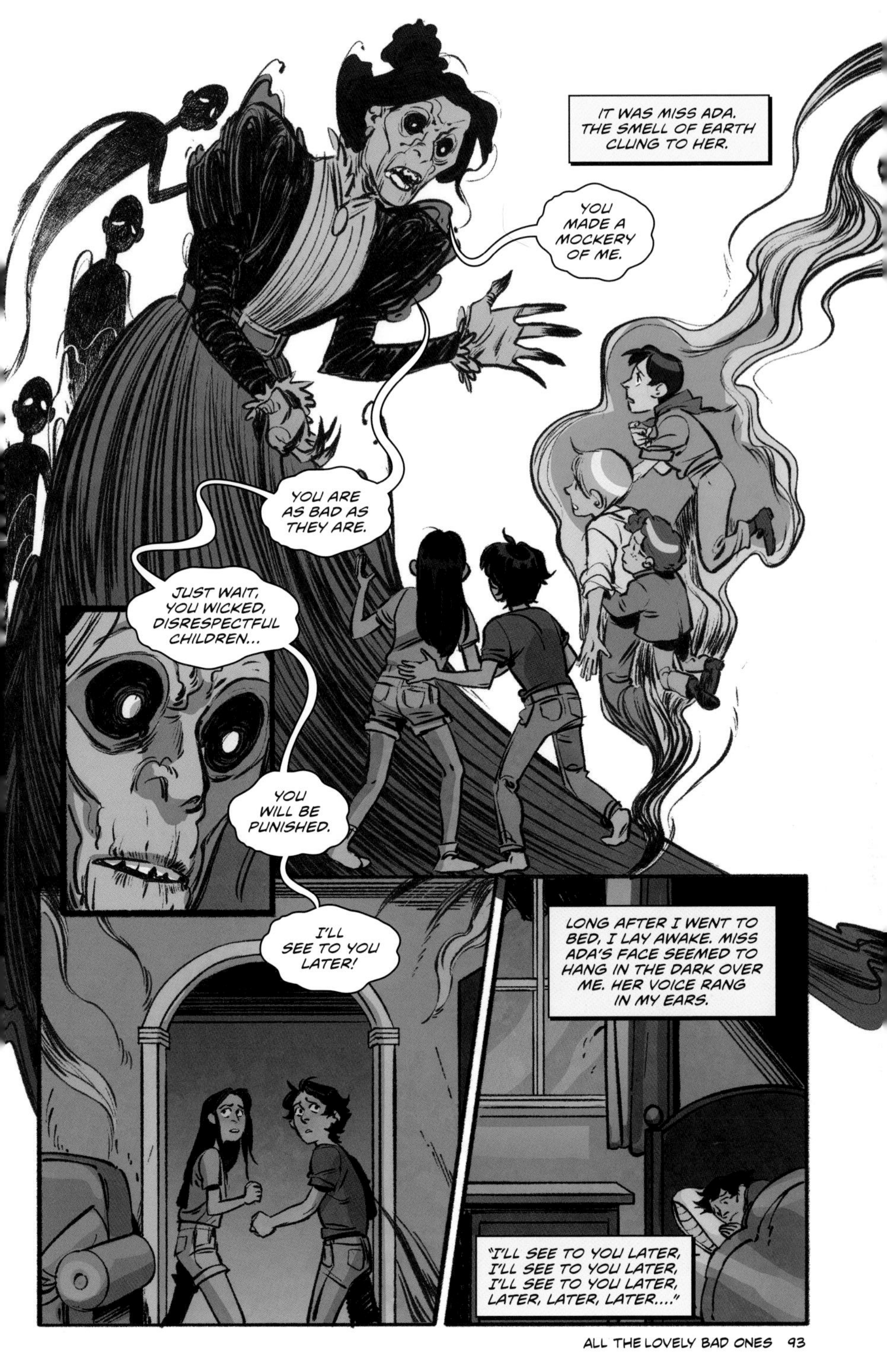
IT WAS MISS ADA. THE SMELL OF EARTH CLUNG TO HER.
YOU MADE A MOCKERY OF ME.
YOU ARE AS BAD AS THEY ARE.
JUST WAIT, YOU WICKED, DISRESPECTFUL CHILDREN...
YOU WILL BE PUNISHED.
I'LL SEE TO YOU LATER!
LONG AFTER I WENT TO BED, I LAY AWAKE. MISS ADA'S FACE SEEMED TO HANG IN THE DARK OVER ME. HER VOICE RANG IN MY EARS.
"I'LL SEE TO YOU LATER, I'LL SEE TO YOU LATER, I'LL SEE TO YOU LATER, LATER, LATER, LATER...."

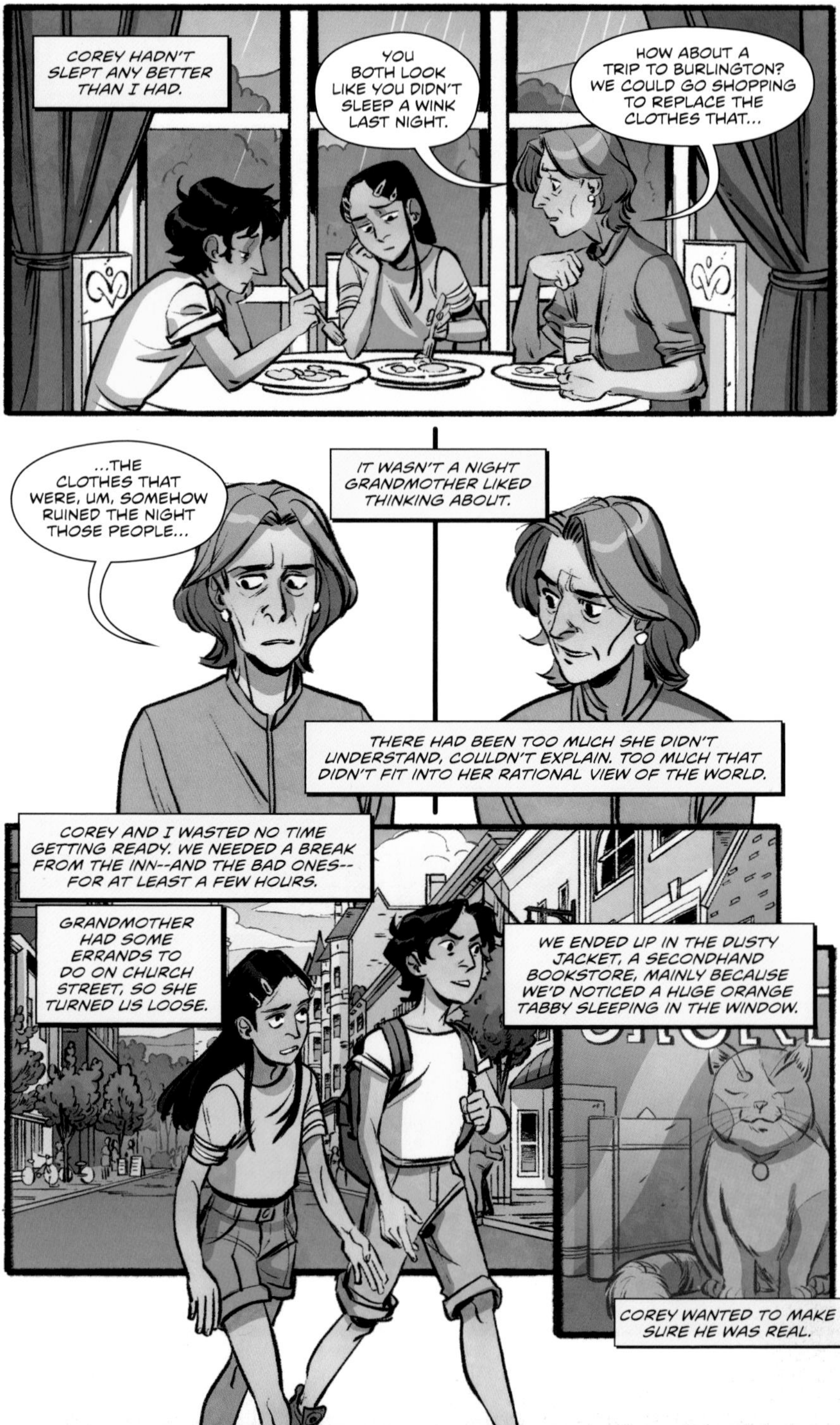
COREY HADN'T SLEPT ANY BETTER THAN I HAD.
YOU BOTH LOOK LIKE YOU DIDN'T SLEEP A WINK LAST NIGHT.
HOW ABOUT A TRIP TO BURLINGTON? WE COULD GO SHOPPING TO REPLACE THE CLOTHES THAT...
...THE CLOTHES THAT WERE, UM, SOMEHOW RUINED THE NIGHT THOSE PEOPLE...
IT WASN'T A NIGHT GRANDMOTHER LIKED THINKING ABOUT.
THERE HAD BEEN TOO MUCH SHE DIDN'T UNDERSTAND, COULDN'T EXPLAIN. TOO MUCH THAT DIDN'T FIT INTO HER RATIONAL VIEW OF THE WORLD.
COREY AND I WASTED NO TIME GETTING READY. WE NEEDED A BREAK FROM THE INN--AND THE BAD ONES--FOR AT LEAST A FEW HOURS.
GRANDMOTHER HAD SOME ERRANDS TO DO ON CHURCH STREET, SO SHE TURNED US LOOSE.
WE ENDED UP IN THE DUSTY JACKET, A SECONDHAND BOOKSTORE, MAINLY BECAUSE WE'D NOTICED A HUGE ORANGE TABBY SLEEPING IN THE WINDOW.
COREY WANTED TO MAKE SURE HE WAS REAL.

INDEED, HE IS REAL.

A WATCH CAT, THAT'S WHAT MOG IS. HE GUARDS THE PLACE AT NIGHT.

HE'S CURRENTLY RESTING UP FOR HIS NOCTURNAL ROUNDS.

DOES HE REALLY CHASE BURGLARS AWAY?

WELL, I'VE NEVER BEEN BURGLED, SO I RECKON HE DOES.

ARE YOU LOOKING FOR ANYTHING SPECIAL?

WHAT WE'D REALLY LIKE TO FIND IS A HISTORY OF FOX HILL.

OUR GRANDMOTHER OWNS IT.

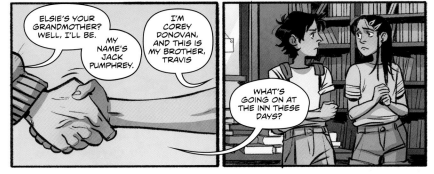

ELSIE'S YOUR GRANDMOTHER? WELL, I'LL BE.

MY NAME'S JACK PUMPHREY.

I'M COREY DONOVAN, AND THIS IS MY BROTHER, TRAVIS

WHAT'S GOING ON AT THE INN THESE DAYS?

DO YOU BELIEVE IN GHOSTS?

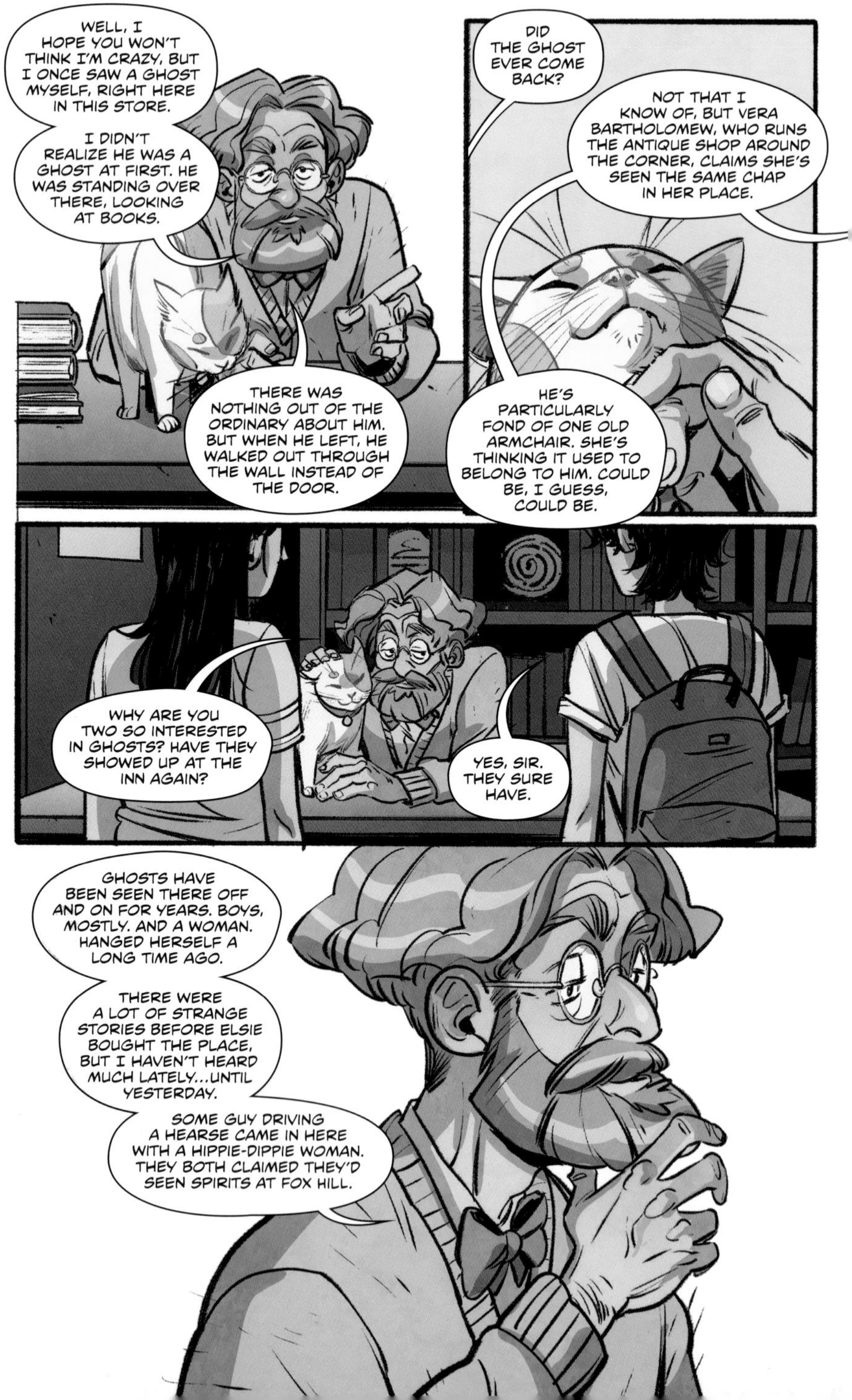
WELL, I HOPE YOU WON'T THINK I'M CRAZY, BUT I ONCE SAW A GHOST MYSELF, RIGHT HERE IN THIS STORE.
I DIDN'T REALIZE HE WAS A GHOST AT FIRST. HE WAS STANDING OVER THERE, LOOKING AT BOOKS.
THERE WAS NOTHING OUT OF THE ORDINARY ABOUT HIM. BUT WHEN HE LEFT, HE WALKED OUT THROUGH THE WALL INSTEAD OF THE DOOR.
DID THE GHOST EVER COME BACK?
NOT THAT I KNOW OF, BUT VERA BARTHOLOMEW, WHO RUNS THE ANTIQUE SHOP AROUND THE CORNER, CLAIMS SHE'S SEEN THE SAME CHAP IN HER PLACE.
HE'S PARTICULARLY FOND OF ONE OLD ARMCHAIR. SHE'S THINKING IT USED TO BELONG TO HIM. COULD BE, I GUESS, COULD BE.
WHY ARE YOU TWO SO INTERESTED IN GHOSTS? HAVE THEY SHOWED UP AT THE INN AGAIN?
YES, SIR. THEY SURE HAVE.
GHOSTS HAVE BEEN SEEN THERE OFF AND ON FOR YEARS. BOYS, MOSTLY. AND A WOMAN. HANGED HERSELF A LONG TIME AGO.
THERE WERE A LOT OF STRANGE STORIES BEFORE ELSIE BOUGHT THE PLACE, BUT I HAVEN'T HEARD MUCH LATELY...UNTIL YESTERDAY.
SOME GUY DRIVING A HEARSE CAME IN HERE WITH A HIPPIE-DIPPIE WOMAN. THEY BOTH CLAIMED THEY'D SEEN SPIRITS AT FOX HILL.

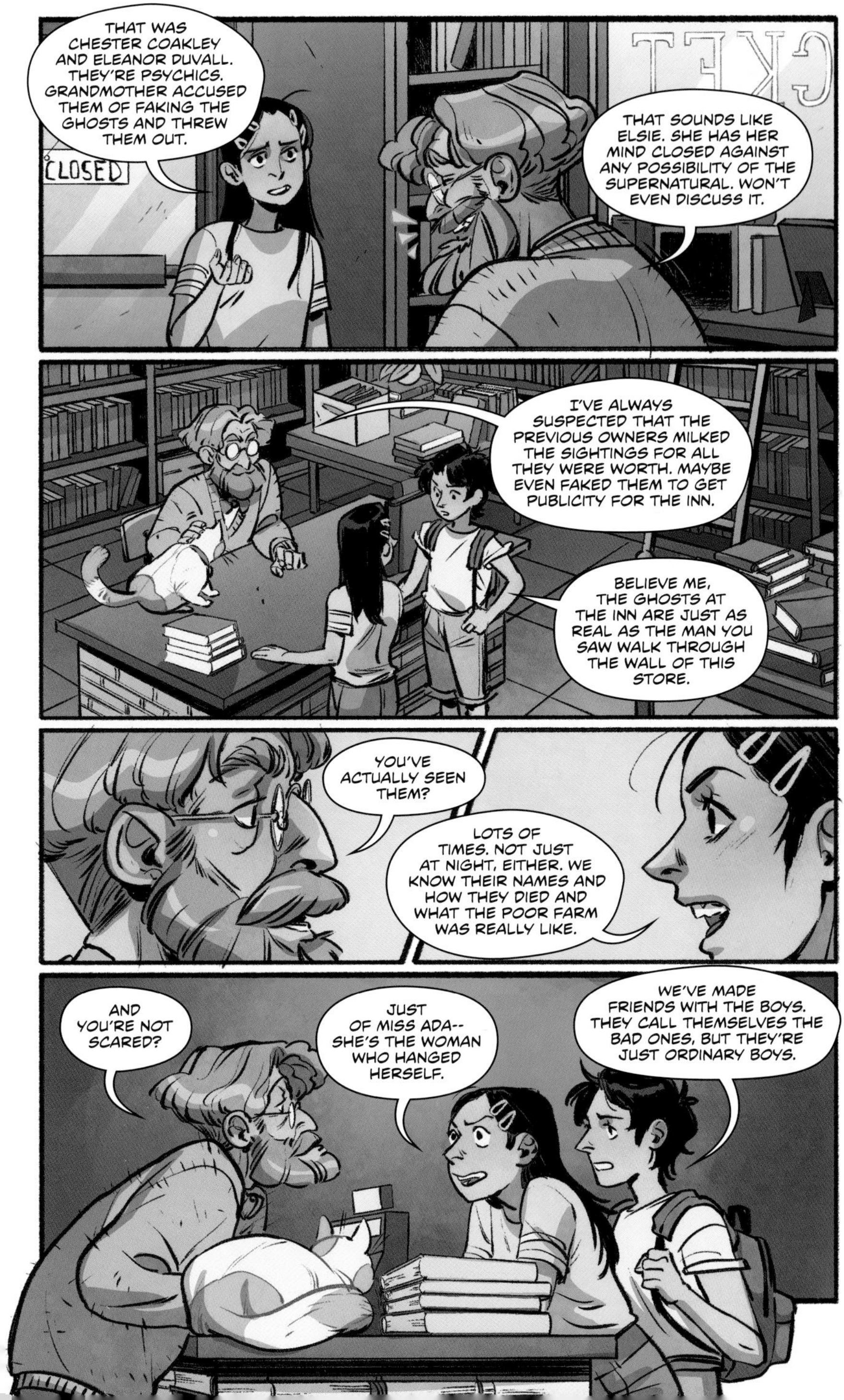
THAT WAS CHESTER COAKLEY AND ELEANOR DUVALL. THEY'RE PSYCHICS. GRANDMOTHER ACCUSED THEM OF FAKING THE GHOSTS AND THREW THEM OUT.
CLOSED
THAT SOUNDS LIKE ELSIE. SHE HAS HER MIND CLOSED AGAINST ANY POSSIBILITY OF THE SUPERNATURAL. WON'T EVEN DISCUSS IT.
I'VE ALWAYS SUSPECTED THAT THE PREVIOUS OWNERS MILKED THE SIGHTINGS FOR ALL THEY WERE WORTH. MAYBE EVEN FAKED THEM TO GET PUBLICITY FOR THE INN.
BELIEVE ME, THE GHOSTS AT THE INN ARE JUST AS REAL AS THE MAN YOU SAW WALK THROUGH THE WALL OF THIS STORE.
YOU'VE ACTUALLY SEEN THEM?
LOTS OF TIMES. NOT JUST AT NIGHT, EITHER. WE KNOW THEIR NAMES AND HOW THEY DIED AND WHAT THE POOR FARM WAS REALLY LIKE.
AND YOU'RE NOT SCARED?
JUST OF MISS ADA-- SHE'S THE WOMAN WHO HANGED HERSELF.
WE'VE MADE FRIENDS WITH THE BOYS. THEY CALL THEMSELVES THE BAD ONES, BUT THEY'RE JUST ORDINARY BOYS.

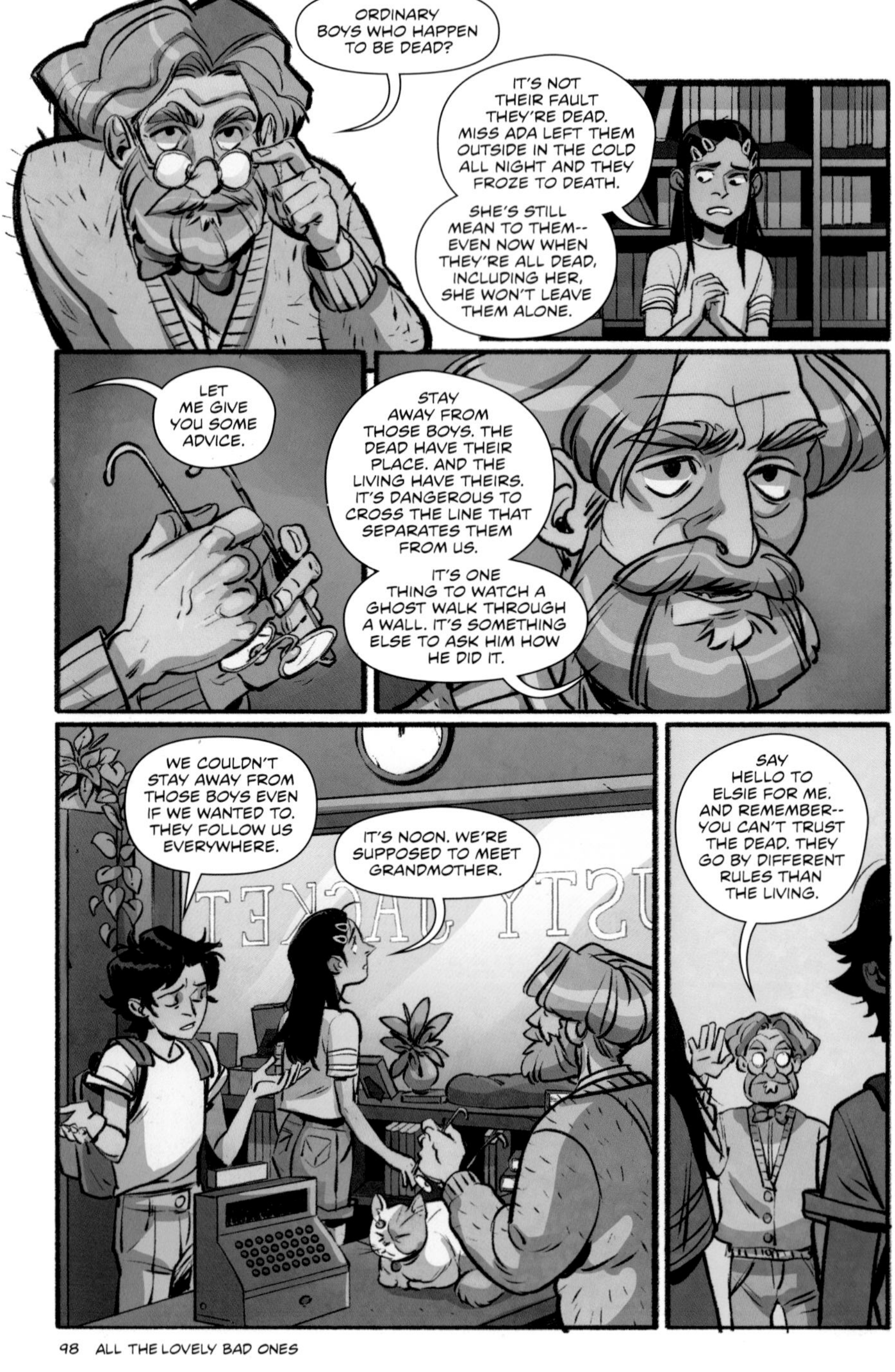
ORDINARY BOYS WHO HAPPEN TO BE DEAD?
IT'S NOT THEIR FAULT THEY'RE DEAD. MISS ADA LEFT THEM OUTSIDE IN THE COLD ALL NIGHT AND THEY FROZE TO DEATH.
SHE'S STILL MEAN TO THEM-- EVEN NOW WHEN THEY'RE ALL DEAD, INCLUDING HER, SHE WON'T LEAVE THEM ALONE.
LET ME GIVE YOU SOME ADVICE.
STAY AWAY FROM THOSE BOYS. THE DEAD HAVE THEIR PLACE. AND THE LIVING HAVE THEIRS. IT'S DANGEROUS TO CROSS THE LINE THAT SEPARATES THEM FROM US.
IT'S ONE THING TO WATCH A GHOST WALK THROUGH A WALL. IT'S SOMETHING ELSE TO ASK HIM HOW HE DID IT.
WE COULDN'T STAY AWAY FROM THOSE BOYS EVEN IF WE WANTED TO. THEY FOLLOW US EVERYWHERE.
IT'S NOON. WE'RE SUPPOSED TO MEET GRANDMOTHER.
SAY HELLO TO ELSIE FOR ME. AND REMEMBER-- YOU CAN'T TRUST THE DEAD. THEY GO BY DIFFERENT RULES THAN THE LIVING.

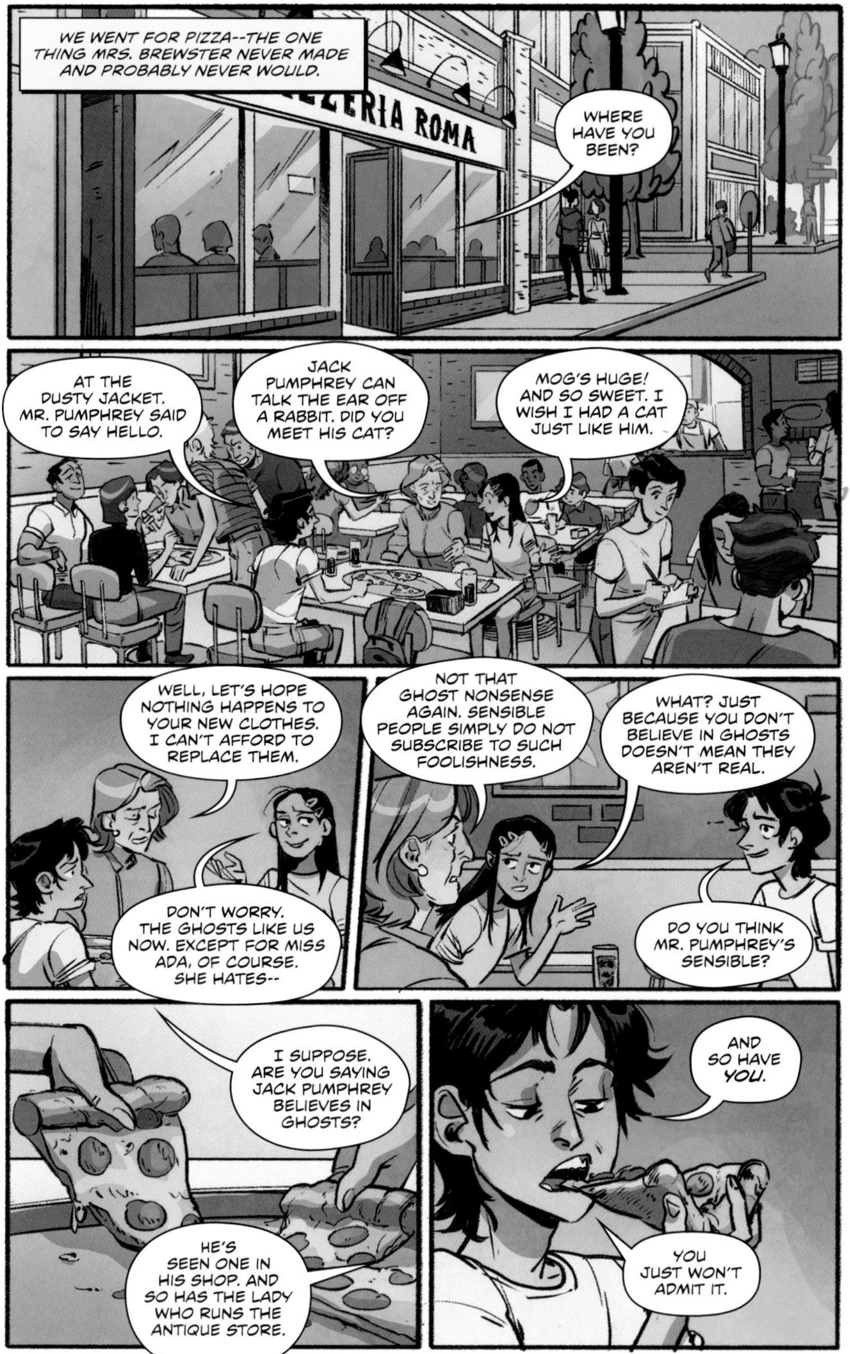
WE WENT FOR PIZZA--THE ONE THING MRS. BREWSTER NEVER MADE AND PROBABLY NEVER WOULD.
ZERIA ROMA
WHERE HAVE YOU BEEN?
AT THE DUSTY JACKET. MR. PUMPHREY SAID TO SAY HELLO.
JACK PUMPHREY CAN TALK THE EAR OFF A RABBIT. DID YOU MEET HIS CAT?
MOG'S HUGE! AND SO SWEET. I WISH I HAD A CAT JUST LIKE HIM.
WELL, LET'S HOPE NOTHING HAPPENS TO YOUR NEW CLOTHES. I CAN'T AFFORD TO REPLACE THEM.
DON'T WORRY. THE GHOSTS LIKE US NOW. EXCEPT FOR MISS ADA, OF COURSE. SHE HATES--
NOT THAT GHOST NONSENSE AGAIN. SENSIBLE PEOPLE SIMPLY DO NOT SUBSCRIBE TO SUCH FOOLISHNESS.
WHAT? JUST BECAUSE YOU DON'T BELIEVE IN GHOSTS DOESN'T MEAN THEY AREN'T REAL.
DO YOU THINK MR. PUMPHREY'S SENSIBLE?
I SUPPOSE. ARE YOU SAYING JACK PUMPHREY BELIEVES IN GHOSTS?
HE'S SEEN ONE IN HIS SHOP. AND SO HAS THE LADY WHO RUNS THE ANTIQUE STORE.
AND SO HAVE *YOU*.
YOU JUST WON'T ADMIT IT.

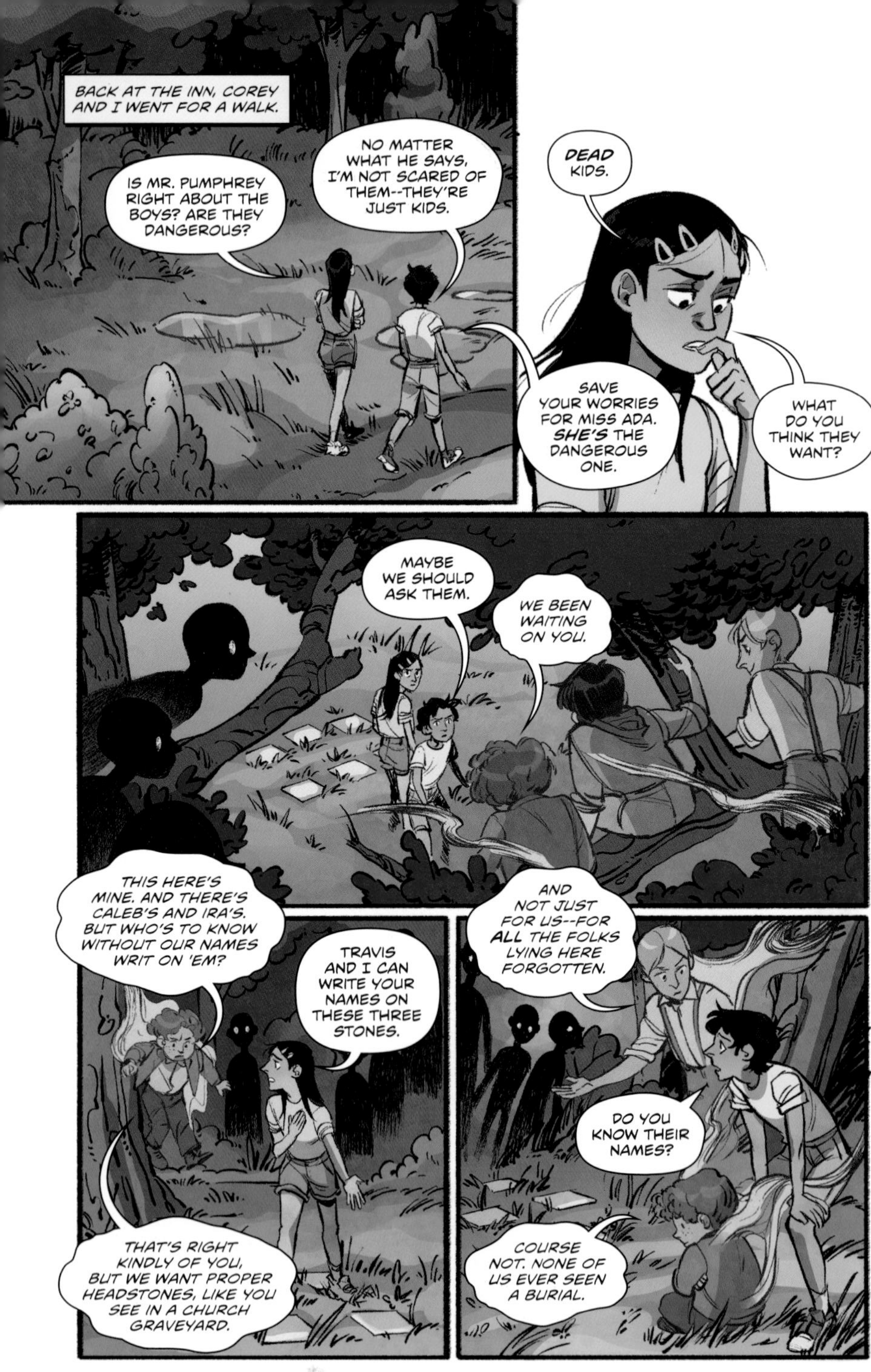
BACK AT THE INN, COREY AND I WENT FOR A WALK.
IS MR. PUMPHREY RIGHT ABOUT THE BOYS? ARE THEY DANGEROUS?
NO MATTER WHAT HE SAYS, I'M NOT SCARED OF THEM--THEY'RE JUST KIDS.
DEAD KIDS.
SAVE YOUR WORRIES FOR MISS ADA. SHE'S THE DANGEROUS ONE.
WHAT DO YOU THINK THEY WANT?
MAYBE WE SHOULD ASK THEM.
WE BEEN WAITING ON YOU.
THIS HERE'S MINE. AND THERE'S CALEB'S AND IRA'S. BUT WHO'S TO KNOW WITHOUT OUR NAMES WRIT ON 'EM?
TRAVIS AND I CAN WRITE YOUR NAMES ON THESE THREE STONES.
THAT'S RIGHT KINDLY OF YOU, BUT WE WANT PROPER HEADSTONES, LIKE YOU SEE IN A CHURCH GRAVEYARD.
AND NOT JUST FOR US--FOR ALL THE FOLKS LYING HERE FORGOTTEN.
DO YOU KNOW THEIR NAMES?
COURSE NOT. NONE OF US EVER SEEN A BURIAL.

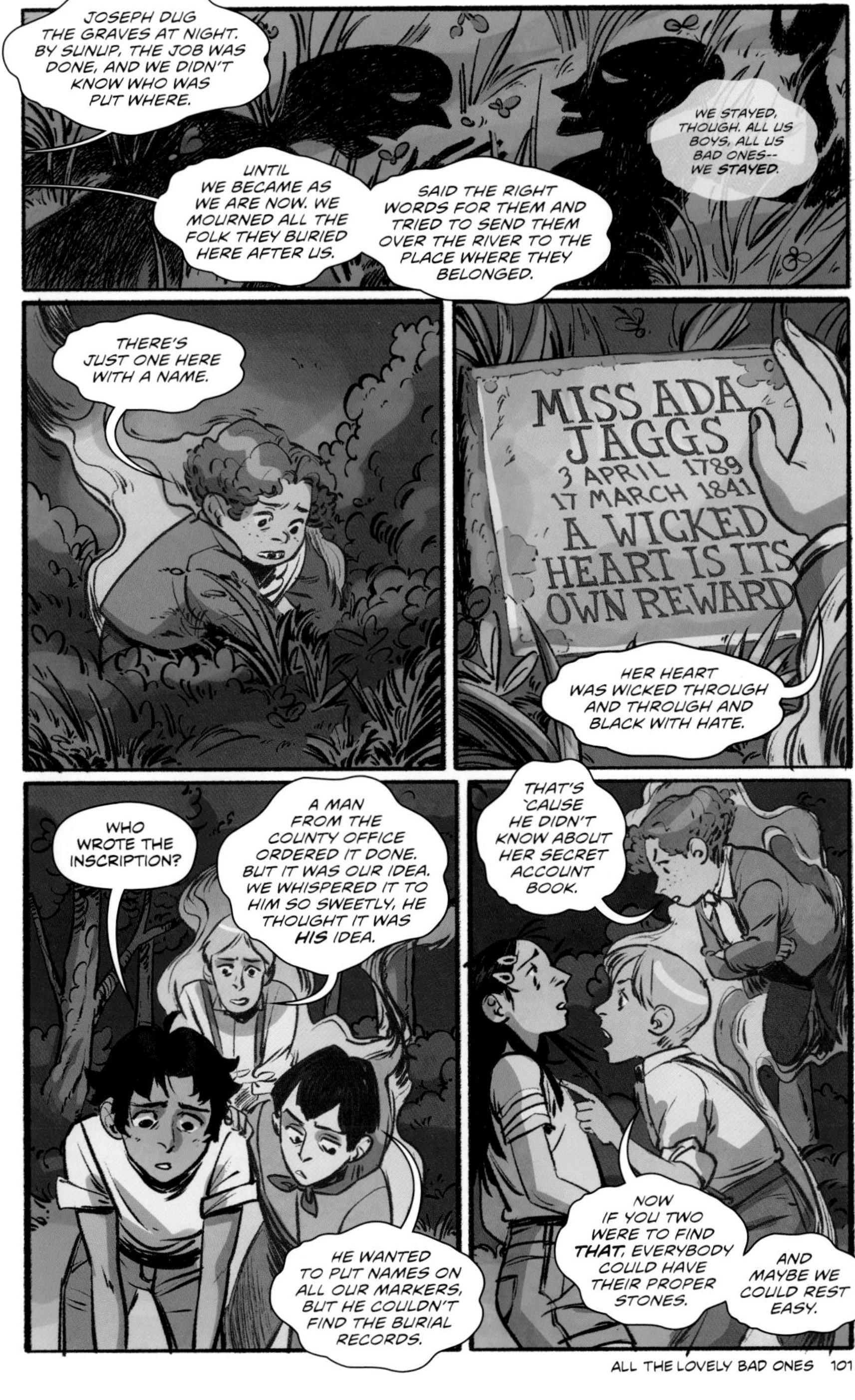
JOSEPH DUG THE GRAVES AT NIGHT. BY SUNUP, THE JOB WAS DONE, AND WE DIDN'T KNOW WHO WAS PUT WHERE.
UNTIL WE BECAME AS WE ARE NOW. WE MOURNED ALL THE FOLK THEY BURIED HERE AFTER US.
SAID THE RIGHT WORDS FOR THEM AND TRIED TO SEND THEM OVER THE RIVER TO THE PLACE WHERE THEY BELONGED.
WE STAYED, THOUGH. ALL US BOYS, ALL US BAD ONES-- WE STAYED.
THERE'S JUST ONE HERE WITH A NAME.
MISS ADA JAGGS 3 APRIL 1789 17 MARCH 1841 A WICKED HEART IS ITS OWN REWARD
HER HEART WAS WICKED THROUGH AND THROUGH AND BLACK WITH HATE.
WHO WROTE THE INSCRIPTION?
A MAN FROM THE COUNTY OFFICE ORDERED IT DONE. BUT IT WAS OUR IDEA. WE WHISPERED IT TO HIM SO SWEETLY, HE THOUGHT IT WAS HIS IDEA.
HE WANTED TO PUT NAMES ON ALL OUR MARKERS, BUT HE COULDN'T FIND THE BURIAL RECORDS.
THAT'S 'CAUSE HE DIDN'T KNOW ABOUT HER SECRET ACCOUNT BOOK.
NOW IF YOU TWO WERE TO FIND THAT, EVERYBODY COULD HAVE THEIR PROPER STONES.
AND MAYBE WE COULD REST EASY.

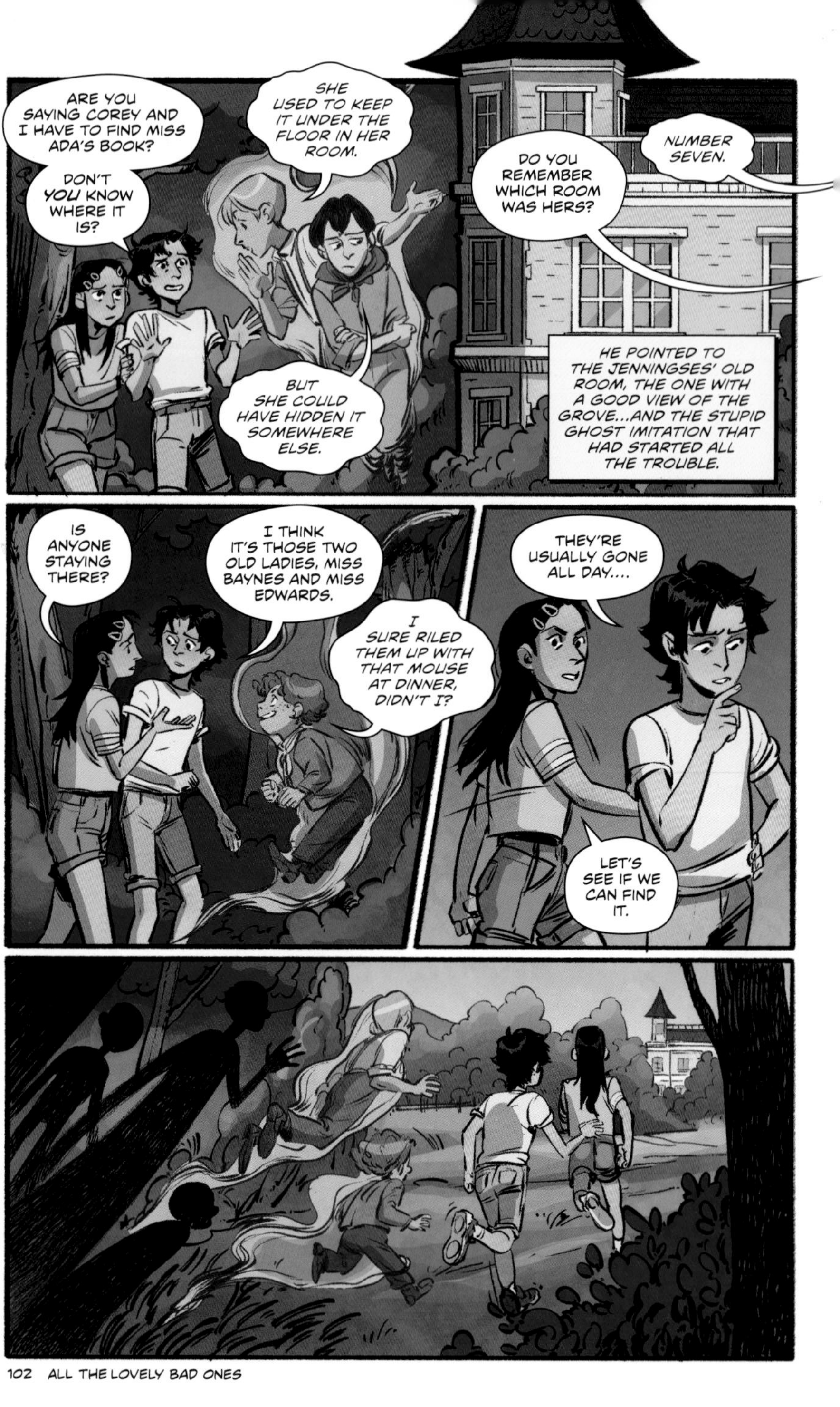
ARE YOU SAYING COREY AND I HAVE TO FIND MISS ADA'S BOOK?
DON'T *YOU* KNOW WHERE IT IS?
SHE USED TO KEEP IT UNDER THE FLOOR IN HER ROOM.
BUT SHE COULD HAVE HIDDEN IT SOMEWHERE ELSE.
DO YOU REMEMBER WHICH ROOM WAS HERS?
NUMBER SEVEN.
HE POINTED TO THE JENNINGSES' OLD ROOM, THE ONE WITH A GOOD VIEW OF THE GROVE...AND THE STUPID GHOST IMITATION THAT HAD STARTED ALL THE TROUBLE.
IS ANYONE STAYING THERE?
I THINK IT'S THOSE TWO OLD LADIES, MISS BAYNES AND MISS EDWARDS.
I SURE RILED THEM UP WITH THAT MOUSE AT DINNER, DIDN'T I?
THEY'RE USUALLY GONE ALL DAY....
LET'S SEE IF WE CAN FIND IT.

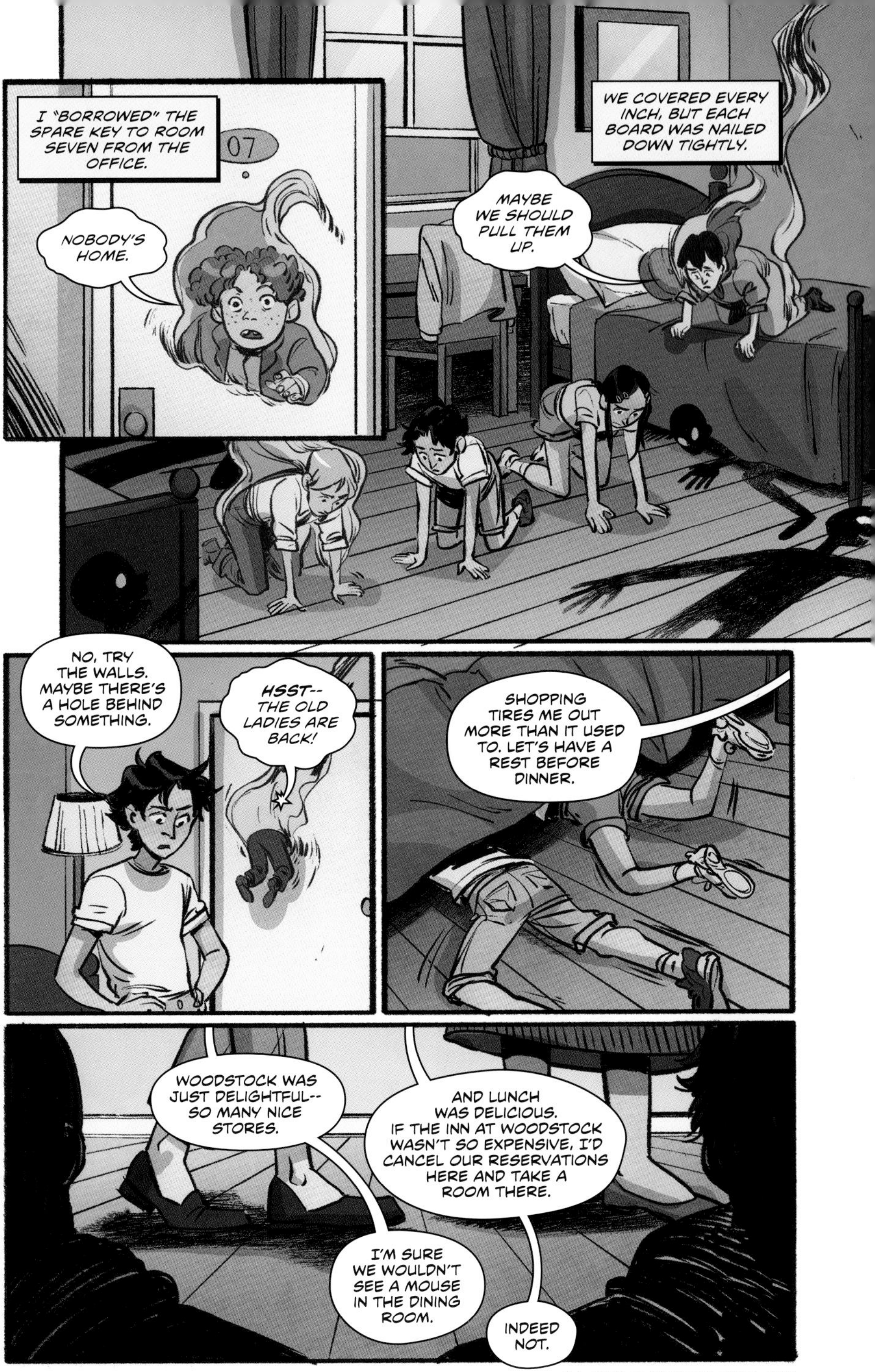

I "BORROWED" THE SPARE KEY TO ROOM SEVEN FROM THE OFFICE.
07
NOBODY'S HOME.
WE COVERED EVERY INCH, BUT EACH BOARD WAS NAILED DOWN TIGHTLY.
MAYBE WE SHOULD PULL THEM UP.
NO, TRY THE WALLS. MAYBE THERE'S A HOLE BEHIND SOMETHING.
HSST-- THE OLD LADIES ARE BACK!
SHOPPING TIRES ME OUT MORE THAN IT USED TO. LET'S HAVE A REST BEFORE DINNER.
WOODSTOCK WAS JUST DELIGHTFUL-- SO MANY NICE STORES.
AND LUNCH WAS DELICIOUS. IF THE INN AT WOODSTOCK WASN'T SO EXPENSIVE, I'D CANCEL OUR RESERVATIONS HERE AND TAKE A ROOM THERE.
I'M SURE WE WOULDN'T SEE A MOUSE IN THE DINING ROOM.
INDEED NOT.

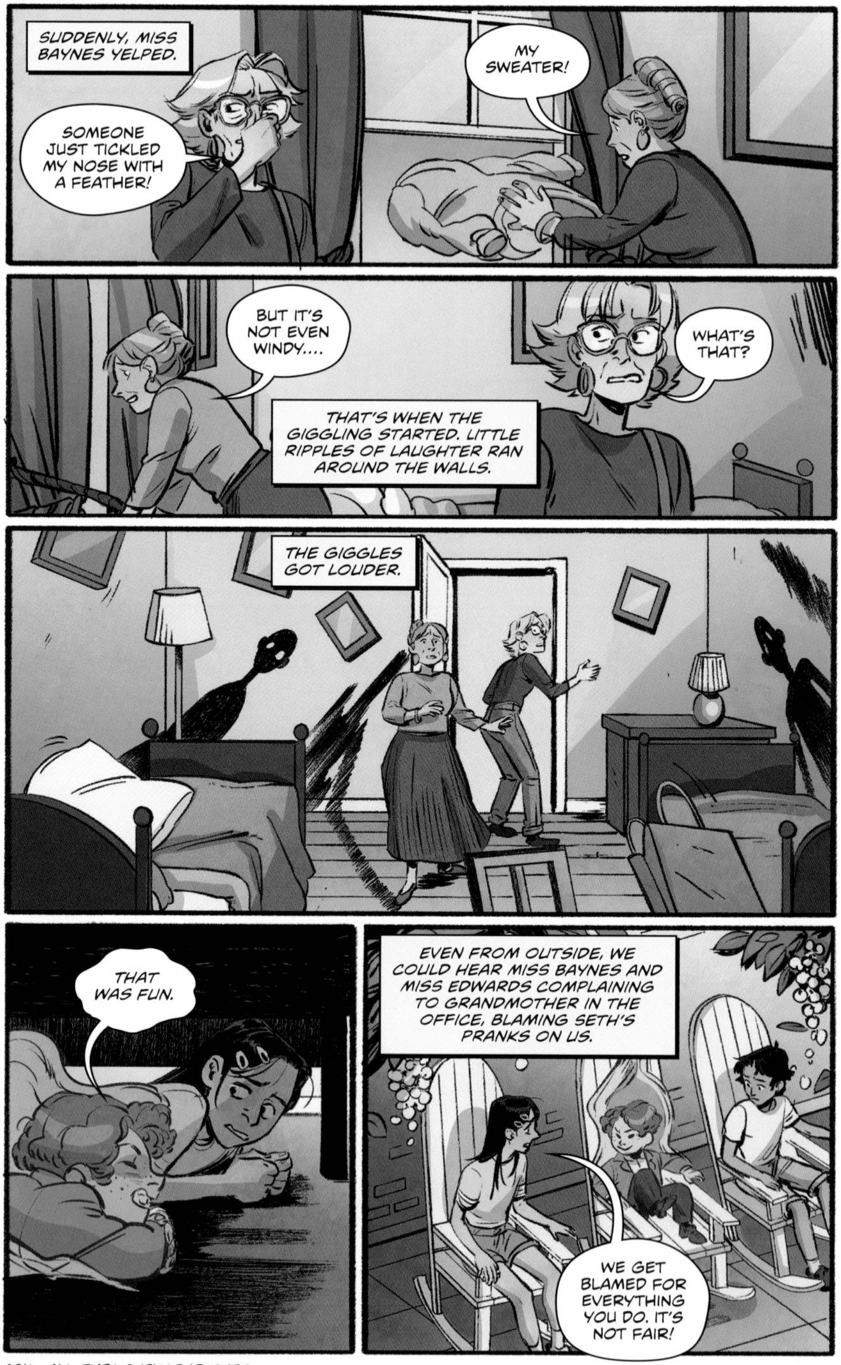

SUDDENLY, MISS BAYNES YELPED.
SOMEONE JUST TICKLED MY NOSE WITH A FEATHER!
MY SWEATER!
BUT IT'S NOT EVEN WINDY....
WHAT'S THAT?
THAT'S WHEN THE GIGGLING STARTED. LITTLE RIPPLES OF LAUGHTER RAN AROUND THE WALLS.
THE GIGGLES GOT LOUDER.
THAT WAS FUN.
EVEN FROM OUTSIDE, WE COULD HEAR MISS BAYNES AND MISS EDWARDS COMPLAINING TO GRANDMOTHER IN THE OFFICE, BLAMING SETH'S PRANKS ON US.
WE GET BLAMED FOR EVERYTHING YOU DO. IT'S NOT FAIR!

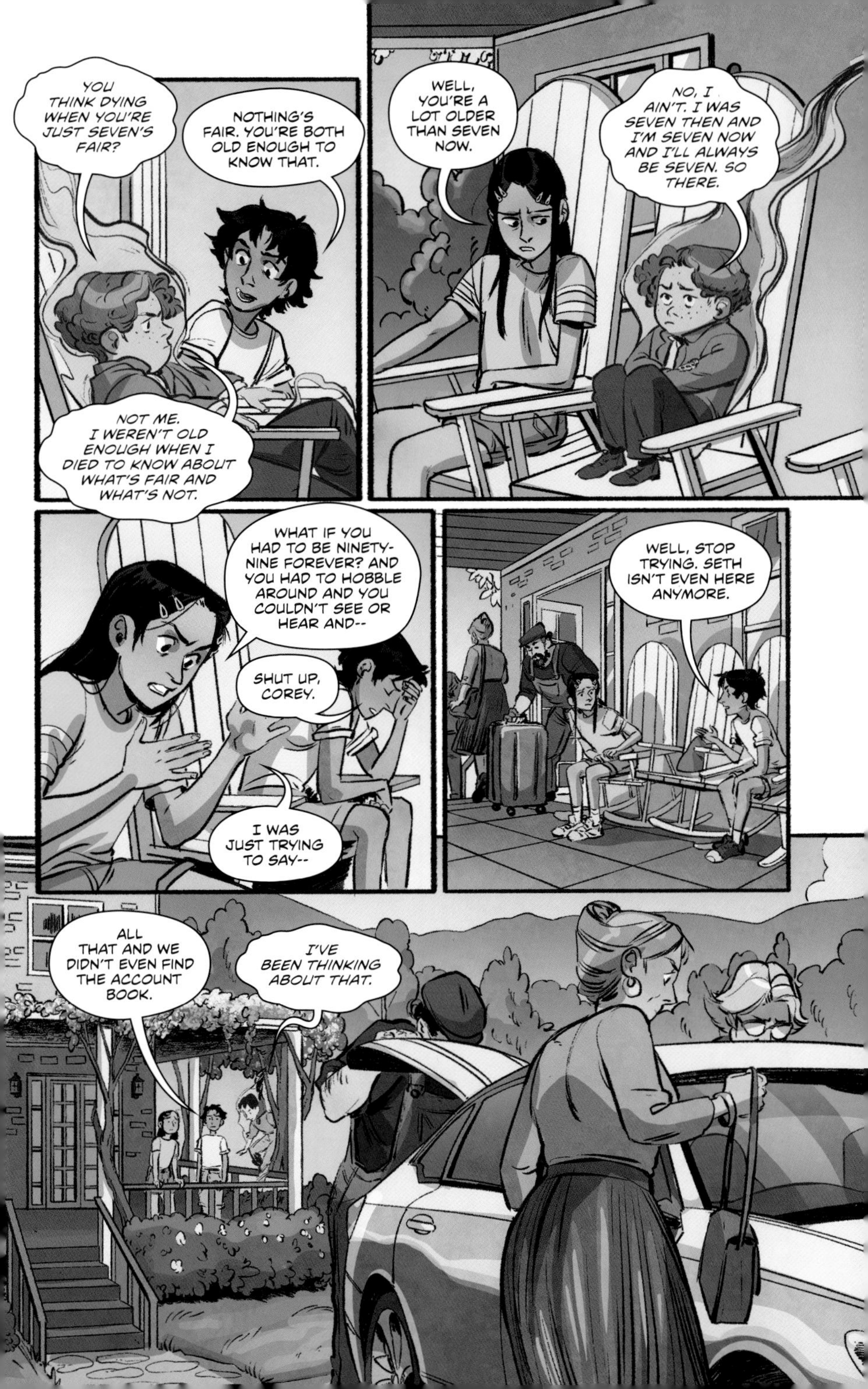
YOU THINK DYING WHEN YOU'RE JUST SEVEN'S FAIR?
NOTHING'S FAIR. YOU'RE BOTH OLD ENOUGH TO KNOW THAT.
NOT ME. I WEREN'T OLD ENOUGH WHEN I DIED TO KNOW ABOUT WHAT'S FAIR AND WHAT'S NOT.
WELL, YOU'RE A LOT OLDER THAN SEVEN NOW.
NO, I AIN'T. I WAS SEVEN THEN AND I'M SEVEN NOW AND I'LL ALWAYS BE SEVEN. SO THERE.
WHAT IF YOU HAD TO BE NINETY-NINE FOREVER? AND YOU HAD TO HOBBLE AROUND AND YOU COULDN'T SEE OR HEAR AND--
SHUT UP, COREY.
I WAS JUST TRYING TO SAY--
WELL, STOP TRYING. SETH ISN'T EVEN HERE ANYMORE.
ALL THAT AND WE DIDN'T EVEN FIND THE ACCOUNT BOOK.
I'VE BEEN THINKING ABOUT THAT.

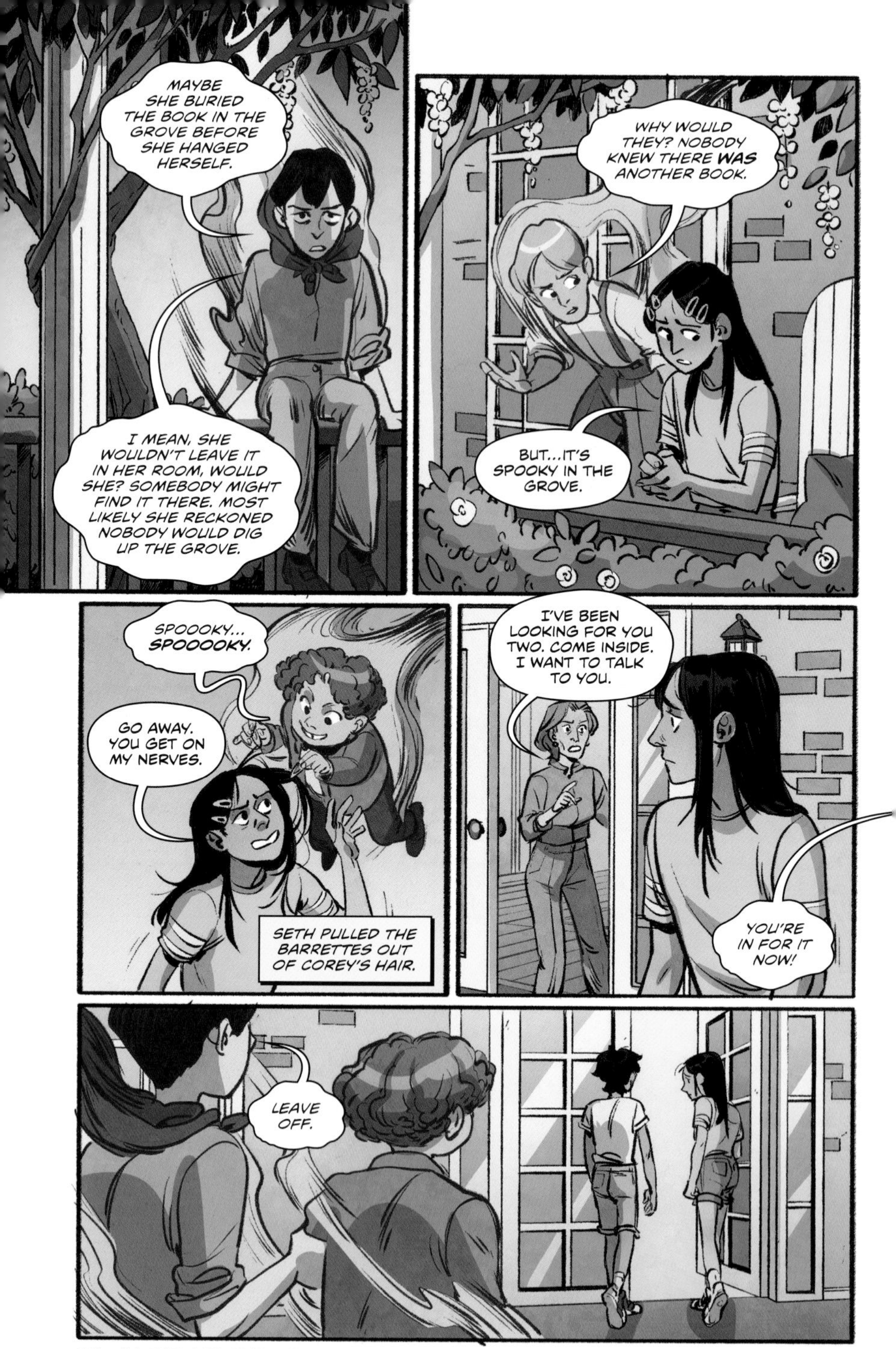
MAYBE SHE BURIED THE BOOK IN THE GROVE BEFORE SHE HANGED HERSELF.
I MEAN, SHE WOULDN'T LEAVE IT IN HER ROOM, WOULD SHE? SOMEBODY MIGHT FIND IT THERE. MOST LIKELY SHE RECKONED NOBODY WOULD DIG UP THE GROVE.
WHY WOULD THEY? NOBODY KNEW THERE **WAS** ANOTHER BOOK.
BUT...IT'S SPOOKY IN THE GROVE.
SPOOOKY... **SPOOOOKY.**
GO AWAY. YOU GET ON MY NERVES.
SETH PULLED THE BARRETTES OUT OF COREY'S HAIR.
I'VE BEEN LOOKING FOR YOU TWO. COME INSIDE. I WANT TO TALK TO YOU.
YOU'RE IN FOR IT NOW!
LEAVE OFF.

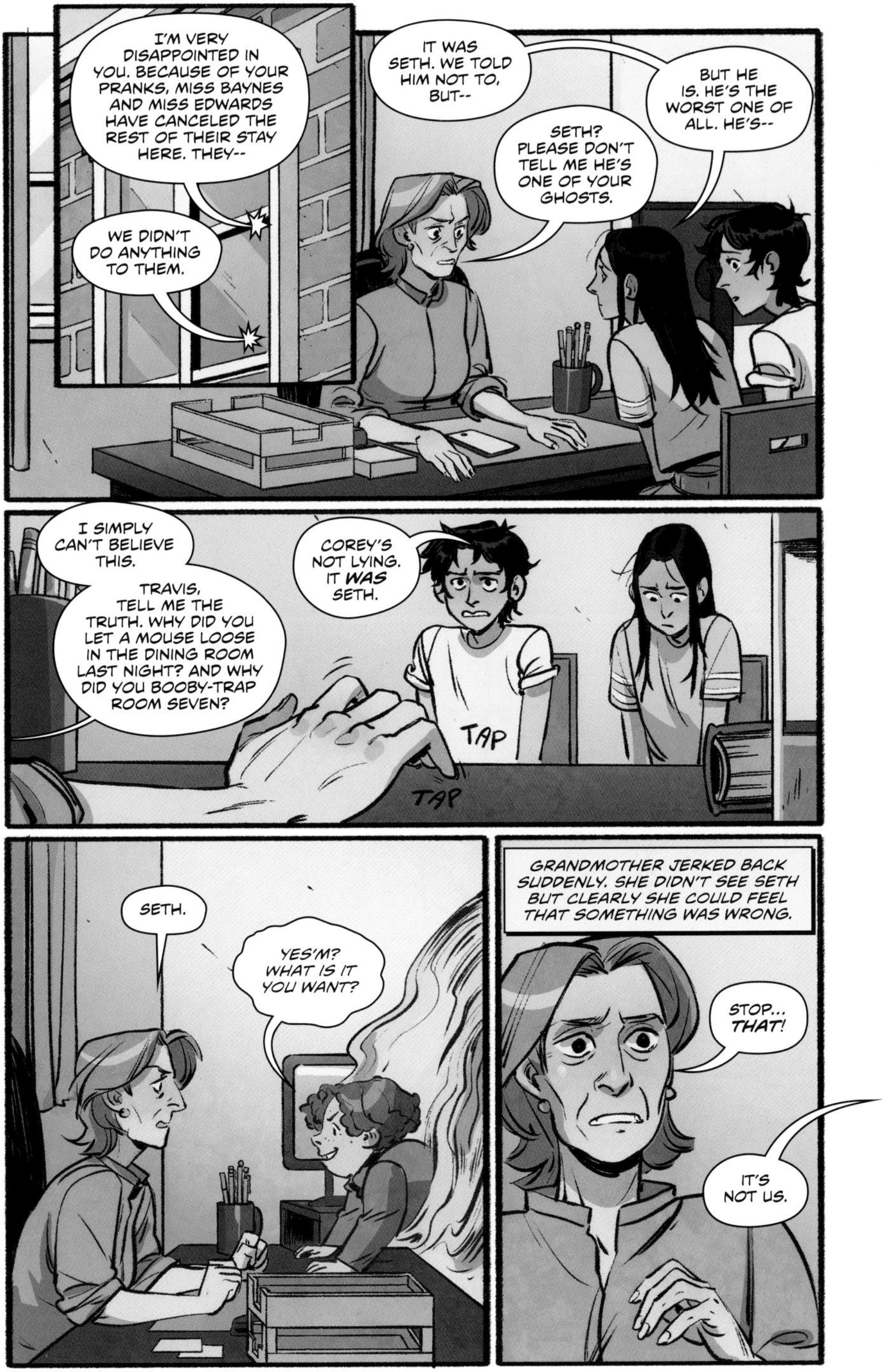
I'M VERY DISAPPOINTED IN YOU. BECAUSE OF YOUR PRANKS, MISS BAYNES AND MISS EDWARDS HAVE CANCELED THE REST OF THEIR STAY HERE. THEY--
WE DIDN'T DO ANYTHING TO THEM.
IT WAS SETH. WE TOLD HIM NOT TO, BUT--
SETH? PLEASE DON'T TELL ME HE'S ONE OF YOUR GHOSTS.
BUT HE IS. HE'S THE WORST ONE OF ALL. HE'S--
I SIMPLY CAN'T BELIEVE THIS.
TRAVIS, TELL ME THE TRUTH. WHY DID YOU LET A MOUSE LOOSE IN THE DINING ROOM LAST NIGHT? AND WHY DID YOU BOOBY-TRAP ROOM SEVEN?
COREY'S NOT LYING. IT WAS SETH.
TAP
TAP
SETH.
YES'M? WHAT IS IT YOU WANT?
GRANDMOTHER JERKED BACK SUDDENLY. SHE DIDN'T SEE SETH BUT CLEARLY SHE COULD FEEL THAT SOMETHING WAS WRONG.
STOP... THAT!
IT'S NOT US.

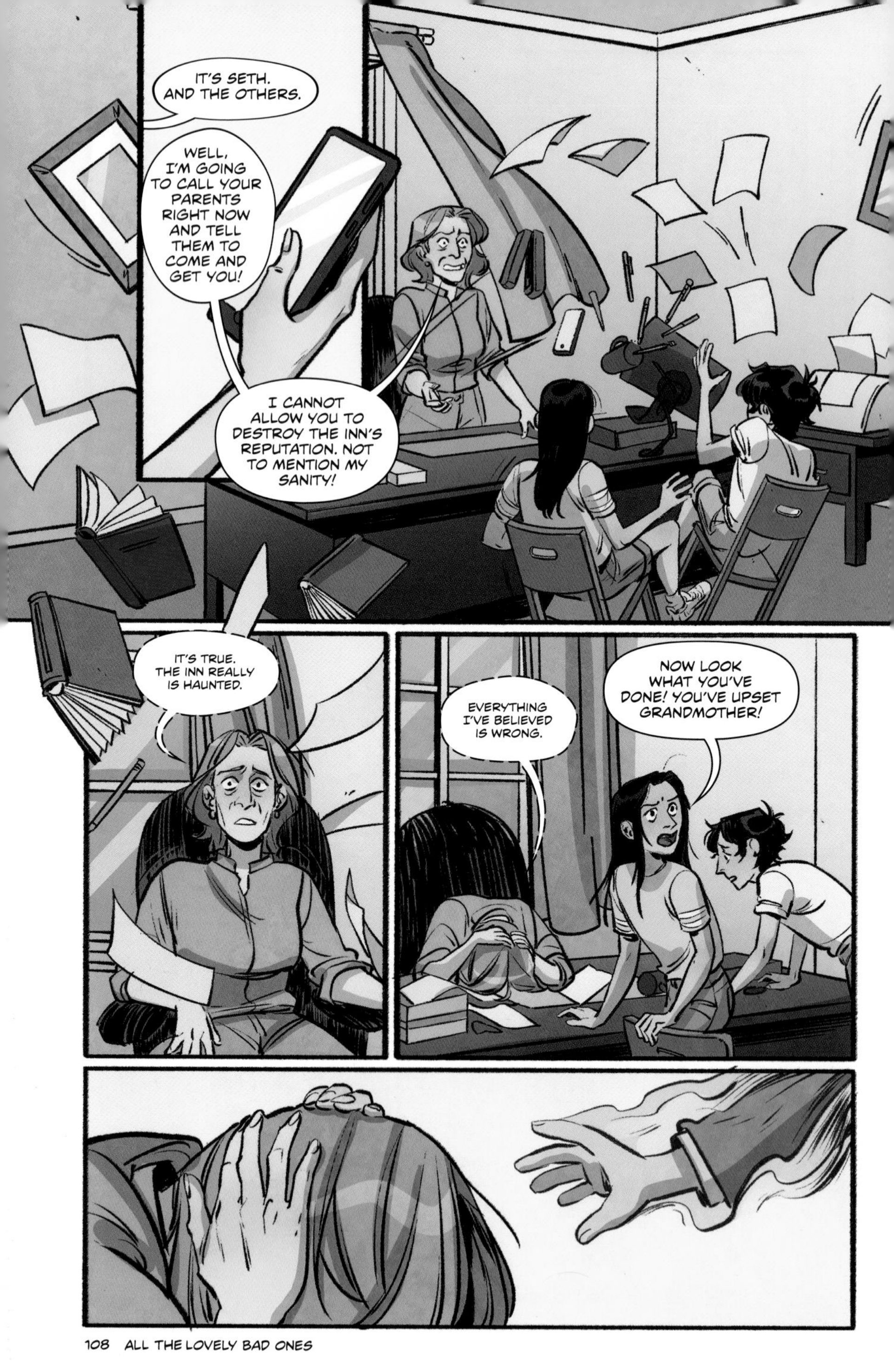
IT'S SETH. AND THE OTHERS.
WELL, I'M GOING TO CALL YOUR PARENTS RIGHT NOW AND TELL THEM TO COME AND GET YOU!
I CANNOT ALLOW YOU TO DESTROY THE INN'S REPUTATION. NOT TO MENTION MY SANITY!
IT'S TRUE. THE INN REALLY IS HAUNTED.
EVERYTHING I'VE BELIEVED IS WRONG.
NOW LOOK WHAT YOU'VE DONE! YOU'VE UPSET GRANDMOTHER!

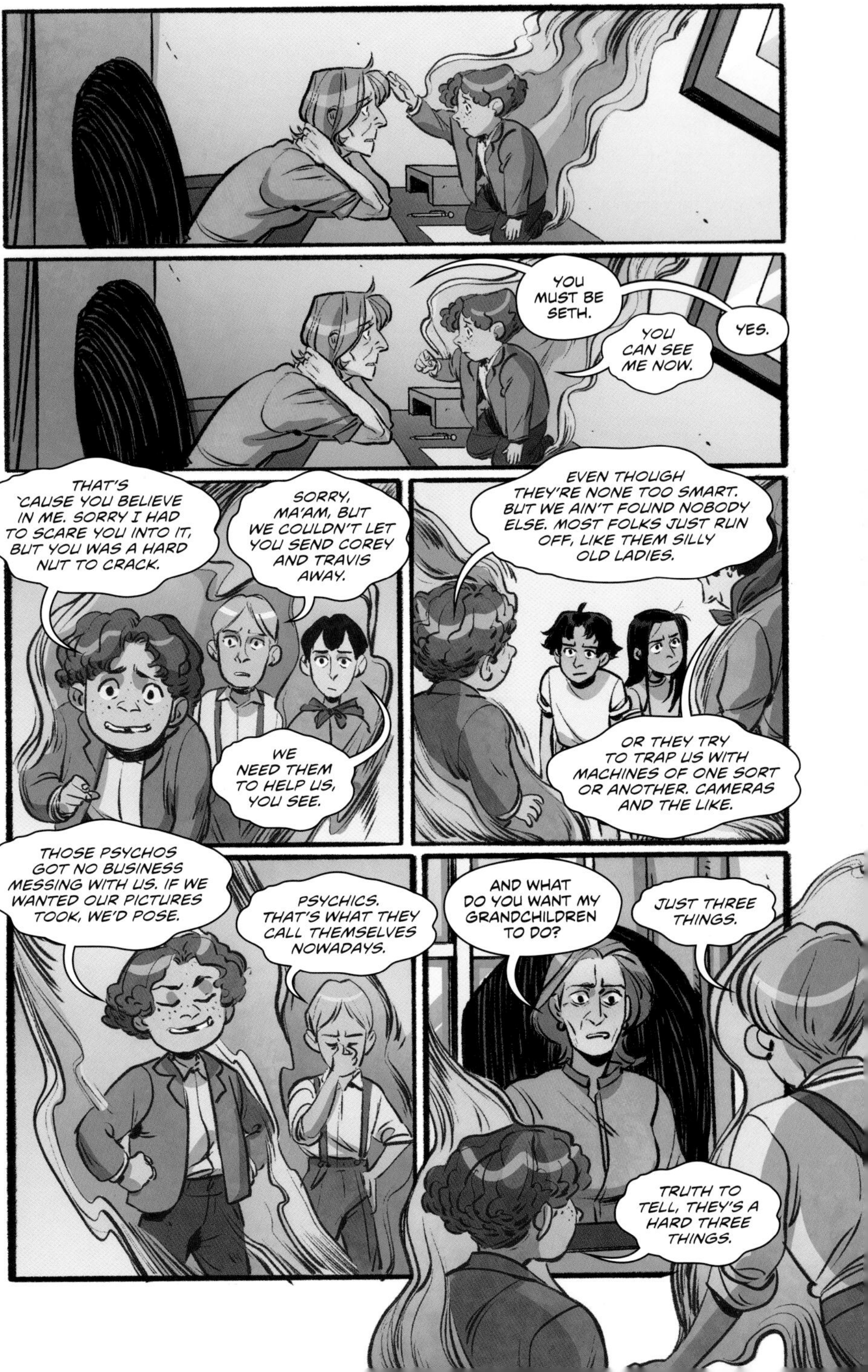
YOU MUST BE SETH.
YES.
YOU CAN SEE ME NOW.
THAT'S 'CAUSE YOU BELIEVE IN ME. SORRY I HAD TO SCARE YOU INTO IT, BUT YOU WAS A HARD NUT TO CRACK.
SORRY, MA'AM, BUT WE COULDN'T LET YOU SEND COREY AND TRAVIS AWAY.
WE NEED THEM TO HELP US, YOU SEE.
EVEN THOUGH THEY'RE NONE TOO SMART. BUT WE AIN'T FOUND NOBODY ELSE. MOST FOLKS JUST RUN OFF, LIKE THEM SILLY OLD LADIES.
OR THEY TRY TO TRAP US WITH MACHINES OF ONE SORT OR ANOTHER. CAMERAS AND THE LIKE.
THOSE PSYCHOS GOT NO BUSINESS MESSING WITH US. IF WE WANTED OUR PICTURES TOOK, WE'D POSE.
PSYCHICS. THAT'S WHAT THEY CALL THEMSELVES NOWADAYS.
AND WHAT DO YOU WANT MY GRANDCHILDREN TO DO?
JUST THREE THINGS.
TRUTH TO TELL, THEY'S A HARD THREE THINGS.

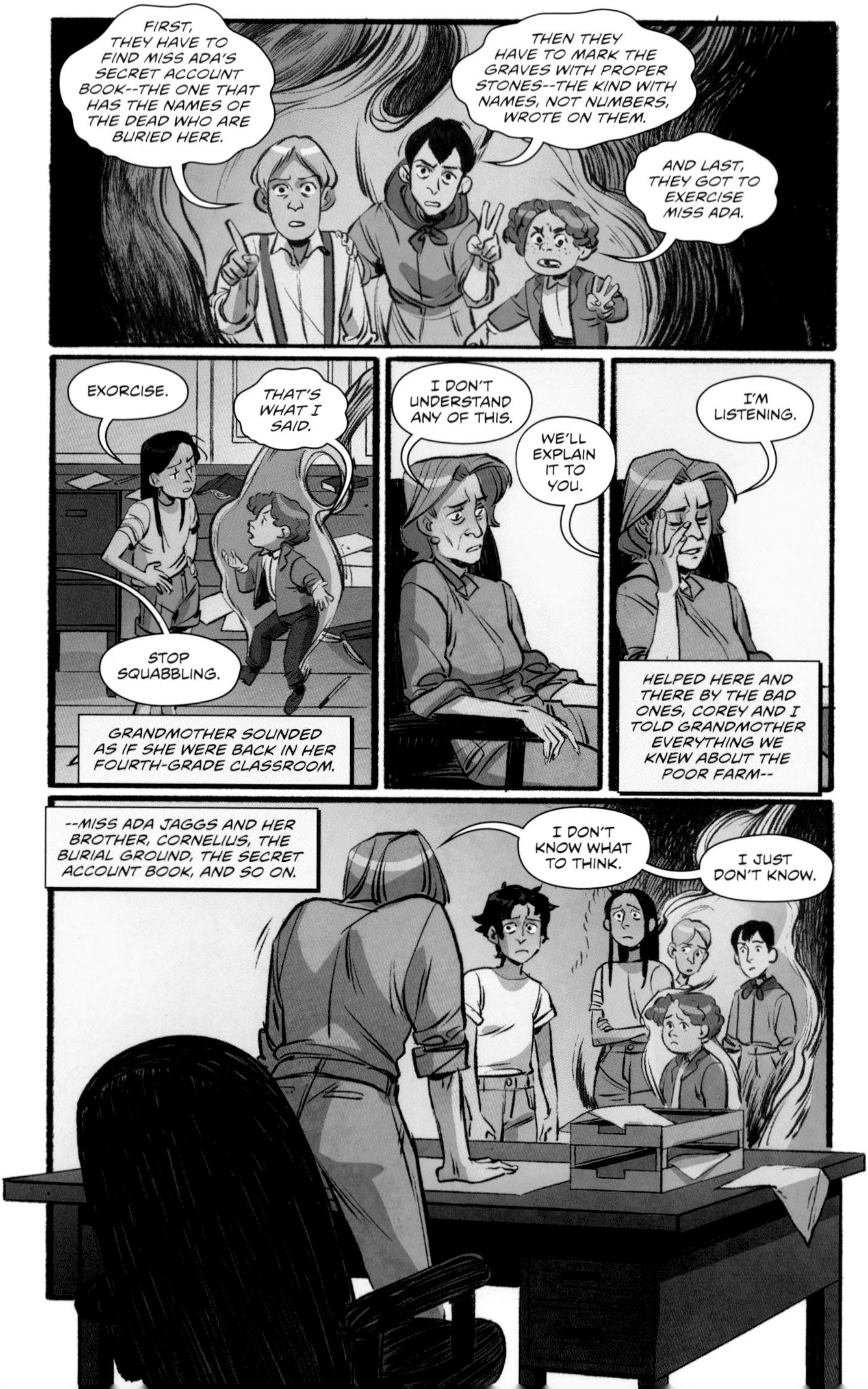

FIRST, THEY HAVE TO FIND MISS ADA'S SECRET ACCOUNT BOOK--THE ONE THAT HAS THE NAMES OF THE DEAD WHO ARE BURIED HERE.
THEN THEY HAVE TO MARK THE GRAVES WITH PROPER STONES--THE KIND WITH NAMES, NOT NUMBERS, WROTE ON THEM.
AND LAST, THEY GOT TO EXERCISE MISS ADA.
EXORCISE.
THAT'S WHAT I SAID.
STOP SQUABBLING.
GRANDMOTHER SOUNDED AS IF SHE WERE BACK IN HER FOURTH-GRADE CLASSROOM.
I DON'T UNDERSTAND ANY OF THIS.
WE'LL EXPLAIN IT TO YOU.
I'M LISTENING.
HELPED HERE AND THERE BY THE BAD ONES, COREY AND I TOLD GRANDMOTHER EVERYTHING WE KNEW ABOUT THE POOR FARM--
--MISS ADA JAGGS AND HER BROTHER, CORNELIUS, THE BURIAL GROUND, THE SECRET ACCOUNT BOOK, AND SO ON.
I DON'T KNOW WHAT TO THINK.
I JUST DON'T KNOW.

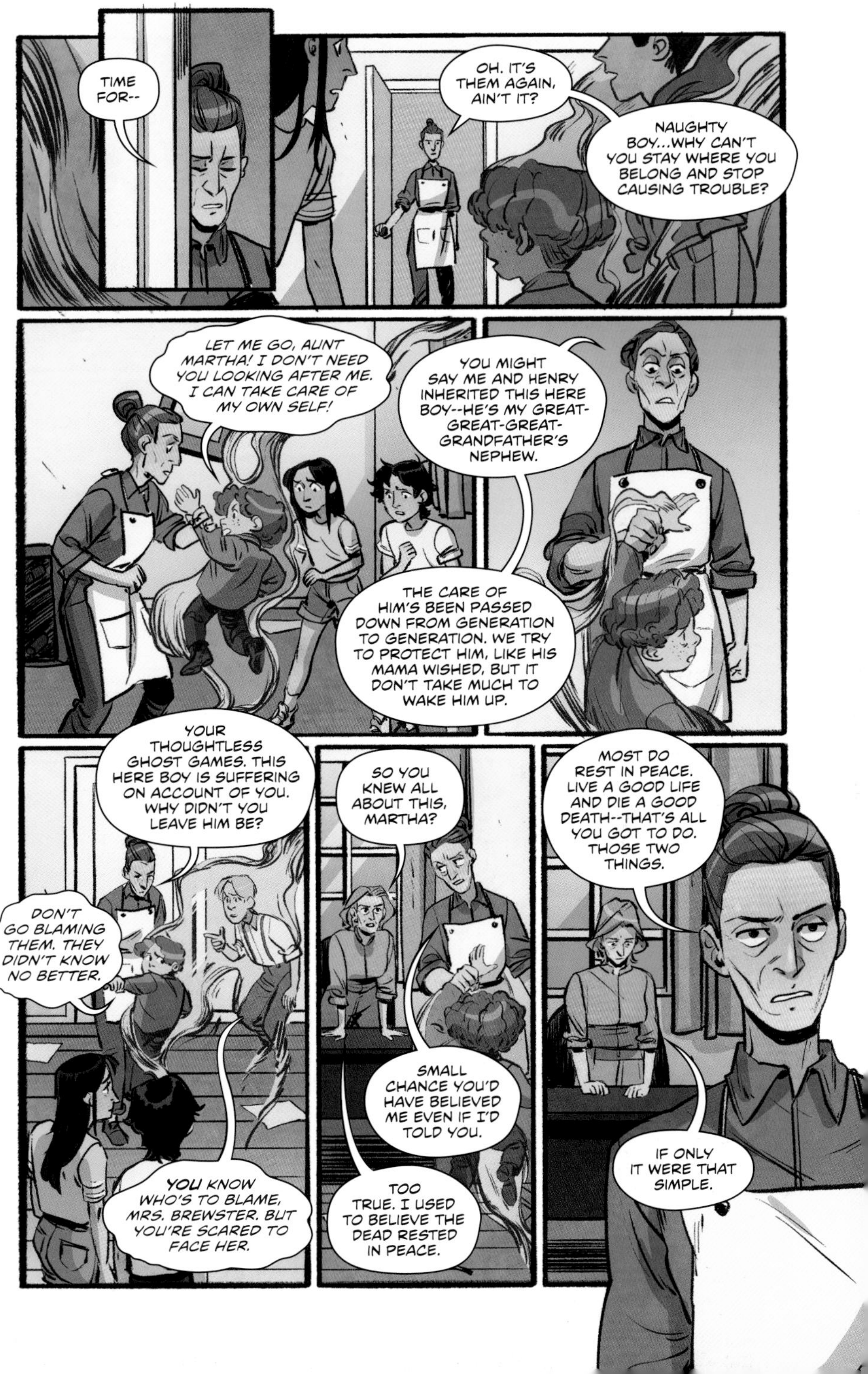
TIME FOR--
OH. IT'S THEM AGAIN, AIN'T IT?
NAUGHTY BOY...WHY CAN'T YOU STAY WHERE YOU BELONG AND STOP CAUSING TROUBLE?
LET ME GO, AUNT MARTHA! I DON'T NEED YOU LOOKING AFTER ME. I CAN TAKE CARE OF MY OWN SELF!
YOU MIGHT SAY ME AND HENRY INHERITED THIS HERE BOY--HE'S MY GREAT-GREAT-GREAT-GRANDFATHER'S NEPHEW.
THE CARE OF HIM'S BEEN PASSED DOWN FROM GENERATION TO GENERATION. WE TRY TO PROTECT HIM, LIKE HIS MAMA WISHED, BUT IT DON'T TAKE MUCH TO WAKE HIM UP.
YOUR THOUGHTLESS GHOST GAMES. THIS HERE BOY IS SUFFERING ON ACCOUNT OF YOU. WHY DIDN'T YOU LEAVE HIM BE?
DON'T GO BLAMING THEM. THEY DIDN'T KNOW NO BETTER.
YOU KNOW WHO'S TO BLAME, MRS. BREWSTER. BUT YOU'RE SCARED TO FACE HER.
SO YOU KNEW ALL ABOUT THIS, MARTHA?
SMALL CHANCE YOU'D HAVE BELIEVED ME EVEN IF I'D TOLD YOU.
TOO TRUE. I USED TO BELIEVE THE DEAD RESTED IN PEACE.
MOST DO REST IN PEACE. LIVE A GOOD LIFE AND DIE A GOOD DEATH--THAT'S ALL YOU GOT TO DO. THOSE TWO THINGS.
IF ONLY IT WERE THAT SIMPLE.

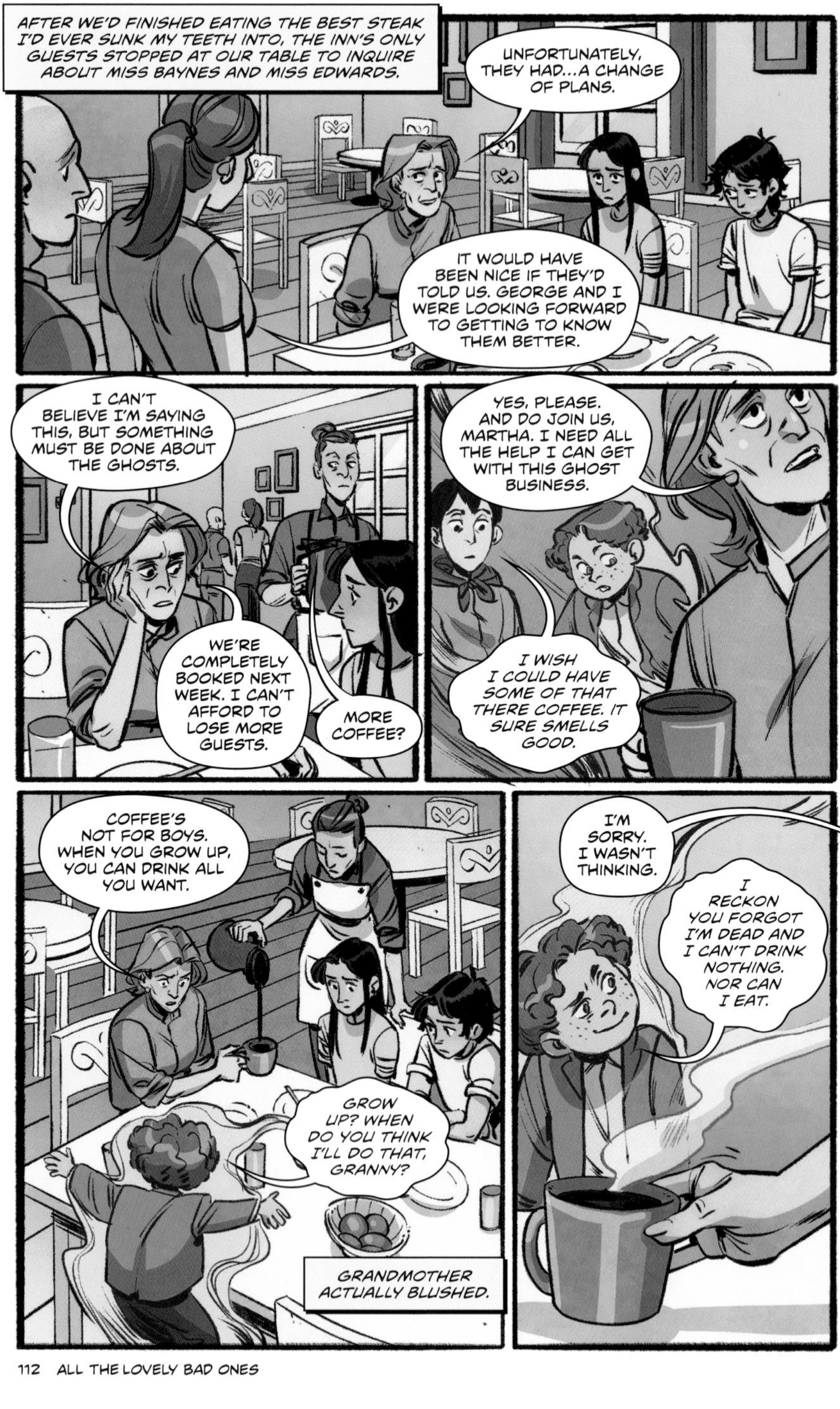
AFTER WE'D FINISHED EATING THE BEST STEAK I'D EVER SUNK MY TEETH INTO, THE INN'S ONLY GUESTS STOPPED AT OUR TABLE TO INQUIRE ABOUT MISS BAYNES AND MISS EDWARDS.
UNFORTUNATELY, THEY HAD...A CHANGE OF PLANS.
IT WOULD HAVE BEEN NICE IF THEY'D TOLD US. GEORGE AND I WERE LOOKING FORWARD TO GETTING TO KNOW THEM BETTER.
I CAN'T BELIEVE I'M SAYING THIS, BUT SOMETHING MUST BE DONE ABOUT THE GHOSTS.
WE'RE COMPLETELY BOOKED NEXT WEEK. I CAN'T AFFORD TO LOSE MORE GUESTS.
MORE COFFEE?
YES, PLEASE. AND DO JOIN US, MARTHA. I NEED ALL THE HELP I CAN GET WITH THIS GHOST BUSINESS.
I WISH I COULD HAVE SOME OF THAT THERE COFFEE. IT SURE SMELLS GOOD.
COFFEE'S NOT FOR BOYS. WHEN YOU GROW UP, YOU CAN DRINK ALL YOU WANT.
GROW UP? WHEN DO YOU THINK I'LL DO THAT, GRANNY?
GRANDMOTHER ACTUALLY BLUSHED.
I'M SORRY. I WASN'T THINKING.
I RECKON YOU FORGOT I'M DEAD AND I CAN'T DRINK NOTHING. NOR CAN I EAT.

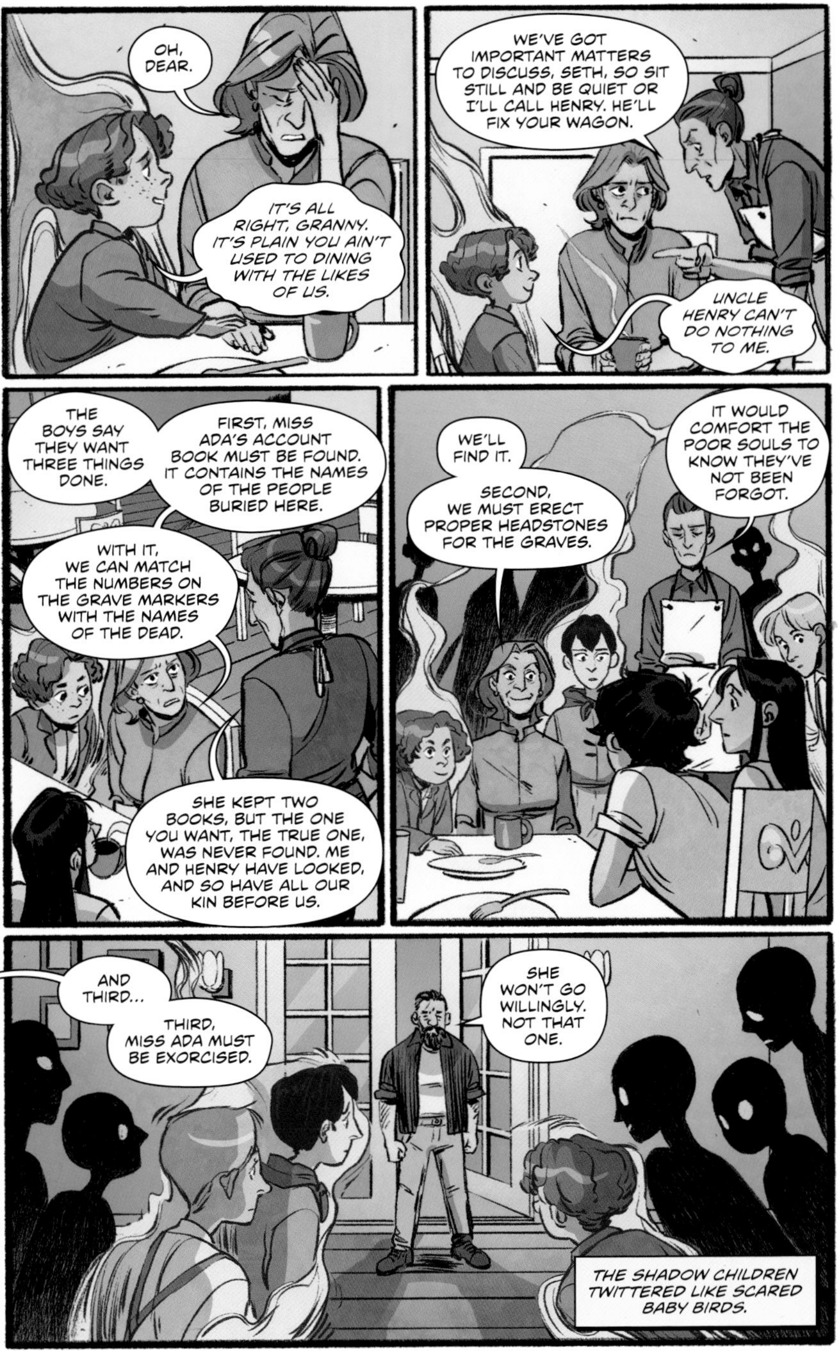
OH, DEAR.
IT'S ALL RIGHT, GRANNY. IT'S PLAIN YOU AIN'T USED TO DINING WITH THE LIKES OF US.
WE'VE GOT IMPORTANT MATTERS TO DISCUSS, SETH, SO SIT STILL AND BE QUIET OR I'LL CALL HENRY. HE'LL FIX YOUR WAGON.
UNCLE HENRY CAN'T DO NOTHING TO ME.
THE BOYS SAY THEY WANT THREE THINGS DONE.
FIRST, MISS ADA'S ACCOUNT BOOK MUST BE FOUND. IT CONTAINS THE NAMES OF THE PEOPLE BURIED HERE.
WITH IT, WE CAN MATCH THE NUMBERS ON THE GRAVE MARKERS WITH THE NAMES OF THE DEAD.
SHE KEPT TWO BOOKS, BUT THE ONE YOU WANT, THE TRUE ONE, WAS NEVER FOUND. ME AND HENRY HAVE LOOKED, AND SO HAVE ALL OUR KIN BEFORE US.
WE'LL FIND IT.
SECOND, WE MUST ERECT PROPER HEADSTONES FOR THE GRAVES.
IT WOULD COMFORT THE POOR SOULS TO KNOW THEY'VE NOT BEEN FORGOT.
AND THIRD...
THIRD, MISS ADA MUST BE EXORCISED.
SHE WON'T GO WILLINGLY. NOT THAT ONE.
THE SHADOW CHILDREN TWITTERED LIKE SCARED BABY BIRDS.

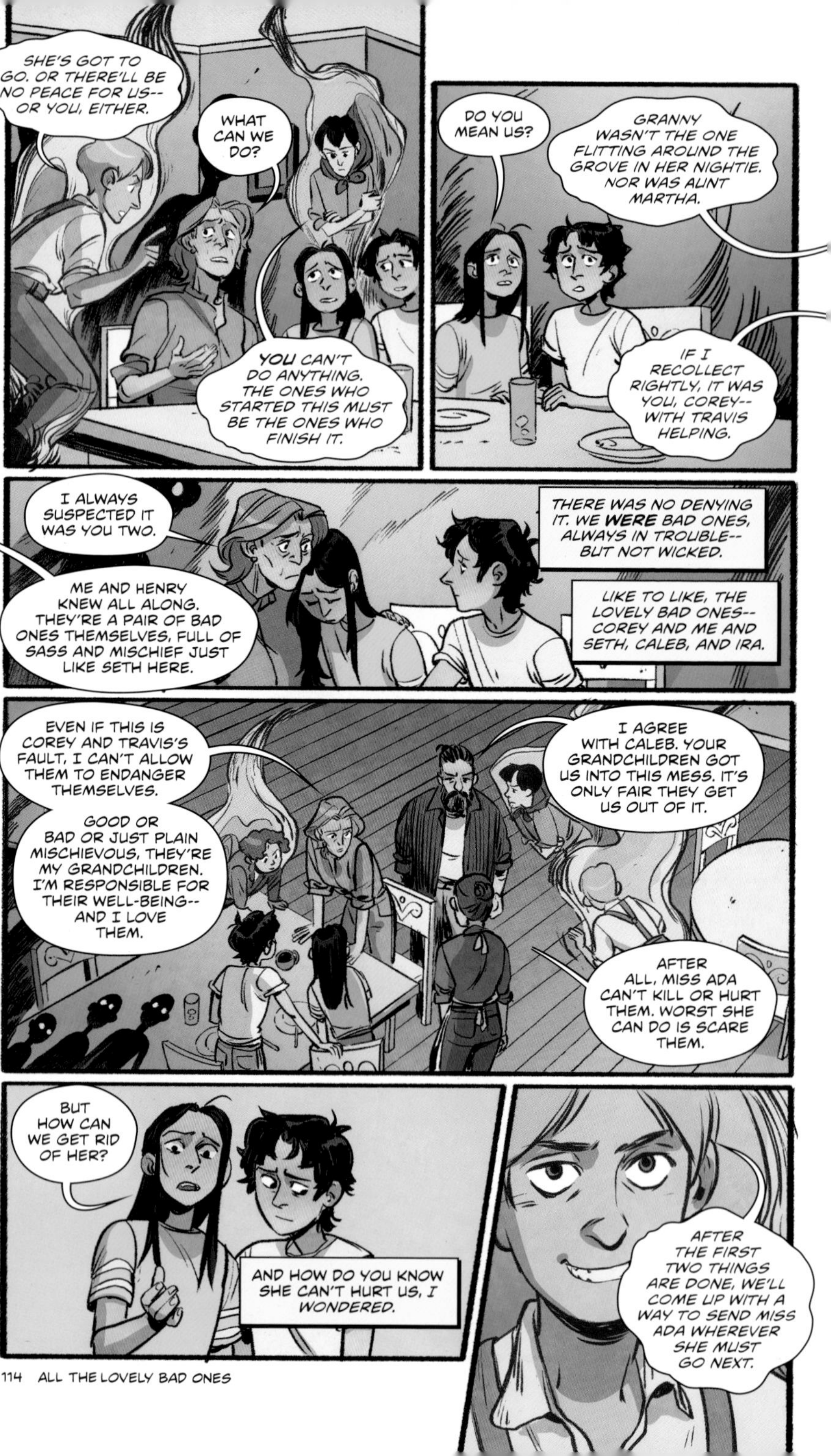
SHE'S GOT TO GO. OR THERE'LL BE NO PEACE FOR US-- OR YOU, EITHER.
WHAT CAN WE DO?
YOU CAN'T DO ANYTHING. THE ONES WHO STARTED THIS MUST BE THE ONES WHO FINISH IT.
DO YOU MEAN US?
GRANNY WASN'T THE ONE FLITTING AROUND THE GROVE IN HER NIGHTIE. NOR WAS AUNT MARTHA.
IF I RECOLLECT RIGHTLY, IT WAS YOU, COREY-- WITH TRAVIS HELPING.
I ALWAYS SUSPECTED IT WAS YOU TWO.
ME AND HENRY KNEW ALL ALONG. THEY'RE A PAIR OF BAD ONES THEMSELVES, FULL OF SASS AND MISCHIEF JUST LIKE SETH HERE.
THERE WAS NO DENYING IT. WE WERE BAD ONES, ALWAYS IN TROUBLE-- BUT NOT WICKED.
LIKE TO LIKE, THE LOVELY BAD ONES-- COREY AND ME AND SETH, CALEB, AND IRA.
EVEN IF THIS IS COREY AND TRAVIS'S FAULT, I CAN'T ALLOW THEM TO ENDANGER THEMSELVES.
GOOD OR BAD OR JUST PLAIN MISCHIEVOUS, THEY'RE MY GRANDCHILDREN. I'M RESPONSIBLE FOR THEIR WELL-BEING-- AND I LOVE THEM.
I AGREE WITH CALEB. YOUR GRANDCHILDREN GOT US INTO THIS MESS. IT'S ONLY FAIR THEY GET US OUT OF IT.
AFTER ALL, MISS ADA CAN'T KILL OR HURT THEM. WORST SHE CAN DO IS SCARE THEM.
BUT HOW CAN WE GET RID OF HER?
AND HOW DO YOU KNOW SHE CAN'T HURT US, I WONDERED.
AFTER THE FIRST TWO THINGS ARE DONE, WE'LL COME UP WITH A WAY TO SEND MISS ADA WHEREVER SHE MUST GO NEXT.

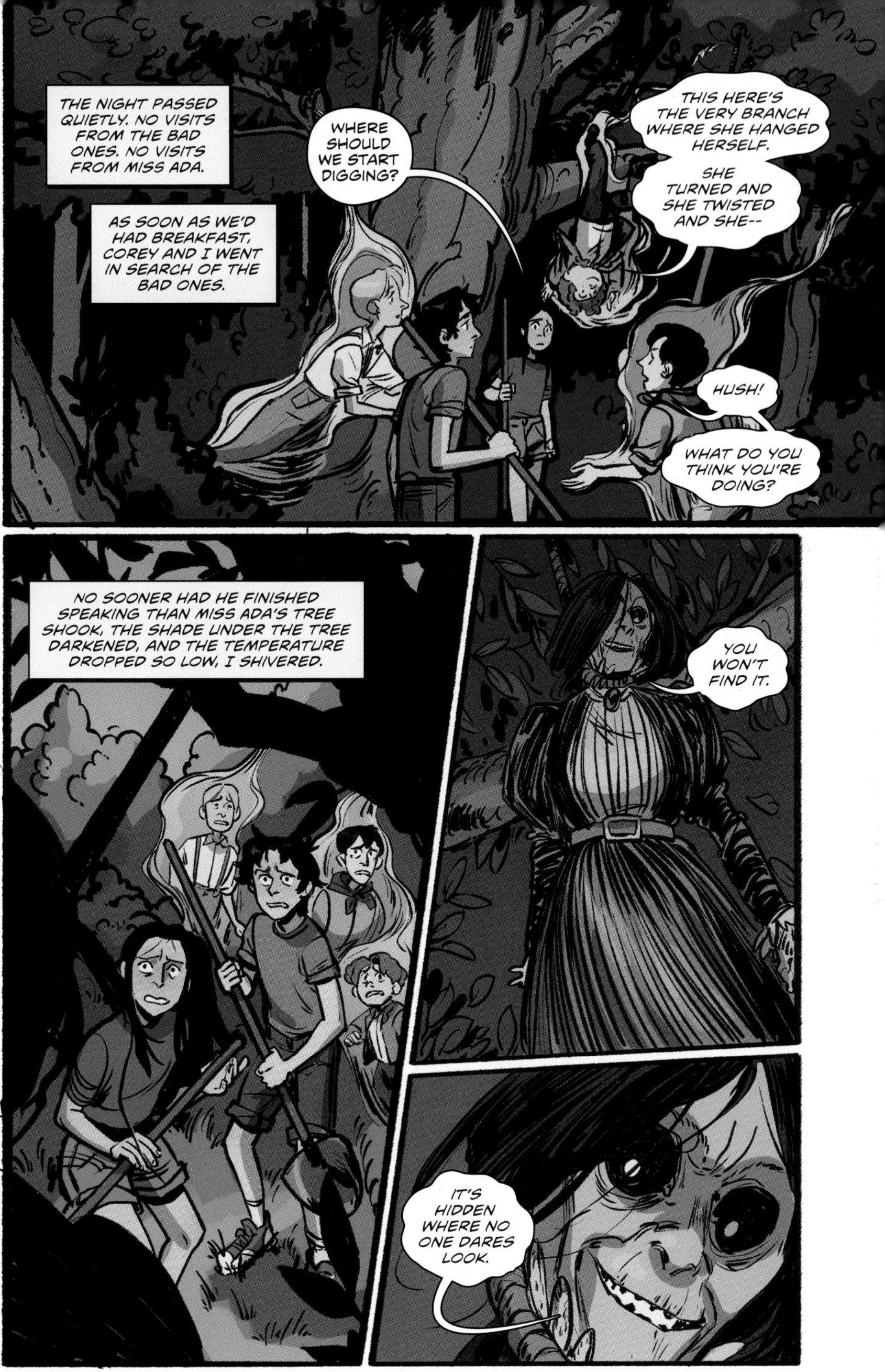
THE NIGHT PASSED QUIETLY. NO VISITS FROM THE BAD ONES. NO VISITS FROM MISS ADA.
AS SOON AS WE'D HAD BREAKFAST, COREY AND I WENT IN SEARCH OF THE BAD ONES.
WHERE SHOULD WE START DIGGING?
THIS HERE'S THE VERY BRANCH WHERE SHE HANGED HERSELF.
SHE TURNED AND SHE TWISTED AND SHE--
HUSH!
WHAT DO YOU THINK YOU'RE DOING?
NO SOONER HAD HE FINISHED SPEAKING THAN MISS ADA'S TREE SHOOK, THE SHADE UNDER THE TREE DARKENED, AND THE TEMPERATURE DROPPED SO LOW, I SHIVERED.
YOU WON'T FIND IT.
IT'S HIDDEN WHERE NO ONE DARES LOOK.

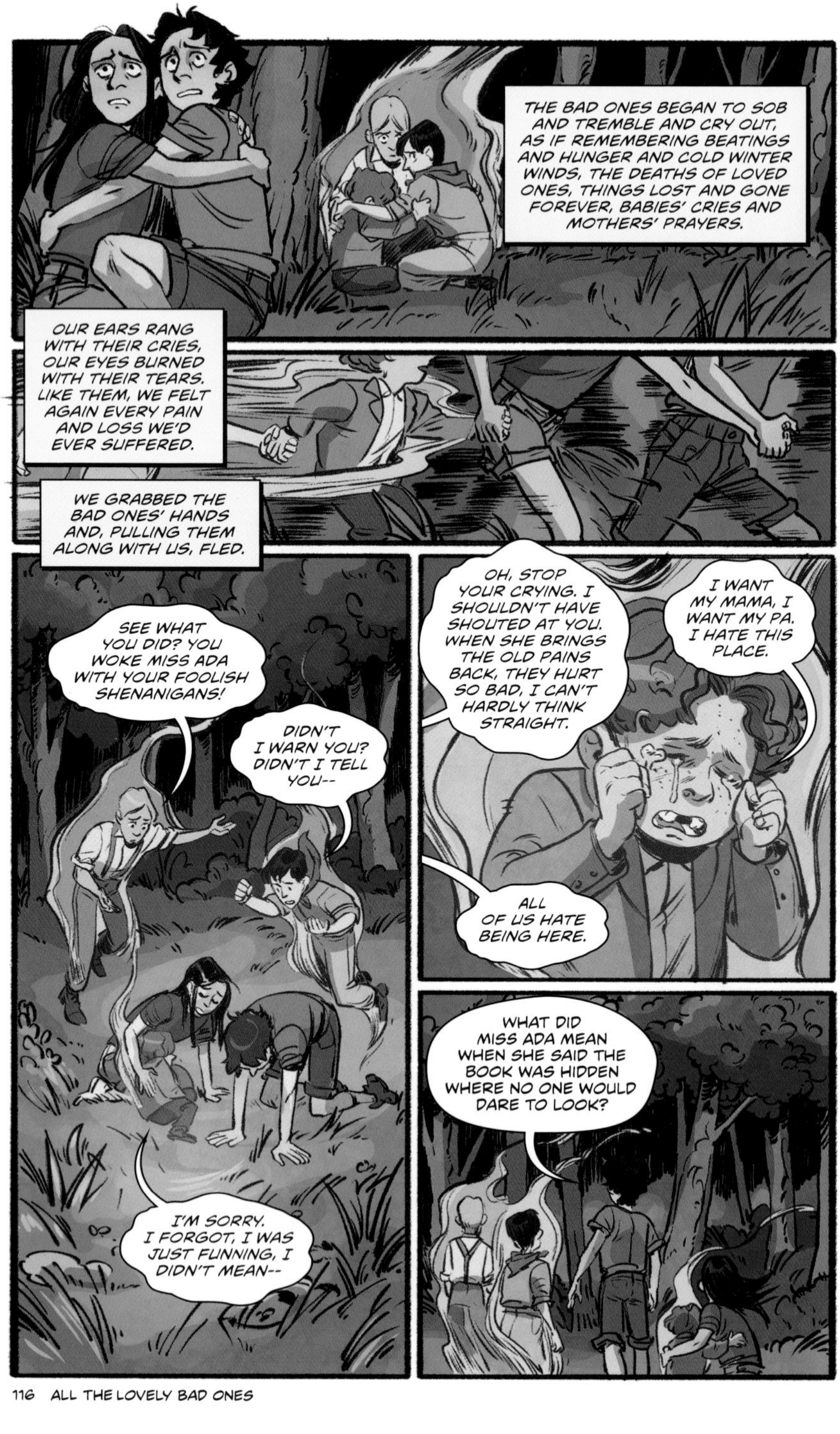
THE BAD ONES BEGAN TO SOB AND TREMBLE AND CRY OUT, AS IF REMEMBERING BEATINGS AND HUNGER AND COLD WINTER WINDS, THE DEATHS OF LOVED ONES, THINGS LOST AND GONE FOREVER, BABIES' CRIES AND MOTHERS' PRAYERS.
OUR EARS RANG WITH THEIR CRIES, OUR EYES BURNED WITH THEIR TEARS. LIKE THEM, WE FELT AGAIN EVERY PAIN AND LOSS WE'D EVER SUFFERED.
WE GRABBED THE BAD ONES' HANDS AND, PULLING THEM ALONG WITH US, FLED.
SEE WHAT YOU DID? YOU WOKE MISS ADA WITH YOUR FOOLISH SHENANIGANS!
DIDN'T I WARN YOU? DIDN'T I TELL YOU--
I'M SORRY. I FORGOT, I WAS JUST FUNNING, I DIDN'T MEAN--
OH, STOP YOUR CRYING. I SHOULDN'T HAVE SHOUTED AT YOU. WHEN SHE BRINGS THE OLD PAINS BACK, THEY HURT SO BAD, I CAN'T HARDLY THINK STRAIGHT.
I WANT MY MAMA, I WANT MY PA. I HATE THIS PLACE.
ALL OF US HATE BEING HERE.
WHAT DID MISS ADA MEAN WHEN SHE SAID THE BOOK WAS HIDDEN WHERE NO ONE WOULD DARE TO LOOK?

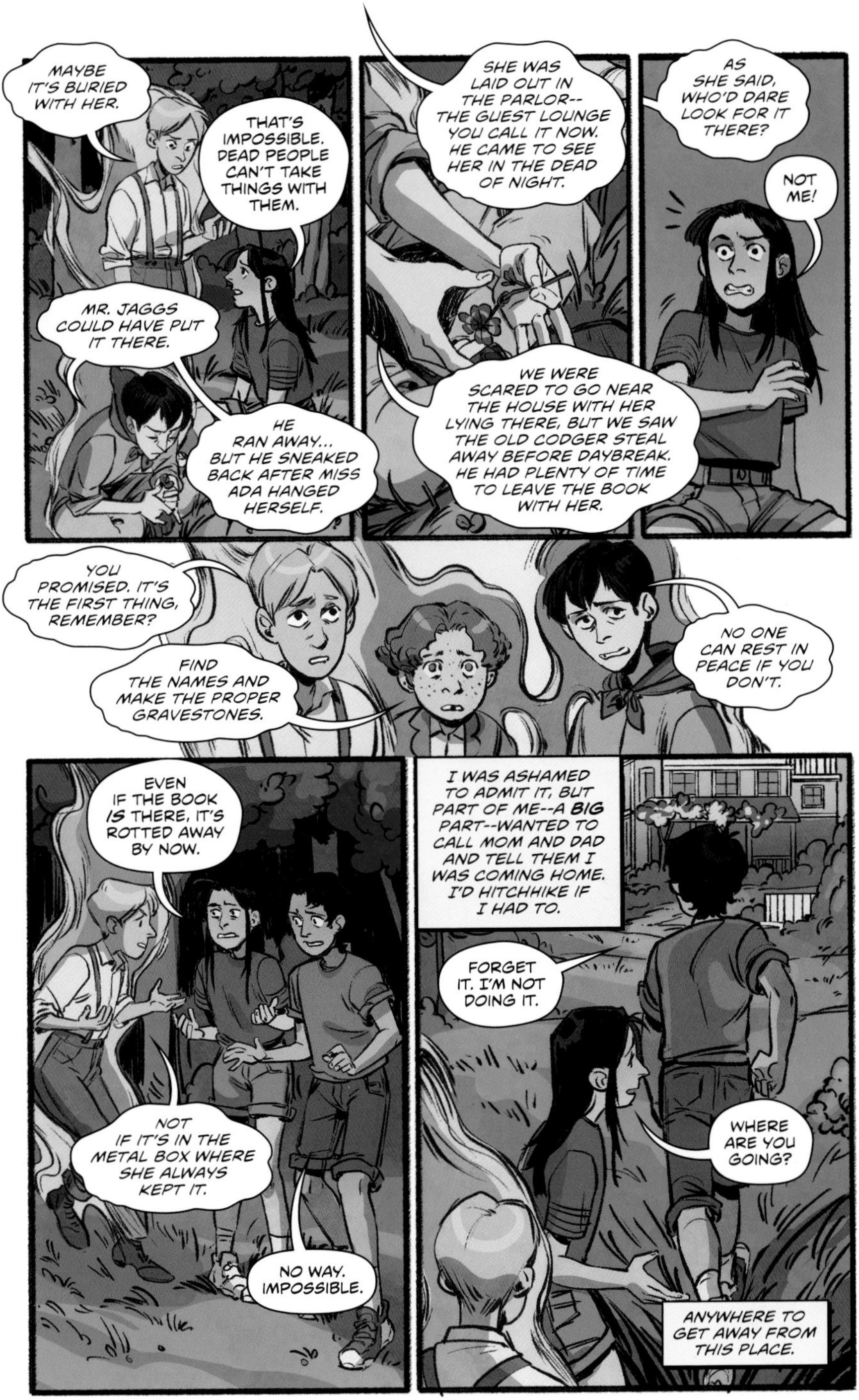
MAYBE IT'S BURIED WITH HER.
THAT'S IMPOSSIBLE. DEAD PEOPLE CAN'T TAKE THINGS WITH THEM.
MR. JAGGS COULD HAVE PUT IT THERE.
HE RAN AWAY... BUT HE SNEAKED BACK AFTER MISS ADA HANGED HERSELF.
SHE WAS LAID OUT IN THE PARLOR-- THE GUEST LOUNGE YOU CALL IT NOW. HE CAME TO SEE HER IN THE DEAD OF NIGHT.
WE WERE SCARED TO GO NEAR THE HOUSE WITH HER LYING THERE, BUT WE SAW THE OLD CODGER STEAL AWAY BEFORE DAYBREAK. HE HAD PLENTY OF TIME TO LEAVE THE BOOK WITH HER.
AS SHE SAID, WHO'D DARE LOOK FOR IT THERE?
NOT ME!
YOU PROMISED. IT'S THE FIRST THING, REMEMBER?
FIND THE NAMES AND MAKE THE PROPER GRAVESTONES.
NO ONE CAN REST IN PEACE IF YOU DON'T.
EVEN IF THE BOOK *IS* THERE, IT'S ROTTED AWAY BY NOW.
NOT IF IT'S IN THE METAL BOX WHERE SHE ALWAYS KEPT IT.
NO WAY. IMPOSSIBLE.
I WAS ASHAMED TO ADMIT IT, BUT PART OF ME--A **BIG** PART--WANTED TO CALL MOM AND DAD AND TELL THEM I WAS COMING HOME. I'D HITCHHIKE IF I HAD TO.
FORGET IT. I'M NOT DOING IT.
WHERE ARE YOU GOING?
ANYWHERE TO GET AWAY FROM THIS PLACE.

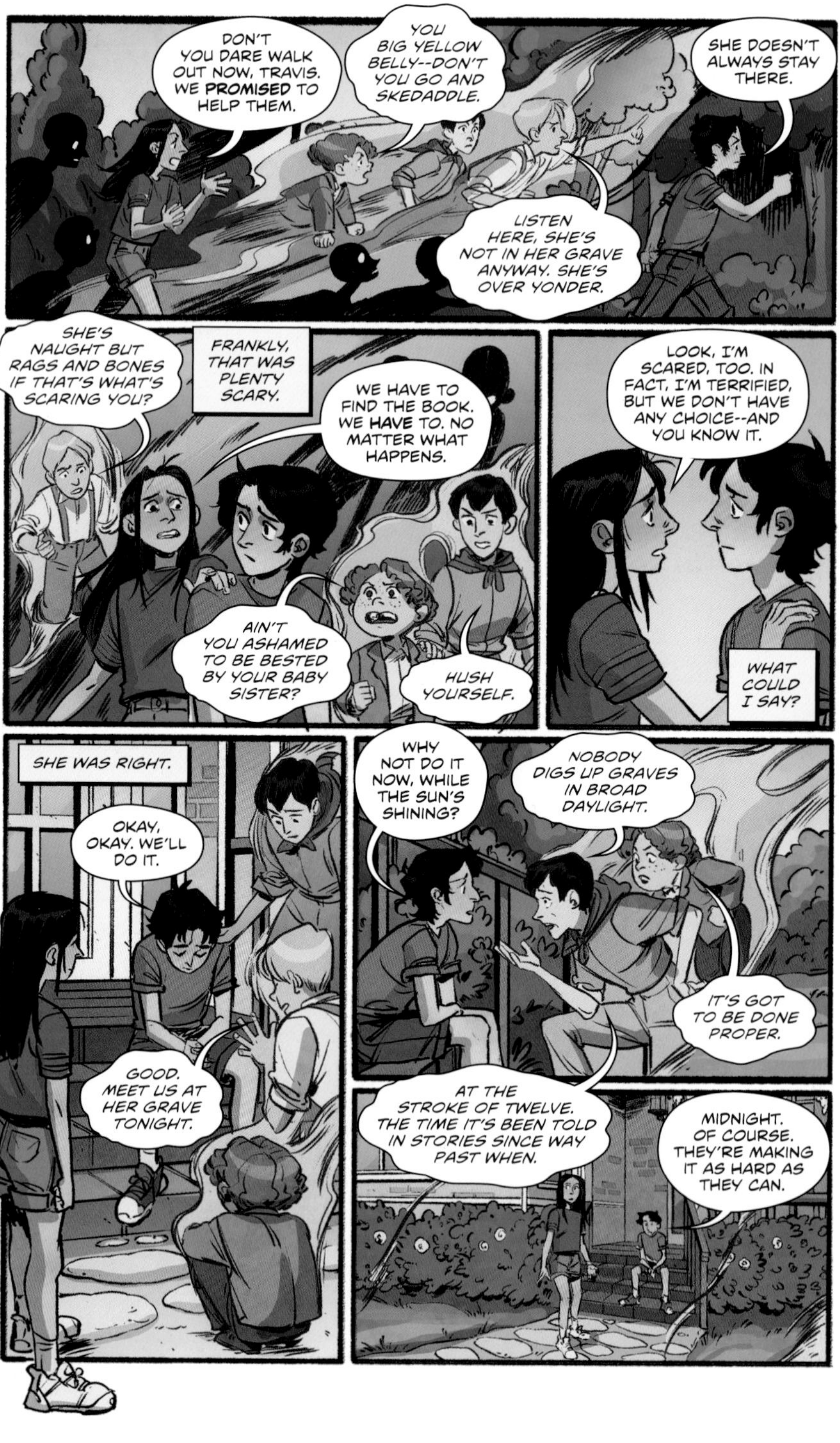
DON'T YOU DARE WALK OUT NOW, TRAVIS. WE PROMISED TO HELP THEM.
YOU BIG YELLOW BELLY--DON'T YOU GO AND SKEDADDLE.
LISTEN HERE, SHE'S NOT IN HER GRAVE ANYWAY. SHE'S OVER YONDER.
SHE DOESN'T ALWAYS STAY THERE.
SHE'S NAUGHT BUT RAGS AND BONES IF THAT'S WHAT'S SCARING YOU?
FRANKLY, THAT WAS PLENTY SCARY.
WE HAVE TO FIND THE BOOK. WE HAVE TO. NO MATTER WHAT HAPPENS.
AIN'T YOU ASHAMED TO BE BESTED BY YOUR BABY SISTER?
HUSH YOURSELF.
LOOK, I'M SCARED, TOO. IN FACT, I'M TERRIFIED, BUT WE DON'T HAVE ANY CHOICE--AND YOU KNOW IT.
WHAT COULD I SAY?
SHE WAS RIGHT.
OKAY, OKAY. WE'LL DO IT.
GOOD. MEET US AT HER GRAVE TONIGHT.
WHY NOT DO IT NOW, WHILE THE SUN'S SHINING?
NOBODY DIGS UP GRAVES IN BROAD DAYLIGHT.
IT'S GOT TO BE DONE PROPER.
AT THE STROKE OF TWELVE. THE TIME IT'S BEEN TOLD IN STORIES SINCE WAY PAST WHEN.
MIDNIGHT. OF COURSE. THEY'RE MAKING IT AS HARD AS THEY CAN.

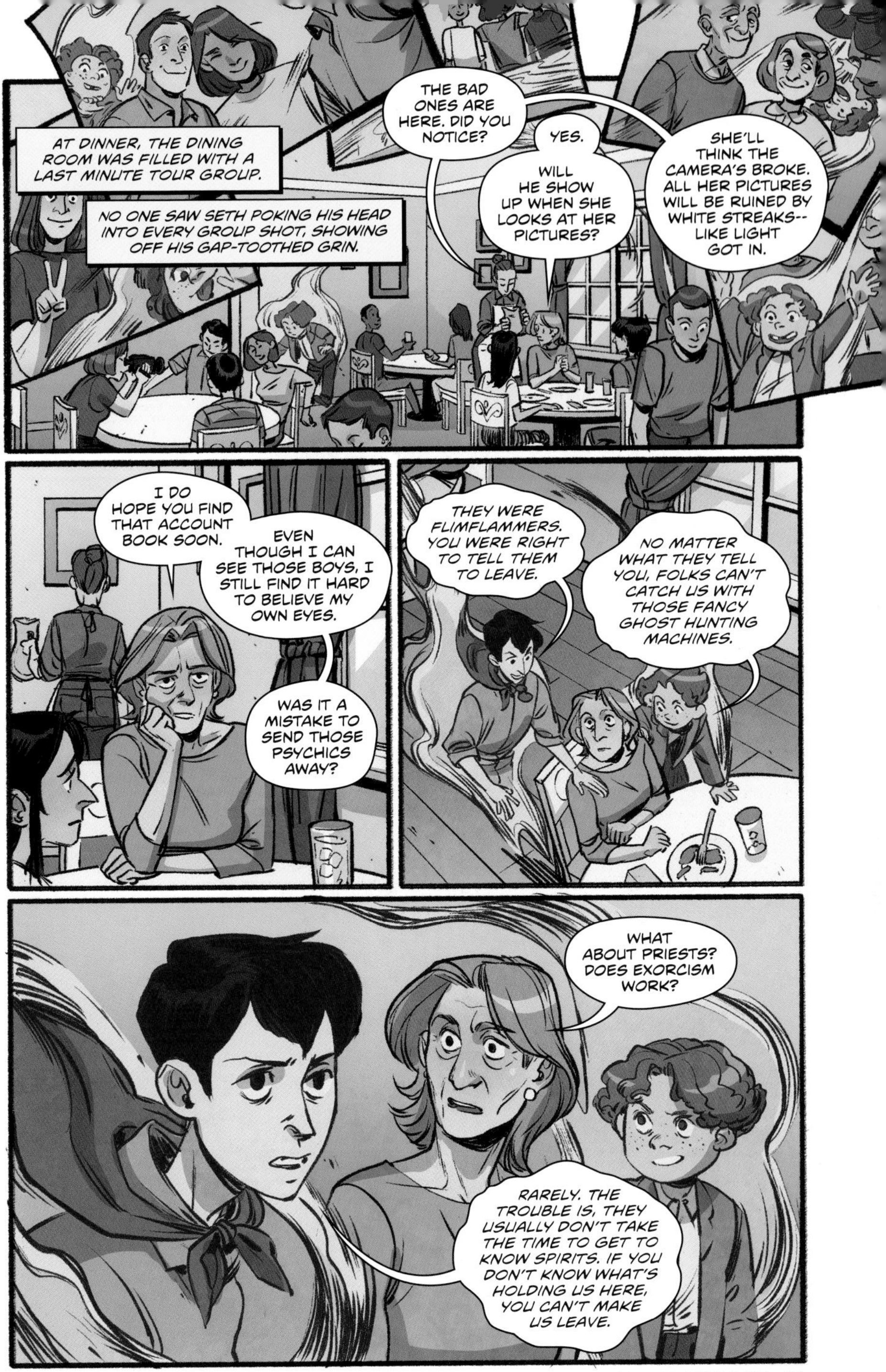
AT DINNER, THE DINING ROOM WAS FILLED WITH A LAST MINUTE TOUR GROUP.
NO ONE SAW SETH POKING HIS HEAD INTO EVERY GROUP SHOT, SHOWING OFF HIS GAP-TOOTHED GRIN.
THE BAD ONES ARE HERE. DID YOU NOTICE?
YES.
WILL HE SHOW UP WHEN SHE LOOKS AT HER PICTURES?
SHE'LL THINK THE CAMERA'S BROKE. ALL HER PICTURES WILL BE RUINED BY WHITE STREAKS-- LIKE LIGHT GOT IN.
I DO HOPE YOU FIND THAT ACCOUNT BOOK SOON.
EVEN THOUGH I CAN SEE THOSE BOYS, I STILL FIND IT HARD TO BELIEVE MY OWN EYES.
WAS IT A MISTAKE TO SEND THOSE PSYCHICS AWAY?
THEY WERE FLIMFLAMMERS. YOU WERE RIGHT TO TELL THEM TO LEAVE.
NO MATTER WHAT THEY TELL YOU, FOLKS CAN'T CATCH US WITH THOSE FANCY GHOST HUNTING MACHINES.
WHAT ABOUT PRIESTS? DOES EXORCISM WORK?
RARELY. THE TROUBLE IS, THEY USUALLY DON'T TAKE THE TIME TO GET TO KNOW SPIRITS. IF YOU DON'T KNOW WHAT'S HOLDING US HERE, YOU CAN'T MAKE US LEAVE.

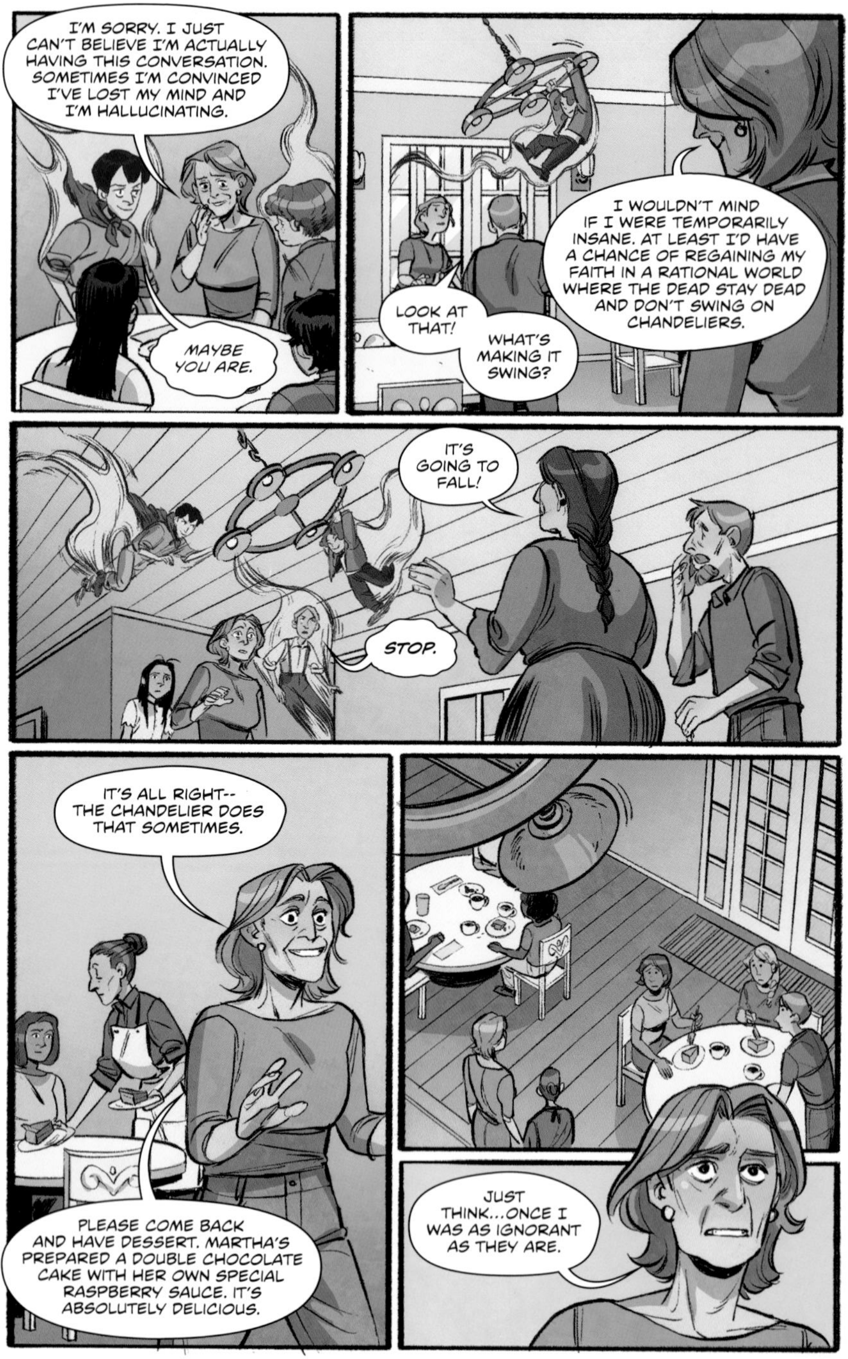
I'M SORRY. I JUST CAN'T BELIEVE I'M ACTUALLY HAVING THIS CONVERSATION. SOMETIMES I'M CONVINCED I'VE LOST MY MIND AND I'M HALLUCINATING.
MAYBE YOU ARE.
I WOULDN'T MIND IF I WERE TEMPORARILY INSANE. AT LEAST I'D HAVE A CHANCE OF REGAINING MY FAITH IN A RATIONAL WORLD WHERE THE DEAD STAY DEAD AND DON'T SWING ON CHANDELIERS.
LOOK AT THAT!
WHAT'S MAKING IT SWING?
IT'S GOING TO FALL!
STOP.
IT'S ALL RIGHT-- THE CHANDELIER DOES THAT SOMETIMES.
PLEASE COME BACK AND HAVE DESSERT. MARTHA'S PREPARED A DOUBLE CHOCOLATE CAKE WITH HER OWN SPECIAL RASPBERRY SAUCE. IT'S ABSOLUTELY DELICIOUS.
JUST THINK...ONCE I WAS AS IGNORANT AS THEY ARE.

AFTER DINNER, GRANDMOTHER WAS SURROUNDED BY THE GUESTS WHO HAD READ *HAUNTED INNS* AND WERE FULL OF QUESTIONS.

HAVE YOU SEEN ANY GHOSTS? HEARD ANY STRANGE SOUNDS? FELT COLD SPOTS?

GRANDMOTHER SHOOK HER HEAD, BUT SHE DIDN'T MEET THE MAN'S EYES. THE OTHER GUESTS CHUCKLED UNEASILY.

WHEN THAT CHANDELIER STARTED TO SWING, I THOUGHT IT WAS GHOSTS, FOR SURE.

THAT WAS THE STRANGEST THING I'VE EVER SEEN.

YOU SAY IT HAPPENS OFTEN?

YOU'LL HAVE TO EXCUSE ME. I'M NOT FEELING VERY WELL.

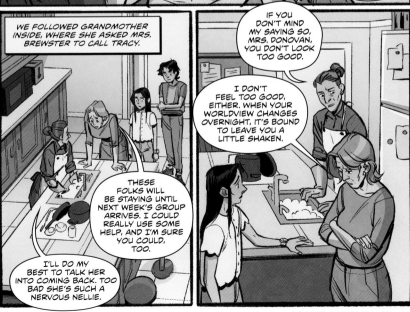

WE FOLLOWED GRANDMOTHER INSIDE, WHERE SHE ASKED MRS. BREWSTER TO CALL TRACY.

THESE FOLKS WILL BE STAYING UNTIL NEXT WEEK'S GROUP ARRIVES. I COULD REALLY USE SOME HELP, AND I'M SURE YOU COULD, TOO.

I'LL DO MY BEST TO TALK HER INTO COMING BACK. TOO BAD SHE'S SUCH A NERVOUS NELLIE.

IF YOU DON'T MIND MY SAYING SO, MRS. DONOVAN, YOU DON'T LOOK TOO GOOD.

I DON'T FEEL TOO GOOD, EITHER. WHEN YOUR WORLDVIEW CHANGES OVERNIGHT, IT'S BOUND TO LEAVE YOU A LITTLE SHAKEN.

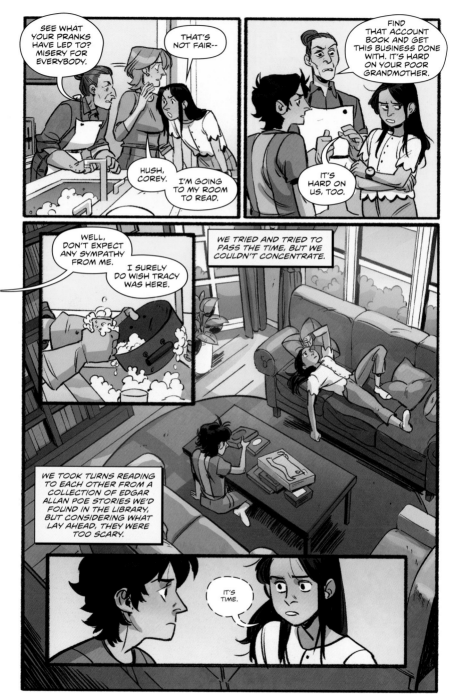

SEE WHAT YOUR PRANKS HAVE LED TO? MISERY FOR EVERYBODY.

THAT'S NOT FAIR--

FIND THAT ACCOUNT BOOK AND GET THIS BUSINESS DONE WITH. IT'S HARD ON YOUR POOR GRANDMOTHER.

HUSH, COREY.

I'M GOING TO MY ROOM TO READ.

IT'S HARD ON US, TOO.

WELL, DON'T EXPECT ANY SYMPATHY FROM ME.

I SURELY DO WISH TRACY WAS HERE.

WE TRIED AND TRIED TO PASS THE TIME, BUT WE COULDN'T CONCENTRATE.

WE TOOK TURNS READING TO EACH OTHER FROM A COLLECTION OF EDGAR ALLAN POE STORIES WE'D FOUND IN THE LIBRARY, BUT CONSIDERING WHAT LAY AHEAD, THEY WERE TOO SCARY.

IT'S TIME.

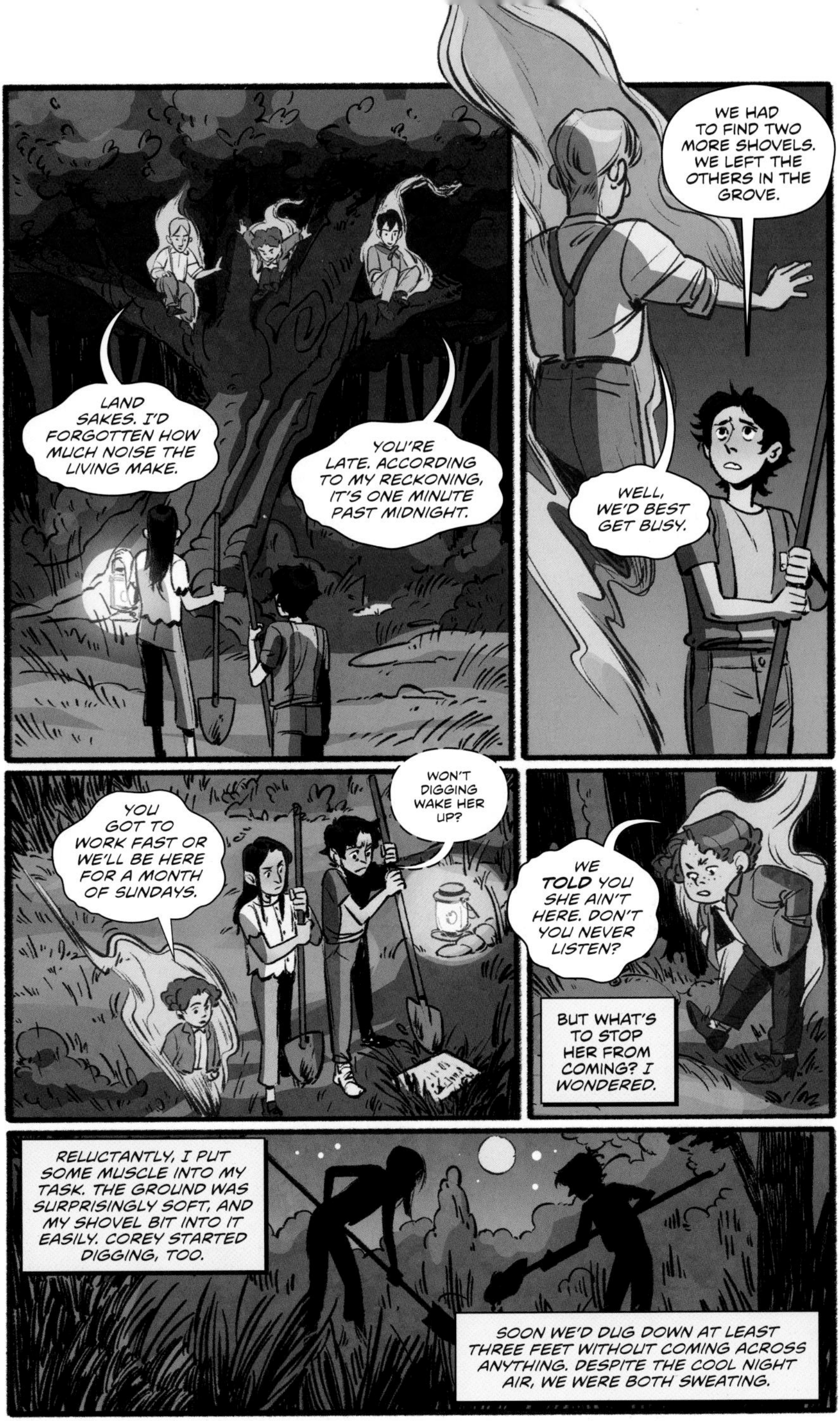
LAND SAKES. I'D FORGOTTEN HOW MUCH NOISE THE LIVING MAKE.
YOU'RE LATE. ACCORDING TO MY RECKONING, IT'S ONE MINUTE PAST MIDNIGHT.
WE HAD TO FIND TWO MORE SHOVELS. WE LEFT THE OTHERS IN THE GROVE.
WELL, WE'D BEST GET BUSY.
YOU GOT TO WORK FAST OR WE'LL BE HERE FOR A MONTH OF SUNDAYS.
WON'T DIGGING WAKE HER UP?
WE **TOLD** YOU SHE AIN'T HERE. DON'T YOU NEVER LISTEN?
BUT WHAT'S TO STOP HER FROM COMING? I WONDERED.
RELUCTANTLY, I PUT SOME MUSCLE INTO MY TASK. THE GROUND WAS SURPRISINGLY SOFT, AND MY SHOVEL BIT INTO IT EASILY. COREY STARTED DIGGING, TOO.
SOON WE'D DUG DOWN AT LEAST THREE FEET WITHOUT COMING ACROSS ANYTHING. DESPITE THE COOL NIGHT AIR, WE WERE BOTH SWEATING.

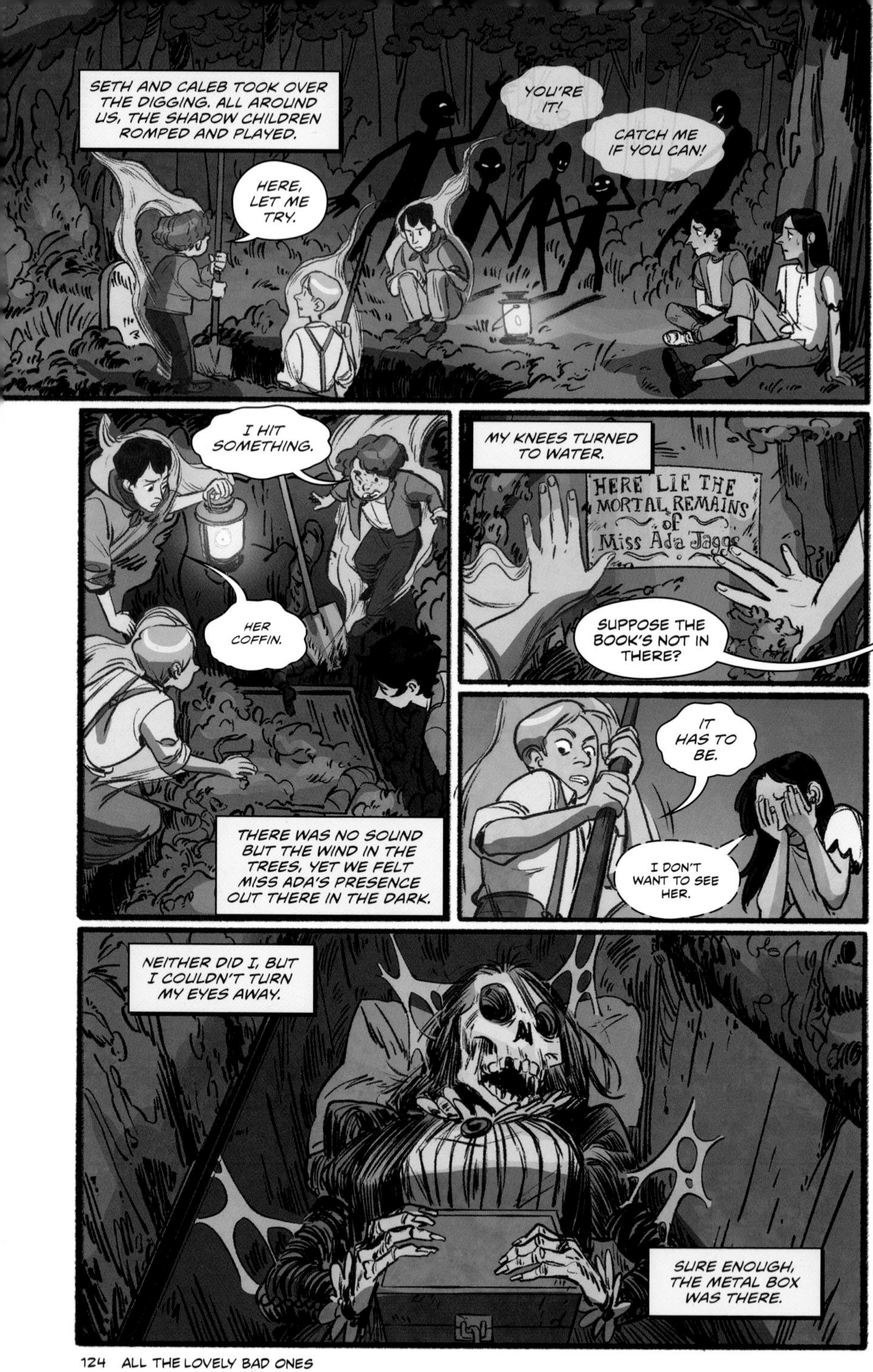
SETH AND CALEB TOOK OVER THE DIGGING. ALL AROUND US, THE SHADOW CHILDREN ROMPED AND PLAYED.
HERE, LET ME TRY.
YOU'RE IT!
CATCH ME IF YOU CAN!
I HIT SOMETHING.
HER COFFIN.
THERE WAS NO SOUND BUT THE WIND IN THE TREES, YET WE FELT MISS ADA'S PRESENCE OUT THERE IN THE DARK.
MY KNEES TURNED TO WATER.
HERE LIE THE MORTAL REMAINS of Miss Ada Jaggs
SUPPOSE THE BOOK'S NOT IN THERE?
IT HAS TO BE.
I DON'T WANT TO SEE HER.
NEITHER DID I, BUT I COULDN'T TURN MY EYES AWAY.
SURE ENOUGH, THE METAL BOX WAS THERE.

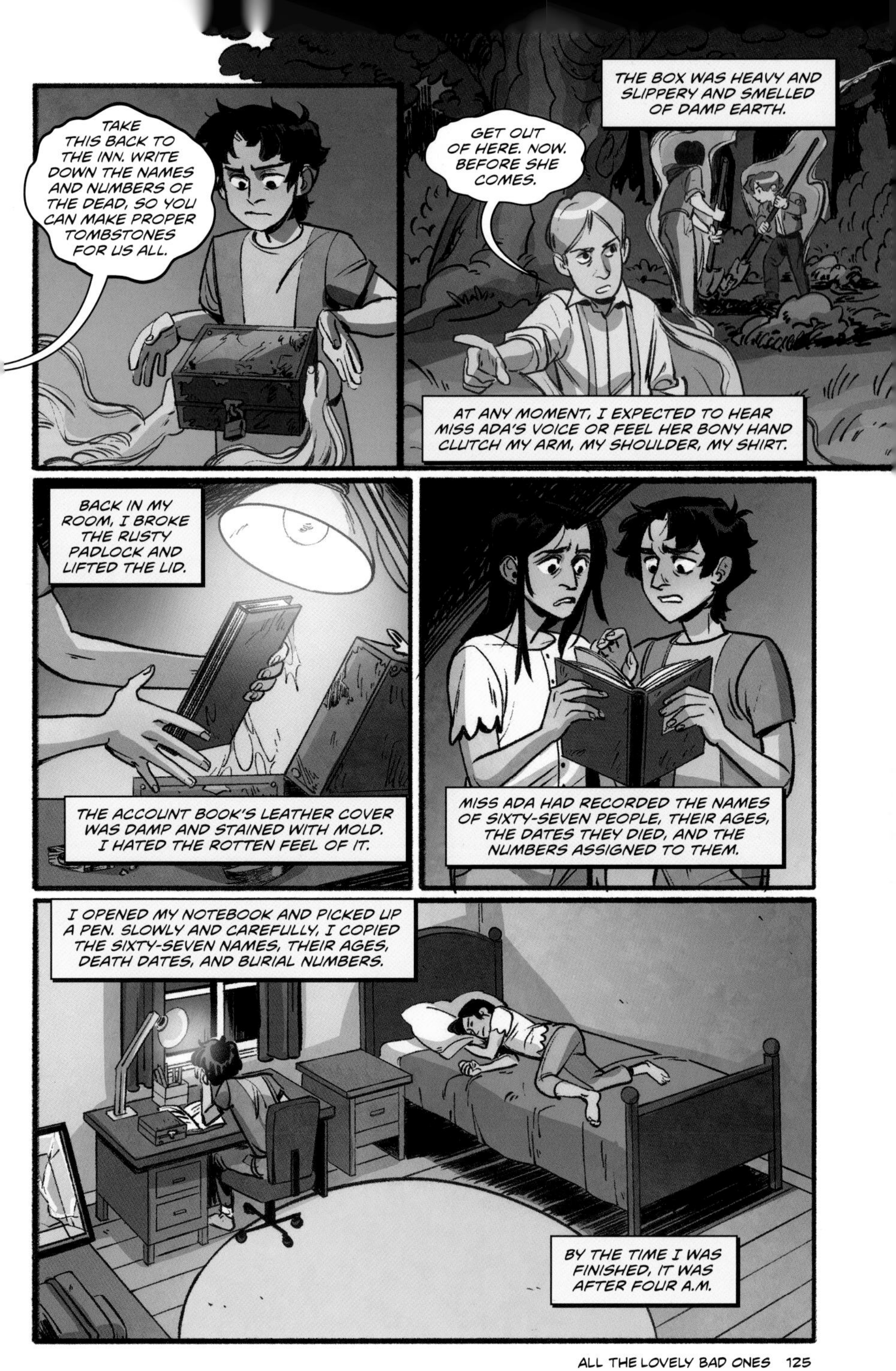
THE BOX WAS HEAVY AND SLIPPERY AND SMELLED OF DAMP EARTH.
TAKE THIS BACK TO THE INN. WRITE DOWN THE NAMES AND NUMBERS OF THE DEAD, SO YOU CAN MAKE PROPER TOMBSTONES FOR US ALL.
GET OUT OF HERE. NOW. BEFORE SHE COMES.
AT ANY MOMENT, I EXPECTED TO HEAR MISS ADA'S VOICE OR FEEL HER BONY HAND CLUTCH MY ARM, MY SHOULDER, MY SHIRT.
BACK IN MY ROOM, I BROKE THE RUSTY PADLOCK AND LIFTED THE LID.
THE ACCOUNT BOOK'S LEATHER COVER WAS DAMP AND STAINED WITH MOLD. I HATED THE ROTTEN FEEL OF IT.
MISS ADA HAD RECORDED THE NAMES OF SIXTY-SEVEN PEOPLE, THEIR AGES, THE DATES THEY DIED, AND THE NUMBERS ASSIGNED TO THEM.
I OPENED MY NOTEBOOK AND PICKED UP A PEN. SLOWLY AND CAREFULLY, I COPIED THE SIXTY-SEVEN NAMES, THEIR AGES, DEATH DATES, AND BURIAL NUMBERS.
BY THE TIME I WAS FINISHED, IT WAS AFTER FOUR A.M.

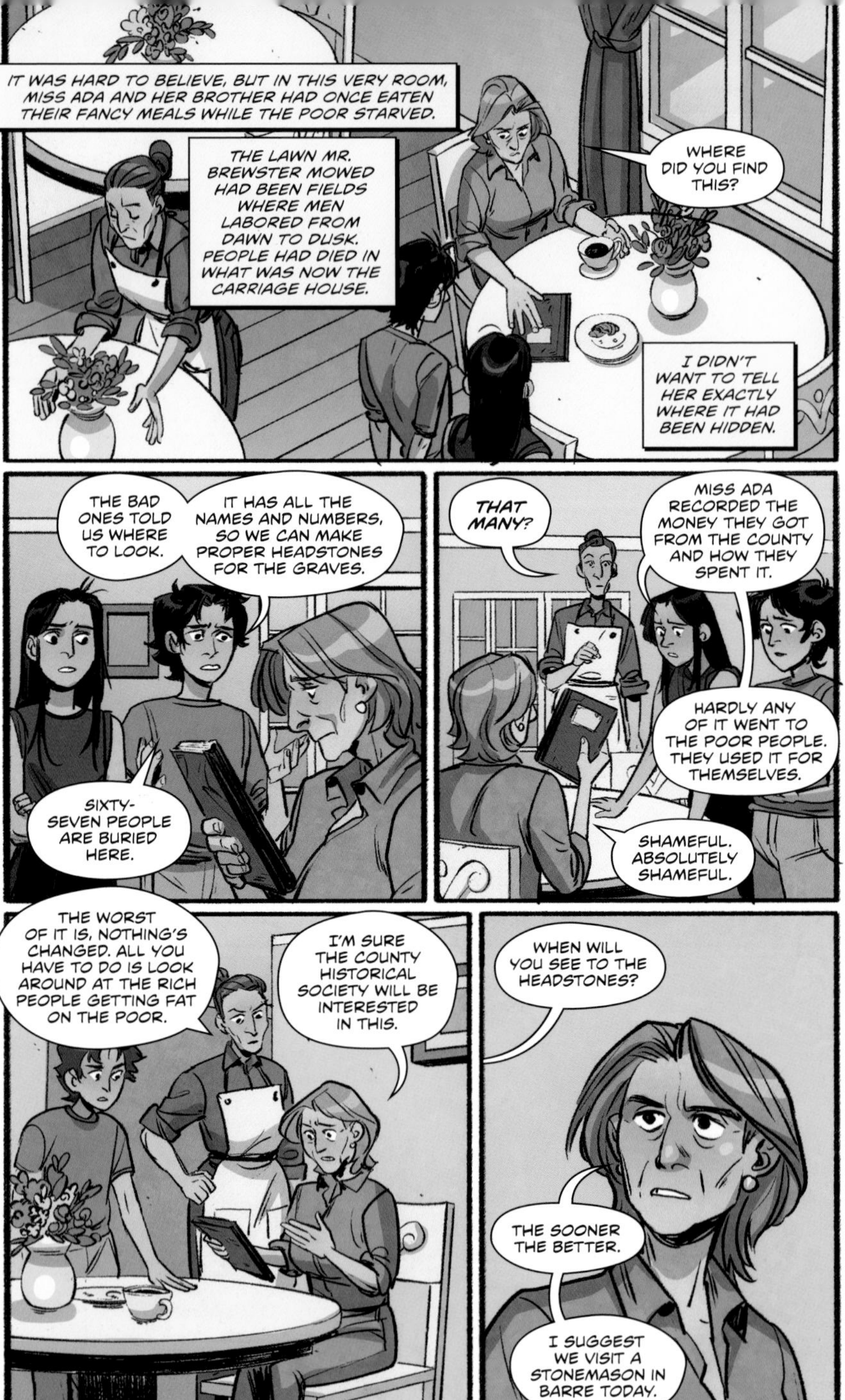
IT WAS HARD TO BELIEVE, BUT IN THIS VERY ROOM, MISS ADA AND HER BROTHER HAD ONCE EATEN THEIR FANCY MEALS WHILE THE POOR STARVED.
THE LAWN MR. BREWSTER MOWED HAD BEEN FIELDS WHERE MEN LABORED FROM DAWN TO DUSK. PEOPLE HAD DIED IN WHAT WAS NOW THE CARRIAGE HOUSE.
WHERE DID YOU FIND THIS?
I DIDN'T WANT TO TELL HER EXACTLY WHERE IT HAD BEEN HIDDEN.
THE BAD ONES TOLD US WHERE TO LOOK.
IT HAS ALL THE NAMES AND NUMBERS, SO WE CAN MAKE PROPER HEADSTONES FOR THE GRAVES.
SIXTY-SEVEN PEOPLE ARE BURIED HERE.
THAT MANY?
MISS ADA RECORDED THE MONEY THEY GOT FROM THE COUNTY AND HOW THEY SPENT IT.
HARDLY ANY OF IT WENT TO THE POOR PEOPLE. THEY USED IT FOR THEMSELVES.
SHAMEFUL. ABSOLUTELY SHAMEFUL.
THE WORST OF IT IS, NOTHING'S CHANGED. ALL YOU HAVE TO DO IS LOOK AROUND AT THE RICH PEOPLE GETTING FAT ON THE POOR.
I'M SURE THE COUNTY HISTORICAL SOCIETY WILL BE INTERESTED IN THIS.
WHEN WILL YOU SEE TO THE HEADSTONES?
THE SOONER THE BETTER.
I SUGGEST WE VISIT A STONEMASON IN BARRE TODAY.

A FEW HOURS LATER, GRANDMOTHER LED US INTO THE OFFICE OF DANIEL GREENE AND SONS, LTD.

SHE PRACTICALLY WENT INTO SHOCK AT THE COST OF PURCHASING SIXTY-SEVEN GRAVESTONES.

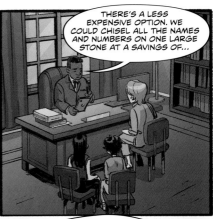

THERE'S A LESS EXPENSIVE OPTION. WE COULD CHISEL ALL THE NAMES AND NUMBERS ON ONE LARGE STONE AT A SAVINGS OF...

HE DID SOME QUICK FIGURING AND CAME UP WITH A PRICE GRANDMOTHER COULD AFFORD.

I'M WILLING TO REDUCE MY PROFIT BECAUSE OF THE HISTORICAL SIGNIFICANCE OF WHAT YOU'RE DOING.

THERE'S MANY A NAME ON THIS LIST WHOSE DESCENDANTS LIVE HERE STILL. THEY DESERVE TO KNOW WHERE THEIR ANCESTORS ARE BURIED.

WE CHOSE A BIG PALE PINK MARBLE SLAB.

HE PROMISED THE MEMORIAL WOULD BE READY AS SOON AS POSSIBLE.

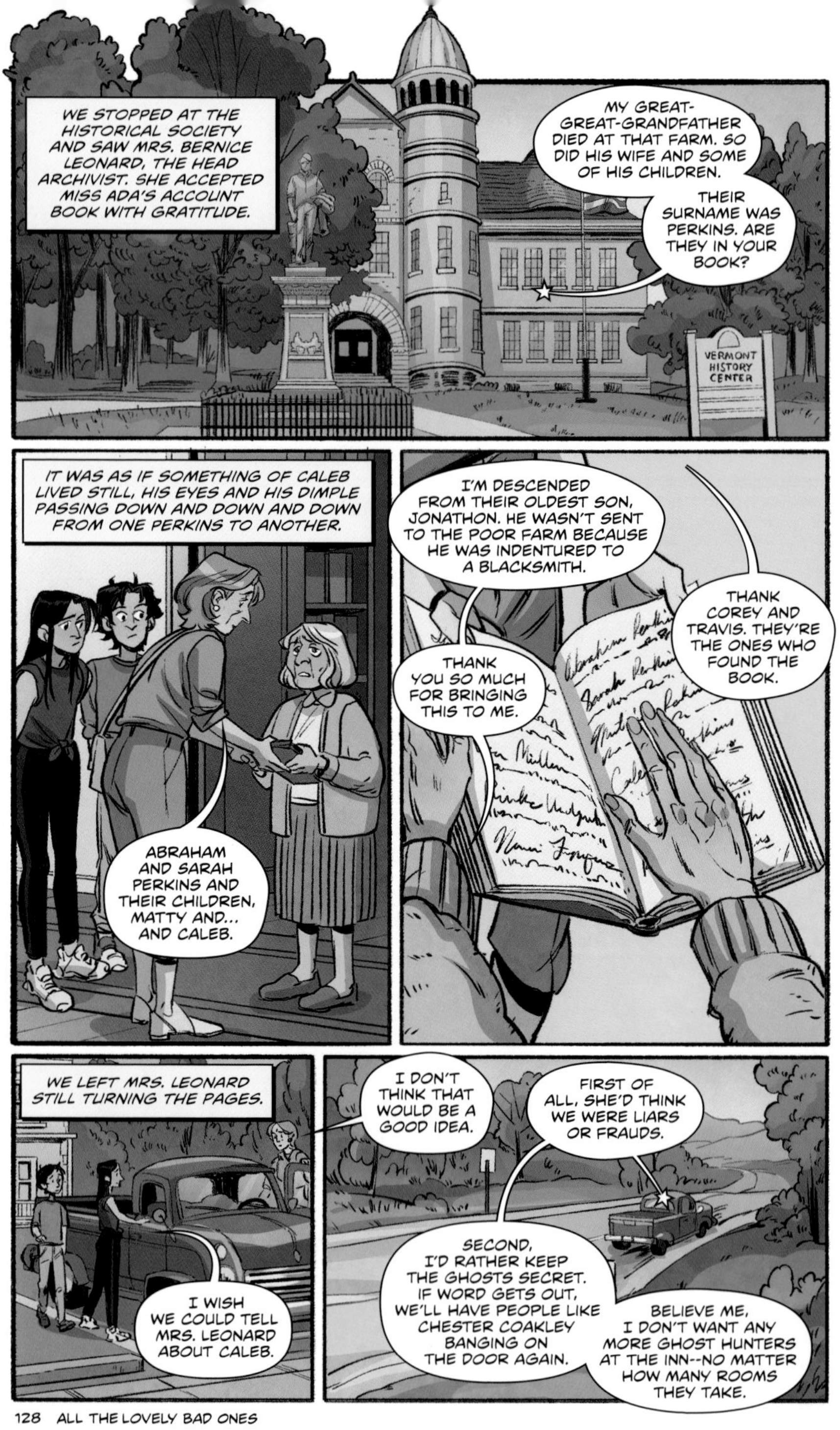
WE STOPPED AT THE HISTORICAL SOCIETY AND SAW MRS. BERNICE LEONARD, THE HEAD ARCHIVIST. SHE ACCEPTED MISS ADA'S ACCOUNT BOOK WITH GRATITUDE.
MY GREAT-GREAT-GRANDFATHER DIED AT THAT FARM. SO DID HIS WIFE AND SOME OF HIS CHILDREN.
THEIR SURNAME WAS PERKINS. ARE THEY IN YOUR BOOK?
VERMONT HISTORY CENTER
IT WAS AS IF SOMETHING OF CALEB LIVED STILL, HIS EYES AND HIS DIMPLE PASSING DOWN AND DOWN AND DOWN FROM ONE PERKINS TO ANOTHER.
ABRAHAM AND SARAH PERKINS AND THEIR CHILDREN, MATTY AND... AND CALEB.
I'M DESCENDED FROM THEIR OLDEST SON, JONATHON. HE WASN'T SENT TO THE POOR FARM BECAUSE HE WAS INDENTURED TO A BLACKSMITH.
THANK YOU SO MUCH FOR BRINGING THIS TO ME.
THANK COREY AND TRAVIS. THEY'RE THE ONES WHO FOUND THE BOOK.
WE LEFT MRS. LEONARD STILL TURNING THE PAGES.
I WISH WE COULD TELL MRS. LEONARD ABOUT CALEB.
I DON'T THINK THAT WOULD BE A GOOD IDEA.
FIRST OF ALL, SHE'D THINK WE WERE LIARS OR FRAUDS.
SECOND, I'D RATHER KEEP THE GHOSTS SECRET. IF WORD GETS OUT, WE'LL HAVE PEOPLE LIKE CHESTER COAKLEY BANGING ON THE DOOR AGAIN.
BELIEVE ME, I DON'T WANT ANY MORE GHOST HUNTERS AT THE INN--NO MATTER HOW MANY ROOMS THEY TAKE.

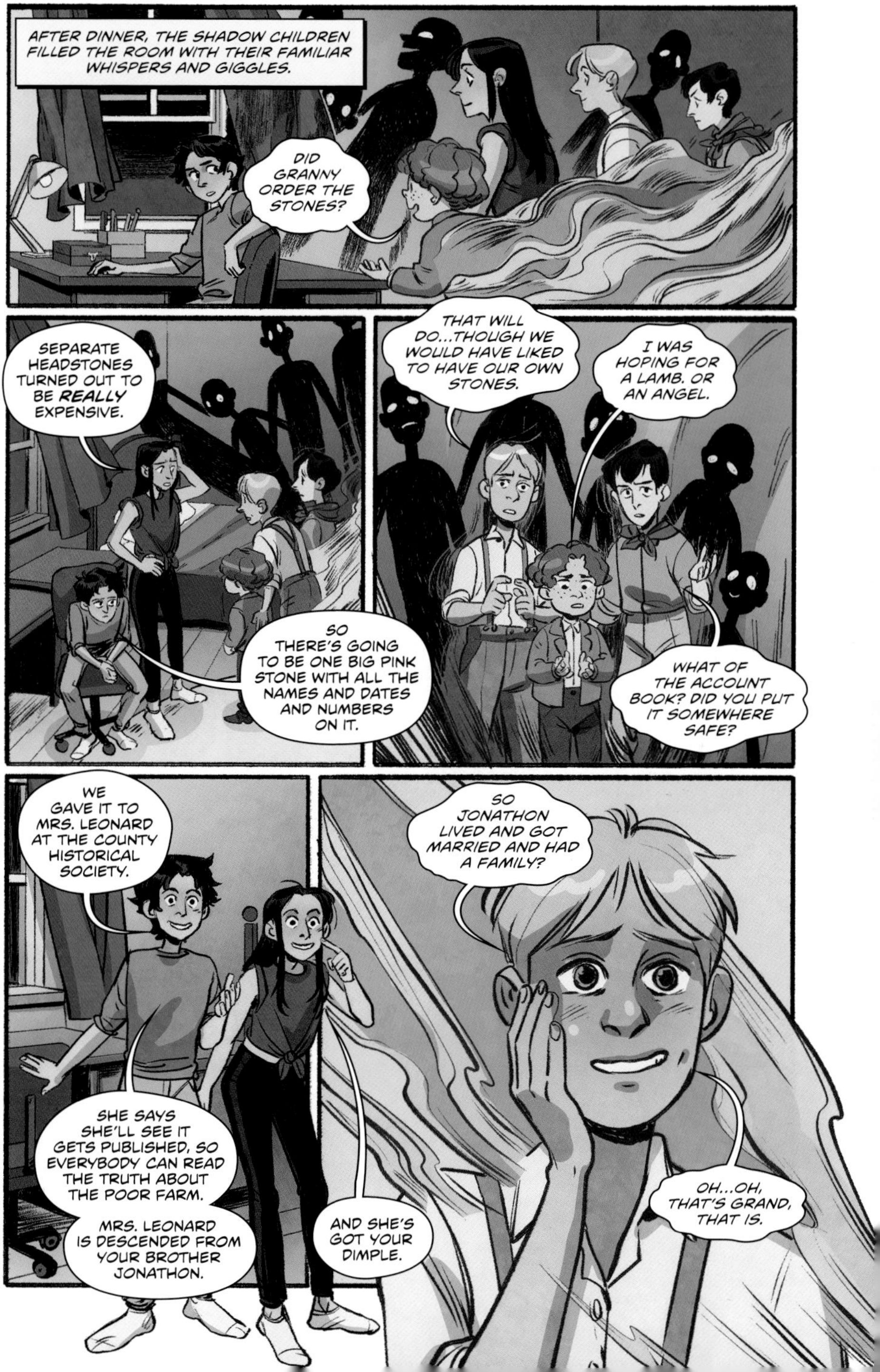
AFTER DINNER, THE SHADOW CHILDREN FILLED THE ROOM WITH THEIR FAMILIAR WHISPERS AND GIGGLES.
DID GRANNY ORDER THE STONES?
SEPARATE HEADSTONES TURNED OUT TO BE **REALLY** EXPENSIVE.
SO THERE'S GOING TO BE ONE BIG PINK STONE WITH ALL THE NAMES AND DATES AND NUMBERS ON IT.
THAT WILL DO...THOUGH WE WOULD HAVE LIKED TO HAVE OUR OWN STONES.
I WAS HOPING FOR A LAMB. OR AN ANGEL.
WHAT OF THE ACCOUNT BOOK? DID YOU PUT IT SOMEWHERE SAFE?
WE GAVE IT TO MRS. LEONARD AT THE COUNTY HISTORICAL SOCIETY.
SHE SAYS SHE'LL SEE IT GETS PUBLISHED, SO EVERYBODY CAN READ THE TRUTH ABOUT THE POOR FARM.
MRS. LEONARD IS DESCENDED FROM YOUR BROTHER JONATHON.
AND SHE'S GOT YOUR DIMPLE.
SO JONATHON LIVED AND GOT MARRIED AND HAD A FAMILY?
OH...OH, THAT'S GRAND, THAT IS.

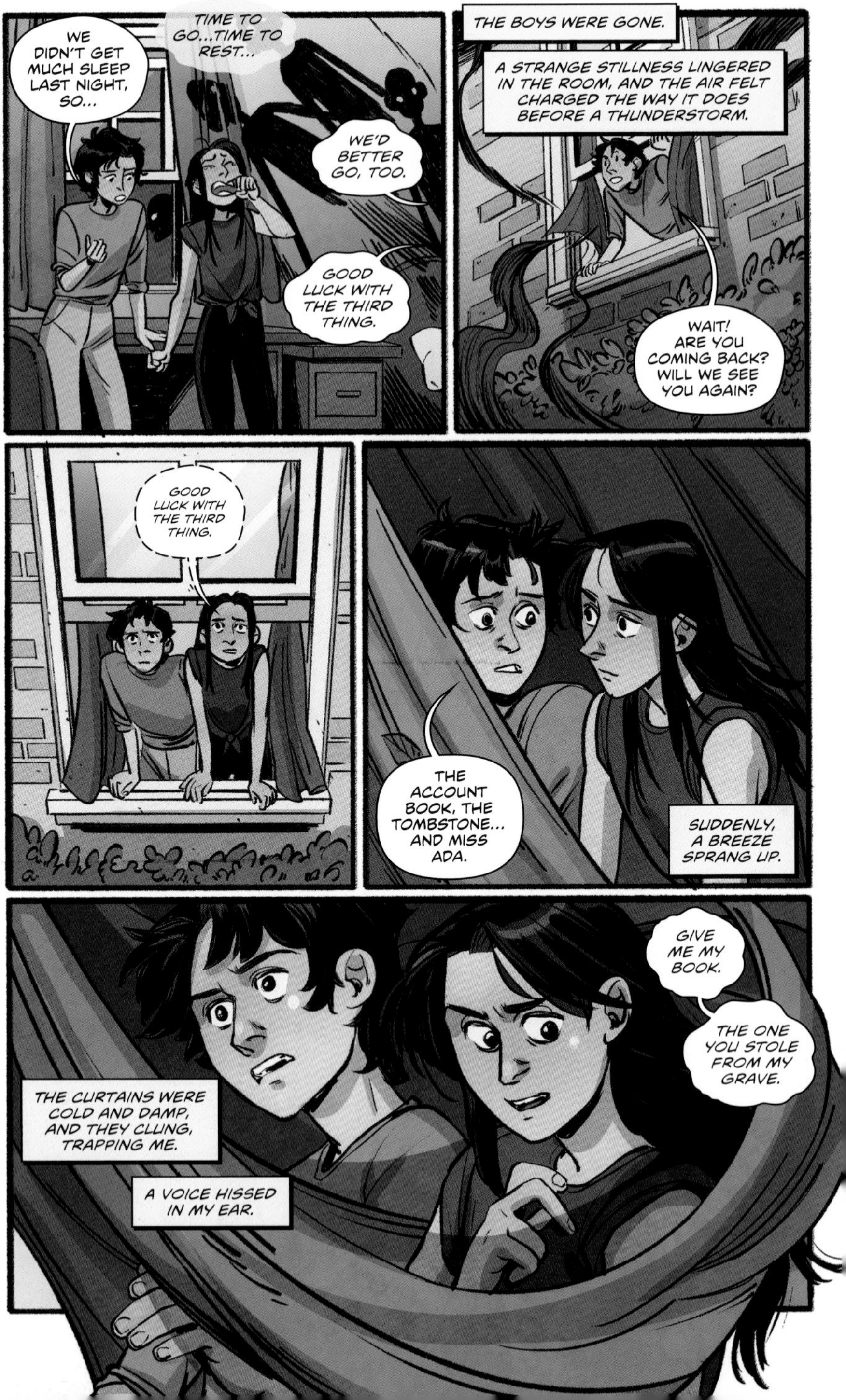
WE DIDN'T GET MUCH SLEEP LAST NIGHT, SO...
TIME TO GO...TIME TO REST...
WE'D BETTER GO, TOO.
GOOD LUCK WITH THE THIRD THING.
THE BOYS WERE GONE.
A STRANGE STILLNESS LINGERED IN THE ROOM, AND THE AIR FELT CHARGED THE WAY IT DOES BEFORE A THUNDERSTORM.
WAIT! ARE YOU COMING BACK? WILL WE SEE YOU AGAIN?
GOOD LUCK WITH THE THIRD THING.
THE ACCOUNT BOOK, THE TOMBSTONE... AND MISS ADA.
SUDDENLY, A BREEZE SPRANG UP.
THE CURTAINS WERE COLD AND DAMP, AND THEY CLUNG, TRAPPING ME.
A VOICE HISSED IN MY EAR.
GIVE ME MY BOOK.
THE ONE YOU STOLE FROM MY GRAVE.

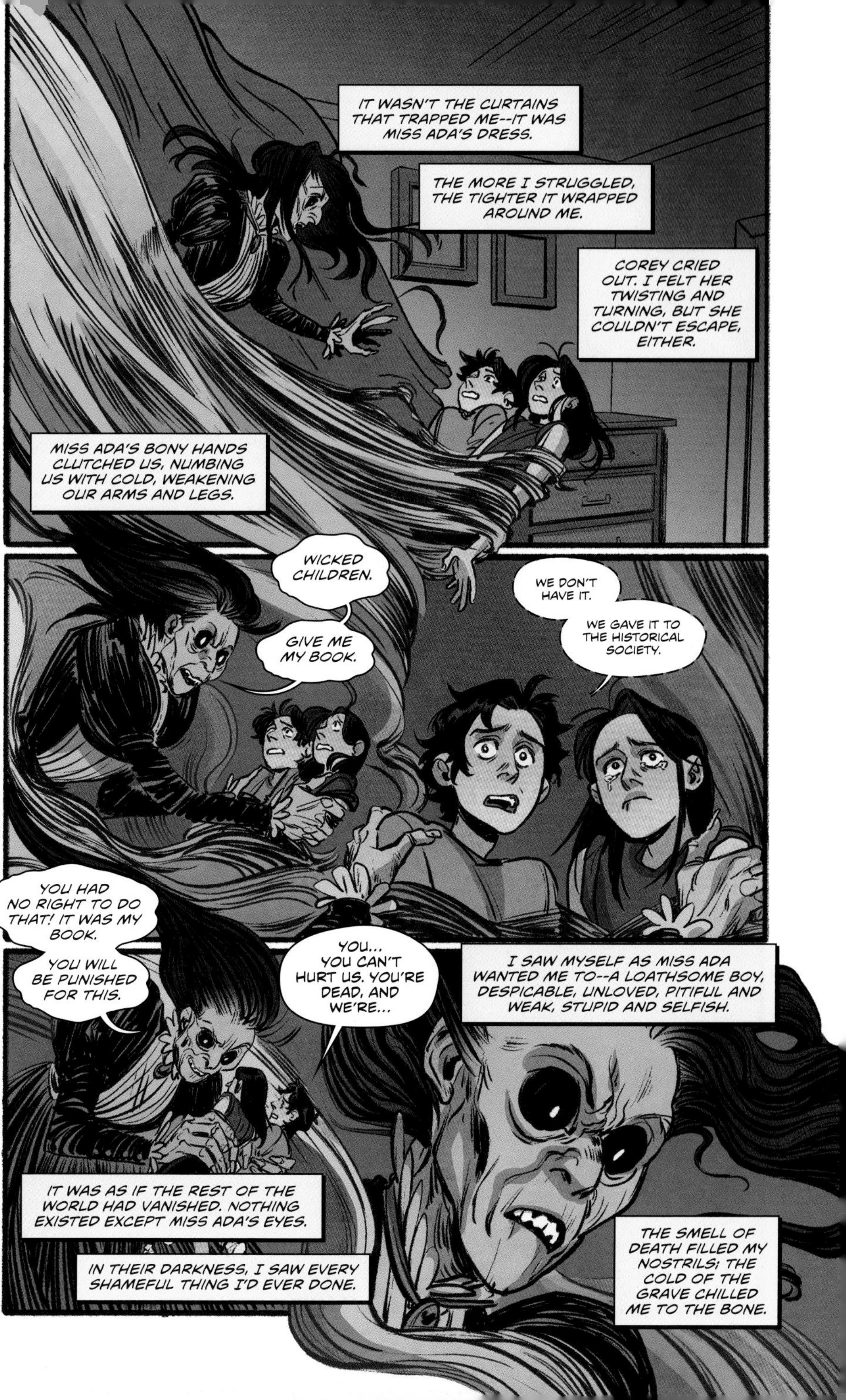
IT WASN'T THE CURTAINS THAT TRAPPED ME--IT WAS MISS ADA'S DRESS.
THE MORE I STRUGGLED, THE TIGHTER IT WRAPPED AROUND ME.
COREY CRIED OUT. I FELT HER TWISTING AND TURNING, BUT SHE COULDN'T ESCAPE, EITHER.
MISS ADA'S BONY HANDS CLUTCHED US, NUMBING US WITH COLD, WEAKENING OUR ARMS AND LEGS.
WICKED CHILDREN.
GIVE ME MY BOOK.
WE DON'T HAVE IT.
WE GAVE IT TO THE HISTORICAL SOCIETY.
YOU HAD NO RIGHT TO DO THAT! IT WAS MY BOOK.
YOU WILL BE PUNISHED FOR THIS.
YOU... YOU CAN'T HURT US. YOU'RE DEAD, AND WE'RE...
I SAW MYSELF AS MISS ADA WANTED ME TO--A LOATHSOME BOY, DESPICABLE, UNLOVED, PITIFUL AND WEAK, STUPID AND SELFISH.
IT WAS AS IF THE REST OF THE WORLD HAD VANISHED. NOTHING EXISTED EXCEPT MISS ADA'S EYES.
IN THEIR DARKNESS, I SAW EVERY SHAMEFUL THING I'D EVER DONE.
THE SMELL OF DEATH FILLED MY NOSTRILS; THE COLD OF THE GRAVE CHILLED ME TO THE BONE.

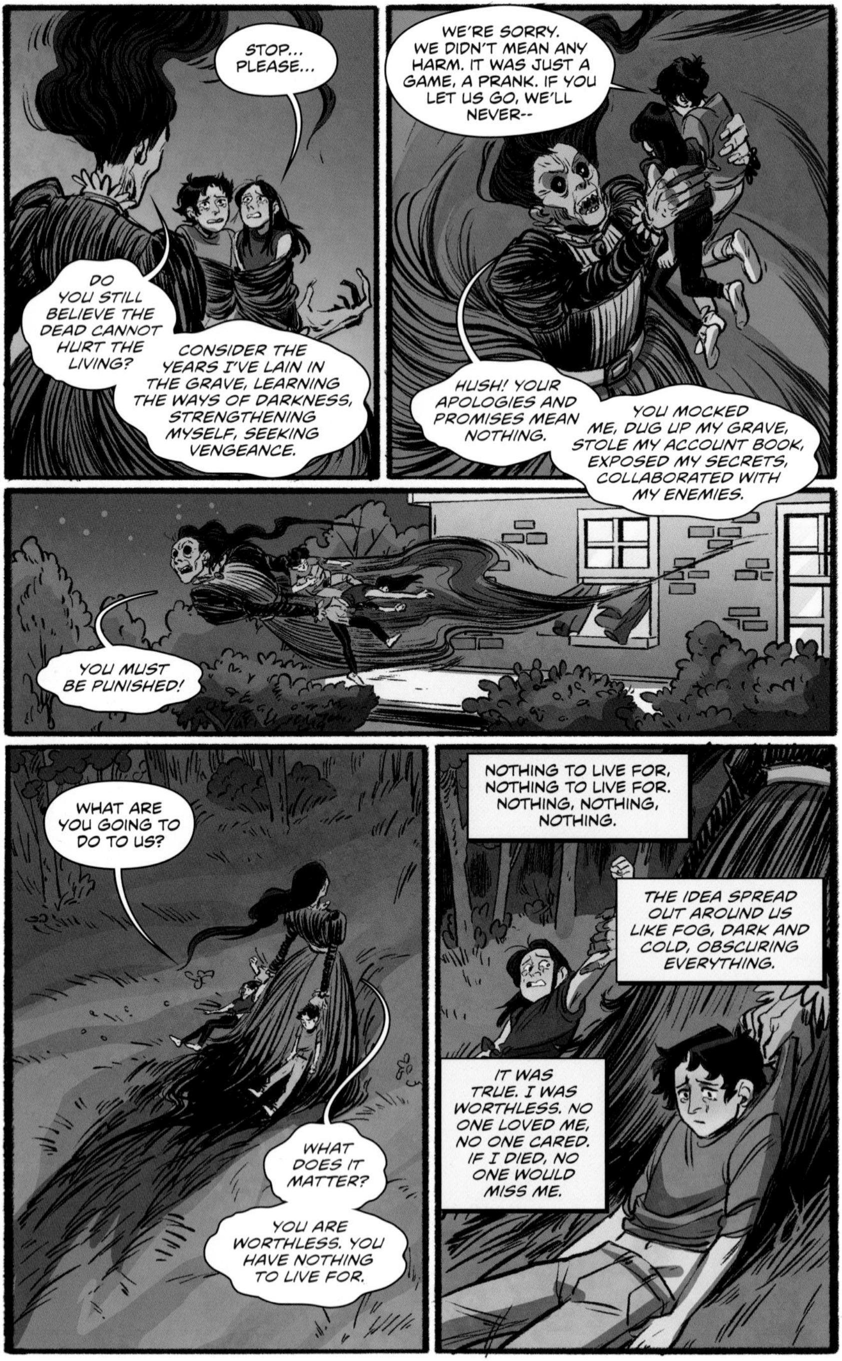
STOP... PLEASE...
DO YOU STILL BELIEVE THE DEAD CANNOT HURT THE LIVING?
CONSIDER THE YEARS I'VE LAIN IN THE GRAVE, LEARNING THE WAYS OF DARKNESS, STRENGTHENING MYSELF, SEEKING VENGEANCE.
WE'RE SORRY. WE DIDN'T MEAN ANY HARM. IT WAS JUST A GAME, A PRANK. IF YOU LET US GO, WE'LL NEVER--
HUSH! YOUR APOLOGIES AND PROMISES MEAN NOTHING.
YOU MOCKED ME, DUG UP MY GRAVE, STOLE MY ACCOUNT BOOK, EXPOSED MY SECRETS, COLLABORATED WITH MY ENEMIES.
YOU MUST BE PUNISHED!
WHAT ARE YOU GOING TO DO TO US?
WHAT DOES IT MATTER?
YOU ARE WORTHLESS. YOU HAVE NOTHING TO LIVE FOR.
NOTHING TO LIVE FOR, NOTHING TO LIVE FOR. NOTHING, NOTHING, NOTHING.
THE IDEA SPREAD OUT AROUND US LIKE FOG, DARK AND COLD, OBSCURING EVERYTHING.
IT WAS TRUE. I WAS WORTHLESS. NO ONE LOVED ME, NO ONE CARED. IF I DIED, NO ONE WOULD MISS ME.

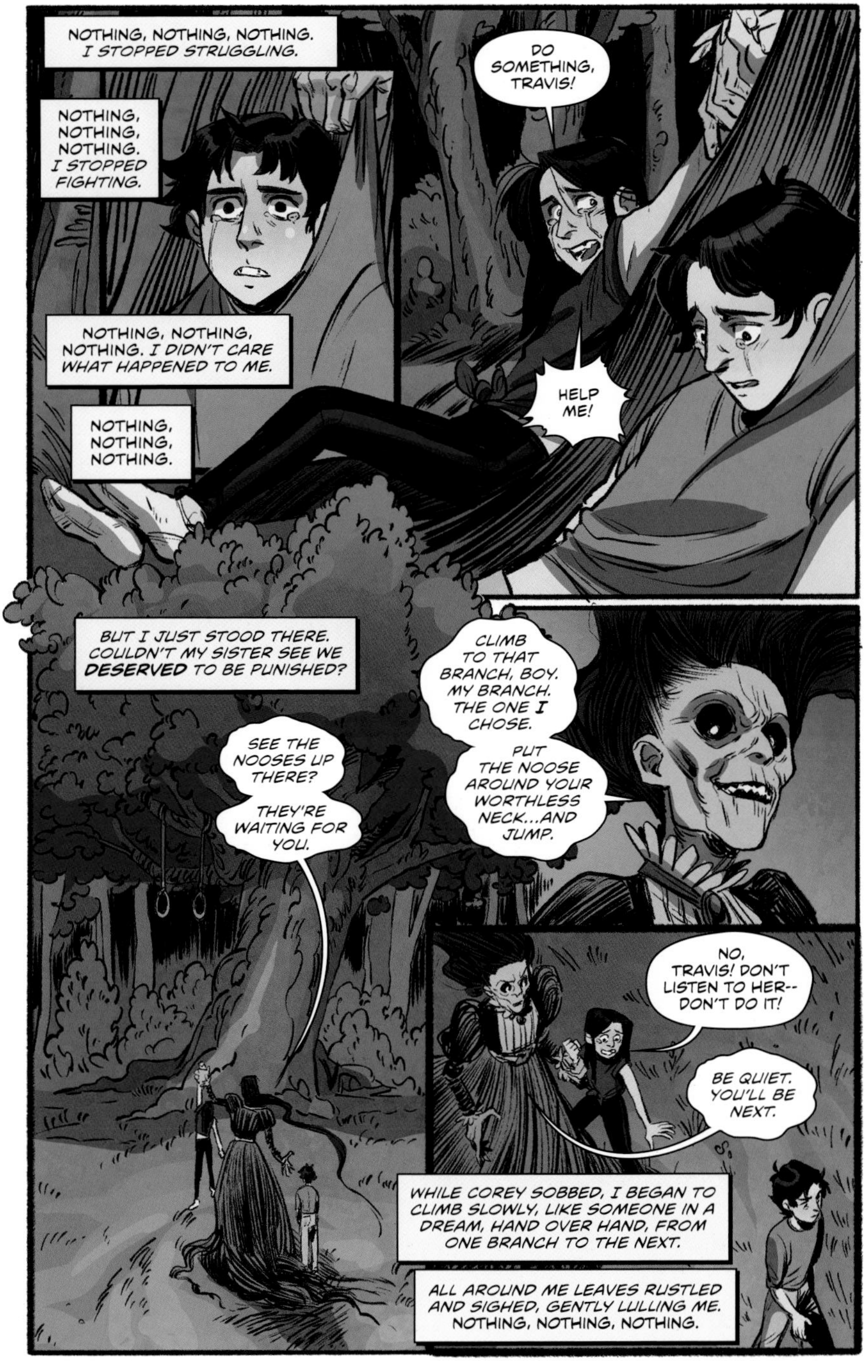
NOTHING, NOTHING, NOTHING. I STOPPED STRUGGLING.
NOTHING, NOTHING, NOTHING. I STOPPED FIGHTING.
NOTHING, NOTHING, NOTHING. I DIDN'T CARE WHAT HAPPENED TO ME.
NOTHING, NOTHING, NOTHING.
DO SOMETHING, TRAVIS!
HELP ME!
BUT I JUST STOOD THERE. COULDN'T MY SISTER SEE WE **DESERVED** TO BE PUNISHED?
SEE THE NOOSES UP THERE?
THEY'RE WAITING FOR YOU.
CLIMB TO THAT BRANCH, BOY. MY BRANCH. THE ONE **I** CHOSE.
PUT THE NOOSE AROUND YOUR WORTHLESS NECK...AND JUMP.
NO, TRAVIS! DON'T LISTEN TO HER--DON'T DO IT!
BE QUIET. YOU'LL BE NEXT.
WHILE COREY SOBBED, I BEGAN TO CLIMB SLOWLY, LIKE SOMEONE IN A DREAM, HAND OVER HAND, FROM ONE BRANCH TO THE NEXT.
ALL AROUND ME LEAVES RUSTLED AND SIGHED, GENTLY LULLING ME. NOTHING, NOTHING, NOTHING.

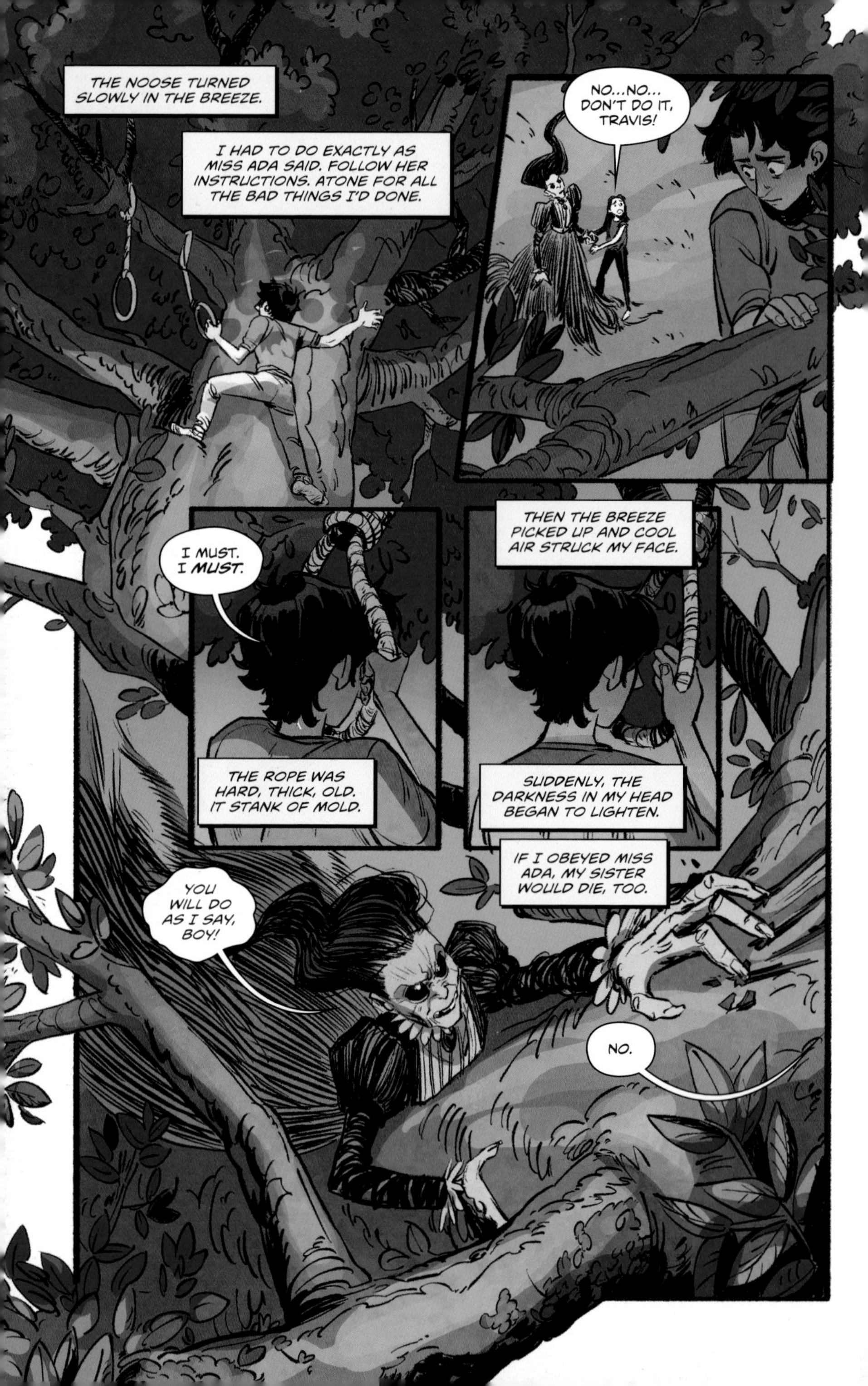
THE NOOSE TURNED SLOWLY IN THE BREEZE.
I HAD TO DO EXACTLY AS MISS ADA SAID. FOLLOW HER INSTRUCTIONS. ATONE FOR ALL THE BAD THINGS I'D DONE.
NO...NO... DON'T DO IT, TRAVIS!
I MUST. I ***MUST***.
THE ROPE WAS HARD, THICK, OLD. IT STANK OF MOLD.
THEN THE BREEZE PICKED UP AND COOL AIR STRUCK MY FACE.
SUDDENLY, THE DARKNESS IN MY HEAD BEGAN TO LIGHTEN.
IF I OBEYED MISS ADA, MY SISTER WOULD DIE, TOO.
YOU WILL DO AS I SAY, BOY!
NO.

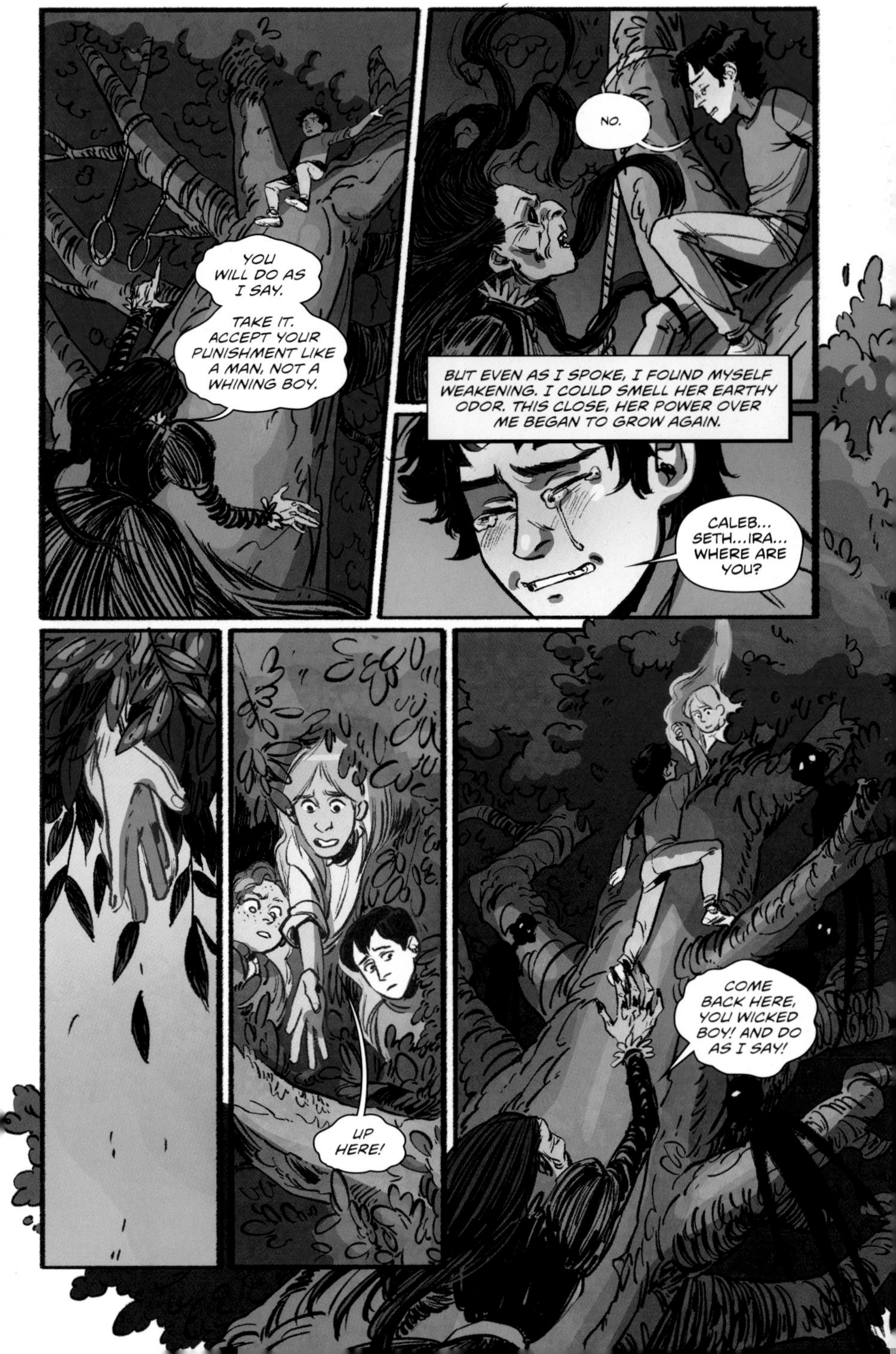
YOU WILL DO AS I SAY.
TAKE IT. ACCEPT YOUR PUNISHMENT LIKE A MAN, NOT A WHINING BOY.
NO.
BUT EVEN AS I SPOKE, I FOUND MYSELF WEAKENING. I COULD SMELL HER EARTHY ODOR. THIS CLOSE, HER POWER OVER ME BEGAN TO GROW AGAIN.
CALEB... SETH...IRA... WHERE ARE YOU?
UP HERE!
COME BACK HERE, YOU WICKED BOY! AND DO AS I SAY!

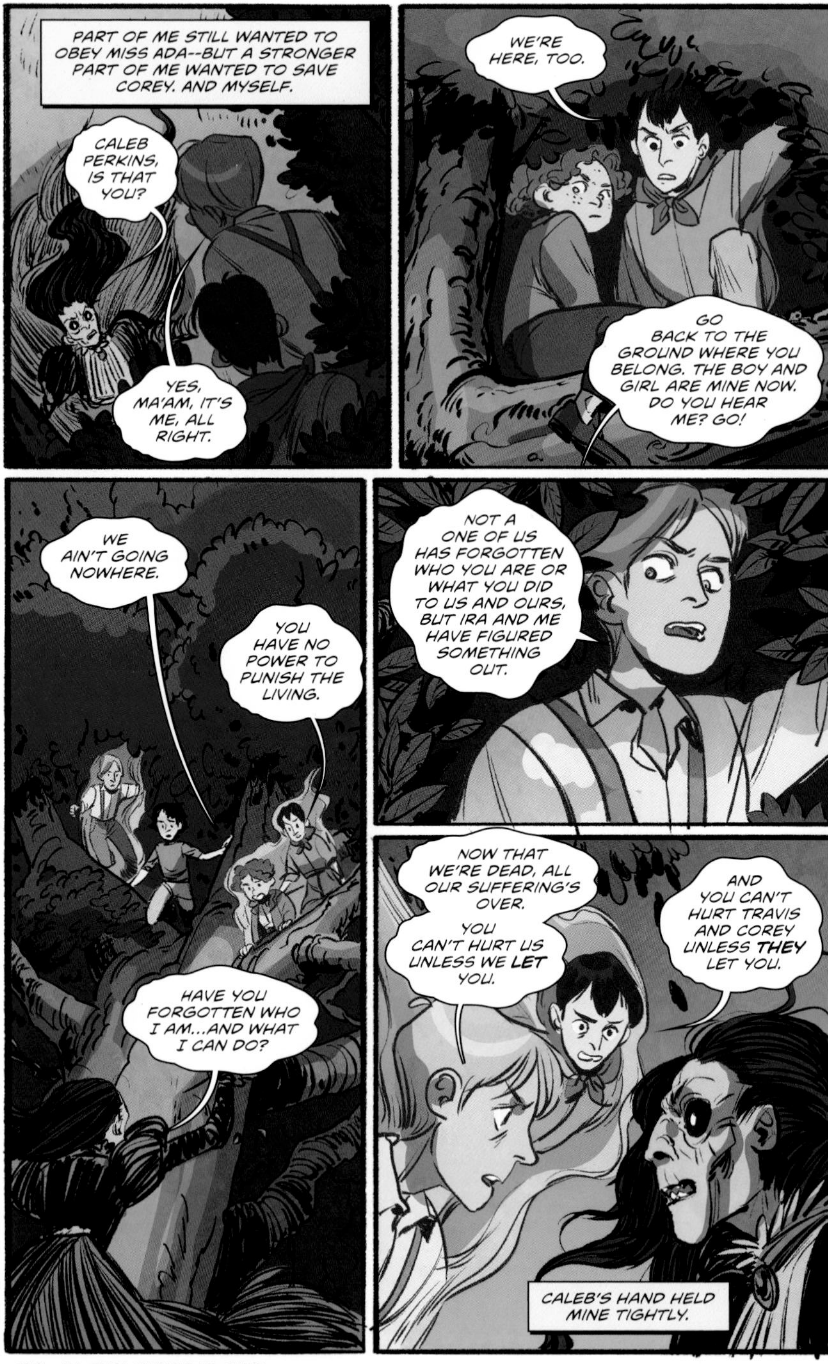
PART OF ME STILL WANTED TO OBEY MISS ADA--BUT A STRONGER PART OF ME WANTED TO SAVE COREY. AND MYSELF.
CALEB PERKINS, IS THAT YOU?
YES, MA'AM, IT'S ME, ALL RIGHT.
WE'RE HERE, TOO.
GO BACK TO THE GROUND WHERE YOU BELONG. THE BOY AND GIRL ARE MINE NOW. DO YOU HEAR ME? GO!
WE AIN'T GOING NOWHERE.
YOU HAVE NO POWER TO PUNISH THE LIVING.
HAVE YOU FORGOTTEN WHO I AM...AND WHAT I CAN DO?
NOT A ONE OF US HAS FORGOTTEN WHO YOU ARE OR WHAT YOU DID TO US AND OURS, BUT IRA AND ME HAVE FIGURED SOMETHING OUT.
NOW THAT WE'RE DEAD, ALL OUR SUFFERING'S OVER.
YOU CAN'T HURT US UNLESS WE **LET** YOU.
AND YOU CAN'T HURT TRAVIS AND COREY UNLESS **THEY** LET YOU.
CALEB'S HAND HELD MINE TIGHTLY.

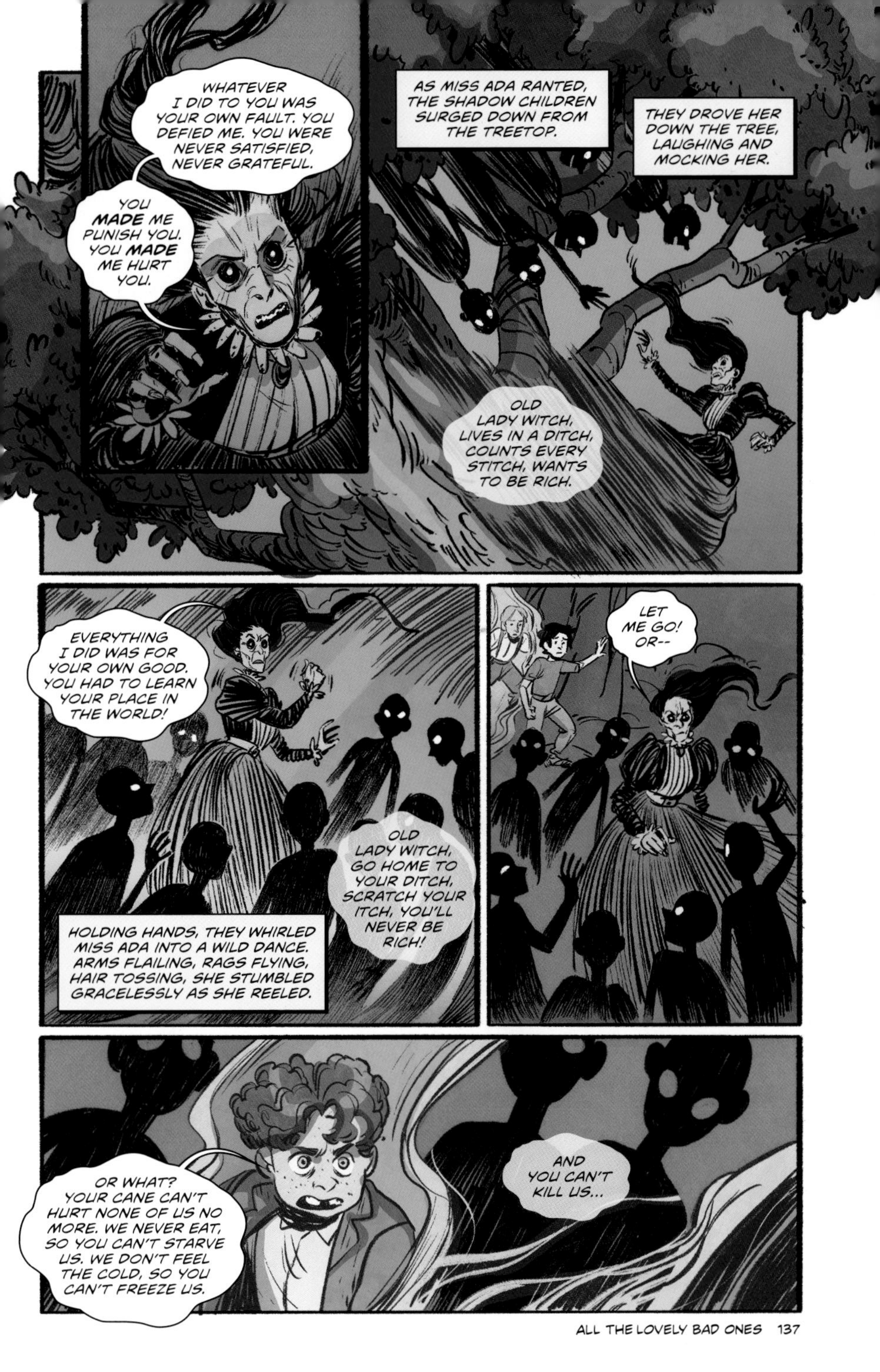
WHATEVER I DID TO YOU WAS YOUR OWN FAULT. YOU DEFIED ME. YOU WERE NEVER SATISFIED, NEVER GRATEFUL.
YOU **MADE** ME PUNISH YOU. YOU **MADE** ME HURT YOU.
AS MISS ADA RANTED, THE SHADOW CHILDREN SURGED DOWN FROM THE TREETOP.
THEY DROVE HER DOWN THE TREE, LAUGHING AND MOCKING HER.
OLD LADY WITCH, LIVES IN A DITCH, COUNTS EVERY STITCH, WANTS TO BE RICH.
EVERYTHING I DID WAS FOR YOUR OWN GOOD. YOU HAD TO LEARN YOUR PLACE IN THE WORLD!
OLD LADY WITCH, GO HOME TO YOUR DITCH, SCRATCH YOUR ITCH, YOU'LL NEVER BE RICH!
HOLDING HANDS, THEY WHIRLED MISS ADA INTO A WILD DANCE. ARMS FLAILING, RAGS FLYING, HAIR TOSSING, SHE STUMBLED GRACELESSLY AS SHE REELED.
LET ME GO! OR--
OR WHAT? YOUR CANE CAN'T HURT NONE OF US NO MORE. WE NEVER EAT, SO YOU CAN'T STARVE US. WE DON'T FEEL THE COLD, SO YOU CAN'T FREEZE US.
AND YOU CAN'T KILL US...

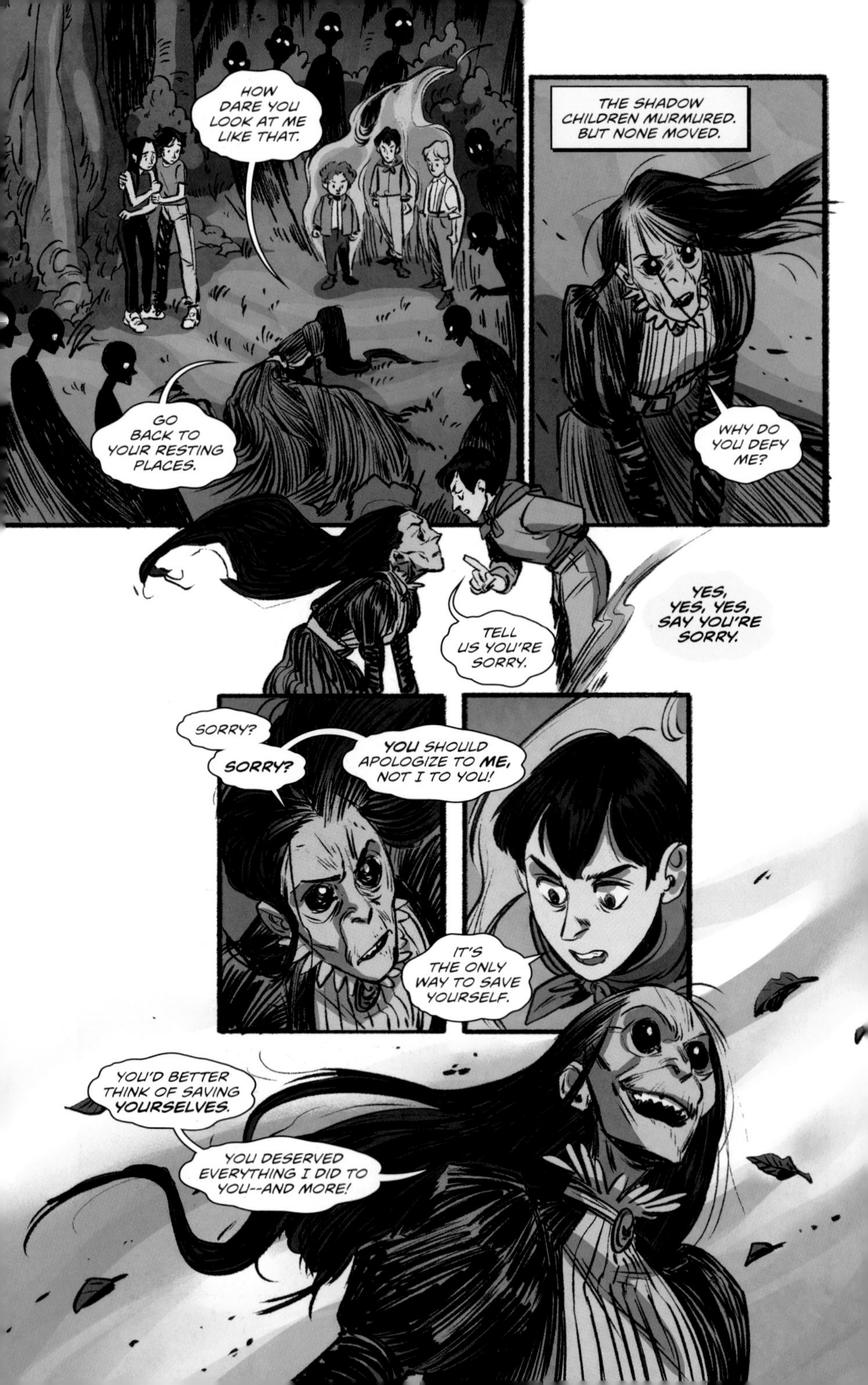
HOW DARE YOU LOOK AT ME LIKE THAT.
GO BACK TO YOUR RESTING PLACES.
THE SHADOW CHILDREN MURMURED. BUT NONE MOVED.
WHY DO YOU DEFY ME?
TELL US YOU'RE SORRY.
YES, YES, YES, SAY YOU'RE SORRY.
SORRY?
SORRY?
YOU SHOULD APOLOGIZE TO ME, NOT I TO YOU!
IT'S THE ONLY WAY TO SAVE YOURSELF.
YOU'D BETTER THINK OF SAVING YOURSELVES.
YOU DESERVED EVERYTHING I DID TO YOU--AND MORE!

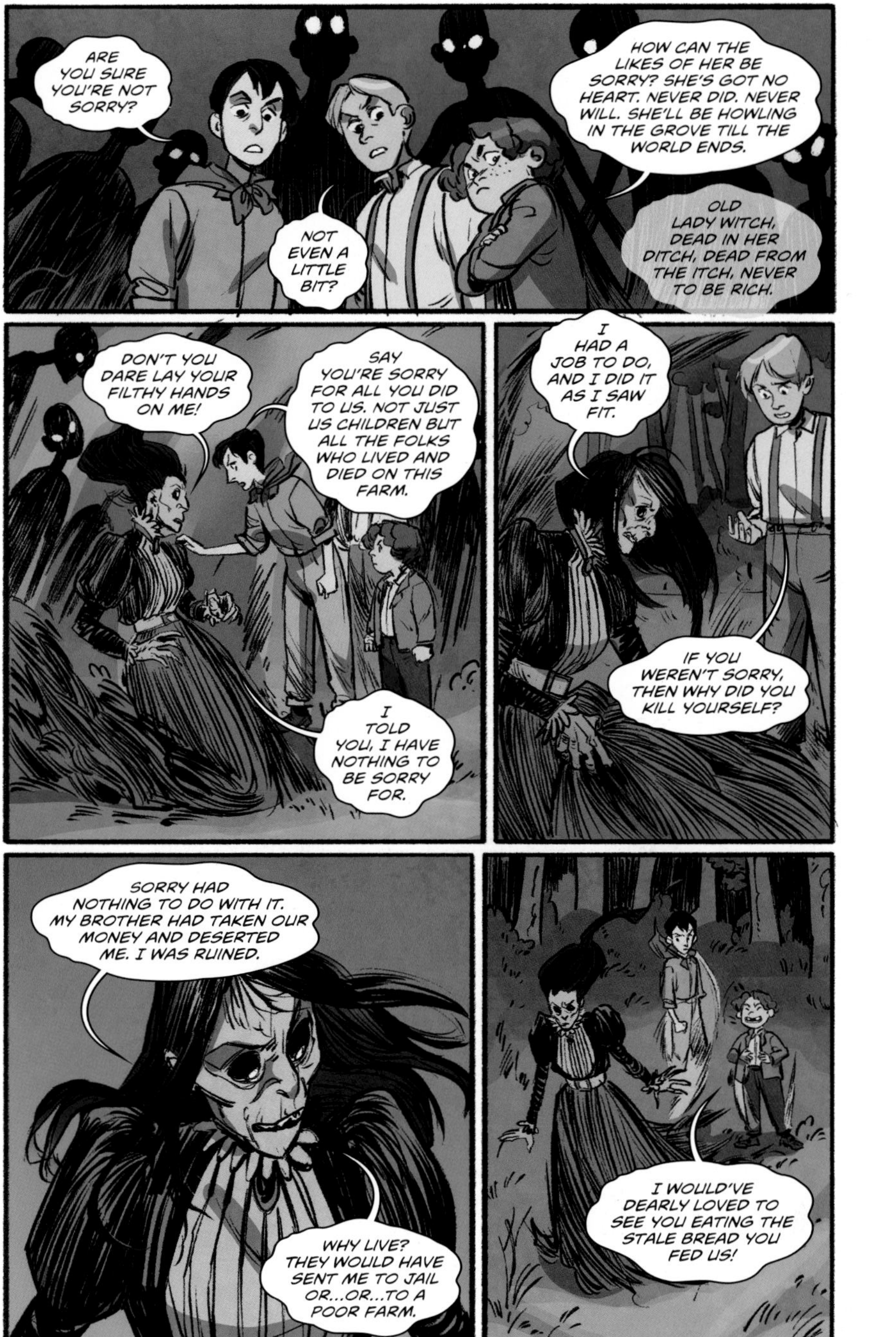
ARE YOU SURE YOU'RE NOT SORRY?
NOT EVEN A LITTLE BIT?
HOW CAN THE LIKES OF HER BE SORRY? SHE'S GOT NO HEART. NEVER DID. NEVER WILL. SHE'LL BE HOWLING IN THE GROVE TILL THE WORLD ENDS.
OLD LADY WITCH, DEAD IN HER DITCH, DEAD FROM THE ITCH, NEVER TO BE RICH.
DON'T YOU DARE LAY YOUR FILTHY HANDS ON ME!
SAY YOU'RE SORRY FOR ALL YOU DID TO US. NOT JUST US CHILDREN BUT ALL THE FOLKS WHO LIVED AND DIED ON THIS FARM.
I TOLD YOU, I HAVE NOTHING TO BE SORRY FOR.
I HAD A JOB TO DO, AND I DID IT AS I SAW FIT.
IF YOU WEREN'T SORRY, THEN WHY DID YOU KILL YOURSELF?
SORRY HAD NOTHING TO DO WITH IT. MY BROTHER HAD TAKEN OUR MONEY AND DESERTED ME. I WAS RUINED.
WHY LIVE? THEY WOULD HAVE SENT ME TO JAIL OR...OR...TO A POOR FARM.
I WOULD'VE DEARLY LOVED TO SEE YOU EATING THE STALE BREAD YOU FED US!

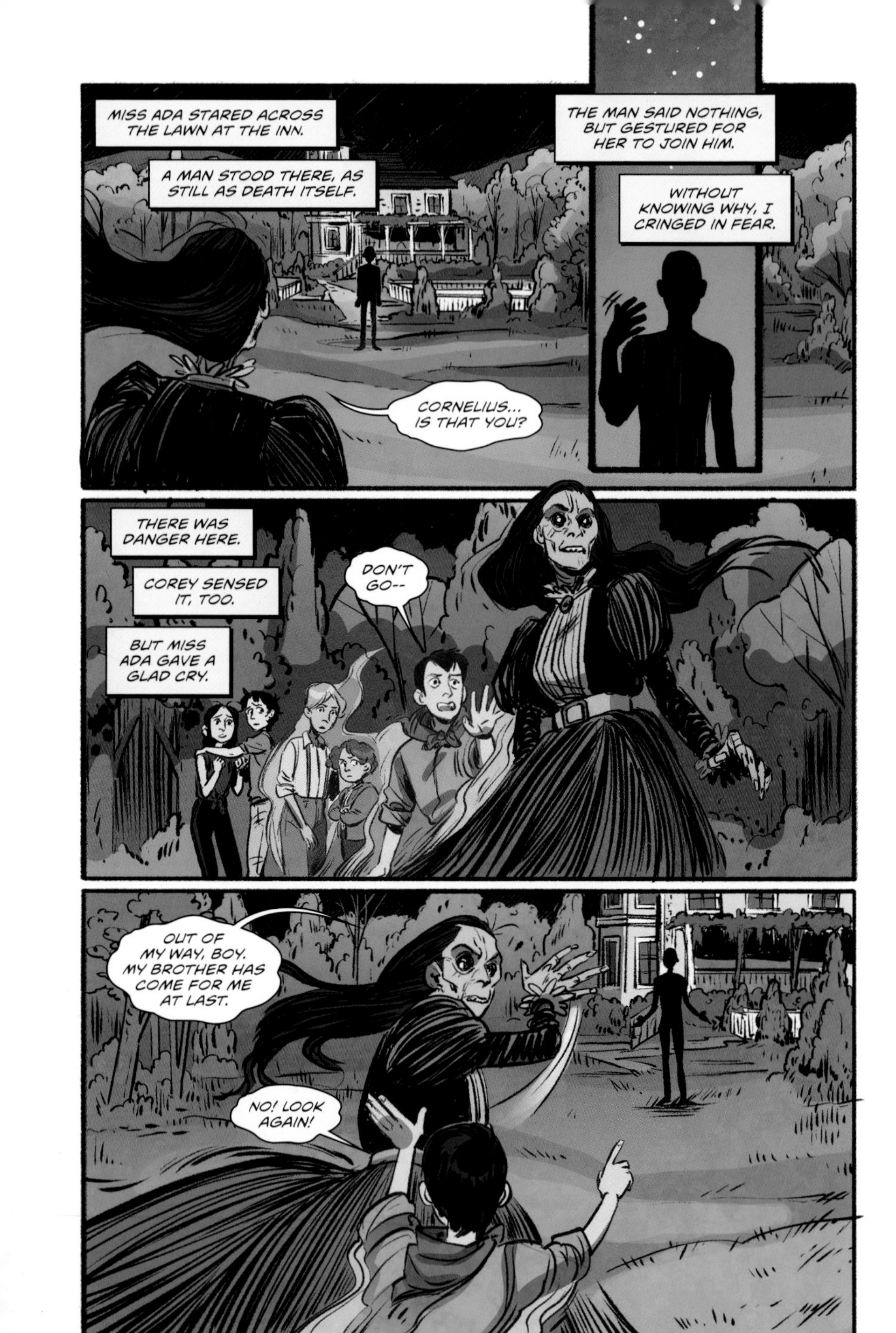
MISS ADA STARED ACROSS THE LAWN AT THE INN.
A MAN STOOD THERE, AS STILL AS DEATH ITSELF.
CORNELIUS... IS THAT YOU?
THE MAN SAID NOTHING, BUT GESTURED FOR HER TO JOIN HIM.
WITHOUT KNOWING WHY, I CRINGED IN FEAR.
THERE WAS DANGER HERE.
COREY SENSED IT, TOO.
BUT MISS ADA GAVE A GLAD CRY.
DON'T GO--
OUT OF MY WAY, BOY. MY BROTHER HAS COME FOR ME AT LAST.
NO! LOOK AGAIN!

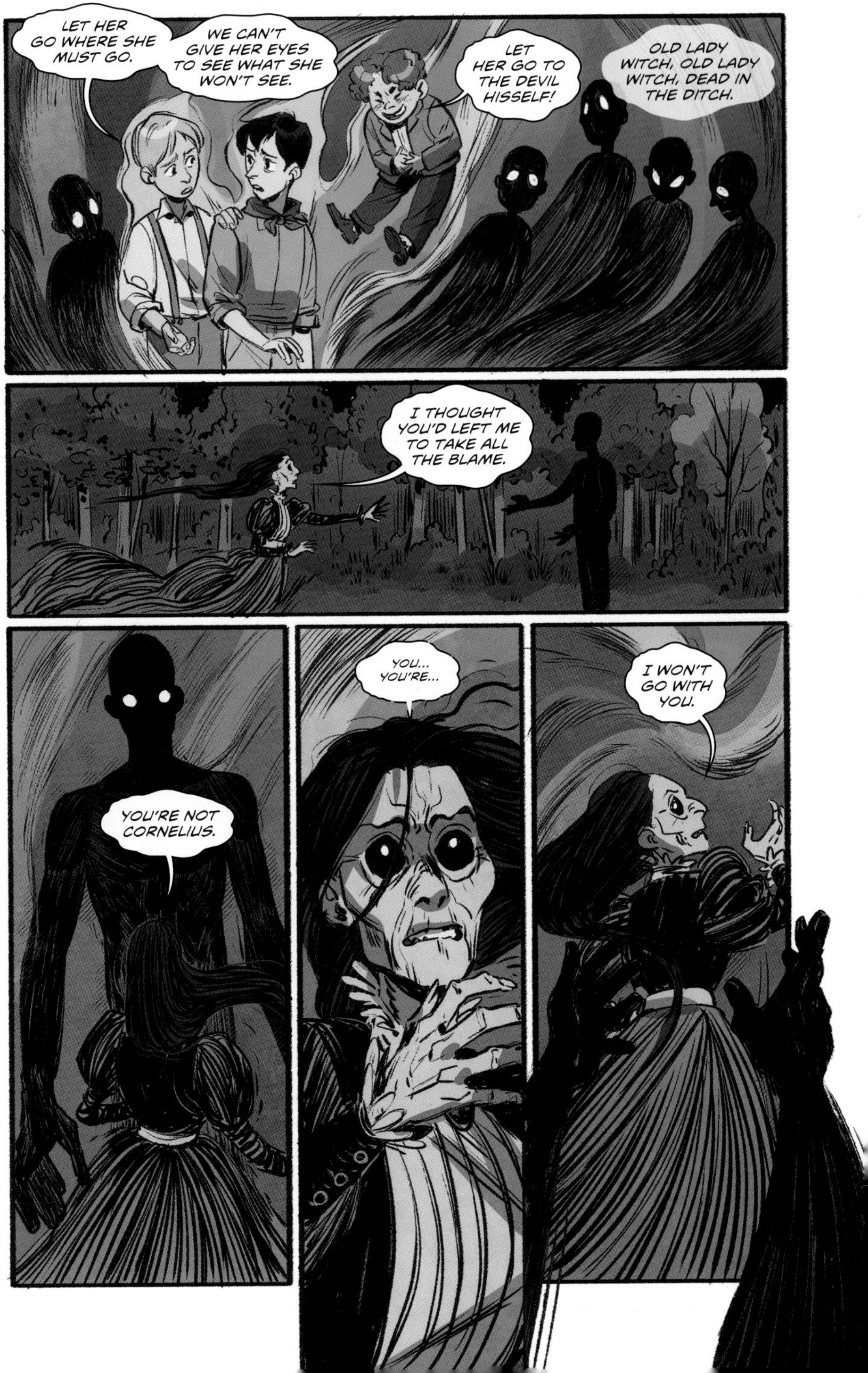
LET HER GO WHERE SHE MUST GO.
WE CAN'T GIVE HER EYES TO SEE WHAT SHE WON'T SEE.
LET HER GO TO THE DEVIL HISSELF!
OLD LADY WITCH, OLD LADY WITCH, DEAD IN THE DITCH.
I THOUGHT YOU'D LEFT ME TO TAKE ALL THE BLAME.
YOU'RE NOT CORNELIUS.
YOU... YOU'RE...
I WON'T GO WITH YOU.

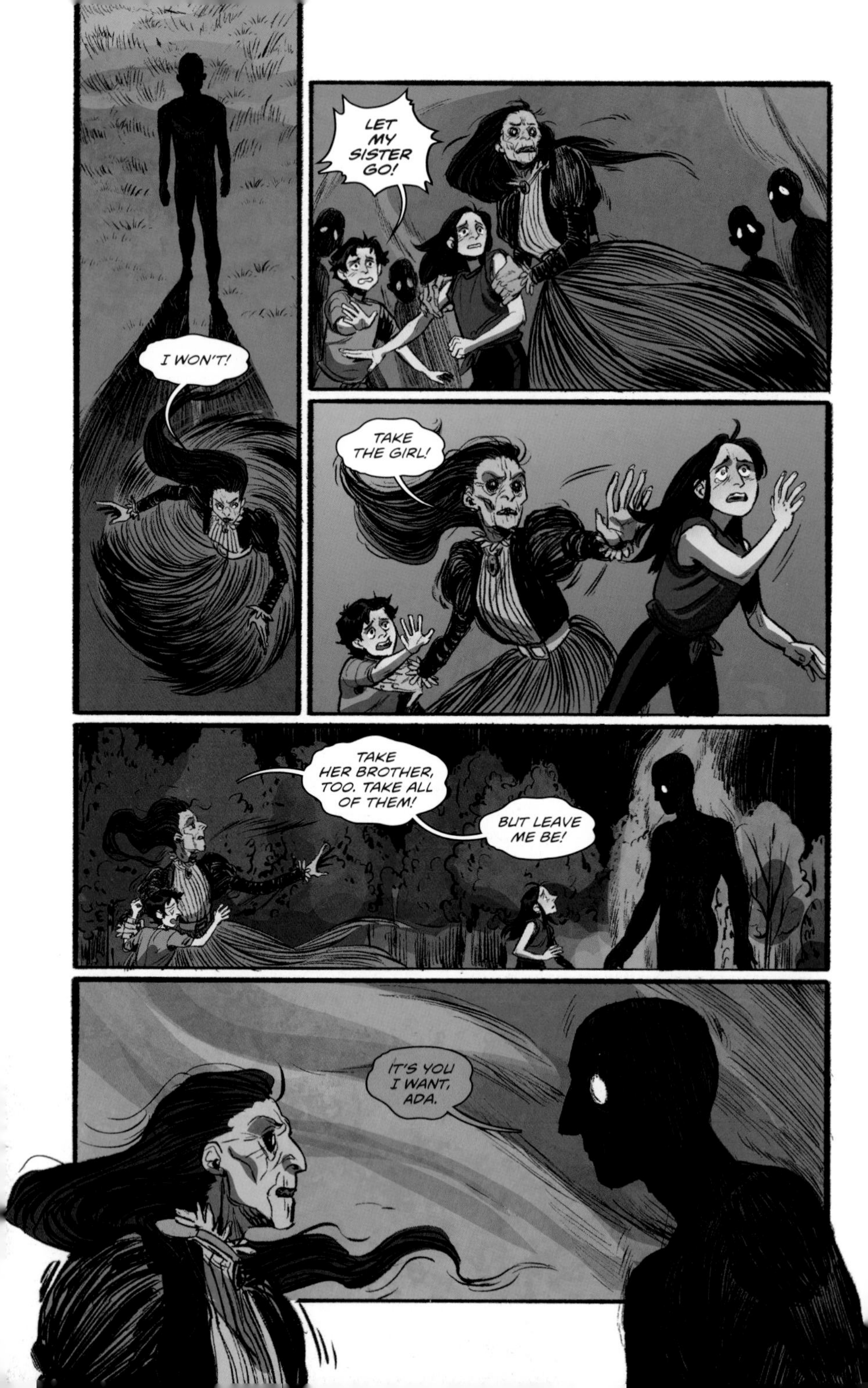
LET MY SISTER GO!
I WON'T!
TAKE THE GIRL!
TAKE HER BROTHER, TOO. TAKE ALL OF THEM!
BUT LEAVE ME BE!
IT'S YOU I WANT, ADA.

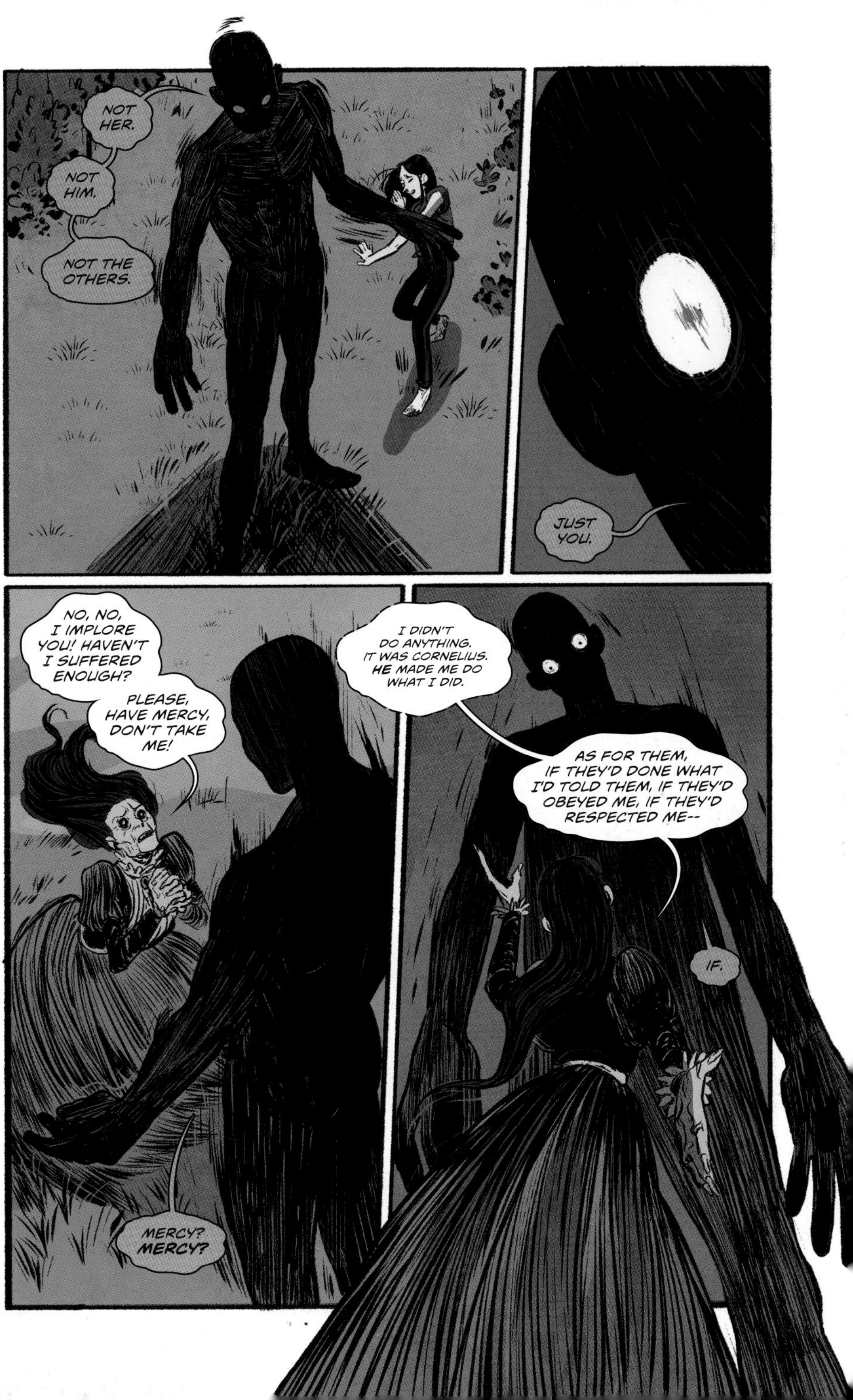
NOT HER.
NOT HIM.
NOT THE OTHERS.
JUST YOU.
NO, NO, I IMPLORE YOU! HAVEN'T I SUFFERED ENOUGH?
PLEASE, HAVE MERCY, DON'T TAKE ME!
MERCY? MERCY?
I DIDN'T DO ANYTHING. IT WAS CORNELIUS. HE MADE ME DO WHAT I DID.
AS FOR THEM, IF THEY'D DONE WHAT I'D TOLD THEM, IF THEY'D OBEYED ME, IF THEY'D RESPECTED ME--
IF.

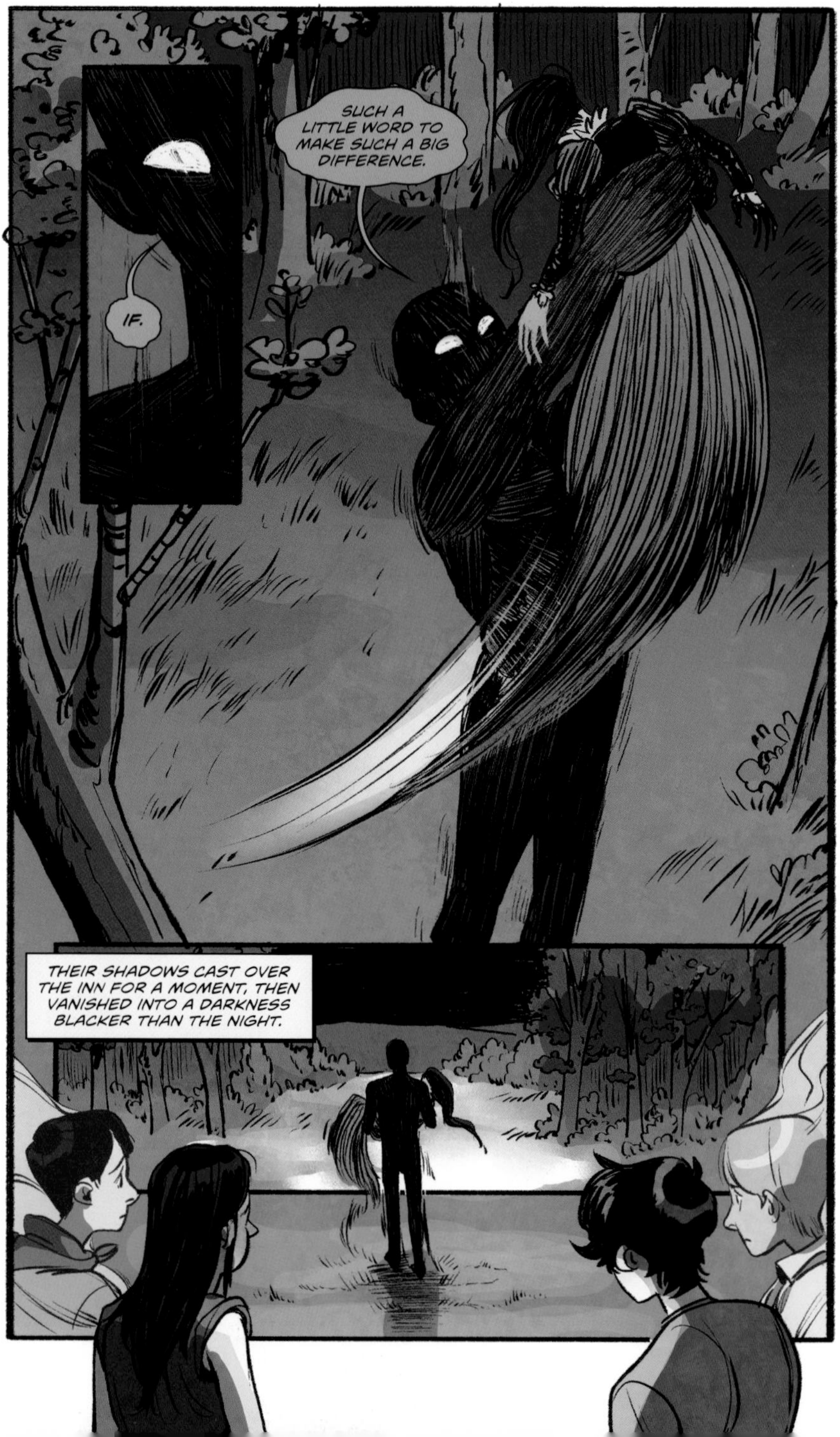
IF.
SUCH A LITTLE WORD TO MAKE SUCH A BIG DIFFERENCE.
THEIR SHADOWS CAST OVER THE INN FOR A MOMENT, THEN VANISHED INTO A DARKNESS BLACKER THAN THE NIGHT.

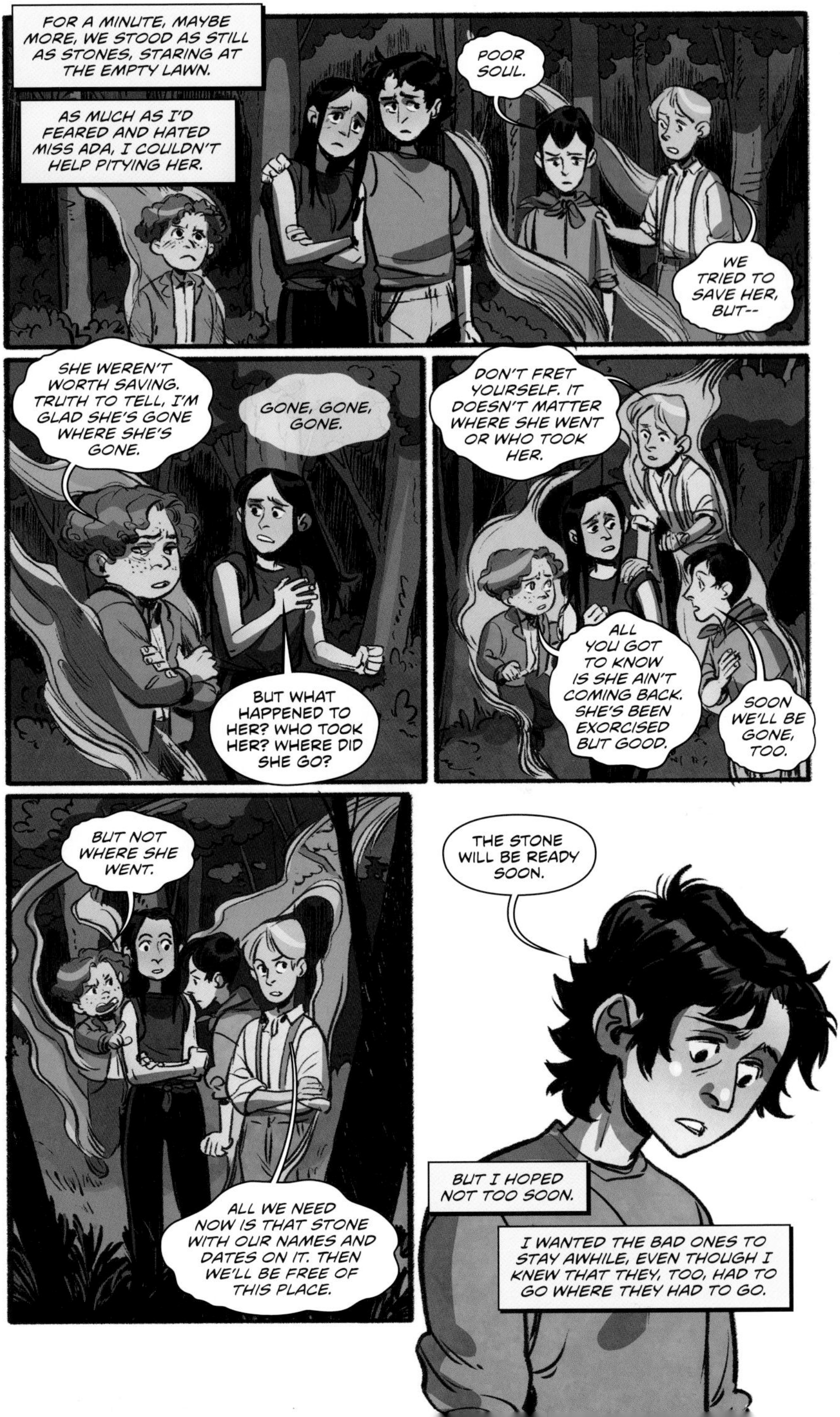

FOR A MINUTE, MAYBE MORE, WE STOOD AS STILL AS STONES, STARING AT THE EMPTY LAWN.
AS MUCH AS I'D FEARED AND HATED MISS ADA, I COULDN'T HELP PITYING HER.
POOR SOUL.
WE TRIED TO SAVE HER, BUT--
SHE WEREN'T WORTH SAVING. TRUTH TO TELL, I'M GLAD SHE'S GONE WHERE SHE'S GONE.
GONE, GONE, GONE.
BUT WHAT HAPPENED TO HER? WHO TOOK HER? WHERE DID SHE GO?
DON'T FRET YOURSELF. IT DOESN'T MATTER WHERE SHE WENT OR WHO TOOK HER.
ALL YOU GOT TO KNOW IS SHE AIN'T COMING BACK. SHE'S BEEN EXORCISED BUT GOOD.
SOON WE'LL BE GONE, TOO.
BUT NOT WHERE SHE WENT.
ALL WE NEED NOW IS THAT STONE WITH OUR NAMES AND DATES ON IT. THEN WE'LL BE FREE OF THIS PLACE.
THE STONE WILL BE READY SOON.
BUT I HOPED NOT TOO SOON.
I WANTED THE BAD ONES TO STAY AWHILE, EVEN THOUGH I KNEW THAT THEY, TOO, HAD TO GO WHERE THEY HAD TO GO.

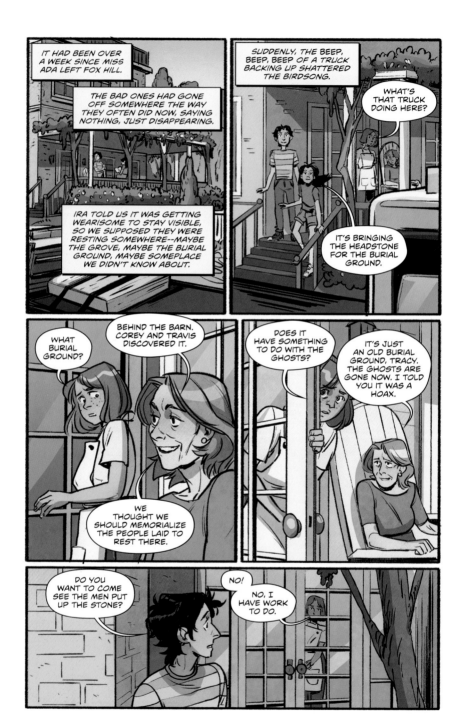

IT HAD BEEN OVER A WEEK SINCE MISS ADA LEFT FOX HILL.

THE BAD ONES HAD GONE OFF SOMEWHERE THE WAY THEY OFTEN DID NOW, SAYING NOTHING, JUST DISAPPEARING.

IRA TOLD US IT WAS GETTING WEARISOME TO STAY VISIBLE, SO WE SUPPOSED THEY WERE RESTING SOMEWHERE--MAYBE THE GROVE, MAYBE THE BURIAL GROUND, MAYBE SOMEPLACE WE DIDN'T KNOW ABOUT.

SUDDENLY, THE BEEP, BEEP, BEEP OF A TRUCK BACKING UP SHATTERED THE BIRDSONG.

WHAT'S THAT TRUCK DOING HERE?

IT'S BRINGING THE HEADSTONE FOR THE BURIAL GROUND.

WHAT BURIAL GROUND?

BEHIND THE BARN. COREY AND TRAVIS DISCOVERED IT.

WE THOUGHT WE SHOULD MEMORIALIZE THE PEOPLE LAID TO REST THERE.

DOES IT HAVE SOMETHING TO DO WITH THE GHOSTS?

IT'S JUST AN OLD BURIAL GROUND, TRACY. THE GHOSTS ARE GONE NOW. I TOLD YOU IT WAS A HOAX.

DO YOU WANT TO COME SEE THE MEN PUT UP THE STONE?

NO! NO, I HAVE WORK TO DO.

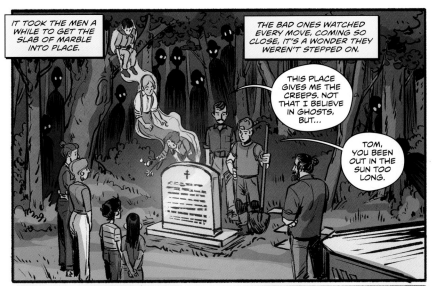

IT TOOK THE MEN A WHILE TO GET THE SLAB OF MARBLE INTO PLACE.

THE BAD ONES WATCHED EVERY MOVE, COMING SO CLOSE, IT'S A WONDER THEY WEREN'T STEPPED ON.

THIS PLACE GIVES ME THE CREEPS. NOT THAT I BELIEVE IN GHOSTS, BUT...

TOM, YOU BEEN OUT IN THE SUN TOO LONG.

WINDY TODAY.

MOSQUITOES FIERCE, TOO.

WORSE THAN USUAL.

PINCHY, PINCHY.

DON'T WORRY ABOUT PAYING NOW, MA'AM. WE'LL TELL MR. GREENE TO SEND THE BILL.

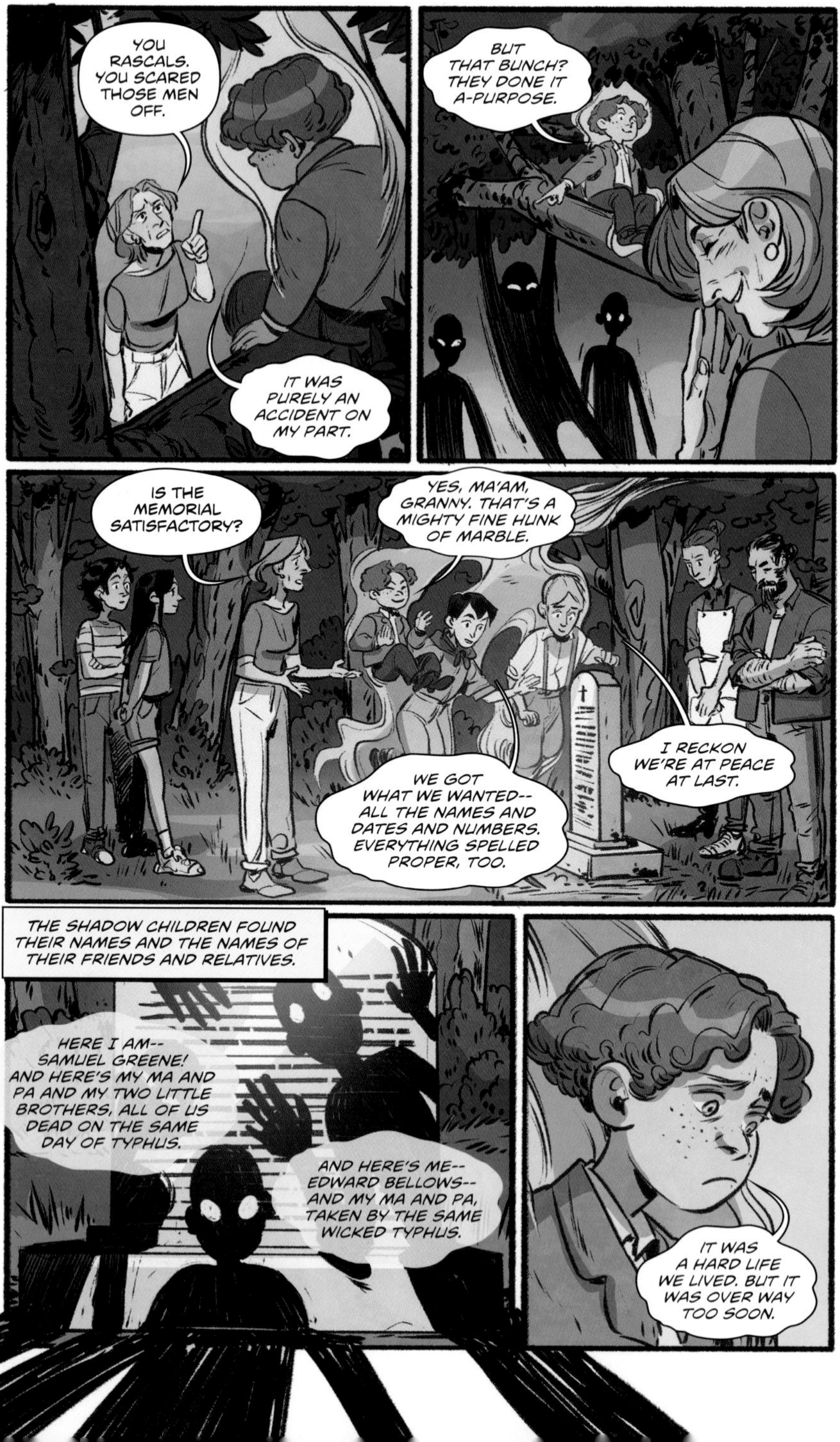
YOU RASCALS. YOU SCARED THOSE MEN OFF.
IT WAS PURELY AN ACCIDENT ON MY PART.
BUT THAT BUNCH? THEY DONE IT A-PURPOSE.
IS THE MEMORIAL SATISFACTORY?
YES, MA'AM, GRANNY. THAT'S A MIGHTY FINE HUNK OF MARBLE.
WE GOT WHAT WE WANTED-- ALL THE NAMES AND DATES AND NUMBERS. EVERYTHING SPELLED PROPER, TOO.
I RECKON WE'RE AT PEACE AT LAST.
THE SHADOW CHILDREN FOUND THEIR NAMES AND THE NAMES OF THEIR FRIENDS AND RELATIVES.
HERE I AM-- SAMUEL GREENE! AND HERE'S MY MA AND PA AND MY TWO LITTLE BROTHERS, ALL OF US DEAD ON THE SAME DAY OF TYPHUS.
AND HERE'S ME-- EDWARD BELLOWS-- AND MY MA AND PA, TAKEN BY THE SAME WICKED TYPHUS.
IT WAS A HARD LIFE WE LIVED. BUT IT WAS OVER WAY TOO SOON.

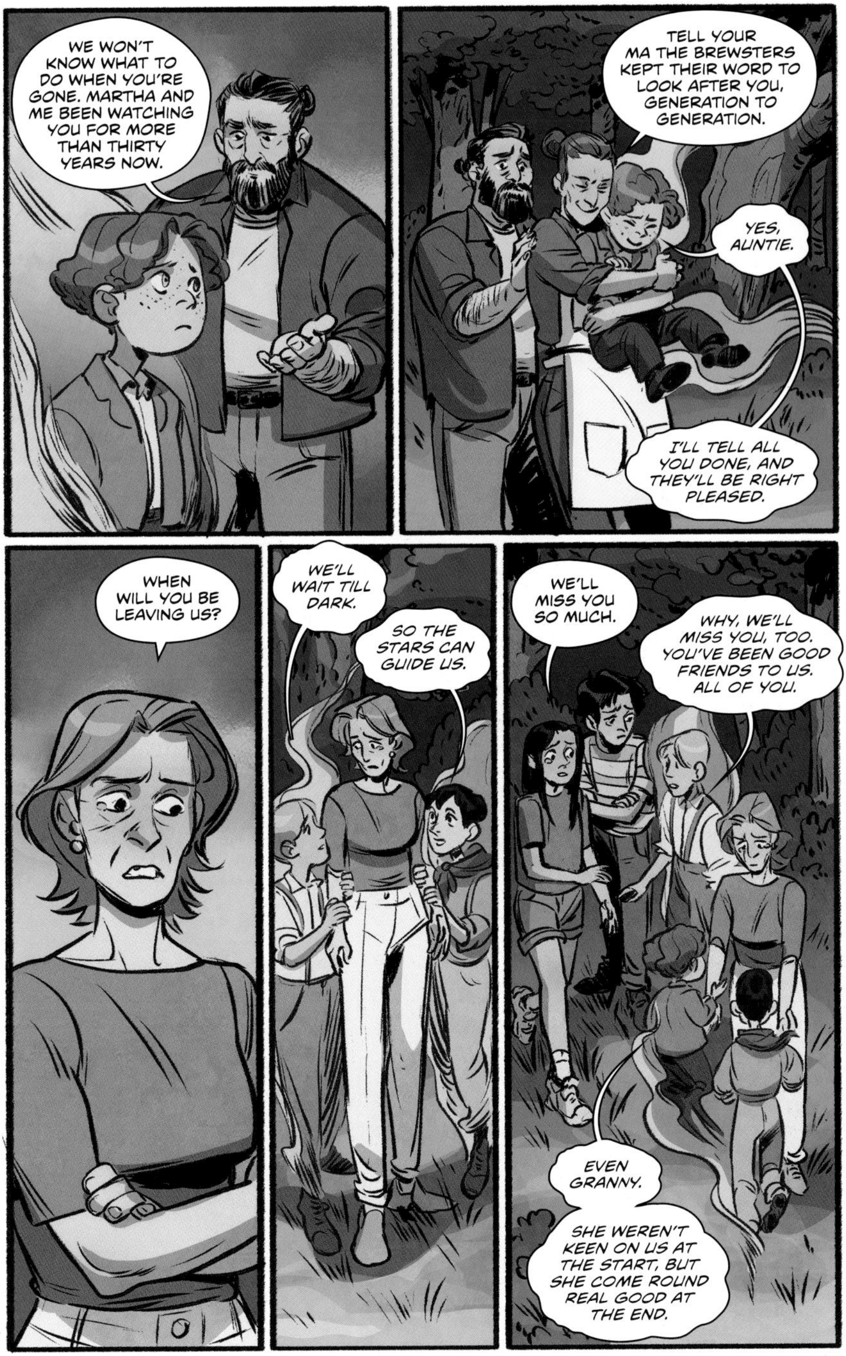
WE WON'T KNOW WHAT TO DO WHEN YOU'RE GONE. MARTHA AND ME BEEN WATCHING YOU FOR MORE THAN THIRTY YEARS NOW.
TELL YOUR MA THE BREWSTERS KEPT THEIR WORD TO LOOK AFTER YOU, GENERATION TO GENERATION.
YES, AUNTIE.
I'LL TELL ALL YOU DONE, AND THEY'LL BE RIGHT PLEASED.
WHEN WILL YOU BE LEAVING US?
WE'LL WAIT TILL DARK.
SO THE STARS CAN GUIDE US.
WE'LL MISS YOU SO MUCH.
WHY, WE'LL MISS YOU, TOO. YOU'VE BEEN GOOD FRIENDS TO US. ALL OF YOU.
EVEN GRANNY.
SHE WEREN'T KEEN ON US AT THE START, BUT SHE COME ROUND REAL GOOD AT THE END.

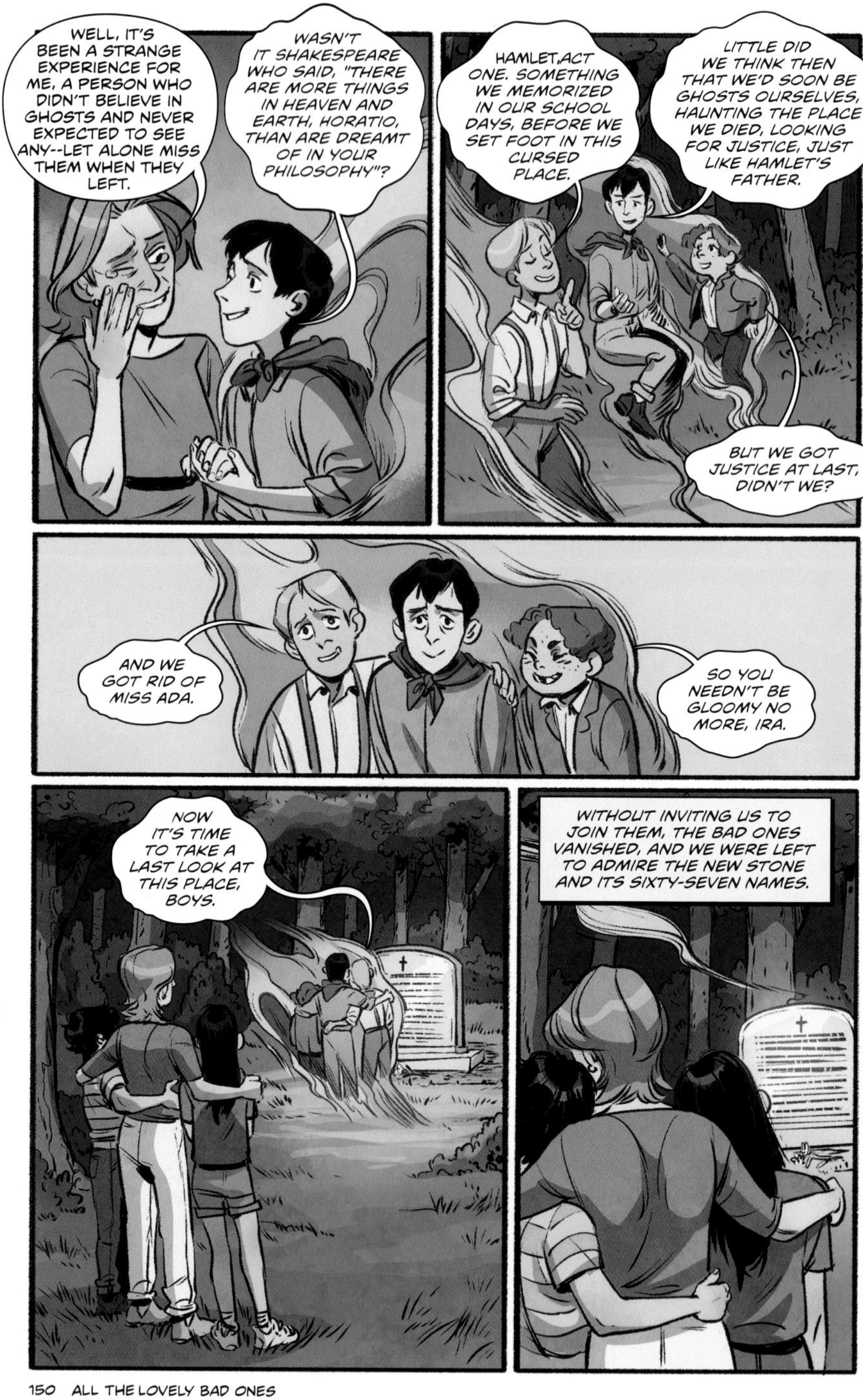
WELL, IT'S BEEN A STRANGE EXPERIENCE FOR ME, A PERSON WHO DIDN'T BELIEVE IN GHOSTS AND NEVER EXPECTED TO SEE ANY--LET ALONE MISS THEM WHEN THEY LEFT.
WASN'T IT SHAKESPEARE WHO SAID, "THERE ARE MORE THINGS IN HEAVEN AND EARTH, HORATIO, THAN ARE DREAMT OF IN YOUR PHILOSOPHY"?
HAMLET,ACT ONE. SOMETHING WE MEMORIZED IN OUR SCHOOL DAYS, BEFORE WE SET FOOT IN THIS CURSED PLACE.
LITTLE DID WE THINK THEN THAT WE'D SOON BE GHOSTS OURSELVES, HAUNTING THE PLACE WE DIED, LOOKING FOR JUSTICE, JUST LIKE HAMLET'S FATHER.
BUT WE GOT JUSTICE AT LAST, DIDN'T WE?
AND WE GOT RID OF MISS ADA.
SO YOU NEEDN'T BE GLOOMY NO MORE, IRA.
NOW IT'S TIME TO TAKE A LAST LOOK AT THIS PLACE, BOYS.
WITHOUT INVITING US TO JOIN THEM, THE BAD ONES VANISHED, AND WE WERE LEFT TO ADMIRE THE NEW STONE AND ITS SIXTY-SEVEN NAMES.

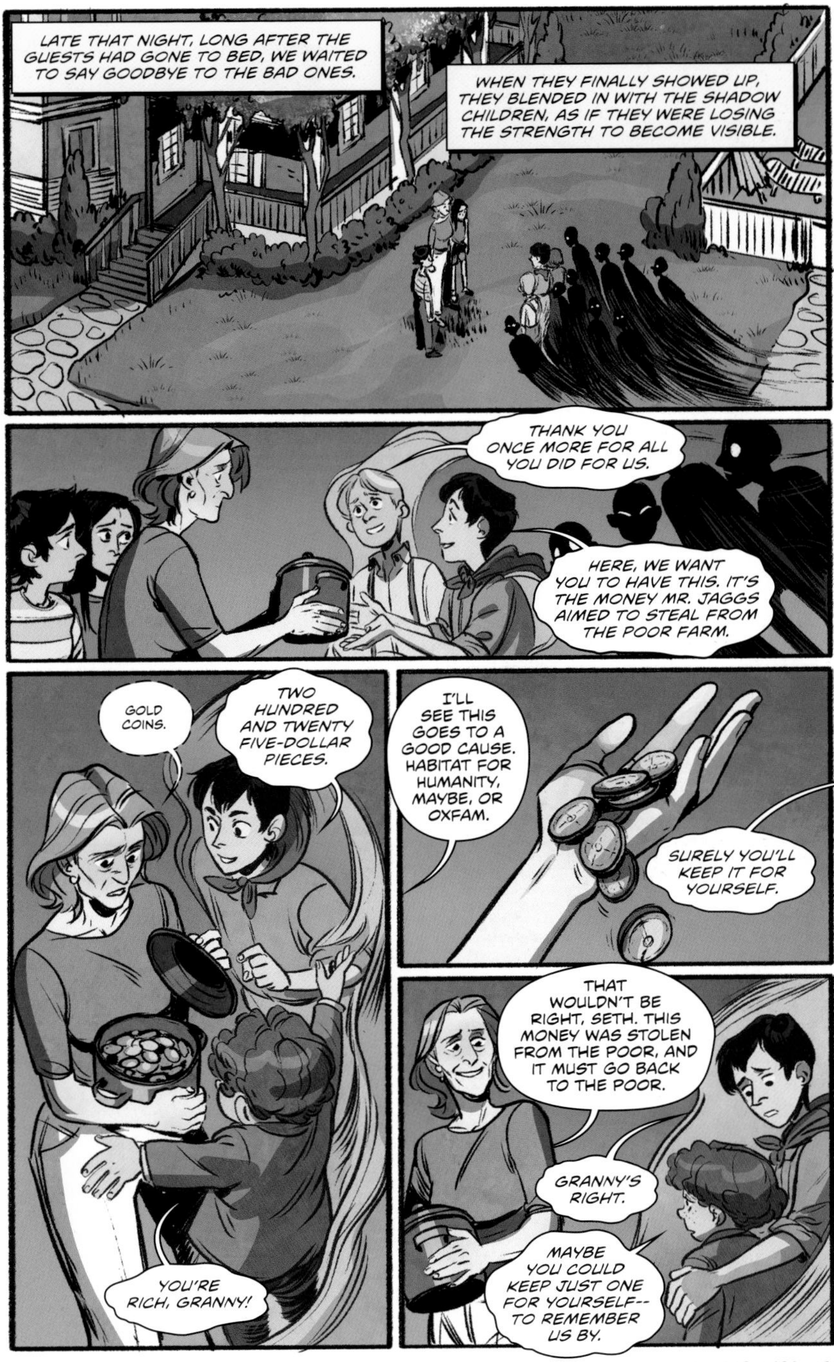
LATE THAT NIGHT, LONG AFTER THE GUESTS HAD GONE TO BED, WE WAITED TO SAY GOODBYE TO THE BAD ONES.
WHEN THEY FINALLY SHOWED UP, THEY BLENDED IN WITH THE SHADOW CHILDREN, AS IF THEY WERE LOSING THE STRENGTH TO BECOME VISIBLE.
THANK YOU ONCE MORE FOR ALL YOU DID FOR US.
HERE, WE WANT YOU TO HAVE THIS. IT'S THE MONEY MR. JAGGS AIMED TO STEAL FROM THE POOR FARM.
GOLD COINS.
TWO HUNDRED AND TWENTY FIVE-DOLLAR PIECES.
YOU'RE RICH, GRANNY!
I'LL SEE THIS GOES TO A GOOD CAUSE. HABITAT FOR HUMANITY, MAYBE, OR OXFAM.
SURELY YOU'LL KEEP IT FOR YOURSELF.
THAT WOULDN'T BE RIGHT, SETH. THIS MONEY WAS STOLEN FROM THE POOR, AND IT MUST GO BACK TO THE POOR.
GRANNY'S RIGHT.
MAYBE YOU COULD KEEP JUST ONE FOR YOURSELF-- TO REMEMBER US BY.

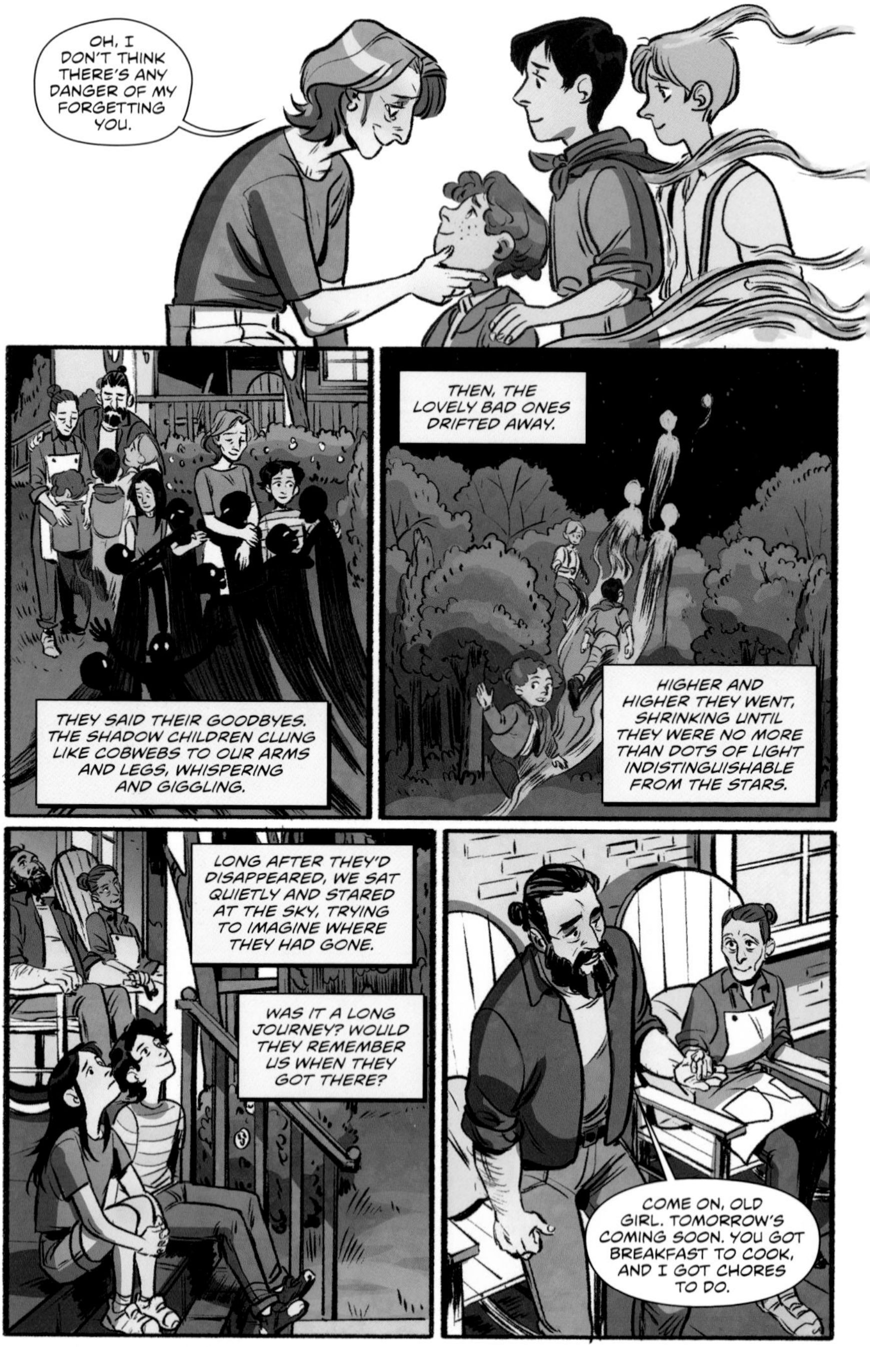
OH, I DON'T THINK THERE'S ANY DANGER OF MY FORGETTING YOU.
THEY SAID THEIR GOODBYES. THE SHADOW CHILDREN CLUNG LIKE COBWEBS TO OUR ARMS AND LEGS, WHISPERING AND GIGGLING.
THEN, THE LOVELY BAD ONES DRIFTED AWAY.
HIGHER AND HIGHER THEY WENT, SHRINKING UNTIL THEY WERE NO MORE THAN DOTS OF LIGHT INDISTINGUISHABLE FROM THE STARS.
LONG AFTER THEY'D DISAPPEARED, WE SAT QUIETLY AND STARED AT THE SKY, TRYING TO IMAGINE WHERE THEY HAD GONE.
WAS IT A LONG JOURNEY? WOULD THEY REMEMBER US WHEN THEY GOT THERE?
COME ON, OLD GIRL. TOMORROW'S COMING SOON. YOU GOT BREAKFAST TO COOK, AND I GOT CHORES TO DO.

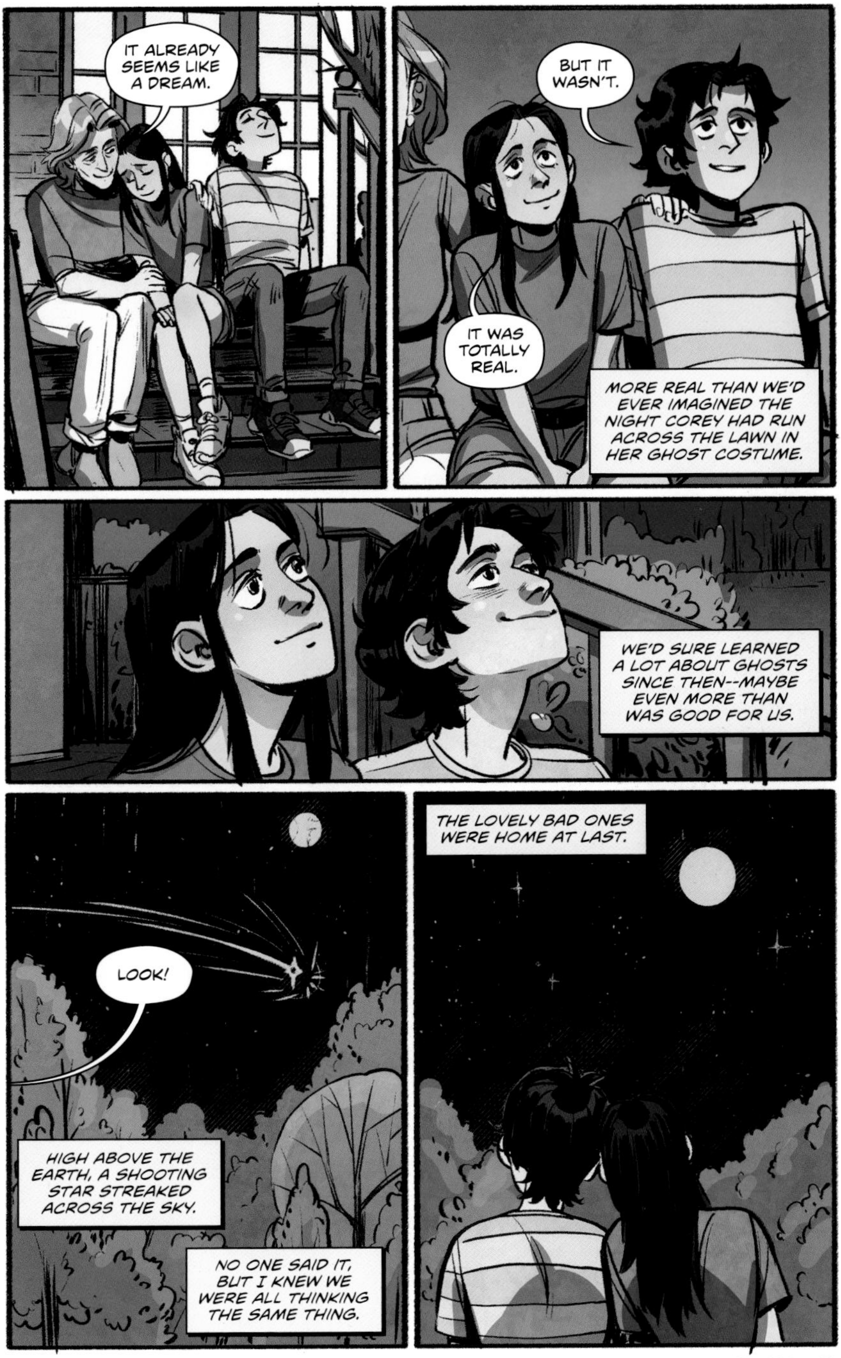
IT ALREADY SEEMS LIKE A DREAM.
BUT IT WASN'T.
IT WAS TOTALLY REAL.
MORE REAL THAN WE'D EVER IMAGINED THE NIGHT COREY HAD RUN ACROSS THE LAWN IN HER GHOST COSTUME.
WE'D SURE LEARNED A LOT ABOUT GHOSTS SINCE THEN--MAYBE EVEN MORE THAN WAS GOOD FOR US.
LOOK!
HIGH ABOVE THE EARTH, A SHOOTING STAR STREAKED ACROSS THE SKY.
NO ONE SAID IT, BUT I KNEW WE WERE ALL THINKING THE SAME THING.
THE LOVELY BAD ONES WERE HOME AT LAST.

# The Creative Team

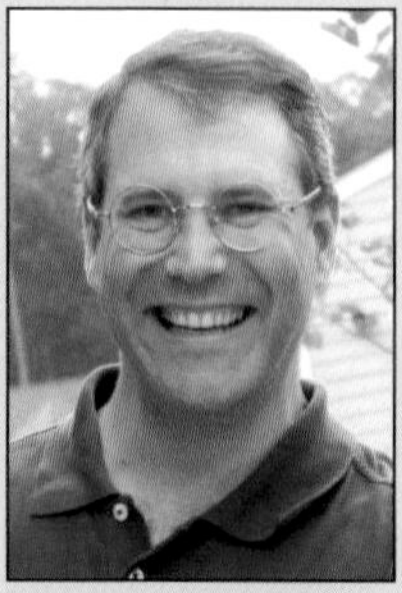

Photo by Scott Peterson

**Scott Peterson** was the editor of *Detective Comics*, DC Comics' flagship title; writer of *Batman: Gotham Adventures*; and co-creator of two Batgirl comics. He has written children's books, webcomics, music reviews, novels, and for animation, and is the author of the acclaimed original graphic novel *Truckus Maximus*. He lives in the Pacific Northwest with his wife, children's book author Melissa Wiley, and their family.

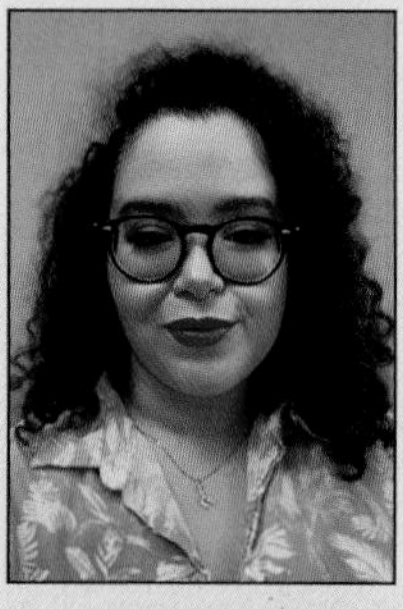

Photo by Naomi Franquiz

**Naomi Franquiz** is a Latina freelance illustrator and comic book artist currently based in delightfully dank Florida. She focuses on diverse and inclusive character-driven narratives that explore concepts such as found family, identity, and independence. Her notable recent work includes *The Unbeatable Squirrel Girl* (Marvel). She is perhaps best known for her expressive character work, as well as her penchant for giving everyone an excellent pair of eyebrows.

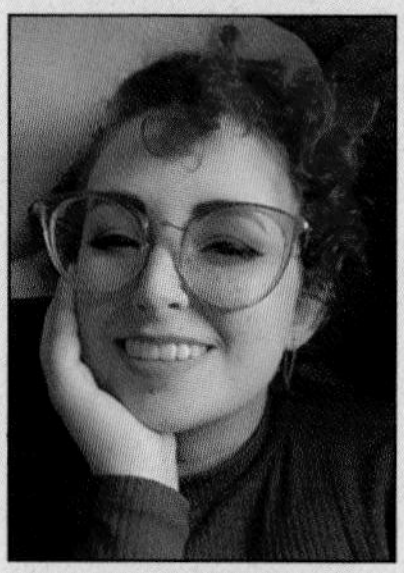

Photo by Brittany Peer

**Brittany Peer** is a comic colorist who likes bright and bold palettes and fun family stories. They spend their free time binging Netflix and getting inspired by frequent hikes in interesting places.

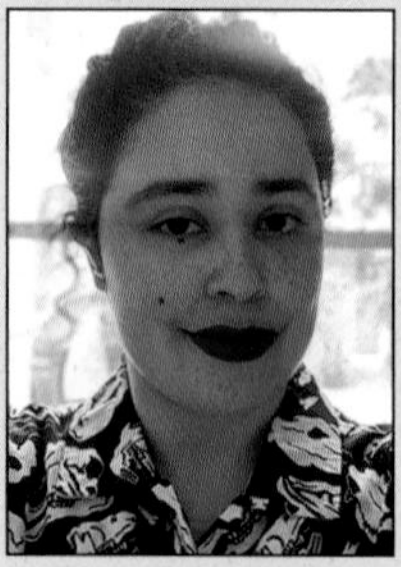

Photo by Joamette Gil

**Joamette Gil** is an award-winning Afro-Cuban cartoonist, editor, and letterer. Her letters grace the pages of titles from Abrams ComicArts, Dark Horse, Oni-Lion Forge, and Macmillan, among others. She's best known for her independent comics imprint centering LGBTQIA+ and BIPOC creatives, Power and Magic Press, publisher of such award-winning titles as *Power and Magic: The Queer Witch Comics Anthology*. Her heart resides in Miami, Florida, while her body does its thing in Portland, Oregon.